PRAISE FOR *IMMORTAL WARRIOR*

"Immortal Warrior will sweep you off your feet [and] have you adding Hendrix to your must-buy list. Shifters, witches, Norse gods, and more make this series unforgettable."
—*Night Owl Romance*

"A bold and beautiful fairy tale for grown-ups: an enchanted story of a stalwart warrior and a feisty lady...Not to be missed!"
—*Romantic Times*

PRAISE FOR THE ROMANCES OF LISA HENDRIX

"A fast, fresh, and funny look at modern love, ancient magic, and new-age zaniness...An enchanting book by a talented storyteller."
—Susan Wiggs, *New York Times* bestselling author of *Snowfall at Willow Lake*

"A fun, fascinating read with the perfect blend of romance, sensuality, and magic. Pick up a copy today and prepare to be dazzled!"
—*Bookbug*

IMMORTAL
WARRIOR

LISA HENDRIX

BERKLEY SENSATION, NEW YORK

THE BERKLEY PUBLISHING GROUP
Published by the Penguin Group
Penguin Group (USA) Inc.
375 Hudson Street, New York, New York 10014, USA
Penguin Group (Canada), 90 Eglinton Avenue East, Suite 700, Toronto, Ontario M4P 2Y3, Canada
(a division of Pearson Penguin Canada Inc.)
Penguin Books Ltd., 80 Strand, London WC2R 0RL, England
Penguin Group Ireland, 25 St. Stephen's Green, Dublin 2, Ireland (a division of Penguin Books Ltd.)
Penguin Group (Australia), 250 Camberwell Road, Camberwell, Victoria 3124, Australia
(a division of Pearson Australia Group Pty. Ltd.)
Penguin Books India Pvt. Ltd., 11 Community Centre, Panchsheel Park, New Delhi—110 017, India
Penguin Group (NZ), 67 Apollo Drive, Rosedale, North Shore 0632, New Zealand
(a division of Pearson New Zealand Ltd.)
Penguin Books (South Africa) (Pty.) Ltd., 24 Sturdee Avenue, Rosebank, Johannesburg 2196, South Africa

Penguin Books Ltd., Registered Offices: 80 Strand, London WC2R 0RL, England

This is a work of fiction. Names, characters, places, and incidents either are the product of the author's imagination or are used fictitiously, and any resemblance to actual persons, living or dead, business establishments, events, or locales is entirely coincidental. The publisher does not have any control over and does not assume any responsibility for author or third-party websites or their content.

IMMORTAL WARRIOR

A Berkley Sensation Book / published by arrangement with the author

PRINTING HISTORY
Berkley Sensation mass-market edition / November 2008

ISBN: 978-0-425-22454-0

BERKLEY® SENSATION
Berkley Sensation Books are published by The Berkley Publishing Group,
a division of Penguin Group (USA) Inc.,
375 Hudson Street, New York, New York 10014.
BERKLEY SENSATION and the "B" design are trademarks of Penguin Group (USA) Inc.

PRINTED IN THE UNITED STATES OF AMERICA

10   9   8   7   6   5   4   3   2   1

To Helen, who made it happen,
and to Kate, who made it happen better.

The Legend

IN THE EARLY *years of the raids upon Britain, it came about that Håkon IronToe, a high chieftain of the Norse, heard tales told among his Saxon thralls that the men of Odinsbrigga, in the Kingdom of Anglia, guarded a great treasure. Determined to have it, he sent his fiercest warriors, led by Brand Einarsson, called Thor's Hammer, to take the village and bring the gold to him. But the treasure was protected not only by the swords of men, but by the sorcery of the witch, Cwen, who conjured warriors from her own blood and sent her son to lead them.*

When Brand saw his men being slaughtered, a great rage came over him, and he gained the strength of ten berserkers. He set upon the ghosts, slashing and hewing until his blade found solid flesh, and he did kill the son of Cwen.

In the fury of her grief, Cwen used her magic to bind Brand and those of his men whose hearts still beat, and she had them carried before the treasure they had come to take, and she cursed them. She turned them into shadow beasts, living half as animal, half as man, each taking the form of his fylgja, *the spirit companion whose image he wore on a chain. When she had done, Cwen took their amulets and scattered them across the face of the earth, and she drove the men off into the forest to be hunted.*

When word of Brand's fate reached Håkon, he trembled in fear and ordered his boats to sail, but a great wave arose and his ship vanished from the face of the sea. He never knew of the greater curse that befell his men, for Cwen also made the warriors immortal, so that their torment should go on and on. Forever.

As the generations passed, the men of Odinsbrigga lost interest in their sport, and Brand searched out his men to gather them together. But those who were beasts set upon those who were men, and were set upon in turn when the sun fell or rose, and the vileness of the magic protected them from death but not from pain. When it grew clear they could not live together thus, each warrior set off to make his own way. Before they scattered, Brand swore a vow to every man that he would hunt Cwen until he found her, and that he would make her pay for what she had done.

The years passed into centuries, and still Brand hunted. One by one, his warriors learned to live among men once more. The first of these was Ivar, son of Thorli, called Graycloak, who spent his days in the form of an eagle . . .

—From the *Dyrrekkr Saga of Ari Sturlusson*
(E. L. Branson, trans.)

CHAPTER 1

December 1095

MADNESS. THAT'S WHAT it was.

Ivar stood before the keep of Salisbury Castle, his heart thudding as though he were going into battle, and wondered what had possessed him to come to this place.

In all the long years since Odinsbrigga, he had never been among so many men. Usually he was called to someplace isolated—a country chapel, a small manor, a forest glade—with only a few trusted men present to know who he was or what he did. On the rare occasions he ventured into a town, he kept to the edges, where the refuge of the forest was only steps away. Now, he was here, in the ward of a mighty castle, with an army camped in the bailey below and an entire city just beyond the walls. Every bone in his body screamed that this place was a trap, that he would be caught here within these walls, that the semblance of a life he had finally pieced together in the past three decades would be shattered.

Yes, it was clearly madness, yet he was going to walk into the tower, because William had ordered him to come and he wanted to know why. Ivar took a deep breath and climbed the stairs to the door.

"Sir Ivo de Vassy," he told the guard, using the name by which he was known to these Normans.

"Solar," the man grunted and pushed the door open.

The sheer crush took Ivar's breath away: nobles and knights and servants mingling and calling to one another; dogs fighting over the bones; a *jongleur* playing; and over it all, the smell of sweat and mead and grease and smoke. The memory of other times and other halls, full of kith and kin now long dead, hit Ivar in the stomach like a mailed fist, and he had to suck in air to keep his knees from buckling. He crossed the hall without glancing to either side and trotted up the stairs. Entering the solar, he stopped a few paces from the ruddy, barrel-shaped man playing at a game of tables and dropped to one knee.

"You are late, de Vassy," said William Rufus, son of the Conqueror and king of all England. "I bade you appear before me on Friday."

"It is yet Friday, Your Grace."

"Only just," growled William, rising. He paced a slow circle around Ivar, his green slippers scuffing on the stone floor, his gaze burning into the top of Ivar's head. "The abbey bells have already rung for Compline."

"Yes, Your Grace. But you are no monk."

The slippers came to a stop at the corner of Ivar's vision, and he braced himself for a blow. This game he played with William was always dangerous and could end badly at any moment—but not tonight. Instead, a snort of laughter escaped the king.

"God's truth, I am not." William thrust a beringed hand before Ivar to kiss and then grabbed him and hauled him to his feet with an impatient, "Rise, man. Rise. The rest of you, out. I wish to speak to my gray knight alone."

The noble lords loitering around the table hesitated, and Ivar knew each now assessed him to see whether this unknown upstart would challenge his position. Small chance of that. A man could provide little challenge to anyone when he spent his days flapping around after pigeons.

"Out!" bellowed William when his barons failed to move quickly enough. He jabbed a finger at a young page. "You. Fill my bowl before you go."

The boy scrambled to comply as the lords filed out. As the door shut behind the page, William lifted the silvered mazer and sipped from it as he paced another circle around Ivar, this time regarding him closely.

"How it is that you change so little from year to year? You look the same as when you first began serving my father."

Trapped. Ivar pushed the thought aside as he accepted the wine William held out. He took a long draught before he answered. "I am fortunate in that I do not have the weight of a crown to wrinkle my brow."

"'Tis a burden most men would carry willingly," said William.

"Most men are fools, Your Grace."

"Including me?"

Ivar met the king's belligerence with a smile. "You were born to the crown, Your Grace. It fits you well, even if it does weigh heavily."

William preened a moment, then pressed on. "And what were you born to? My heralds found no record of your birth in France or England."

"I assure you, I was born, Your Grace." *He'd had his heralds search? He was up to something.*

"But where? And who was your father?"

"Will my answer make a difference to how well you think I serve you, Your Grace?"

"It will not," William roared, laughing. "Thanks to you, de Mowbray, Tyson, and the rest are in chains, and we hold the north firmly again. Your aid gave us quick victory and allowed me to shift my attention to the matter in Wales. You could be the Devil's own spawn and you would still have my gratitude."

Ivar dipped his head in acknowledgment and to hide his smile. Devil's spawn, indeed. The king had no idea how close he was to the truth. He gave William what he wanted to hear. "My father was a *riddari*—a knight, in our land. Your lord father changed my name when I first became his man. He said he wanted those I dealt with to be certain I was not Saxon. As did I."

"And well you should. They are little more than animals," said William. He sat back down at the board and started pushing men idly from point to point. "Tell me how you managed to bring me de Mowbray's plans. Every other man I sent either failed or died."

"Yes, Your Grace. I saw some of them die."

"There are those who claim you killed them yourself."

"Only Montrose."

William's expression suddenly darkened. "You d-dare to admit murder to your k-king?"

Ivo ignored the stutter that arose when William was angry. "Murder in defense of my king. He would have betrayed you."

Fury hoisted William up off his stool. Spittle flew as he roared, "Aldaric M-montrose was no t-traitor!"

"No. But he was careless," said Ivar, giving no ground even though William was mere inches from his face. "I did not do it lightly, Your Grace. He had been taken and was being . . . questioned. A single arrow saved you considerable trouble, and saved him from the hands of William of Eu."

William's rage cooled as quickly as it had arisen and he backed off, turning to walk the few paces to the hearth. He stared into the dying flames for a long moment, his jaw working with some emotion Ivar didn't care to identify. The fair Montrose, it was rumored, had been more than friend to the king. True or not, a confession of sodomy extracted from the man under torture might have meant the end of William's rule—and Eu employed a torturer of some skill.

"I will have Eu's balls for a n-necklace," William vowed so softly that Ivar barely heard him.

"Would you like me to bring them to you, Your Grace?"

A long moment passed before William answered. "No. I will tend to it myself, and take great d-delight in it."

He drew himself up and turned to face Ivar, every bit the king once more. "You have served me well once again, *messire*, even if not as I intended. What will you ask as your reward this time?"

Gold. It was what Ivar always asked and always got, in quantities enough to make his life tolerable and occasionally pleasant, and it was on the tip of his tongue to ask for it again. But a shout of bawdy laughter rang up from the hall below, once more conjuring visions of home and the company of friends. How long had it been since he had laughed with other men?

"Land," he said abruptly, and once the thought was spoken, it took form. He wanted land and a home, even if only for a while. They would cost him, he knew. Sooner or later he would be seen changing, or William would demand he appear at the *Curia Regis* by daylight, or some other mishap would find him out. He would have to vanish into the wilds and start over again, in some other place and time when memories had faded. But for a while . . . He would trade his soul for even a month. "An estate."

To his astonishment, William simply nodded. "Then it is good my father renamed you. The peasants will never guess you are not one of us."

Ivar's head throbbed as though he had downed an entire cask of wine. "What peasants would those be, Your Grace?"

"Those of Alnwick and whatever other estates Gilbert Tyson held in Northumberland. I had already thought of settling part of his lands upon you before you came up the stairs in that gray mantle of yours. Your honesty only confirms my mind on it. To tell a king the truth even when you know he will not like it—that is a rare courage, *messire*. You shall have Alnwick, and you shall build me a castle to hold off those bastard Scots."

"Your Grace, I—" *A castle?*

"Ah, where is that wit of yours now?" demanded William, laughing. He strode across the room, threw the door wide, and bellowed into the hall below. "Attend me, all of you. Fetch my sword and a priest. And a scribe. By the by," he said, turning back to Ivar as the great barons of England began filing in. "Tyson has a granddaughter, a pretty red-haired creature, I'm told. You are to seal your hold on his lands by marrying the girl."

A wife? By the gods, he had not considered the possibility that William would give him a wife. Ivar's nails curled into his palms as he contemplated the pleasure and the danger inherent in that word, *wife.* How was he to keep the truth from a wife, even for a little? This truly was madness.

But there was no stopping William now as he began introducing Ivar to the men who would soon be his peers. "Step forward, Lord Ivo of Alnwick. 'Tis time for you to come out of the shadows where you have hidden for so long."

IT TOOK SIX nights of hard riding and six days of flying in unfamiliar woods for Ivar to reach the forests where Brand still hunted Cwen, and half another night to find his camp. It was Ari who finally led him there, dropping acorns and chattering from high in the trees, as noisy a raven as he was a man.

Finally, Ivar spotted the glow of a fire at the bottom of a narrow dene. He dismounted to lead his horses down to it, and as he did, a blade glinted and a voice growled, "Hold or die."

Ivar froze. "Easy, friend. 'Tis only me."

"Ivar? By Thor, Ivar! It is good to see you."

Ivar suddenly found himself lifted off the ground by arms that could crush a bull.

"And you," he said as Brand set him down.

"Hang on. I was about to take a piss," Brand said. He turned his back on Ivar and proceeded to do just that against the nearest tree. "You shouldn't sneak up on a man."

"I didn't think I was, with that bloody raven chattering."

"Bah. He does that all the time. It's when he gets quiet that I worry." Brand fastened his breeks and dropped his tunic back into place. "Come, sit by the fire where it is warm. Share my roasted squirrels."

"I have bread and a skin of wine," Ivar said.

"Good wine?"

"The king's. I stole it myself."

"Good enough, then. We will make a feast."

Brand led the way down into the ravine, pausing to rinse his hands in the brook that trickled along the bottom while Ivar hobbled his horses and carried the wine and loaf to the fire. They settled in before a half-crumbled hut, and Brand prodded the squirrels with the tip of his scramasax. "Not done yet."

"This is a good place," said Ivar, looking around. "I couldn't see your fire until I was nearly on top of you."

"Sometimes I come here when the weather is cold. The walls cut the wind, and there are dens nearby where the bear can sleep."

Ivar snorted. "You get a den, while I freeze my balls off in the top of some tree."

"The *fylgjur* choose who they choose," said Brand. "But tonight you should be warm enough, at least. Pass the wine."

They drank a little, and ate, and then drank a little more, and finally Brand leaned back. "Why have you come?"

"You know I have been working for the Norman kings."

Brand nodded. "The current one is not much loved by the few men I speak with. Especially the monks."

"He's not much loved by anyone, but he pays well."

"A man can forgive much for enough gold."

Ivo took another drink from the wineskin and passed it to Brand. "This time he did not give me gold. He gave me land. A manor in the north called Alnwick."

Brand's eyes widened with surprise. "And you took it?"

"Worse. I asked for it. Then I found out he wants me to build him a castle." He heard the mice scuttling through the leaves over Brand's silence. "I know. 'Tis madness."

"No. But it is foolish. You know it will end badly."

"It always ends badly, no matter what we do or how we

try to hide ourselves. How many times have you been chased out of a forest? I want to sit in my own hall once more, even if only for a while."

"Then you should do so," said Brand. "You may even make this last a little. You move among them more easily than the rest of us."

"Not well enough to do this alone. Come with me," said Ivar. "Your French is surely good enough now. You had lessons from that hermit."

"It is passable, but I cannot go. I have not yet found her."

Ivar shook his head. "It's time to stop hunting, my friend. Cwen is long dead."

"No. She used her magic on herself when she finished with us. Ari saw it. She lives."

"Ari saw wrong. She is dead," said Ivar more firmly. "I need you both to help me hold Alnwick. The former lord stood against William. I cannot walk into his hall with no one at my back. And I need Ari to be my voice during the day."

The silence again. Brand's face grew taut in the firelight, and Ivar knew that his friend, too, longed for the old days and the noisy halls of Vass.

"Come with me," Ivar urged again. "Fight with me, if need be. And when it goes badly, as it must, and we have to vanish into the woods again, I will come hunt Cwen with you. In the meantime there will be warm fires and good food and the company of men."

The raven chortled softly as Brand groaned. "It has been a long time. You tempt me."

"If you will not stay, then at the least come stand with me at my wedding," said Ivar. "William gave me a wife as well."

"*Gave* her?" Brand's brow lifted. "Is she *thir*?"

"No, no slave. She is noble born."

"Yet this king gives her as though she were chattel?"

"Under Norman law, she is. William took her grandfather's lands by forfeit, and now he gives me the maid to confirm my hold on them."

"What if she doesn't want to marry you?"

"She has no choice. Neither do I. The king has decreed it."

Brand muttered something dark and unpleasant about the parentage of men who would treat their own women so. Slaves and captives were one matter, but free women quite another. By both law and custom, Norse women were not forced to wed against their will.

"No wonder you want us there," said Brand. "If the old lord's men do not stick a knife in your back, your wife surely will. What is this maid's name?"

"Alaida."

It was the first time Ivo had spoken her name aloud, and as he did, his body tightened with desire. A woman of his own, for more than a quick tup.

"Is she pretty?" asked Brand.

"I don't know." It didn't matter. She was *his*. He could spend the long winter nights coming to know her scent and her laughter, and drawing out her cries of pleasure. "Any woman's pretty enough when she's under you.

"So will you ride with me?" he asked Brand once again, suddenly more anxious to get to Alnwick.

"I will. *We* will. But you'd better have good ale and plenty of it."

"That I promise you. By the by, the Normans know me as Ivo de Vassy. You'll both have to call me that, so long as we're there."

"Ivo de Vassy," said Brand, testing the sound of it. "I suppose we'll have to 'm'lord' you now and again, too."

"You are my war-leader and my captain. I would not ask that of you."

"I released you from those vows long ago. Besides, in this, you are the leader. We will do what we must to help you." Brand looked up at the patch of sky overhead, reading the time in the stars. "We won't get far before dawn, Lord Ivo de Vassy."

"Then we'll start tomorrow, as soon as we're men again."

By Odin. A castle and a wife and good friends, Ivar thought as he tore off another chunk of bread.

For now, he would simply think of that, and not of what would happen when Alaida of Alnwick discovered she was married to a man who became an eagle with the break of every day.

CHAPTER 2

January 1096

THE CANDLES IN the solar flickered in the bitter wind that seeped past the shutter and tapestries. Alaida shivered and continued to squint at her embroidery frame. The cloth on it was intended as an altar cover for the chapel, but the figures of pilgrims looked too stark on the plain ground of the cloth.

"Perhaps a chevron of the blue wool," she mused aloud.

"That would be lovely, my lady," said the old nurse, Bôte, as she lifted the lid to a nearby chest. "Or the green would do as well."

Alaida held up a hank of each, but could not choose. She would have to look at it again in the morning light.

It was late, and around her the maidservants busied themselves dragging the bedding from the chests and cupboards. They would all sleep in the solar, curling up on cots and straw pallets around the great bed where Alaida and her nurse slept, their presence an impenetrable layer of femininity that would protect Alaida and her reputation from the siege of bachelors below.

No sooner had news of her grandfather's capture worked its way around Northumberland than landless knights and lesser lordlings had started turning up, each hoping to win her hand and the lands she held as his heiress. Even after rumor spread that William had confiscated Alnwick for the Crown, some had stayed on, ever hopeful that the king would gift the lands to whoever won Gilbert Tyson's granddaughter—although why they thought she'd have one of them now when she had never wanted one before was a mystery. Most had gone on their way, but three of the most determined still lingered below, making free with the wine.

She despised them to a man. Vultures they were, picking over her grandfather's carcass before he was dead. Any day now, William would forgive her grandfather, along with de Mowbray and the others, just as he had eight years ago when Northumberland had rebelled in support of Robert Curthose for king. Then *Grand-père* would be back to take his rightful place at the head of the table, and he would toss these jackdaws out on their ears.

Preparations for the night were nearly complete when a quiet knock came at the door. Bôte opened it a crack, whispered briefly with the guard who stood on the stairs, then opened the door a wedge more to let one of the stableboys slip in.

"What is it, Tom?"

"Oswald sent me to say there's two men at the gate asking for you, m'lady. He said to be quiet about it, so as not to cause a stir in the hall."

"What sort of men?"

"Knights, I think, m'lady," said Tom. "One of them rides a very handsome horse."

"'Tis only more of *them*, my lady," said her maid. "Let them freeze. We can serve them to the others and save butchering a hog."

"Hadwisa!" Alaida had to bite her lip to keep from laughing with the others. "Tom, tell Oswald I will come. I wish to see these men for myself before we decide whether to let them in."

"Lady, you should not," said Bôte.

Alaida ignored her. "Go, Tom. But quietly."

"Yes, m'lady." He cracked the door and slipped out as silently as he'd come in.

Alaida reached for the gown she'd just laid aside. "Help me. Quickly."

Bôte obeyed, muttering all the while. "Any man who would come so late can be up to no good. Let them find shelter in the village. You'll catch a chill, you will."

"I am mistress of Alnwick in my grandfather's absence. It is my place to welcome travelers—or to send them on their way," said Alaida as she slipped into her shoes. She pulled her cloak around herself while Bôte did the same. "The rest of you stay here and bar the door behind us."

The wine had done its work. Men sprawled all over the darkened hall, some on benches, some on pallets wrapped in blankets or furs, a few simply curled up in their own cloaks on a mound of rushes. She passed through them, touching the shoulders of a half-dozen of the Alnwick men as she went. They roused, saw her with a warning finger to her lips, and came quickly but quietly to their feet.

Outside, Oswald, her grandfather's aging marshal, had already gathered a few men from the guardhouse and stables. With those she'd brought and the men already on duty, they had enough to deal with anything short of outright invasion. Several of the servants grabbed up torches and lit them while the others armed themselves. Those without swords or spears took up what was at hand—a club or pitchfork here, an axe or scythe there—as Alaida peeked through a gap between the timbers.

Their visitors were indeed knights, and one of the horses was indeed handsome, with a striking white mane against a dark coat that matched its rider's pale hair and dark clothes. She could see little of the second man in the moonlight, except that he was huge and carried a large bird on his shoulder.

"Who are they?" she asked Oswald, keeping her voice low.

"They will say only that they come from the king and would speak to you. The one does talk like a nobleman."

"Is there any sign of trickery?"

"No, my lady. I have Edric watching the verges. He sees nothing."

If Edric saw nothing, there was nothing to be seen—the man had the vision of an owl. "Let them in, then," said Alaida. "But on our terms. The postern gate."

The men arrayed themselves around the side gate, their arms at the ready. Alaida drew her own knife from the sheath at her waist and gripped it low, nearly out of sight under the edge of her cloak. Oswald nodded, and the men at the gate drew the bar and swung the gate open.

The postern gate was made to pass a horse without a rider, so the strangers had to dismount and lead their animals through single file. The leader, the man with the pale hair, stepped into the circle of torchlight and stopped, glancing around at the blades pointed toward him until his eyes fell upon Alaida.

"Your caution is wise, Lady Alaida."

"Who are you?" she demanded. "And by what right do you demand to see me at this unholy hour?"

"I am called Ivo de Vassy, and I take my right from the king, as the new baron of Alnwick." He glanced down at the knife in her fist, then back up to meet her eyes. One brow went up, and she had the unnerving sense that he was holding back a laugh.

The second man didn't bother to hold it back, snorting mightily when he saw her blade. "I told you," he said to the first, then turned to Alaida's men. "Why are you still on your feet? Kneel to your new lord."

The guards and servants dropped immediately, save Bôte, who stood firmly at her mistress's heel. Oswald also held his position, his short sword gripped tightly in his hand.

"I said kneel," growled the second knight, putting a hand to the hilt of his sword. As though sensing trouble, his bird—a large raven—flew off to sit on the wall.

"A man can claim to be anything," said Oswald with a calm he surely must not feel. "I have seen no royal writ, and until I do, Gilbert Tyson is lord of Alnwick, and I serve him and Lady Alaida."

"Fair enough." The pale knight reached into a pouch hanging from his saddle and produced a folded parchment. "Do you read Latin, my lady?"

"Well enough for this." She returned her knife to its sheath, took the document, and with de Vassy following, carried it to one of the large standing torches. The scribe's hand was clear, and even in the flickering light, she could make out the important words: *Ivo de Vesci. Barô. Dominus. Alnwick.* And that was the king's great seal imprinted in the wax; she recognized it from letters held by her grandfather. The sense of dread she had held at bay through these last months flooded over her. Her voice was barely a whisper as she asked, "Is my grandfather dead, then, *monseigneur?*"

"No. Imprisoned at Windsor with de Mowbray, but alive and well at last word."

"Thank you, my lord." She collected herself, turned, and lifted her chin to announce to the others, "This is from the king. Bid welcome to your new lord."

"Saints save us." Bôte crossed herself and did a quick courtesy.

Oswald sheathed his sword, and with an apologetic glance toward Alaida, knelt to his new master. "Forgive me, my lord. I sought only to protect my lady."

Lord Ivo brushed away his apology with a flick of his gloved hand. "I expect no less diligence in the future. What is your name?"

"Oswald, my lord. I serve as marshal of Alnwick."

"On your feet, then, Oswald Marshal, and the rest of you, as well. Someone see to our horses."

Young Tom dashed forward to grab the reins of his handsome horse, while one of the grooms took the other animals and led them off. Lord Ivo walked to the center of the yard, then turned a slow circle, taking in every stone and timber, surveying, measuring. Finally, his eyes came to rest on Alaida with the same assessing look.

Damn William. He'd given her to this usurper; she knew it as surely as she knew her own name. Well, this new-made lord would find she was not a willing bride—if he could find her at all. She had just enough silver of her own to buy sanctuary at some nunnery, and she could petition for her grandfather's release from there. She would be away at first light.

Except this Ivo's eyes said he knew precisely what she was thinking. He tugged off one glove and put out his hand. "Come, my lady. Show me my new hall."

Show him his new hall, as though it were as simple as that, when it meant the very earth had shifted beneath her feet. Look at the way he stood there with his hand out, expecting her to come to him. She clenched her fists at her side and glared her defiance back at him. Let him whip her. She was not his dog.

His eyes narrowed. In three strides he was before her, so close she could feel his breath on her cheek. But instead of striking her, he leaned closer, his lips nearly against her ear.

"Do not let things begin so between us, my lady."

His voice was low and full of warning, but a note of something else underlying that warning—kindness? hopefulness?—so disarmed her that when he stepped back a pace and put his hand out again, she found herself laying her hand in his palm. His fingers closed over hers, claiming her. It suddenly became very hard to breathe, and she vowed to herself that this surrender was only temporary, a way to put him off his guard so she could escape more easily come morning.

"Will I find resistance within?" he asked as he led her toward the door. His companion, Oswald, and the rest of the Alnwick men fell in behind them.

She ignored his double meaning. "Not from our men—I mean *your* men—once they see Oswald at your side. But there are several knights bachelor inside who have been loitering about, hoping Alnwick would be theirs."

"Only Alnwick?"

"No." Her cheeks flamed as she heard herself add, "Now they are disappointed in both regards."

"Brand. Did you hear?"

He stepped up to take his place at Ivo's right. "I did. Shall I just gut them now, or do you want to be civilized?"

"I would be pleased to help to do the gutting, my lord," volunteered Oswald. Behind him, several of the others muttered their agreement.

So it was like that, thought Ivo. He'd suspected it as soon as he'd heard the disgust in Alaida's voice when she said *knights bachelor*. "How many are there?"

"Three," said Oswald. "And eight men between them."

"Do I owe any regard to their fathers or grandfathers?"

"No, m'lord."

"Then let us be rid of them," said Ivo. "But leave their guts intact unless they're too foolish to keep them. No use starting any unnecessary wars."

They reached the door and Ivo shoved it open hard, so it hit the wall with a crack. The dogs began barking, and Oswald whistled to silence them. A few men stirred and pulled their covers tighter in the chill draft. One lifted his head groggily. "Shut the door, ye pig's ass."

Before his head hit his arm again, Ivo had hauled the offender to his feet. "Mind your tongue, oaf, or I will have it tanned for a purse. Now light the torches. All of them." He shoved the man on his way. "Everyone, awake."

The man had the sense to obey. The hall stirred to life as the torches flared. *My hall*, Ivo thought with a sense of satisfaction deeper than he'd had in years. "On your feet!"

When they didn't move quickly enough, he nodded to Brand, who strode through the room, bellowing and yanking blankets off stragglers. One man came up off his pallet with fists swinging; Brand swept his legs out from under him with one foot and moved on without breaking stride. Oswald followed in his wake, urging the Alnwick men to some order. By the time they reached the low dais at the front of the hall, even Alaida's would-be suitors were awake, their eyes red-rimmed and bleary from drink. They reached for their weapons and started forward.

Ivo left Alaida by the door and swept across the path Brand had cleared. One of the leeches met him at the edge of the dais, his sword half out of the scabbard.

The flash of Ivo's blade at his throat stopped the man cold, and his friends with him. Some of their men in the hall started forward. Brand rounded on them, defending Ivo's back. Several Alnwick men rushed to his aid, and there was a brief tussle as they confiscated weapons.

"You dare to draw your sword against your host?" demanded Ivo hotly.

"What the devil? Who are you to speak to me so?"

"Ivo de Vassy," he pronounced the name very clearly, so they would be sure to remember it. "Baron of Alnwick. You are in my hall, and you will stand down."

"Baron of . . . ?" The man struggled to wrap his wine-soaked brain around the words, but when he managed at last, the color drained from his face. "It cannot be so."

"And yet it is. I have seen the letter patent myself," said Alaida clearly from her place near the door, undoubtedly as much for the benefit of her own men as for these louts. "Now sheath your weapons, *messires*, before I ask the baron to make me a gift of your ears. I am sure I would find them in fine condition, seeing how little they have been used in the past month."

The knights' faces went scarlet as laughter echoed through the hall, but they yielded, slowly returning their swords to their scabbards.

"My actions were unwise, my lord . . . Ivo, is it?" The man held his palms out and spread wide in surrender, but his oily tone still challenged. "Forgive me. I was asleep and dreaming of war. Being awakened so, I thought the dream was real."

"Perhaps you would have gentler dreams if you slept elsewhere," said Ivo. "Tonight."

The knight's lips thinned and he drew himself up. "Come, friends. We are no longer welcome here."

"Ye never were," muttered Oswald.

"You would have us leave now?" asked the shortest of the three, his eyes wide with the thought. "At *night*?"

"I just traveled the road from Morpeth and found it safe enough," said Ivo. He tipped his blade slightly toward Brand, who stood there with his sword in his fist, looking every bit as though he would still enjoy gutting someone. "However, my friend here is not afraid of the dark. He would be happy to escort you."

"We need no escort," growled their leader. He stalked toward the door, his companions on his heels and their men trailing after. He slowed only long enough to spit an insult in Alaida's direction. "Well done, m'lady. You found a champion as ill mannered as yourself."

"But not half so rude as you, sir," she snapped back, then went to the open door to call after them, "Be warned, if I hear of so much as a single egg cracked in the village, I will ask for your ears after all."

Ivo laughed. The maid had a quick wit and a tongue to go with it. He was going to have to watch her, lest he find himself married to a shrew.

She turned back to the hall, flush with victory, her eyes flashing, and her red hair blazing in the torchlight. The wind lifted loose strands and whipped them around her brow like tongues of flame. *Eisa, goddess of the hearth.* The ancient image leapt into Ivo's mind. *She was fire itself.* He suddenly very much wanted this woman, and it had nothing to do with land or king or anything beyond a desire to see how all that heat might warm him.

"I will see they don't get lost between the hall and the gate," said Brand, fetching him back to the business at hand. A grinning Oswald signaled his small troop of Alnwick men to bring the weapons they had taken, and they followed him out.

The door had barely shut behind them when the hall

erupted. Ivo's new men crowded forward to kneel and offer
their loyalty. Like that, he had them, and Alnwick was no
longer in Tyson hands. Alaida's high spirits faded as the fact
of it struck her.

"He's done it, my lady," said Bôte, excited. "He's sent
them packing."

"But who will send *him* packing?" Alaida wondered
aloud.

No one. He looked too right standing there in what used
to be her grandfather's spot, accepting his due—powerful
and commanding. Noble, from the angular cut of his features to how he held himself. Even his clothes singled him
out from the others. In the crowd of shapeless browns
and blues, his were a rich, dark gray, the cloth barely dis-
tinguishable from his mail shirt except by the latter's
dull gleam. With his white-gold hair capping his head like
a halo, he looked like some sort of warrior saint—Saint
George, perhaps—except no saint ever looked at a woman
the way Lord Ivo looked at her over the heads of his men,
like he would possess her right there. Her cheeks burned,
but she refused to give him the satisfaction of looking
away.

"He will make a good lord," prattled Bôte. "I can see it in
his eyes. He's strong, but he knows how to wield his
strength."

"I hope you are correct," said Alaida quietly. "Ask Geoffrey to come to me."

When Geoffrey came along, she gave her last orders as
the lady of Alnwick: to clear the bedding from the floor and
send for the women to come down to greet their new lord; to
bring out the lord's great chair and a bowl and ewer for him
to wash; and to see that he was offered bread, meat, and
wine. Finished, she waited until Lord Ivo was at last distracted, and then slipped off to the solar, unwilling to watch
any longer and anxious to pack what she intended to carry
away with her to the convent.

* * *

IVO WASN'T SURE when she had disappeared, just that he looked up from the line of men kneeling to pledge their loyalty to find her gone. He frowned, and the eyes of the man before him grew round with concern.

"Have I offended, my lord?"

"What? No, no, it's not you. Go. We will finish this another time." He turned to Brand. "Where is she?"

"Upstairs. I saw her go as I was coming in. From the look on her face, I thought you had told her."

"Not yet, but she surely knows. I had better get it over with."

"Shall I go up and take that little blade of hers first? She might not be able to kill you, but it would hurt—although in truth, her tongue might cut more deeply. Those knights we routed may never swagger again."

Ivo grinned. "She did take their balls off, didn't she? What confounds me is why she didn't do it before and send them on their way."

"That sort only listens to steel." Brand's smile faded. "A bride so quick could make this venture very short, my friend."

"Then it will be short. However, if I do not take her to wife as William commands, it will never begin at all."

"Then go and talk to your lady. I will stay here and enjoy your fire and make sure our raven friend stays out of the wine."

"You remind me." Ivo motioned Oswald and the steward, Geoffrey, over. "I will ride out before dawn to survey my lands."

"I'll have a guard ready to ride with you, my lord," said Oswald.

"No!" said Ivo, too quickly. He took a deep breath and spoke more carefully. "No. Brand is all the guard I need. We will cover more ground that way. While I'm gone, another of my men will arrive, by the name of Sir Ari. He is my left hand, as Sir Brand is my right, and will be seneschal and steward over the castle to be built, while you, Geoffrey, will remain steward of the manor. Know this: he and Sir Brand both speak with my voice in all things. Obey them and grant them each the respect due to me, and see that every man and woman on this manor does the same."

"Yes, my lord." They both bobbed their heads at him and at Brand, and were gone.

Ivo stood, stretched, and shook out the kinks. He had a final sip of wine. He stretched again.

"You delay like those stairs lead to the gallows," laughed Brand. "Are you truly ready for this?"

Ivo closed his eyes, picturing her as she'd looked there by the door, her color high and her red hair blazing in the torchlight. Brand was right. She was too quick by half for comfort. But she was also fair beyond pretty, and more to the point, she was his. He blew out a long sigh. "I may never be ready for her, but by the gods, I do want her."

He took the stairs two at a time. Below him, he heard Brand, still chuckling.

CHAPTER 3

SHE WOULD TAKE nothing that was not her own.

Alaida ignored the silk chainse that was part of her grandfather's court dress and dug to the bottom of the big chest to find her own best sindon chemise. There would be no use for it at the abbey, of course, but the holy sisters could sell it as part of her dower. Her best gowns plus her jewels would surely be enough to buy her a place in one of the wealthier chapters. She would go to Durham . . . or farther south, perhaps. She'd heard of an abbey at Helenstowe in Oxfordshire. He would never find her there.

"Where are you going, my lady?"

She whirled, startled, clutching the soft linen to her breast. Behind her, the lid to the chest crashed down and she jumped. "Oh."

"I do not bite. At least, not after a good meal." The amusement in Ivo's voice made her blood roil. Twice already he had laughed at her, and he had not yet been here one night.

"You startled me, *monseigneur*, that is all. I did not hear you enter."

"You had your head deep in that chest."

Presenting a charming view from the door, no doubt. She released her death grip on the chemise and draped it more loosely over her arm in an attempt to look less embarrassed. Or guilty. "Do you want something, my lord?"

"Yes, you . . . to answer my question. Where are you going?"

"Nowhere," she lied.

"Odd." He picked his way past the women's bedding and over to the foot of the great bed, where a stack of neatly folded clothing lay next to a small wooden casket. He picked up the corner of a gown and fingered the embroidered hem, then tipped open the lid of the casket and lifted up the silver girdle that lay on top. "You appear to be packing for a journey."

"I only thought to remove my things." Her heart was pounding so loudly, surely he must hear. "The chamber is yours now, like the rest of Alnwick." She failed to keep the bitterness out of her voice.

"There is no need." He dropped the girdle back in with the other things. "I will rest in the hall tonight."

"Tomorrow, then, I will—"

"Tomorrow, you will not need to remove your things. Tomorrow, we will be married. That is what I came to discuss."

"There is nothing to discuss."

"You must know the king has gifted you to me along with the land."

"The king! The king is . . ." She could not summon words to describe what she thought of William. "I am not a chair to be given away so some knight can sit more comfortably in my grandfather's hall."

"The marriage will strengthen my claim," he admitted, running his hand down the heavy green linen that curtained the bed. "But that is not the only reason I wish to wed."

His meaning was clear, as he intended. She felt the heat crawling up her neck and turned away so he would not see.

Or at least, she tried to turn away.

Her gown was caught on something, so firmly she could move only inches. With his gaze still fixed on her and the color creeping into her cheeks, she reached behind herself, trying to trace the source of the snag.

"Well, I do *not* wish it," she said, groping about, flustered. "Find some other woman who will have you willingly. You will gain even more land."

"I have land enough for now."

"And you have it with or without me, so what difference if I g—" She stopped herself too late.

He jumped on her error. "So you were planning to run. Where?"

"Nowhere."

Glowering, he started toward her. "Do not lie to me, woman. Where were you going?"

Alaida tugged at the yards of wool. "I will not . . ."

The sentence went unfinished as he reached for her and she jerked away. Her skirts pulled her off balance, and he caught her as she started to fall, one arm around her waist, and pulled her hard against his chest.

She froze, and a long moment of silence stretched, in which she could see the anger in him fading, only to be replaced by something far more dangerous. She wanted to look away, but she found herself trapped by the dark blue flint of his eyes, by the tangy smell of sweat and steel, and most of all, by the warmth of his body, even through all the layers of cloth and mail between them. Or was it her own heat? She was suddenly unsure.

"You are caught," he said softly.

He threaded his other arm behind her and lowered his head. He was going to kiss her, she thought, and her breath hung in her throat on a soft *ah*.

But no, he kept going, leaning past her shoulder as he reached behind her. There was a groan of metal, and she was free—but not from Ivo. He kept his hold as he straightened.

"The lid had closed on your gown," he explained.

"M—" She had to swallow to find her voice. "My thanks, my lord."

"I ask again, where were you going?"

"Nowh—" His arm tightened slightly, just enough to warn her she would not win this battle. "To a convent."

"I can think of few women less suited to life as a nun."

"You know nothing of me and what I am suited to." She tried to push free, but she might as well have been shoving against a wall. "You know nothing of me at all. Release me."

"You are going nowhere, Alaida. Resign yourself to that fact." He adjusted his hold slightly, but kept her caught there, so she was forced to look up at his stern face, just inches away. "And as for what I know . . . I already know you have a tongue that can be sharper than a carter's whip. I know you have a spirit that would fester in a nunnery. And I know that, even though you would deny it, you wonder why I didn't kiss you a moment ago and what it would have been like if I had."

"Bah. You are as full of yourself as Sir Neville."

"Is that his name? Did *he* kiss you?"

She shuddered, just thinking of it. "No."

"Good," said Ivo. And then he did, briefly, but enough to send sparks flying through her blood. She tried to keep from showing its effect, but she could tell by his smile that he knew he'd proved his point.

"No convent," he said.

She didn't answer, and his smile faded.

"By all that . . ." His jaw clamped as he visibly worked to tamp his temper down. When he spoke, his voice was clipped with the effort. "I would be within my rights to make you wife within the hour, and you sorely tempt me to do so." He ran a callused thumb across the apple of her cheek as though smudging away some mark. "But I vowed before I arrived that I would give you a day to reconcile yourself to this marriage. Do not make me regret the courtesy. I do not wish to spend the next fortnight tearing down an abbey stone by stone."

"You would not dare."

"I would, and not for the first time," he said darkly, and Alaida knew in her heart he told the truth. He said again, "No convent. Swear it."

What kind of man was he, to attack an abbey? The answer was too clear: William's man. William, who ravaged entire shires simply to prove his power. What would this de Vassy do to prove his? What if he took his wrath out on the village? Suddenly frightened, she gave in—but still she hedged.

"No convent." There were places other than convents for a woman to find refuge. There must be.

"Good," he said, and satisfied, settled her firmly on her feet. "Come. I want the men to see you at my side before they sleep tonight."

It was the last thing she wanted, but resistance would serve little purpose. "Yes, my lord."

"No argument?" His brow furrowed in suspicion.

"First you demand resignation, and then you question it," she snapped. "Truly, my lord, you must make up your mind."

"Ah, there we go." Chuckling, he took her hand and led her toward the hall.

There he kept her until well past midnight, taking homage from the rest of the household with her at his right, so every man would know she acknowledged his position. Then, as the women drifted back to the solar and the men retrieved their bedding and settled in for the night, he had the accounts brought out, and he and Brand pored over them, asking her and Geoffrey and Oswald countless questions. By the time he finally released them to bed, she was so exhausted that she fell asleep as her head touched the pillow.

Even then he harried her, though, filling her dreams with kisses and her nightmares with visions of burning abbeys and ransacked villages. By the time she woke, well past midday, she knew she could not run—even if she somehow did manage to think of a place to hide besides a convent.

So she summoned Bôte and Geoffrey and told them to prepare for a wedding.

"We already prepare, my lady," said Bôte, beaming.

Geoffrey confirmed this. "Lord Ivo said we are to be ready for your wedding feast when he returns."

"Returns? From where?"

"He rode out before dawn with Sir Brand, my lady. He said to expect him late, likely after sunset."

"And you are to be married then," added Bôte. "Though I've never heard of a wedding at night. In the morning it should be, with the feast to begin at a proper hour. Odd, it is."

More than odd, but nothing about this situation was usual. "He's gone? For the entire day?"

"Yes, my lady."

"Up all night and still riding out today to see his lands," said Bôte. "I tell you, he will make a good lord, if we must have a new one, and a good husband, too."

For one brief moment, Alaida considered hieing off to Helenstowe while he was gone, but pushed the thought aside. She would not leave Alnwick and its people to the whims of this new lord—but neither would she sit here and listen to Bôte prate on about his virtues.

"Do what you must. I am going for a walk." She retrieved her purse and yanked her cloak from its peg.

"'Tis foul out there, my lady, and cold as a dog's nose," said Bôte. "You will catch a chill."

"Then I shall sneeze my vows."

"But you must prepare, my lady," said Hadwisa. "Which gown will you wear?"

"God's truth, I do not care," said Alaida, and she escaped.

THERE WERE TIMES, Ari thought, when he wished he could be a raven by day. Like now. It would be most convenient to be able to fly up to the lady's window and see what plots she was hatching. Of course, as a raven, he wouldn't be able to stop her from hatching them, but at least he would know.

He was having a hard time believing she had bent so easily to Ivar's will, yet the buzz of activity as the household prepared for a wedding told him otherwise. Women had swept the dirty rushes from the floor and strewn fresh, mixed with rosemary to make the air sweet. A rider had been dispatched to Lesbury for the priest, and boys had dragged in boughs and vines to garland the hall. Fresh torches and candles perched in their holders, ready to be lit, and the tables, already on their trestles, bore enough fresh white linen to provide sails for a dragonship.

And all of this done since Ari had arrived at mid-morning—a ruse to convince watching eyes he had ridden in from Morpeth. Nearly every man had still been snoring when he'd entered the hall, and most yawned even now.

It was no wonder, as late as Ivo and Brand had kept them up. With so little time to live as men, they had all learned to make do with little sleep, and often with none but what their beasts snatched. The people of Alnwick would quickly adjust to their new lord's hours, Ari guessed, staying up unnaturally late and thus sleeping later as well—which would suit Ivo perfectly. The fewer eyes open to see him and Brand ride out each morning, and Ari ride back in, the better.

But today the manor folk could only scramble to make up the lost time. For his part, Ari stayed out of their way, lounging in the hall while he waited for Ivo's lady to appear. He had been waiting a long time; he'd composed most of a wedding poem in his head.

He was considering the final verse when a door slammed. Ari looked up, spotted Alaida at the same instant she spotted him, and came to his feet. She stopped. Her eyes narrowed with suspicion.

"Lady Alaida, I take it." Ari stepped forward and knelt. "Good morrow. I am—"

"If you're another bachelor come to try to win me, you're

too late," she interrupted, her voice as tart as a quince. "I will be married in a matter of hours."

"Ah, I would try to win you, fair lady, but Ivo would have my manhood for my efforts, and I have grown most fond of it."

"You are his man, then? You are too bold."

"I am. I am. And I am Ari," he said, rising. "My lord's steward for the castle."

"Good. Then stew." She swept down the stairs, out the door, and across the yard toward the gate.

Laughing, Ari went after her. He signaled to one of the guards at the gate, who stepped aside to let them pass. "Where are we going, my lady?"

"Are you steward or jailer?" she demanded.

"Jailer is a harsh word. Let us say . . . escort." Tiny shards of sleet beat against his cheeks, and he thought of the bear and the eagle freezing in the woods.

"I need no escort. I will not run."

"Good. Then we may enjoy a pleasant walk together, if there is any pleasantness to be found in this weather. Where did you say we're going?"

"I didn't say, but if you must know, I'm going to the village to remind myself *why* I will not run."

The people of Alnwick loved their lady, Ari discovered as she marched through the village. Cold-blanched faces brightened as she passed; greetings and good wishes followed her chilly progress. She led him to the far edge of the scattering of cottages, to the poorest of the lot. There she stopped long enough to stir up the fire and feed a bowl of pottage to the cottar's ailing wife, then laid seven silver deniers on the table. She moved on to the next tiny hut, barely a hen richer than the last, where she repeated both the kindnesses and the charity.

As they left the third cottage, Ari gave in to his curiosity. "Why do you give alms now, instead of *after* the wedding, my lady?"

"Because I can."

"I'm sorry, my lady, I do not understand."

"This is *my* money," she said. "After I'm wed, it becomes *his* money. I will give up many things tonight, but this, at least, I give on my own terms."

"You have little understanding of the man you marry if you think he would take your purse."

"He warned me himself what sort of man he is," she said tightly. "He boasted he once tore down an abbey."

Over two hundred years ago, Ari thought, but he could hardly tell her that. "It was in war and the monks were well armed. They split more than a few skulls, as I recall."

"Monks? Not nuns?" She seemed surprised, but waved it off. "No matter. He said he would do it again, if I joined the holy sisters."

Ari swore softly at Ivar's thickness. Threats were no way to woo a maid—but then again, from what he'd seen last night, this was not one of England's more delicate flowers.

"Then he probably would, if he wanted you enough," he granted. "He can be a hard man."

"No doubt. He is William's man, after all."

"William is king. All knights and nobles are his men, and if they are not, they quickly find themselves no longer knights and nobles."

"Like my grandfather."

"I am sorry, my lady," he said when he saw the stricken look on her face. "But yes, like your grandfather. However, Ivar is not like the king. He is not cruel for sport."

"Ivar?"

"What?"

"You called him Ivar."

Ass. Ari kicked himself. He'd been able to keep the new name straight all morning, and to misspeak now, with her . . .

He thought quickly. "There was an old man called Ivar in my village when I was young. Sometimes my tongue slips." For good measure he added, "I am not Norman-born."

"Ah, that explains it. You have an accent I don't know. Even when you speak Saxon to the peasants, it sounds odd. Like Sir Brand."

"Brand and I come from the same region."

She seemed satisfied and didn't ask where, or about Ivar—*Ivo*—thank the gods. Apparently his mastery of the Normans' French was more perfect, or else he hadn't spoken enough for her ear to catch anything peculiar.

Freshly wary, he followed her as she did the rest of her almsgiving, largely keeping his mouth shut as he chanted to himself, *Ivo, Ivo, Ivo.*

The wind had died by the time they finished, but the clouds had lifted enough to let the air cool as the sun settled lower. Ari calculated how long until dusk with an ease honed by centuries of necessity. He would have to slip away soon, but first he wanted to know something.

"Now, my lady, will you tell me, how did this good work remind you of why you do not run?"

She stopped and looked at him, as though measuring his worth. She must have found him satisfactory.

"I had a dream last night," she said. "I had run, and your lord burned the village to the ground to punish me for leaving. I want to carry my people's faces with me to the church door, to strengthen me when I say my vows."

"Ah, lady." Ari shook his head at the fear his friend had somehow wrought in this poor girl. "It was a false dream. I fought beside Ivo for years, and to see a man in war is to know him. He would never make the village pay for your acts. Do not go to the chapel tonight out of fear. Go because you want a good husband and a fine lord for Alnwick."

She cupped her hands over her mouth, briefly warming her fingers before turning solemn, brown eyes up at him. "Will he be those things?"

"He will, my lady, I swear it. And if he is not, I will help you run away myself." He screwed up his face as though in great pain. "We will have to flee to Byzantium to escape him—well, perhaps only to Rome—but I will help you."

His exaggeration brought a slight smile to her lips.

"That is better. Now, go, my lady," he said. "Here are the manor gates, and you have but little time to prepare for your groom."

She started forward, then stopped and turned. "Thank you, Sir Steward. You have been a most kind escort."

Ari stood by the gate until she disappeared into the hall, then turned to one of the men loitering nearby and sent him to fetch his horse. As he waited, he wandered over to the well and dipped into the bucket for a drink. He would have preferred something warm, plus time in which to scribble down the verses he'd constructed earlier, but the sun was dropping like a stone and he had to be away.

Well, his poem might go unheard, but at least the raven would see this wedding he had just promoted. He was staring into the bucket, thinking of the strangeness of the afternoon, when the water suddenly darkened and swirled. His heart began thumping wildly.

A vision. They had been common in his youth—a fact that had brought him great grief, since magic was the domain of women and unsuited to a warrior—but they had grown rare since Odinsbrigga. He hadn't had one for years. He resisted for a moment, unwilling to slip into that netherworld where the visions lived, but the haze settled over him.

Surrendering to what must be, he calmed his heart and let himself drift into the half-dream that beckoned him. Images slowly formed on the mirrored surface of the water. He grasped at them, but they shifted, fleeting, too thin to see. *A bird. Was it him or Ivar? An eagle. And then a woman, slowly swirling into view. Alaida, perhaps. Or not. Was that an infant? The eagle again.* The images would not settle. They eddied, twisting one into the other and then into the next, without giving him a chance to read their meaning. He again reached out with his mind to try to catch one. Just one.

"My lord? Are you ill?"

"What?" The vision shattered and vanished. "No. No. I'm fine."

"You were staring for so long, I thought you were having a fit."

"I'm fine, I tell you." Ari looked up, the fog only slowly

lifting from his mind. The sun was lower yet, barely a finger's width above the horizon. He had lost time and had nothing to show for it.

He spilled the bucket onto the ground in frustration, grabbed the reins away from the man, and threw himself into the saddle. As he tore out the gate, his mind raced ahead of the animal. There was too much to do in the moments remaining before dark. He must reach Brand and Ivar. He must leave them a message before the curse turned him raven for the night.

And most important of all, he must figure out what the gods were trying to tell him with their damnable vision.

CHAPTER 4

THE LAST GLEAM of the passing day still lingered on the horizon as Ivo and Brand rode out of the wilds and onto *demesne* land. Ivo had rushed after regaining human form, throwing on his clothes and urging Hrimfaxi toward Alnwick almost before his friend could follow. But now, here at the edge of the orchard, where the frost-covered trees stood like skeletons against the evening sky, he reined to a stop.

Brand rode up beside him, his hand on the hilt of his sword. "What is it?"

"Nothing. Just wondering if I'm going to have to run her to ground."

"She'll be there. Ari would not let her escape so easily."

"He had to leave well before sunset," said Ivo, glancing at the bird on Brand's shoulder. "She's had time to slip away."

"Then we'll find her and bring her back."

"I don't want a prisoner, I want a *wife*—and a willing one, at that." Ivo shook his head in disgust at the situation William had put him in, then touched the scrap of bark knot-

ted into his sleeve. "Come, let's find some light and see
what Ari had to say."

This time, the gate swung wide as they approached, and
a half-dozen men stepped forward to welcome them. Another two score or so hung back around the fire that blazed
in the yard. It took Ivo a moment to realize they were the
freemen of the village, come for the wedding feast, but also,
he realized, to see what sort of man the king had set in Gilbert Tyson's place. He greeted them, singling out the reeve,
Wat, who had been in the hall the night before, then turned
to his steward. "What news, Geoffrey?"

"The hall and food are ready, my lord. The village men
have arrived, as you see, and Father Theobald waits in the
chapel."

"And Lady Alaida?" Ivo kept his voice easy and avoided
glancing toward Brand.

"In the solar with her women, my lord, preparing."

The knot in Ivo's belly began to untangle itself. "Good. I
will send for her shortly. Tell Oswald to have the men stand
by."

"Yes, my lord." Geoffrey excused himself and disappeared off toward the kitchen. Ivo and Brand went inside
and wove their way past the tables and scurrying servants to
warm themselves by the hearth.

The message from Ari was brief and hard to make out,
having been scratched into a scrap of bark with the point of
a knife.

Gave all her money to poor. Feared you would take.
Near 10s. Stop scaring.

Ivo reread the runes twice, then again, trying to make
sense of them. He handed it to Brand, scowling at the bird
on his shoulder. "You'd think a *skald* would be better with
words."

"It looks like he ran out of light," said Brand. "'Feared
you would take'? What did you do to the girl?"

"I don't know. Nothing. Warned her not to run off to her

convent. We barely spoke a dozen words. Frey's pillock!" Ivo crumbled the bark in his fist and dropped it into the flames. "I've been in the forest too long. I used to know how to handle a woman."

"That you did," Brand agreed. He sucked on his teeth a moment, thinking. "Remember that sailmaker's daughter in Kaupang?"

A smile spread across Ivo's face as a vision of the girl's ripe curves formed in his mind. "Ingigerd."

"She began with no more love for you than your Alaida. Yet as I recall, it cost you a barrel of salted fish and a pound of silver when her father caught you giving her a ride in the sail loft."

"She was worth every coin and cod," said Ivo fondly. But even as he recalled Ingigerd's enthusiastic gallop, his imagination strayed to thoughts of Alaida and how she might feel astride him, there on the big bed in the solar. He shifted to ease the sudden heaviness in his groin. "That was long ago—very long ago—and I had time to woo Ingigerd."

"So woo Alaida."

It had taken most of one summer to win over Ingigerd, Ivo thought. He would be lucky to have a month with Alaida, and he wanted every night of it in her bed. Plus there was the king to consider. "William so desires this castle that he waived the relief and pledged a hundred pounds to aid the building, but he waits for word that Alnwick and its lady are firmly in hand. I must bed her tonight, or she may yet run to a convent and have the wedding annulled."

"Mmm. Well, you have 'til after supper," said Brand, as though that should be ample time. "There's some fire to her. It shouldn't be too hard to kindle a full blaze. A little wine, a few sweet words . . . Of course, if she's too much for you, we can ride away now. The king will find another lord to take her land and her maidenhead, and we can go back to hunting Cwen."

Ivo didn't bother to answer. "You." He jabbed a finger toward a passing maid. "Fetch me some hot water and a clean chainse. And send Geoffrey to me."

"I guess not," said Brand to the bird. "Ah, well. At least she didn't run. Perhaps she's more willing than you think."

"Perhaps," Ivo conceded, though the worm of doubt wriggling up and down his spine said otherwise.

It did seem Brand might be right, however, when Ivo sent for Alaida a short while later. She appeared at the top of the stairs promptly, her serving women close behind her, and though her face was pale and strained against the frame of her wimple, she came down with only a slight hesitation.

"You have no male relative to make the marriage contract," he said for the benefit of the gathered witnesses. "Will you sign it with me, Lady Alaida?"

"*Oui, monseigneur,*" she answered quietly.

No, not quietly. *Meekly*. And with downcast eyes. And when she took his hand, her fingers were cold as sea ice and trembled on his palm.

Ari was right. She was afraid of him.

He didn't like it. He didn't like it at all. Some men might want wives who cowered, but he preferred a woman with more spine, like the fiery maid who had snapped her threats at Neville or the rebellious one who had plotted her escape and demanded that he make up his mind what he wanted from her.

Ransacking his brain for a reason for Alaida's change, he led her toward the high table where the contract lay waiting. It was there, as the witnesses gathered around, that Ivo looked down at his bride and saw it. The severe white wimple. The plain linen showing at her neck and sleeves. The shapeless gown of rough, black wool tied with a simple braided belt from which hung a small, wooden cross.

The little vixen.

She might, indeed, be a little afraid of him, but beneath that fear, her rebellious streak still lurked, straight-backed as ever.

Disguised in the habit of a nun.

* * *

EVEN WITHOUT SEEING his face, Alaida knew by the way de Vassy's fingers tightened around hers that he had deciphered her choice of dress. She had expected he would—whatever the man was, he was surely no fool—but now that she felt the rage that shook him, she rued the impulse that had led her to order Hadwisa to bring out one of her grandmother's old gowns.

The gesture had seemed harmless enough there in the solar, a way to show she was beaten but not cowed, but now it only seemed foolhardy. What if Sir Ari had been wrong about his lord? And where, by the by, was the seneschal, he and his easy assurances of aid? Cowardly wretch.

No mind. She had baited the bull, and now she would face him down. When Ivo's fingers tightened again, she took a fortifying breath, composed her face, and looked up, hoping to appear as serene as the Holy Mother in the chapel triptych.

"Is something amiss, my lord?" she asked, honey sweet.

His eyes narrowed and she felt herself blanch. Then an odd glint made her look more closely at the way his jaw and mouth worked. Was that a smile he was trying to tame?

It was. God's thumbs, it wasn't anger that shook him, it was laughter, barely contained. He was laughing at her yet again.

Her resolve to submit obediently flashed away like rain on a hot coal. The Devil take him. She would not play his fool. She snatched her hand out of his and stepped forward to take up the quill.

"Would you not have the contract read out first, my lady?" asked Geoffrey in surprise.

"It would serve no purpose. The king commands this union, and I bend my will to his for the good of Alnwick."

She scrawled her mark and threw the quill down, leaving a splatter of ink across the bottom of the parchment. Before she could back away, Ivo stepped up close behind her. The grin he'd been fighting spread across his lips with a wicked curl as he slid his arm around her waist.

"Patience, sweet leaf." Voice rippling with amusement, he tugged her backward, bringing her hips firmly against his loins. "You will enjoy Alnwick's *deep* appreciation soon enough."

She gasped, and the watching men joined in the laughter that finally burst out of Ivo as he reached around her to scribe his name next to hers.

Pinned between him and the table, she could only stand there, held fast against his body, her face as red hot as the wax Ivo spilled over the blot she'd left. He pressed his ring into the puddle to imprint his seal, and three witnesses quickly stepped up to make their marks.

Still laughing, he led her off the dais. "Come, my lady. The priest awaits, and the sooner we say our vows, the sooner you can bend to *my* will."

Another gale of laughter carried them across the hall and out the door, where Ivo let Alaida's giggling women surround her, wrap her in her cloak, and sweep her off toward the manor's little chapel. The men, full of bawdy good humor, grabbed up torches and trailed after them, their laughter echoing across the yard as Ivo's words were repeated to those who hadn't heard.

"You have an odd way of wooing a woman," shouted Brand over the tumult as he and Ivo followed along after the others.

"She tweaked me."

"Well, now she's ready to slit your throat."

"That will pass."

"And if it doesn't?"

"Then better an angry woman in my bed than a fearful one."

"Better yet a laughing one," Brand pointed out.

"Aye," Ivo agreed, then added with a wicked grin, "But best of all, a moaning one."

Brand nodded ahead to where Alaida stood at the chapel door. "I wager my best arm ring you'll draw neither laugh nor moan from those lips tonight."

Ivo looked at his bride, at the fury that hardened her face and the clenched fists she held stiffly at her side. She was at least as angry as she had been last night.

And yet last night . . . That little hitch in her breath as he'd bent to kiss her—that wouldn't be so hard to draw out again, to turn into a moan.

"That," he said to his friend, "is a wager I will take."

WHORESON. PAUTONNIER DE linage felon. *Base-born pig swiver.*

A life lived amid Norman knights and Saxon peasants had taught Alaida a multitude of curses in two languages. She ran through the entire litany in her mind without finding anything foul enough to describe Lord Ivo de Vassy.

God, that she were a man and a knight, she fumed as she watched him swagger toward her, his gray cloak flapping behind him like the wings of some great bird. She would beat that randy grin off his face, then take up the sword to ride against him and the king that had given him lordship over Alnwick. But she wasn't a man, and de Vassy did have dominion, so when he reached the chapel step and took his place at her right, she bit back the stream of curses, pulled her cloak more tightly against the cold, and prepared to do what she must.

De Vassy leaned over as if to kiss her cheek. "Smile," he whispered, half jest, half command. "Lest that scowl frighten the good father."

A moment later Father Theobald, who had gone ahead of them to pray, came to the chapel door. His eyes widened as he caught a glimpse of her face. He hesitated.

"Quickly, priest," grunted Sir Brand from his place at his friend's side. "Before we all start pissing ice."

Amid the hoots of laughter, Father Theobald quickly crossed himself and asked, a bit doubtfully to Alaida's ear, "Do you both come willingly to be married in the sight of God and man?"

"We do," said Ivo, not giving Alaida a chance to say otherwise. He twisted a ring off his little finger and took her hand. "I, Ivo, take you, Alaida . . ."

She let him slip the ring onto her finger and spoke her vows without emotion, and soon Father Theobald was sprinkling them with hyssop-scented holy water. "*Ego conjugo vos in matrimonum. In nomine Patris et Filii et Spiritus Sancti. Amen.*"

This time when Ivo bent, it truly was to kiss her. Alaida forced herself to remain still while his lips touched hers to seal their vows. It was no more of a kiss than the night before—but no less of one either, and once more she had to steady herself as he broke away. Ivo glanced over her head and grinned as though to share some jest with Sir Brand, and the big man's chuckle mixed with the good wishes that rose from the witnesses.

And so they were wed, except for the Mass to be said in the chapel. Whether because of Brand's earlier remark or his own frozen bones, Father Theobald raced through the Latin. They were back in the warmth of the hall almost before the last Amen. In behind them trooped the men and women of the manor and village, chattering and laughing and ready to feast.

Before anyone would eat, however, Alaida had one more trial to endure, one that would have taken place at the chapel but for the cold: to commend herself to her husband as lord of Alnwick by doing homage. This was the more difficult part, the act by which she would grant him power over her grandfather's lands. Knowing it was mere show, that Lord Ivo had already made the vows that mattered by kneeling to the king, didn't make it any easier to walk with him to the front of the suddenly quiet hall.

Kneeling, Alaida ignored the chill seeping into her bones and lifted her hands as if in prayer. Ivo enfolded them between his. His eyes locked with hers.

"Will you make yourself completely mine?"

A buzzing filled Alaida's head, as though a hive of bees had suddenly swarmed out of the rafters and settled about her ears. She stared at Ivo dumbly. *Completely his?* The lord's request for submission was part of doing homage, but he hadn't asked the question in this manner last night when the men knelt to him. Not in these words, with their layers of meaning.

"My lady?" coaxed the priest.

It was mere formality, she told herself, ignoring the tightening low in her belly that said otherwise. It was part of the ritual. She shook off the noise in her head and lifted her chin.

"I will." Her voice came out husky and low. She cleared her throat and spoke again, more firmly. "I, Alaida, do hereby become your liege woman in all things, holding to you against all men. I acknowledge you as rightful lord of Alnwick and"—her voice broke, and again she had to clear her throat—"and I will have you as my lord and be subject to you and submit myself to you. So I swear before God and these witnesses."

"I accept your homage and hereafter call you mine," said Ivo. He released her hands, but his eyes stayed on her, softer now. "In return I confirm your dower of one-third portion of my holdings as well as those gifts named in the marriage contract we each signed. For these, I ask only your oath of fealty. Will you give it?"

Dower? Gifts? She had assumed the contract only confirmed Ivo's rights, not her own. He held the advantage, after all. For what was she about to pledge? "Yes, my lord."

Ivo cocked one eyebrow as if to ask, *Don't you wish you had let Geoffrey read it to you?*

Father Theobald held out the huge volume of the Gospels for Alaida to kiss, and she laid both hands on the bejeweled cover. "I promise that from this day forward I will be a . . . a true and faithful vassal to you as my lord." Caught off guard, she stumbled through the rest of the words. Then with Ivo's nod, it was over. Alnwick was his, as was she in all ways but one.

As he put out his hand to help her rise, the knowledge of that final surrender made her belly clench again. Angrily, she pushed the thought away. She would have to deal with it soon enough, but she refused to let her mind travel that path now.

When they had washed and taken their places at table, the horn blew, and servants began carrying in the food, lading the tables with meats and savories until the trestles fair groaned. Considering how little time there had been to prepare, Geoffrey had done his new lord honor, Alaida noted without cheer. Those in the hall would eat almost as well as at Christmas, and those gathering at the gate—the poorest of the cottars and whatever beggars were in the area—would have rich orts to carry off. By morning, Ivo de Vassy would be known as a generous lord. Whether that held true over time, they would all see.

Being without a squire, Ivo asked Oswald to carve for them. Wielding the knife like the master bladesman he was, the marshal quickly piled their shared trencher with the choicest slices of mutton and pork. He laid a fillet of salmon and a pair of herrings on the side, then twisted off the leg of a goose like it was no more than a leaf and laid it among the rest. Finally, he cut into a plump pie.

"No pigeon," said Ivo firmly. "Take it away."

Oswald motioned for a boy to remove the pie, added a glistening eel to their portion, then placed the trencher between Ivo and Alaida and left them to their meal.

Ivo sliced off a bit of the crunchy, herbed rind of the pork and held the morsel out to Alaida. Such courtesy was the proper service of a knight for a lady, a swain for his lover, or a husband for his wife. He had probably been looking forward to it.

Alaida had not. She would sooner starve than eat out of the man's hand.

Ivo shrugged and popped the sliver of pork into his mouth. "You will have to unclench sooner or later."

She looked up sharply.

"Your hands," he said, gesturing toward her lap. "And your jaw. I'm surprised it doesn't pain you."

"Only one thing pains me."

"I have seen men die from a jaw less locked," he said, ignoring her jab. He took a hearty drink of the perry and offered her the bowl, which she also refused. "Come, Alaida. You have had your jest, and I have had mine. Let us call truce before you starve."

"Jest? Is that what you call it? Bend to your *will*. Do you think I didn't know you meant your . . . ?" She waved her hand vaguely in the direction of his privates.

"You began this battle, my lady, with your nun's robes and your little speech. I only returned blow for blow." The grin crept back onto his lips. "Though with better humor."

She glared at him even as her anger subsided a little. He was right. She had started this tonight, and for all that his gibes had embarrassed her, they were no worse than she'd heard at other weddings. What's more, she had challenged him before the hall, for which some men would have struck out with a fist rather than words and laughter.

"As you wish, my lord. Truce." She thought once more of what would come after supper and added, "For now."

"For now," he agreed. "But we must seal our pact." He hooked a finger under her chin and leaned close. "With a kiss."

No, she wanted to say, but in the spirit of truce, she once again closed her eyes and waited for him to take his kiss.

And waited.

She opened her eyes. He was still there, inches away, his finger still under her chin, grinning at her, clearly expecting her to kiss him. This was no truce. This was another demand for surrender.

He waited her out, and she felt every eye in the hall waiting with him.

"Come, Alaida," he murmured. "*Pax*."

Seething, she leaned forward and pecked the briefest possible kiss on his mouth. "There. And *pax* upon you."

His laugh shook the air. "By God, woman, your kisses may lack, but as quick as that tongue is, I will enjoy teaching you better."

When she thought of it later, she wasn't sure what made

her do it. All she knew was that in that moment, suddenly, she was tired. Tired of being at the disadvantage. Tired of being the butt of his humor. Tired of him being . . . him. She wanted that smirk off his face. And she wanted her hall back.

"Your lessons will not be necessary, my lord." In one motion, she snatched her knife from its sheath and drove it into arm of his chair, inches from his thigh. Instinct brought his leg up to protect his groin, and in the eyeblink he was off balance, she grabbed him by the collar and pulled him to her lips. His mouth opened in surprise. She slipped her tongue in, found his, and taunted him with a slow, circling, in-and-out until a growl of pleasure rumbled up beneath her hands. As soon as she felt it, she pushed him away, retrieved her knife, and turned back to the table, leaving Ivo hanging there, a stunned look about him.

Much like she must have looked in the solar, she thought with satisfaction.

"I said Neville had not kissed me," she said lightly as she cut herself a bit of mutton. "I did not say no one had."

The hall erupted in laughter, Sir Brand's loudest of all. This time, gratifyingly, she found it didn't bother her.

As Ivo continued to gape, Alaida crooked a finger at the varlet who stood by to serve them and pointed at the mazer.

"See this stays full," she commanded. "And bring that pie back." She turned and gave her dumbfounded groom a scathing look. "My lord husband may not like pigeon, but *I do*."

WHAT MAN HAD taught her to kiss like that?

A thousand questions churned through Ivo's head as he sat bemused, watching Alaida eat her pigeon pie, but most of them amounted to the same thing. Who had kissed her? Why had she let him? Where could he find the whoreson, and how much would he scream as he died?

Some small corner of Ivo's mind was grateful for the skill the unknown knight—he'd better be at least a knight—

had taught Alaida, but the rest of him wanted to rip the man's lungs out and fly them from the gate as pennants. Strangely, none of that fury spilled over to his thoughts of Alaida. Jealousy, yes, that some other man had tasted those lips before him, but not anger.

She was a puzzle, this wife of his, so changeable he couldn't predict from one breath to the next what spirit possessed her. First she'd been angry, then resigned, then fearful, then outraged, and now . . . what?

Confident. That's what it was. Confidence.

There she sat, enjoying her meal, ignoring him so thoroughly, he could be another servant. Somehow, that kiss had given her back a measure of the spirit that he'd admired in those first moments last night.

That made it a good kiss. One he could work with. One he just might parlay into a new armband.

That decided, Ivo settled back to watch his wife and figure out how best to approach her. How to woo her. How to make her laugh.

How, precisely, to make her moan.

CHAPTER 5

IGNORING THE PRICKLES of awareness that crawled over her flesh like so many mites, Alaida examined the sweets on the tray being offered her. She could see Ivo from the corner of her eye, leaning back as he studied her, his lips working in and out as though he puzzled over some deep riddle. She had seen the same look on her grandfather's face a thousand times, over chess or merels or plans for war. They were all the same to men: games. The fact that one of their games involved violence and death mattered little.

Now she was the game. Or the battle, as the case may be.

Fine. Better he think of her as an adversary than as property. At least her ill-considered kiss had bought her that much. She selected a wedge of almond gastel and nibbled at one corner as she considered a battle plan of her own.

She'd barely swallowed the first bite when Ivo set aside the bowl he'd been nursing and rose. "It grows late, my lady. We will retire."

So. It began.

Conscious of the laughter that rippled down the tables,

Alaida put down her cake, gathered her feet and her dignity, and rose. To her relief, the women swarmed forward and swept her upstairs before she had to take the hand he offered. The men followed, laughing and joking.

"The wedding posset," said Bôte, holding up a large drinking horn. "Ale, spiced for desire, in the horn of a bull for my lord's manhood. Drink up, both of you."

She took a sip to show it wasn't poisoned and offered it to Ivo. He drank deeply while the men cheered him on, then passed the horn to Alaida, whose reluctant sip drew hoots from all.

"Ach, that's not enough, my lady," scolded Bôte. She stood there, hands on hips, 'til Alaida downed a good swig, then a second and a third. "There. You'll be wanting all that and more, if I judge your lord husband rightly."

Her words brought yet more laughter. As it trailed off, Father Theobald was pushed forward to bless the bed. In the warmth of the solar, his prayer took on the flowery wording he had avoided in the chapel. With any luck, Alaida thought, he would go on all night.

But no. When he mentioned fruitful loins for the third time, Sir Brand cleared his throat in a pointed way. Father Theobald quickly found the end of his blessing and, naming the Trinity, swung the censer to send its smoke swirling over the furs.

"Fruitful loins," mused Wat the Reeve into the silence after they'd all crossed themselves. "I've always thought that sounds like something they'd serve at a feast."

"Aye," agreed Edric. "With butter."

"And sauce," added a voice from somewhere in the back, with a lewd slurp that made the men laugh and the women squeal and cover their cheeks with their hands. Poor Father Theobald looked as though he'd like to go out the roof hole with the smoke.

Alaida glanced over toward her groom and thought she might join the rising smoke as well, scorched away by what she saw. The bemused expression he'd worn earlier had vanished. His eyes burned like they had those first moments in the hall the night before, like those of some beast on its prey. Bright. Possessive. *Hungry.*

Without taking his gaze off her, he passed his belt and sword to Sir Brand. "Clear the room."

Voices rose in protest. Brand cut them off with a slash of his hand, but Oswald stepped forward. "Your pardon, my lord, but 'tis custom to see the bride put to bed."

"Your custom, not mine. My wife's bounty is mine alone," said Ivo. Relief washed over Alaida, even as the men grumbled at the loss of their sport. "Her serving women may stay. The rest of you, out."

"You heard his lordship," rumbled Brand. "Back to your feasting. There's plenty of good ale to ease the sting."

The room emptied quickly, though with a great many snickers and knowing looks. Only Father Theobald lingered, looking somber again, as though he might launch into the sermon he'd neglected to give at the chapel. Something about marital temperance, no doubt. Alaida smiled encouragement.

"You, too, priest." Brand put a hand between his shoulders and steered him toward the door with a none-too-gentle shove. "There'll be no more need for your services tonight."

"I'm not so certain, *messire*," said Oswald from the doorway. He spoke loudly, so his voice would carry to those in the hall. "The father here is a fair hand in the fields. I wager he could teach a man a bit about keeping his blade sharp and his furrow straight, even though he does not plow for himself."

Brand's response was lost to the roar from below as he followed the others out. His departure left only Alaida's laughing women, whose job it was to ready her for her husband. She struggled to keep her balance as merry fingers plucked away her wimple and belt and pulled her gown over her head. Someone loosed the plaits from her hair while Hadwisa and Bôte knelt to remove her shoes and hose. On the far side of the room, Ivo stripped off his cote and tossed it aside, then turned to watch as her women gathered the hem of her chainse.

That heat again. This time it reached across the gap to scorch her, as though she'd wandered too near the smith's forge. Alaida held herself tall, determined neither to look away nor to cover herself when they stripped her.

"Dismiss your women," said Ivo, his voice rough with desire. "I would be alone with you now."

The women froze. Alaida stood there for an eternity, her chainse bunched to the middle of her thighs, before she found her voice.

"Leave us." Her fingers felt clumsy as she tugged the garment away and let it fall back into place.

"But, my lady." Hadwisa blinked like a mole at midday. "We haven't . . . That is, you're not . . ."

"Hush, girl," said Böte. "I wager his lordship knows how to undress a woman. Away with you lot." She shooed Hadwisa and the others along, but stooped to pick up one of Alaida's shoes and put it at the head of the bed, a reminder that she was to submit to her husband. Then she turned and gave her a fierce hug.

"Ah, my lamb." She raised up on tiptoe to place a kiss on Alaida's forehead. "I have slept by your side each night for nigh to a score of years, but now I give you up to your husband in good joy." She leaned close to whisper, "Have some more posset if you're frightened."

"I'm not," said Alaida firmly.

"Good. Good." Suddenly Böte's face crumpled. She snatched up the corner of her headrail and blotted at the tears that dribbled down her ruddy cheeks. "Oh, my lamb, my babe, gone to wife. It seems but yesterday your lady mother put you in my arms and—"

"God's legs, woman. *Out!*"

Ivo's snarl startled Böte out of her tears. She backed away and made her escape, pausing just long enough to give Alaida an encouraging smile before she slipped out the door and pulled it firmly shut. It was a heavy door, made of oak bound with iron, and it had a bar meant to keep out the most determined invader. It cost Alaida a great deal to stand there as Ivo crossed to drop that bar into place. Whatever he intended for her, she thought, no one would stop him. The walls themselves would fall before that door gave way.

When he turned back to her, he wore an odd expression, still heated, but tempered by a wry smile. "I fear I have little patience for crying women."

"You will not be burdened with my tears, *monseigneur*."

"We are so very pleased, *madame*," he answered, mimicking her formality. He turned to the tall iron candlestick by the door and began pinching out the flames one by one. "Did I hear the old woman aright? You are twenty?"

"Near one and twenty."

"So young," he mused. "And yet old to be going to wife for the first time."

"Very old, my lord. Ancient. You should call Father Theobald back and ask for an annulment before you find yourself saddled with a crone."

"But such a pretty crone." Chuckling, he pinched out another flame. "How is it you come to marry so late?"

"To my mind, it is yet too early."

He glanced at her, one eyebrow lifted in question. "You did not wish to marry at all, then?"

"Only to you, my lord," she said bluntly. "I was betrothed at fourteen, and willingly, to a man my grandfather chose. A brave and *honorable* man."

Her cut had no effect. He simply kept at his candles. "Where is this paragon, that he never married you?"

"The marriage was much delayed because of warring, and he was killed before we could wed."

"Not at table and by a lady's knife, I hope?"

"In a melée, by a broken neck. *He* did not mock me, as you seem driven to do."

"He likely never saw you dressed as a nun." He moved to another candlestick and continued. "Is he the man who taught you to kiss?"

"No. Though I think he might have liked to."

"No doubt. Then who?"

She recalled a certain May Day and a passing knight who had joined the woodland revels for an afternoon before he rode on. "No one you would know, my lord, nor anyone you're likely to meet."

"How unfortunate." Another flame died between his thumb and finger. "I wish to thank him."

"More likely have Sir Brand gut him."

He paused over a candle, and though the smile stayed on his lips, his voice hardened. "No, I would do that myself. But only if there was more to his lessons than kissing."

"Never fear, William gave you a virgin," she said drily. "Besides, if there had been more, my grandfather would have gutted him for you."

"Good." He continued to work his way around the solar, extinguishing candles until the edges of the room receded into shadow. As he crossed to the last candlestick, his path brought him near Alaida, and as he passed, he stopped abruptly.

"It *is* you." His fingers closed around her arms, gripping them so she couldn't turn to face him. He inhaled deeply. "That scent has tickled my nose all evening, but I thought it was the rush-herbs. What is it?"

What was this distraction? Brows knit in suspicion, Alaida sniffed, first the air and then, realizing what he smelled, at the sleeve of her chainse.

"Wormwood and rue . . . and tansy, I think," she said, trying not to let on how distracted she was by the pressure of his hands. "For moths. They were on the gown I wore."

"Ah." He sniffed near her ear and it tickled. "I thought you might have doused yourself in some strange perfume in an effort to drive me away."

"I had not thought of it. Would it work?"

"No." Bending to the curve of her neck, he inhaled deeply once more. "I am not a moth."

The words warmed her skin as he breathed them out. She

turned her head away to escape the heat, but that only exposed more skin to him, skin over which he brushed a kiss. The contact was like steel to flint, and the sparks it produced scattered over her skin, spreading until she had to dig her toes into the rug to stop them. He pressed another kiss to the spot, then released her and stepped away, leaving only the swirl of chill air to take his place. A moment later, the bed creaked as he sat and began taking off his boots.

The first boot plopped to the floor. "If Geoffrey has done his job, there is a small gift for you on the tray."

More distraction. He truly was playing some game with her, trying to put her off guard with these feints, though to what end she wasn't sure. Chary but curious, she shook off the last of the sparks and sidled over to the table. There, between the oil lamp and the horns of ale and posset, lay a fat leather pouch. Coins jingled as she hefted it.

"Silver?" She let the purse fall back to the table with a thump that echoed her disgust. "I am not a whore, my lord, that you must pay for access to my bed."

"I never buy what is already mine." The second boot hit the wall as he tossed it aside in exasperation. "By the saints, woman, must everything be a battle with you? I said it is a gift. Ten shillings, to replace what you gave as alms today."

"Oh." She sagged a little, the wind out of her sails. "I didn't think you . . . But of course. Sir Ari told you."

"He did."

"He was very kind." He was also right about his lord not taking her purse, and Alaida wondered what else the seneschal had correct. More to the point, what else did she have wrong? She'd presumed much about this man before her, and thus far was being proved wrong at every turn. Feeling ever more the fool, she wrapped her arms around herself and stared down at her bare toes for a long while before adding with reluctance, "You are . . . also . . . being very kind."

Ivo snorted. "Pains you to say that, does it?"

"A little." Her mouth twisted ruefully. "*Kind* is not a word that has been much on my mind since you arrived at my gate."

"*My* gate," he corrected. "Is it so strange an idea, that a man might be kind to his wife?"

"No, my lord. But many men are not, especially to a wife who does not want them." She sounded small even to her own ears, but pushed on. "And I did not want this marriage."

"So you have made clear. Numerous times." The creak of the bed as he rose made Alaida look up. He had rid himself of his hose without her noticing, and now his chainse went, too, tossed aside so that he wore only his braies. He stretched vigorously, like a warrior about to begin combat. "And yet you have it. So now you must decide what you will do with it. With me."

"I will not fight you, my lord, if that is what you mean."

"Wise. But I want more from you than simply not fighting." Holding her eyes, he flipped back the furs to reveal the fresh linens. "Much more."

Alaida's mouth went as dry as old parchment. Blindly, she reached for the nearest horn. She'd gulped down several mouthfuls before she tasted Bôte's spices.

Ivo padded over to the last candlestick and slowly put out the final tapers, leaving her standing in the thin pool of light thrown by the fire and the lamp. Beyond its edge, her lord and husband was a ghostly figure against the blackness, with eyes that glinted like shards of glass as he turned toward her.

She looked away, just for a moment, and when she looked back, he was barely a pace away and the wall of his chest filled her vision, all planes and muscles and pale gold skin.

"You're trembling," he said, taking the posset horn from her hand and setting it back in its rest.

"I'm cold."

"You will find it warm in my arms." He stepped closer, and as his hands spanned her waist, the heat billowing off his body proved that he, at least, was not lying. "God's truth, Alaida, I would rather spend the night pleasuring you than sparring with you. Tell me what it will be. Will you make yourself completely mine?"

He used the same words he had in the hall, but filled them now with invitation rather than challenge. The trepidation that had been lying in her belly like a rock suddenly thinned and softened into a warm, smoky mist that curled though her.

"That was the vow you demanded, my lord, and the one I gave. I will honor it." Her voice grew rough as his thumbs traced lazy circles below her ribs, but she saw the triumph that lit his eyes and fought back in what small way she could. "Though I do not see what pleasure I will find in it."

"Do you not?" he asked softly as he lowered his head. "Then I must help you hunt."

His mouth covered hers, gentle at first, then more determined, until she parted her lips to his probing tongue. *I can do this,* she told herself. She could let him take what he wanted without letting it touch her.

"No." He broke off the kiss and brought one hand up to grip her chin. "You gave yourself away with that kiss, Alaida. I know that you know better. I know that you *want* better." He tilted her face into a better position, then lowered his lips to within a hair's breadth of hers. "Now kiss me, wife. Properly."

She had little choice but to give him the kiss he commanded, the kind she'd so foolishly demonstrated in the hall. This time, though, he kissed back from the first, his tongue parrying with hers, and to her shock, he tasted good, like Bôte's spices but better. And astonishingly male.

How had she missed that earlier?

Her blood began to stir despite her intentions, and as she sought to bring herself back in hand, he changed his attack, shifting off her mouth to kiss his way down her neck and back up to her ear, where he proceeded to do things with his teeth and his tongue that sent shivers down her spine. Waves of shivers, which continued to wash over her even after he finally returned to her lips. And what he did to her then was even worse.

Or better. Alaida suddenly wasn't certain. She tried to

separate herself again, but couldn't find the place where his lips left off and hers began.

It was the posset, she thought. Bôte's spices. That must be why her body was behaving so traitorously, why it was turning all warm and liquid when she didn't wish it to.

Or perhaps it was the kissing. She liked kissing, what she knew of it, and he did it well, nipping and sucking at her lower lip and then soothing away the ache he created with yet more kisses. Her May Day knight had not used that particular trick, nor had he made her knees go so weak. If he would just keep to kissing . . .

But of course he didn't. He began to explore her body, his hands moving over her with confidence but also with a gentleness she hadn't expected. Slowly, she realized she hadn't lied to Bôte. She wasn't afraid of him. Nervous about what would happen once he took her into the bed, but not afraid of the man himself. So when he stepped back a half pace and reached for the opening of her chainse and said, "Time to be rid of this," she blushed, but she nodded.

"Yes, my lord."

"Ivo," he said. Carefully, he spread the opening. It parted to reveal a wide wedge of neck and shoulder but would go no further. He placed a kiss at each edge. "You have yet to say my name, except in your vows. I would hear it from your lips."

"The neck is too narrow, *my lord*," she said softly, defiant even as she told him how to undress her. "It will not go that way."

"No?" He dipped his fingers in and brushed his knuckles over her breasts, smiling as her eyelids fluttered, then took the cloth in both hands and gave a sturdy tug. It tore to her navel. "I think it will."

She blushed more deeply, but stood fast. "Perhaps you are right, my lord."

"Ivo." He dipped a hand into the tear and flattened it against her belly. Awareness quivered through her as he slid it lower. She tensed, waiting for that touch, *there*, but he switched directions, slowly tracing a line up her belly with his fingertips, trailing fire between her breasts and up over the soft skin of her throat. Carefully, he tipped the chainse off her shoulders. It slid to her hips and hung, barely. Letting it be, he took his fill with his eyes, then slowly slid his hands up to cup her breasts. She gasped as his thumbs circled the peaks, and his eyes darkened with desire.

He bent to taste her, and that was when she discovered that kissing could be more than lip to lip, that a tongue could do things to her body she'd never imagined in her most sinful daydreams. Sensation spiraled out from where he suckled, joining with the spices to make her giddy with want. Such want. With a harsh, almost unwilling sigh, she curled her fingers into his hair.

He had her. Ivo would have crowed his victory, except his mouth was full of her summer-sweet flesh and he had no wish to give her up. He tongued over her again and shifted to the other breast, working both until her breath came in uneven gasps.

By Freyja, it was going to be hard to go slow, with his body already screaming to be buried in her. There was a hunger on him he hadn't expected, keen as the edge of his sword and growing sharper with every breath. He could slake it easily enough, carry her down onto the bed and simply have her, but he wanted more than simple release. The memory of women long ago, women like Ingigerd, who had lain with him not for money or out of obligation but for the joy of it, drove him even more than his wager with Brand.

"Come lie with me, Alaida," he whispered. She nodded, and he scooped her up and carried her the few feet to the bed. Kneeling over her, he looked down at the woman who would be his, her lips and breasts smudged and swollen from his mouth, and her fair skin carrying the flush of a woman ready for a man. He reached for the tie to his braies, but thought better of it. If he bared himself now, he would be in her in a heartbeat, maidenhead or no.

"I will not hurt you," he vowed to them both as he reared back and dragged the torn kirtle from her hips.

Her legs splayed a little as he yanked the linen free, enough for him to see the shadowed gate to her womanhood. Reddish curls, the same rich copper as her hair, surrounded it, begging for his touch, and only force of will kept him from falling on her like the raider he had once been. Like the eagle he was.

To slow himself, he started with her lips and kissed his way down, pulling another gasp out of her as he locked his lips over her breast again. She reached out for him and he let her pull him down, twisting to land beside her instead of on her, so that he retained both his sanity and free range of her body. His hands wandered over her skin as he suckled her again, making her fingers clutch at his back and his hair. He shifted and kissed his way to her belly.

"My lord," she panted, tugging at his hair, trying to bring him back to her breast.

"Ivo," he said into the soft mound of her belly. He dipped his tongue into the almond shape of her navel and felt her shiver. "Say my name."

He turned his head to watch her face while he slid his hand down and filled it with all that copper. She stilled. Her eyes got very wide, and her mouth opened in a round *Oh*. She clamped her thighs together.

As if that would stop him.

Grinning at her innocence, he curled his fingers down to find the tender bud he knew was the source of pleasure in womankind, took possession, and began to toy with it as he had her breasts. It swelled to his touch, and as it did, her legs began to churn restlessly, gradually easing apart. The scent of her curled up and grabbed him. Musky. Woman-y.

With a groan of surrender, he pressed her thighs apart and put his mouth to her. She arched and cried out in shock, pushing at his head. "What are you doing?"

Chuckling, he caught her hips and held her as she tried to scoot away. "It is the sweetest part of love-play, Alaida. The sweetest part of the hunt for pleasure. Let me show you." He let his breath warm the place he'd kissed. "Give yourself over to it. You will see."

He lowered his mouth to her again. She held herself rigid at first, but before long, she relaxed and slowly opened to him, and he settled in to enjoy himself as he helped in her hunt. She began to stir, to shift and squirm under his tonguing and the gentle exploration of his fingers. He looked to her face again to see if it was pleasure or unwillingness that made her move. She had squeezed her eyes shut, as women oft did in their passion, and was biting down on her lip. It was pleasure, for certs, and if he had any doubts, they burned away as she suddenly lifted to take his fingers into her. Her dew flooded over his hand, warm as summer honey.

By the gods, for all her supposed reluctance, she was as wet and heated as ever he'd known a woman to be. And yes, she was virgin. With a smile, he swirled his tongue down into the folds to taste her more deeply.

That's when he heard it, a distant keening that faded as quickly as it rose. He stilled, not sure it was truly there or that it came from her. Testing, he rasped his tongue across the same spot. The sound rose again, faint and low, but real. With mounting excitement, he closed his lips over the spot and drew her into his mouth.

And then the most amazing thing happened.

She moaned.

The sound was guttural, almost vicious with need, and as it broke from her lips, the need to make her truly his thudded through his veins like life itself, shattering what little remained of his patience. He wanted that heat she held within her. He needed it. It suddenly became impossible to wait. To breathe. To think.

In one motion, he stripped away his braies and was over her, pressing her down as he positioned himself and slid into her, just a little.

She froze, then squirmed, trying to escape him.

"Be still, Alaida. I can't . . ." He slipped in a bit more. He was hurting her, he knew he was, but with her moving like that, he couldn't help himself. He tried to pull back.

"No." Her nails dug into his shoulders, and she squirmed again.

"Shh, sweet leaf. Shh," he soothed. He fought to move slowly, to do it the way he'd planned, but she was so warm, so alive, so young and sweet. She moved like flame beneath him, bucking and writhing, drawing him deeper even as she tried to throw him off. He pinned her hands down, kissing her, ready to demand again that she lie still so he could do this properly, but she lifted again and in a heartbeat he was buried in her, too fast. She cried out, but still she wouldn't stop moving and the lust was on him and there was nothing he could do.

He came suddenly and hard, shoving into her, taking her, claiming her.

His. His wife.

For as long as the gods would let him keep her.

His.

SAINT PETER'S KNEES, what had just happened?

Alaida stared up into the draperies, a single tear dampening the corner of each eye. For all her high words, she wasn't able to stop those two tears.

Just like she hadn't been able to stop herself from moving against him, showing him she was a whore, after all, and for naught. She hadn't found it, whatever it was he had set her seeking. It had been there, almost, and then gone as he came into her, dissolved in the stretching fullness, her cry of disappointment following it away.

And now she had to lie here beneath him as his passion ebbed and his breathing slowed. He would roll off her soon and fall asleep, if what little she'd heard of these things was true, and she would be able to ease away from him and find some way to take herself back. She closed her eyes and waited.

He stirred atop her, and she felt a rush of warmth where their bodies still joined. "Alaida?"

Unwillingly, she opened her eyes again, this time to find him peering down at her. The dim flicker of the lamp made his face a dance of shadows. He touched a finger to the corner of one eye and held it up so the drop glinted. "Tears?"

"You have my apologies, *monseigneur*."

"Have we gone back so far?" he asked with a sigh. "It is I who should apologize. I said I wouldn't hurt you, and I did."

She said nothing.

"It had been a long time since I had a woman. Things went too quickly. And you, my sweet leaf." He kissed the tip of her nose, then her mouth. "You did not help your cause."

She frowned. "What do you mean?"

"Sometimes a man needs a woman to lie still while he . . . collects himself. You would not."

"I could not," she confessed, suddenly wanting him to understand.

"Because I hurt you," he said.

"No, my lord."

He rose up on his elbows and looked down at her. "But you cried out."

"Not with pain."

He pondered this. "Then why?"

"It was . . . I was . . . Are there no words for these things?"

A smile ghosted across his face. "Many, and I will teach you all of them. But just now, use the ones you know."

The need to explain suddenly faded. She wanted to crawl under the covers and forget the entire matter, but he hung there, over her, in her, waiting.

"It felt good," she finally managed, and once she'd started, she thought she might as well finish. "But then you"—she searched for a word—"mounted me and the good went away, and that's why I cried out, not because you hurt me, and it seemed I could get it back but . . ."

"But I came too quickly."

"Came? Is that the word for spilling your seed?"

He grinned down at her. "Aye. And for what you were hunting for as well."

"Women spill seed?" She raised an eyebrow at that one.

"No, but they come, if their man does things properly. You will see. I promise, I will do it properly the next time."

"And I will try not to move," she promised, vaguely disappointed.

Chuckling, he shook his head. "That is not what I want either."

"But you said my moving is what made you too quick."

"Only in that moment. If you had let me calm myself a little, you could have moved as much as you wanted. In fact, your moving makes it better for me, too."

"Does it?" A great sense of relief washed over her, followed by a curiosity that made her bold again. "Are you calm now?"

He made an odd choking noise, and she felt a surge within her. "Not as calm as I thought I'd be," he answered cryptically. He shifted again, settling more firmly between her legs, then kissed her gently, almost chastely she would say, except for how their bodies fit together.

Gaze locked with hers, he began to rock slowly, side to side. At first she wasn't sure what he was doing, but after a while she began to drift back toward where she had been before. She felt fuller, too—he was hardening again, without ever leaving her. She hadn't known such a thing was possible, but it felt wonderful. His kisses deepened, drifted from her mouth to her throat to her ear and back. She began to move. She *needed* to move.

"Tell me what you want," he commanded in a ragged voice. "Tell me, Alaida. Use the word."

"I want . . ." She gasped as he pressed into her. "I want to come."

With a groan, he wrapped his arms around her and tumbled, a quick roll that put her on top, still joined to him.

"Move," he urged. "Find what pleases you."

He showed her how, his broad palms cupping her bottom

to guide her over him, then shifting her a little so it felt even better. Understanding now, she moved on her own, tested different ways, different rhythms, slowly learning how to use his body to find the pleasure in her own. His hands wandered over her skin, helping her, touching her, stoking the slow fire that rose inside her. She closed her eyes and swirled her hips, seeking that perfect motion. Her whole world shrank to the bed, then to the two of them, then down to the fevered place where her body joined his. She trembled on the edge of that thing she wanted, smoldering, still not knowing what it was.

"You're there, sweet leaf. Come." His thumbs rolled over her nipples and pure raw heat burst through her. She writhed over him, twisting and arcing like the flames that seared her. "Come for me," he urged again, watching her burn with keen eyes. A final blaze of pleasure made her cry out, and she collapsed onto his chest, whimpering and boneless, shaking as he murmured for her to come, to come, to give herself, to say his name.

He gathered her close and began to move, first gently, letting her finish, then harder, more insistently as he sought his own release. Slowly the world enlarged again to include him. She found the rhythm with him, and as she answered his urgency with the same words he'd used to her, he suddenly lifted up, pulled her down hard, and poured himself into her with a shout.

Later, when it was long over and she lay beside him, hiding behind closed lids, she couldn't figure out where that wanton heat had been born, whether it came from Bôte's spices or had been in her all along, waiting for him to find it. All she knew was that it had taken her, consumed her, and left her as fragile as a leaf burned to ash. If he touched her, she was sure, she would fall into a thousand pieces.

"Alaida?" he whispered against her hair.

"What, my lord?"

"Aargh." He pushed her to her back and shifted over her, so they were nose to nose. "Look at me."

Face hot, she opened her eyes.

"Ivo. Say it."

She clung to that single piece of herself she could keep from him. "*It.*"

His eyes narrowed. "You are stubborn."

"I have often heard that, my lord."

He considered her a long moment, then slowly, deliberately, slid down her body so his mouth hovered over her breast. "We will work on that."

She didn't fall apart after all. Not until he wanted her to.

CHAPTER 6

A ROOF OVER your head. A real bed. Your woman's steady breathing in the night.

Simple things, thought Ivo as he lay beside Alaida in the hour before dawn. Things the meanest peasant enjoyed. Things Cwen had stolen, so long ago.

He couldn't count the years since the last time he'd held a woman while she slept. Alaida had granted him even that prize, drifting off in his arms in perhaps the sweetest surrender of all. The fine gold brooch he'd had Ari buy for a morning gift as they'd passed near Durham now seemed as worthless as pot metal next to what she'd given him, in just this one night. She shifted sleepily, curling into his body so that her bottom tucked against his loins, warm and soft, and he closed his eyes and reveled in the rewards of life as a man.

He was lying there trying to convince himself to get up when claws skittered across the roof. A moment later the harsh *kaugh* of a raven echoing down the chimney told him he'd tarried too long already. He eased his arm from beneath

Alaida's head and slid out of bed. She mumbled a little and rolled onto her stomach, her hips a tempting swell beneath the furs.

Ivo closed his eyes to the sight. There would be time enough for that when he rode back out of the woods tonight. Time to take his leisure over her, time to teach her about pleasuring him. Time every night, at least for a while, to enjoy being lord over Alnwick and its lady—but only if he left her now.

He dressed quickly and was reaching for his boots when the raven screeched again, louder. Ivo whistled back this time, the high-low call of the cuckoo, a signal they'd used in the raiding days. There was more scraping and the sound of wingbeats fading. He pulled on his boots, then leaned over the bed to press a kiss to the back of Alaida's tousled head. She smelled of her moth-herbs and of sex, and he breathed it in deeply so he could carry it with him.

"I would stay if I could, sweet leaf. Dream of me."

She sighed and burrowed down into the furs. With a sigh of his own, Ivo drew the bed curtains closed to shelter her as best he could. He retrieved his sword from the corner where Brand had put it, then took a moment to quaff down some ale and break off a fistful of bread before he left his sleeping wife.

The hall below was nearly dark, the torches and most of the candles having long since burned out. Two men huddled over their cups at the low table, insensible and barely upright. The rest lay sprawled like corpses, some on tables, some on the floor, with the smell of stale ale and sweat rising as thick as the smoke and the snores. The women must have taken refuge in the pantry for the night, for there was no sign of them in the hall as Ivo picked his way through the bodies and out into the night.

Brand stood in the yard with the horses, their breath curling around their noses in moonlit streamers. "You're late."

"I was distracted."

Brand tossed Ivo his cloak as the raven glided down out

of the night sky and settled onto his shoulder with a rustle of feathers. "I thought you might be. That's why I sent this one."

"Good idea. He can wake me every morning." Holding the bread between his teeth, Ivo pinned on his cloak and quickly checked Fax's girth. "Come. We need to be away. Gate!"

"My lord?" The guard stepped out of the shadows, another man at his heels. "We didn't expect you up and about this early."

There was a question under his words, a question Ivo expected would be asked many times that day as word spread that he'd left his bride before dawn. Thank the gods the sheets bore clear evidence of both consummation and Alaida's virginity, for he had no desire for either his manhood or her reputation to be challenged. Still, there would be questions. Witness this oaf.

"I have spent too many years riding out at this hour for a woman to change the habit," said Ivo, even as he wished one could. He swung up on Fax. "Least of all a wife."

The men chuckled knowingly, of one mind on the proper place of wives. Confident his words would be repeated and turn away at least some of the curiosity, Ivo motioned for the men to open the gate. Moments later, he and Brand were headed toward an untracked area the eagle had spotted as he flew yesterday.

They were nearing the edge of demesne land before Brand finally cracked.

"Balls, man. Did you or didn't you?"

"Did I or didn't I what?" asked Ivo over his shoulder, enjoying this more than he should have.

"Make her moan. Or laugh." He reined Kraken to a stop. "Or anything."

Grinning, Ivo turned Fax in a tight circle and pulled up facing Brand. He put out his hand. "I should have wagered on each instance. I could give her one, too, and have an extra for trade."

"Balls," repeated Brand. Laughing, he pushed up his sleeve, took off his arm ring, and handed it to Ivo. "Imagine if the woman actually liked you."

"I think," said Ivo as he slipped the ring onto his arm, "that if she liked me, I might be dead of it."

Brand grunted. "If it were that easy for us to die, I would get me a wife tonight and set about killing myself."

On his shoulder, the raven chortled his agreement.

"THERE'S NO USE pretending, my lady. I know you are awake."

Alaida had been lying there behind the drawn curtains of the bed for a good while, coming to terms with a body that felt strange and tender and with the fact that she had woken alone. As she'd lain, she'd listened to the scuffle of Bôte and the others moving about the room. She'd heard the clatter of wood being fetched in, the slosh of water poured from ewer to bowl, the thump of the shutters being thrown open, the sounds of all the things that her servants did every morning, as though this morning were no different than any other. Except that it *was* different, for she'd also heard the titters over the torn chainse that lay on the floor and the whispers that Lord Ivo had ridden out early.

That was how she learned he was truly gone, not simply down in the hall breaking his fast, and that was when the anger started to rise, anger that grew sharper as she heard the pity in her servants' voices.

She understood the pity—she felt it for herself, and it stung far more than the ache between her legs—but she had no desire to see it on their faces. So she'd feigned sleep, nursing her growing fury in the shadows of the bed, and eventually the others had completed their chores and left the solar.

Bôte, however, had not. "Come, my lady, it is a fine day, and well past time for you to be up and about."

Alaida cracked one eyelid to see her nurse's creased,

round face peeping through the draperies. "Leave me. I do not wish to be disturbed."

Bôte only laughed and pushed the curtains back. Sunlight and chill morning air flooded into the recess. "The whole manor knows he's ridden out, my lady. The question is, did he do his husband's duty before he left?" With no warning, she swept the covers off. Her glance raked over the sheets and Alaida's naked body. "Aye, I'd say he did, and right well, by the look of it."

Alaida snatched for a fur to cover herself and sat up. "Begone, you old fool, before I have you whipped. Recall that I am married now and have no need of a nurse."

"*Ssst.*" Bôte waved off what they both knew was an empty threat. She'd been all but mother to Alaida for too many years to be set aside so lightly. "Perhaps 'tis better Lord Ivo is gone, else he might discover what a devil you are when you wake. Get you dressed, my lady. Others need to see that the marriage is true."

"You will *not* parade the men through this chamber," said Alaida flatly.

"You must have witnesses, my lady. Sir Ari waits on the stair, with Geoffrey and Oswald and Wat."

"No!"

"Then I shall hang the sheets out the window as they did in the old days, for all the village to see your virgin's blood. You must have witnesses," Bôte repeated stubbornly.

"By Saint Peter and Saint Paul. I know I'm well and truly married. Why cannot the rest of the world be satisfied of it?"

"Because you are a lady and he is a lord, and there can be no doubts, nor any excuse for him to claim the marriage is not true." Bôte opened the cupboard and pulled out a fresh chainse and a squirrel-lined robe to go over it. "Come, lamb. You know they must see the sheets, as they would even if he were at your side."

"But he is not." Bitterness tinged Alaida's voice. "What sort of man leaves his wife the very morning he weds her?"

"Lord Ivo's sort," said Bôte simply. "I wonder that it vexes you so, when you claimed you did not want him."

Alaida flinched as her own words came back at her. Was that why he had left her to face this mortification alone? "Want him or not, he is now my husband. His absence dishonors me."

"Only if you let it. Hold your chin high, my lady. Keep that temper of yours on a leash and show all that it is no concern to you that he is gone, for you know he will be back in your bed tonight. And he will be, mark my word. He's full of vigor, he is, and 'tis clear he enjoyed lying with you." She shook out the chainse and held it out to Alaida. "Now, put this on, unless you wish the men to see you in naught but that pelt. I will tie your hair back, and we will comb it out after and get you cleancd up."

"Bah," said Alaida, but she crawled out of bed and let Bôte help her dress.

The men were as embarrassed as she when they shuffled in a few moments later. None of them would so much as meet her eye except her husband's brash young seneschal, and even he went red when Bôte turned the furs back once more.

"Your pardon, my lady. We have seen all we need." Sir Ari signaled the others to leave, while he stayed behind. "My lady, I—"

"Thricc!" came Wat's voice, carrying up the stairs over the tread of their boots. "And a bride that fair and still he left her before dawn? The man must have balls of steel and a heart to match."

Ari whirled toward the door with a snarl. "Braying ass! I will shut that mouth."

"Hold, steward," said Alaida sharply. "Let him be."

"But he—"

She cut off his protest with a flick of her hand. "If I were as foul-tempered of a morning as my nurse claims, I would leave him to your mercies. But I am not, and it is my wedding morning. I am inclined to be generous." Besides, any insult in the reeve's comment was to her husband, not her. She rather liked that. "He only says what all of you think. Ah, see his cheeks, Bôte? I am right."

"Aye. 'Twould appear you are." Bôte chuckled merrily as chagrin twisted the seneschal's smile.

"Perhaps," he admitted. "Nonetheless, you have my apology. After last night, I should have known to select a man with more sense to bring in here."

"Wat has ample sense where it matters," said Alaida, stepping closer to the fire to warm herself. She would let manor business distract her a little—manor business and this pleasant young knight, who, she reminded herself, was not responsible for his lord's behavior. "The harvest and threshing were done in good order last fall, with little waste. Every mare is in foal that should be, and he has seen to the making of enough rope for all we need, with more to sell for profit. Even the walls and ditches are in better repair since he became reeve. The villagers work well for him, and he knows how best to use them. That buys much tolerance from me, as it should from you, if you intend to build this castle."

"Nevertheless, I will warn him to watch his tongue. The wedding sport is done, and he *will* show respect." Sir Ari crossed to the window and stood looking out over the open meadow that sloped down to the bridge and the desmesne lands beyond the river. He studied the view for a long while before turning back to her. "You know a great deal about the workings of the manor, my lady."

"Alnwick has been mine to keep in my grandfather's absence, though I thought I was keeping it for him and not a husband." *A filthy dog of a husband.*

"I will gladly take whatever advice you would share," said Ari. "It has been too long since I oversaw either men or lands."

"My advice will come dearly after your abandonment."

"My apologies, my lady, but my duties took me away. I returned only in time to come up here." His glance flickered toward the bed then back to her, and his lips worked as he fought a smile. "I trust you didn't find it necessary to flee to Rome."

"Not yet, at the least," she allowed. "But where were you if I had? You owe me a forfeit for decamping, sir."

"And the price of this forfeit?"

Alaida thought a moment. "I heard you humming as we walked yesterday. Do you sing? We have not had a *jongleur* come to Alnwick in many months."

"I am better poet than singer, my lady, and better story-teller than poet. And no poet at all in French."

"Then you shall tell me a story as your fine. Something with dragons. I greatly enjoy tales with dragons." She smiled at the way his brows suddenly knit in concentration. "Do not look so pained, steward. You needn't pay your debt today. I will wait a little.

"As to the advice, it is simple," she continued. "We have good officials at Alnwick. Put your trust in them and you will not go far wrong. But not too much trust. A careful eye to the accounts will serve you well, for all that Wat keeps his with marks cut on sticks."

"I know the method well, my lady." He grinned widely, his straight white teeth flashing in his comely face. "We will get by."

It struck Alaida that her husband and his men were all fairer than most. She had not seen them all side by side yet, but Ari clearly bore the finest features of the three, so well formed he was almost pretty—especially when he smiled, as he did so much of the time. Towering Brand, despite his untrimmed hair and beard and the scar marking his cheek, had a sparkle in his sky blue eyes that could make a maid sigh. And Ivo, of course, bore that chiseled face, all angles except for the curve of his full lips.

Desire crackled through her body at the thought of those lips and where they had traveled, an echo of the spasms that had racked her as he put his mouth to her. Dismay followed close behind, followed by anger at herself. What was she, that even in her humiliation her body warmed for him?

"I will take my leave, my lady," said Ari, drawing her attention back. "I only stayed to say I will be taking Geoffrey and Wat with me to ride the bounds while the weather holds."

"That is usually done on Saint Mark's Day," said Alaida.

"And so the proper riding will be. Today is merely for my knowledge. Also, your lord husband left a message. He says"—he looked up, as though Ivo's words might be carved into the beams—" 'Tell my lady that my absence could not be avoided. Say that I will return soon after sunset, and ask her to wear something pretty tonight at supper, for I have a gift to give her and it would not look well on a nun.' "

Tell him he can piss on his gift, for all I care. The words leapt to Alaida's tongue, but for once in her life she took Bôte's good advice, bit them back, and merely smiled. "My thanks, *messire.* Be good enough to send Hadwisa up as you go."

There was a breath when she thought he would say something more, but he simply nodded. "Yes, my lady. I will put my mind to your dragon. By your leave."

Bôte turned to her as the door shut, nodding sagely. "See, Lord Ivo is no happier about going than you are at having him gone. He will return as I said he would, and then you will have a gift and all will be aright."

"*Phfft.* He will not appease me with some bauble. Fetch the soap. I would wash him off me."

"Proud and stubborn as when you were a babe," muttered Bôte. "Be careful, lest your anger does you even less honor than his going. A smile would serve you better."

"I am such a happy bride," mocked Alaida, fixing a bland smile to her face for a heartbeat before she let it fall away. "The soap."

By the time Hadwisa turned up, Alaida had washed and dressed and was sitting at the table, picking at the remains of the bread and cheese. Hadwisa quickly untied the ribbon holding back Alaida's hair and took up the comb.

"I will try not to hurt, my lady, but the rats have made a terrible nest here in the back."

Bote eyed Alaida mischievously. "Had you thrashin' a bit, did he?"

"Bôte!" Alaida tried to look stern, but she *had* been thrashing, and more than a bit. Recalled heat flashed through her again and burned up her neck before the flame curled back on itself and settled between her legs.

"You blush, my lady," said Hadwisa, giggling. "Even your ears are red."

"That, girl, is the color of a well-tupped bride," said Bôte. Grinning, she tipped Alaida's face up and peered into it. "Enjoyed him as much as he enjoyed you, I venture. Good. 'Tis how it is meant be."

"I vow I will get me a *real* waiting woman," muttered Alaida as she pushed Bôte's hand aside and pressed her palms to her blazing cheeks. "One who knows her place and when to keep silent."

Bôte only laughed, but she held her tongue after that and set to work helping Hadwisa. Their hands were deft and gentle despite the tangles, and as they combed and smoothed, Alaida finally had time to consider what Bôte had said. The old woman was right; she would be better served by pretending all was well, at least until she heard what her husband offered as reason for his absence. That decided, she was able to relax under the women's hands and let her thoughts drift, first to Ivo's message and then to the messenger. They had begun the long plaits when what the steward had said hit her: *After last night, I should have known* . . . How the devil did he know what Wat said last night?

"What was that, my lady?" asked Hadwisa.

"Hmm? Oh. I must have been thinking aloud." Alaida would have left it there, but both women had stopped their work and looked at her expectantly. "'Tis nothing. Sir Ari said that after last night, he should have known to pick someone with more sense than Wat to bring as witness. I only wondered how he knew what was said, when he was not here."

"Men talk," said Bôte. "Especially about such foolish-ness as went on last night. They're all boasting of their wit this morning, even the ones who have none."

"But when would Sir Ari have heard the tale? He said he had only just returned." Alaida's thoughts leapt ahead of themselves. "And if he did just return, how did he come to have a message from my husband?"

"Aye, that is strange," said Hadwisa. "Lord Ivo was away well before Sir Ari came. Before dawn, Penda said."

"Hush," said Bôte sharply. "They must have met in pass-ing, that is all."

"Oh, of course," said Alaida as reason finally caught up with her anger-stoked imagination. "My mind is as thick as honey in winter. I must be tired."

"Tired," muttered Bôte. "There's a name for it." Hadwisa giggled again as color flooded into Alaida's cheeks, and Bôte joined in the laughter. "Here. Let's have those ribbons. We must get you off to Mass. Father waits."

Sweet Mother, thought Alaida as they wove the ribbons into her hair. Mass. Father Theobald. And all while smiling and pretending nothing was amiss. Sweet Mother.

She should have stayed abed.

"AND THE CAIRN marks the end, with a straight line back to where we began," said Geoffrey. He tapped his staff on the pile of rocks then swung it to point back toward the south and east. As he did, a movement overhead caught his eye and he glanced up. His jaw dropped open. "I vow, that eagle has followed us since we left the gate."

A smile curved Ari's lips as he twisted to watch the bird carving circles overhead. "Are you certain 'tis the same one?"

"Aye. See the crooked feather in his tail?"

Geoff had good eyes. They had been under Cwen's curse for years before Ari learned to tell Ivar by that crooked feather. "Perhaps he wants to learn the bounds as well, to know where he may fly."

"Just so he hunts outside them," said Geoffrey. "If he starts taking lambs or hens on manor land, an arrow will find him."

An instant later, the eagle stooped and whisked past Geoffrey's head, so close they could hear the wind whistle in his feathers. The others ducked and cursed, but Ari only laughed, pleased to know Ivo could hear from that high. A raven's ears were not quite so keen.

"Tell the men to look to their lord's shield before they think of killing any eagle," he said. Understanding dawned on three faces: Ivo's black shield bore a silver eagle.

"But what if there are losses, *messire*?" asked Wat.

"They will be made good, and if an eagle must be killed, Lord Ivo will assign a man to do it. Now, let us see if I have any kind of memory." He rattled off the markers they had touched so far, Geoff and Wat nodding as he got them all correct. "We will finish another day. Be on your way. By now Lady Alaida will likely have recalled she wants to see the marriage contract. I will stay here a little to think, then ride out to meet Lord Ivo and Brand as they come in."

Oswald and Geoffrey started off, but Wat hung back. "I truly did not mean for her to hear me," he said as soon as the others were out of hearing. "I would not purposely do the lady hurt for all the gold in Christendom."

"You've heard all I have to say, Reeve, and your lady has already forgiven you. Go on."

Wat opened his mouth as if to say something else, but thought better, snapped it shut, and kicked his fat little pony into a trot that carried him toward home. Perhaps he was learning.

Ari waited until he was well away, then turned to look up at the nearby tree where the eagle settled.

"He saw the three stains on the sheets and said you must have balls of steel and a heart to match. He was out of the room, but she overheard." He wasn't certain how much Ivo took in while in the eagle's form but knew it was something.

Ari considered himself fortunate in that regard. Whether

by some flaw in Cwen's magic or because the raven was the sacred messenger to Odin, he retained full awareness even when he was in bird form. The others lost a part of themselves to their beasts: some less, like Ivo, who could recall enough of what he saw through the eagle's eyes to help him in his spying for the king, and some more, like Brand, who vanished into the bear completely each night, often to discover the next day that the animal had done great harm without his ken. Ari had never been able to speak to either man about it and knew only what he saw the beasts do or heard about later from Brand's shoulder. As much as he missed what Cwen had taken, he was grateful for what had been left him.

The eagle leapt into the sky with a shriek, circled once, then wheeled away after a flock of gulls and was soon lost in the distance. For his part, Ari sat studying the manor a bit, then turned his mount west, toward the wood. He had passed a pool there as he'd ridden in this morning, and now that the day's business was done, he had need of its quiet waters.

He soon found the spot, dismounted, and hobbled his horse with a twist of rope. As the animal began to crop at the grass, Ari knelt on a dry hummock at the water's edge and rested there while he prepared his mind. When he was ready, he rose up on his knees, took out his knife, and touched the blade to his palm.

"Father of All, I call on you for aid." He lifted his eyes and hands to the heavens. "I have tried, but I do not understand your message. Help me, Odin. Help me see what you and Vör mean for me to see."

With a slash, he laid his palm open. Blood welled and gathered. He held it high for the gods to see, then tipped his hand and let it stream into the still waters and swirl away into the depths.

Odin liked blood and sacrifice. If there were enough of both, he might answer. Ari waited.

After a time, the blood began to slow and clot, and the sting in his palm faded to become one with the dull throb in his upraised arms. Still he knelt there, his arms high, the pain growing. Only when agony drew a haze over his eyes did he finally let his hands fall to his side.

"I am ready, Odin," he called once more before he settled back on his heels and turned his eyes to the bloodred waters of the pool, waiting for the vision to come.

CHAPTER 7

TAKE THAT. WITH a grim smile, Alaida stabbed the eye of the little man she was stitching, the one she had given yellow hair and an eagle shield.

She had grown angrier as the day passed, irritated by the sideways stares and whispers that had trailed after her as she moved around the manor. It would have been appalling enough to walk through the world on her husband's arm, with everyone knowing what they'd been doing all night. Facing it by herself had simply proved too much, especially when combined with the pity. She had retreated to the solar not long after dinner and created this little man to torture. It amused her.

A change in the voices that rose from the hall caught her ear, and she left her needle in the eye of her little lordling. "Is that Geoffrey I hear?"

Hadwisa cocked her head to listen, then rose and went to the doorway to check. "Aye, my lady. He and Oswald are below. I do not see Sir Ari."

"'Tis Geoff I want. Tell him to bring the marriage contract to me."

At some point, she had recovered her ability to think beyond the moment and remembered she needed to know what the devil she'd signed. Unfortunately, this realization had taken place after Ari had stolen away the steward, and she'd been forced to while away the afternoon with her embroidered tortures. Her limited patience was now wearing thin, and it threatened to fray entirely as she waited for Hadwisa to do her bidding. She plucked the needle out and poked it in lower, right at the spot where the little lordling's legs met. Even better.

Geoffrey soon appeared with the document in question, a rare smile on his face that waned as he saw her glowering. "Sir Ari guessed you would be ready to see the contract by now. Would you like me to leave it, or shall I read it out?"

"Read it. I am of no mind to puzzle out your hand today."

"As you wish, my lady." He came to stand near the window, where the light was better. "There is a bit at the first about the authority for the contract. God and king. The usual. I assume you want to hear the endowment." He waited for her nod.

"Let me see, then . . . Ah, here. 'Therefore I, Ivo, Baron of Alnwick, by my authority and according to ancient practice, give thee, my wife Alaida, by this document, everything of mine within the vill of Chatton.'—And here it is all listed out, my lady, from the lands and the men down to the doves in the cote and the bees in the skep—'And I give thee in the vill of Houton five oxgangs of land, which you may choose of the best of the *demesne* excepting the orchard, and I give as well the mill and the perquisites of the hallmote, and the profits of its wool. And I give thee in the manor proper of Alnwick, the pasture called Swinlees and its herbage. All these things I cede in perpetuity to thee, my wife Alaida, to have, to sell, to give, or to do whatever you wish with them at your will, saving only the obligations of fealty . . .'"

There was more, including a section detailing the one-third portion that made up her dower, but Alaida barely heard it. At some point, along about the mention of doves and bees, her hands had begun to tremble. By the time Geoffrey listed out the names of those who had signed and witnessed, they were shaking so hard she had to twist them into her skirts to keep them from flapping about like crows.

"He gave me all of that?" she asked when he came to the end, surprised to hear that her voice was not shaking as well.

"Yes, my lady, all of it. That first night, after you went upstairs, he looked at the accounts again and told me what he wished you to have. I set it down as he said."

Alaida tried to absorb it. A manor—a small one, worth only a half knight's fee, but a manor—and the largest parts of the income from another, plus land of her own within the *demesne*. Even the marriage contract her grandfather had made had not secured so much for her outright. She had money and property now, of her own right, and all thanks to this husband she barely knew, whom she had fought at every turn, and who had ridden off this morning and left her to a day of humiliation. What was she to make of him?

There existed a more pressing problem, however. "I was foolish last night, Geoffrey. I do not have good witnesses to this."

"Oswald and the others were in the hall as Lord Ivo commanded me what to write, my lady," said Geoffrey. "They heard what he said. Their witness is sound, with or without the reading."

"Nonetheless, I will have you read it out again at supper for all to hear. It will do me well to protect myself, even if I am late at it."

"Very well, my lady. I will see that Wat and Edric are in the hall with Oswald to affirm their marks."

"Good. Leave the parchment as you go. I wish to read it for myself after all. And have the accounts brought to me so I may see the value of what I own."

Geoffrey left, and Alaida turned to where Bôte sat in the corner, hemming a gown and grinning to herself. "You are unnaturally silent, old woman. Out with it before you burst."

"I have naught to say, my lady."

"And I have a pig's ears. Fetch me a wax tablet."

"As you say, my lady." Bôte broke off her thread and held her work out to admire before she rose. "As you say."

EVERY EYE SWIVELED toward Ivo as he and Brand walked into the hall that night. Half of them asked the same question that had hovered beneath the guard's words that morning, a question he was now going to have to answer for Alaida. The others—men mostly—were filled with a kind of open admiration, owing to Wat's mouth, no doubt. A fierce scowl sent them all back to their business.

"I don't see her," said Brand. He lifted the raven off his shoulder and set him carefully on a perch. They had noticed the bird seemed to be favoring one wing and suspected an owl or hawk had hit him. "Perhaps your lovemaking drove her to the convent after all."

Ivo scanned the hall. "She must be upstairs."

Brand grunted. "Bad sign, that."

"What?"

"Losing your sense of humor over a woman. And a wife, at that."

"Hmm?" It took Ivo a moment to come back around to what Brand had said. "Oh. Lovemaking. Convent. Very funny. Ha-ha."

Chuckling, Brand thumped Ivo on the shoulder with enough force to rattle his teeth. "Go on. See to your lady and make that pretty speech you've been practicing in your head all the way home. I will find me some ale and a place to read this saga your new steward left." Brand patted the spot where Ari's latest message hung in a pouch from his belt. "He must be trying to show you he's good with words after all."

"I heard much of it already. Tell me if he says anything

important," said Ivo. As Brand bellowed for ale, he trotted up the stairs, unpinning his cloak as he went.

Brand was right. Ivo had been playing out various explanations for his absence in his head and finding none of them satisfactory—especially the part where he had to tell her to expect him to leave every day before dawn. There was no way to do it, just as there had been no way to tell her last night amid the love play that he would not be beside her come morning. He should never have come to Alnwick, never have married Alaida, never have expected this madness to work, but he was here and he didn't have it in him to leave until the gods or Cwen's magic forced him to. He would tell her somehow.

When he pushed the door to the solar open, he found Alaida alone and bent over a thick book and a sheet of parchment that lay spread out on the table. She pursed her lips in concentration as she traced out a line of script with one finger then scribed a few marks onto a wax tablet with a stylus. Ivo watched her for a moment, enjoying the peace of it, until she heard some small noise and looked up. The crease between her eyebrows deepened.

"My lord."

Not the cheerful greeting he'd hoped for, but neither was it the hostility he'd expected. He hung his cloak on a peg and pushed the door shut so their words would not feed the gossip. "Is that the marriage contract?"

"Yes, my lord. And the accounts."

"I hoped you would take time for it today." He went over and picked up the wax tablet. She had been tallying rents, by the look of it. "Are you satisfied?"

She nodded. "I am. I have asked Geoffrey to read it out at supper, for Oswald and the others to confirm their witness."

"I will confirm it as well, for all to hear." He handed back the tablet. "Never again sign a contract without knowing what is in it, Alaida. You are my vassal now, as well as my wife, and you owe me care in your dealings."

"I have always been careful until now, my lord." She

looked down at her lap, so he couldn't see her face. "I let my anger make me foolish."

"Well, you are being wise now, and that is what is important." Her words made him hopeful, and he dragged a stool around so he could sit before her. "Does this sudden wisdom mean you're no longer angry with me?"

"Yes. No." She raised her head to meet his eyes, and her lips thinned as she considered the question. "I do not know."

He wasn't sure what to say to that, so he waited.

"You confuse me, my lord. You threaten and yet you're kind. You force yourself into my life and yet you woo me with a gentle hand. You take everything, even myself, and yet I discover you have done this." She touched the contract almost reverently, as though it were some sort of holy relic. "This most generous thing. Few men would have given so much when they held the advantage that you hold over me."

"My father always told his sons that too much of an advantage is a bad thing in a marriage, that a husband should be openhanded with his wife. The king gave me much and took all from you. The lands and monies are to . . . balance things a little, as well as to ensure that you are protected, no matter what comes." *Like your husband suddenly disappearing,* he thought.

Her eyes narrowed and she looked at him aslant. "You wish to protect me," she said doubtfully.

"You are my wife."

"And yet you leave me here alone while your men come in to examine the stains of our lovemaking." She shook her head. "It is strange protection you offer, my lord."

Her voice was calm and even, but her words fell like a lash on Ivo's guilty conscience. He pushed to his feet before she could see the blood she had drawn rise into his neck and ears. "Ari was here, as were your women. You were safe."

"I was humiliated."

"That was not my wish."

"And then I had to go to Mass," she continued without acknowledging him, working herself into a fine rage, no matter what she said about not being angry. "Also without my husband at my side. And there I knelt, trading blushes with Father Theobald while you galloped around the countryside. Was your hunting good, my lord? That's what I told him you were doing. I thought it sounded better than saying I had no idea where you were or why you had gone. I decided lying to a priest was no more of a sin than some of the things we did last night."

"It wasn't a lie, and it wasn't s—"

"So you *were* hunting?" Her outrage lifted her off her stool. "You left me to go *hunting*?"

"No. I left for other reasons, but I did hunt a little while I was out, which means you did not lie to the priest. Nor did you sin with me."

"That's not what Father Theobald said. He spoke this morning of the intemperate acts husband and wife should avoid. We missed very few last night, I think."

"For a man who has forsaken women, Father Theobald has over many opinions on the subject." He fought to keep his voice calm. He was getting angry, and he was not the one wronged. "Nothing a husband and wife enjoy together is sin in any reasonable man's religion. As to the humiliation, all I can do is say again that it was not my intention, and tell you I would not have left without good reason."

"What reason?" she challenged.

He shook his head. "You would not understand."

"I am not witless, my lord. Explain it so I can. Was it punishment for my sharp tongue?"

"No."

"Did I displease you so much in bed?"

"No! God's legs, Alaida, is that what you've been thinking all day? You pleased me beyond words. Surely you know that."

"Then why?" she demanded.

"I cannot tell you."

"Cannot or will not?"

"Both," he snapped back before he could stop himself. "And you may as well know now that I will ride out every day, without fail." *There. It was out. Poorly, but out.*

She looked as though he'd slapped her, open mouthed with shock. "*Every* day?"

"Every day, all day, fair or foul, and for the same good cause which has nothing—nothing!—to do with you or whether I am pleased or displeased. It is not my choice. It is . . . what I must do."

"But why?" she fairly shouted.

"Because I must. Stop asking, woman. That is all the answer you will get."

"It is—" she began, but Ivo moved toward her, warning in his eye, and she snapped her mouth shut again. With a "*Hummpf,*" she stalked over to the embroidery frame that sat near the window.

"'Because I must. Because I must,'" she repeated to herself, catching his tone precisely. She reached down, snatched up her needle, and jabbed it into the cloth. "*Coillons!*"

The sound of Brand's favorite curse coming from the mouth of his lady wife—even this termagant of a wife and even in French—caught Ivo off guard. He started to laugh, and when she whirled on him, ready to do battle, it only made him laugh more. "I knew you would make no nun—unless nuns now talk like sailors."

She choked on something that could have been either another profanity or a strangled laugh, and the fire suddenly drained out of her. She pressed her fingers between her brows as though her head pained her. "This is what I mean, my lord. You announce you will be husband only by night, you mock me, and yet you expect me to laugh with you."

"Which you nearly did," he pointed out, for which he earned a quick flash of almost-smile followed by a frown so sour it could have curdled milk. He tried a different tack. "Many men are husband only by night, and many of their ladies are glad of it."

"Many ladies wish they had no husbands at all." She heaved a sigh that sounded for all the world like she might be one of them, but when she spoke again, it was in resignation. "I am not going to change you in this, am I, my lord?"

"No."

"And I suppose I am to wave farewell obediently each morning as you ride off."

"I doubt you ever do anything obediently," said Ivo. She looked up sharply, but he raised his hands in surrender before she could find reason to rage again. "I leave long before dawn, Alaida. I do not expect you to wake."

"Before dawn," she repeated in disbelief. "Every morning?"

"Yes. But I will return each night, and I promise you, the return will be more willing than the leaving."

"So you say."

"So I swear." He ventured a little closer to her, and when she didn't back away, closer still, so he could take her hands in his. "I do not wish to leave you, sweet leaf, but I must. I cannot tell you any more. You will have to trust me in this."

"Trust you?" Her question carried a note of bitterness. "I barely know you, my lord. You are a stranger to me, for all that I lay beneath you last night. I have exchanged more words with your seneschal than with you."

"That will change," he vowed firmly, ignoring the flicker of envy that rose at her mention of Ari. Ari, who had already seen the sunlight touch her face, as he would never do. "You will come to know me over the next days and weeks, and trust will come with knowing."

"And in the meantime?"

"In the meantime, I can offer only this as my pledge." He swept her into his arms before she could protest and kissed her until he heard that little catch in her breath and felt her melt against him. When he finally set her back on her feet, her eyes had gone all smoky, in a way that made him feel reckless, like he would carry her off into the woods and keep her for his own no matter what came. "Do you understand?"

She swallowed hard. "I believe so, my lord."

"Good. Now, would you like the gift I brought you?"

"I would not refuse it," she said carefully. "But I did not put on a pretty gown as you asked. I was not happy with you when I dressed."

"I suspect you are not happy with me, even now." Ivo took in her plum-colored gown, laced just tight enough to show the curve of her body, and the pale yellow underdress that brightened her neck and wrists. On her head, instead of the head-swathing wimple, she wore a simple *couvre-chef* that let her plaits show. He nodded in approval. "'Tis plain, but better than that horror you wore last night. Hold out your hand."

He pulled a pouch from his belt, unknotted it, and spilled its contents into her palm. A dozen small, dark green stones glinted within the knot of gold vines that formed the brooch.

"Emeralds!"

The surprise and delight in that one word was worth the fat purse it had cost him. "I'd been told you had red hair and thought you might have green eyes."

"I am almost sorry I do not, even though they would likely mean even more freckles." She held the brooch up, tilting the bruted stones against the firelight. "They are as if the leaves had turned to stone."

As Alaida pinned her brooch in place and found a bronze mirror in which to admire it, Ivo glanced down at the piece on her embroidery frame. He immediately picked out his shield among the army of figures on the tapestry. He was beginning to puff up a bit at the idea that she had already stitched his image, when he noticed where her needle sat— where she had stabbed it so viciously only moments before. *Coillons, indeed.* His crotch throbbed as though she'd stabbed him instead of this bit of cloth. Wincing, he looked to his wife and the blade hanging at her waist, trying to decide whether he needed to disarm her before he sat beside her again. Then she turned, and thoughts of knives and needles faded in the glow of pleasure that lit her eyes.

"I have long wanted an emerald," she said softly. "And now to have so many."

"You like it, then?"

"I do, my lord, though once again I find myself lost in confusion, this time of my own making." The light in her eyes dimmed a little as she touched the spot at the base of her throat where the brooch rested. "I vowed I would not be appeased with a bauble."

"It was meant to please, not appease. I would have given it no matter what your mood."

"Then you have accomplished your intent, my lord, for I am most pleased."

"Good. Now, let us go show off your new jewels and have the contract read. I wish for every man in the hall to know how much I value my wife on all counts. Come." He stepped out from behind her frame and held out his hand, and she crossed the few steps to lay her fingers on his palm. This time they were warm and steady. "Afterward, we will come back up here and I will try once more to convince you to say my name. Perhaps twice more."

The gold of the firelight made the blush that rose in her cheeks look like sunrise. For the first time that evening, she smiled an honest smile, a woman's smile. "If you must, my lord."

It was as though she'd reached out to take him in her hand, so quickly did he harden. Supper was going to be a very long meal.

CHAPTER 8

"I CANNOT GRASP it. Three knights, one of them a baron, and all without squires." Alaida contemplated the two men before her over folded hands. "You do not dance, sing, or hawk. Next you will tell me you do not play chess."

Ivo laughed. "Not enough to be good at it."

Aladia looked to Brand. "And you, *messire*?"

"Not at all, my lady," he said, reaching for his cup of ale. With the wedding behind them, he had taken his place at Ivo's right hand. By custom, Sir Ari should have been at the high table as well, next to Alaida, but he seemed to have vanished again shortly before supper, and Father Theobald sat in his place. It was Alaida's comment on the missing seneschal, and on Oswald carving again, which had started this conversation and exposed the sad lack of graces among her husband and his knights. Why, even Neville and his pitiful friends had squires—and even their squires played chess. These two seemed to have been fostered by wolves.

"And what of Sir Ari?" she asked. "Does he play?"

Ivo looked to Brand, who shrugged. "I don't think so."

Alaida frowned. "What sort of land do you two come from, *messire*, that its noble knights do not play chess?"

Ivo shot Brand a glance as if in warning, but when he met Alaida's eyes, his expression was bland. "What do you mean?"

"Sir Ari said he and Sir Brand are not Norman, and it is clear they are not English," she said. She leaned forward so she could see Brand better. "But he did not say from where you do hail."

"Uh . . ."

"Guelders," said Ivo easily.

"Aye, Guelders," echoed Brand.

Ivo took Alaida's hand and began tracing lines down each finger, one at a time, in a way that sent shivers racing up her arm. "How did you come to ask Ari where he's from?"

"We were talking of you, that first day, and he called you Ivar," she said. His touch was distracting, but not so much so that she failed to notice the glances that passed between him and Brand again. Something about the topic made these two wary. She watched their faces carefully as she recounted the rest of her conversation with the seneschal.

Brand's face grew more shuttered as she spoke, then suddenly brightened. "I remember Ivar! He was a good man—the kind you want by your side in battle—but a devil with the maids."

"Really?" Alaida cocked an eyebrow. "Sir Ari said he was old."

"Oh. Well, he probably seemed so to Ari. He's much younger than I." The corners of his eyes crinkled with good humor. "But I knew Ivar when he was still in his prime, and the women loved him as much as he loved them, and that was a great deal. He would find a willing wench near every night and—"

"Brand," Ivo cut him off. "This is not a proper tale for my wife."

"No. I suppose not," Brand agreed even as his grin grew

wider. "'Tis no wonder Ari thought of him, though. Ivar looked a lot like Father Theobald here."

Alaida turned to eye the priest, with his belly like an ale-pot and his thinning hair the color of damp straw—not the sort she would have thought of as wenching his way through a village, even if he were not a priest. Her doubt must have shown on her face, for Father Theobald suddenly flushed, and Ivo and Brand burst out laughing. She felt her color rise, but then their laughter caught her and she fell into a fit of giggles.

"I am sorry, Father. It is just . . ." She realized she couldn't explain without making things worse and succumbed to a full laugh. Father Theobald, bless him, simply looked down, patted his belly, and joined in.

When the laughter had died away, Brand addressed Alaida again. "So, my lady, you say that if I am to be a knight, I must learn to play chess."

"The sooner, the better." A few brisk orders sent two men upstairs for the chessboard and set other servants to clearing the tables.

As Alaida directed the placement of the board and chairs, Ivo stepped up behind her and rested his hands lightly on her shoulders. "What are you doing, wife?"

"Preparing to teach your man chess, my lord."

He leaned forward to put his mouth next to her ear. "You are due for lessons of your own, if you will recall. Learning to say my name?"

If he had spread her legs right there, he could hardly have caused more havoc in her mind or her body. Desire swamped her, as it had earlier in the solar, when Lucifer himself had whispered into her ear that it might be pleasant to skip supper in favor of her husband's lessons. She teetered on the edge of that wantonness as she answered, "I only try to do as you asked, my lord. Come to know you better."

"By teaching *Brand* chess?"

"A man's men are a reflection of his character," she said neatly, but he only ground out a profanity that showed how much he disliked her argument. A few steps away, Father Theobald studied them with open curiosity, likely watching for any sign of intemperance to address the next time he had her at Mass. His concern was clearly warranted. Alaida affixed a neutral smile to her lips. "I cannot leave now, my lord. It would be ill mannered." *Not to mention obvious.*

"Show him the pieces and how they move," said Ivo. "Then ask someone else to take over and excuse yourself."

A part of her bridled at his high-handed order, but that other part of her, the part he had already taught to crave his touch, made her nod. "Yes, my lord."

He squeezed her shoulders gently, and she heard the smile in his voice as he said, "Ivo."

Then he was gone as Brand drew him aside for some conversation, and she was left wondering just how quickly she could explain the basics of the game and whether Father Theobald would be willing to help, considering how Sir Brand goaded him.

"WHERE THE DEVIL is Guelders?" demanded Brand in a low voice as soon as they reached a corner out of earshot of the others.

"Between Flanders and Saxony, I think. We can't say we're Norse. Memories are too fresh along these coasts."

"And what do I do if I meet a man who really is from Guelders and he wants to talk of home?"

"Tell him you fostered elsewhere. Did Ari have any news?"

"I never got to his message. Oswald wanted to talk about getting him, er, you, more fighting men—it seems your king has all your knights in prison—and I found some other small distractions." His gaze wandered, and Ivo followed it to a pair of golden-haired women who were stripping down a table. Their breasts bobbled merrily beneath their gowns as they shook out the cloth, and Brand sighed. "To my mind, all that Danish seed has improved the English."

"They would not agree." Ivo glanced around the hall.

He'd barely taken note of any of the servants he hadn't had to deal with directly, but Brand made a point. "Pick one out if you want. That one with the wide hips has a friendly look to her."

"I just may do that." Grinning, Brand pulled the parchment from his sleeve and smoothed it against his thigh. He tilted it to catch the best light from the torches and began to read. "It looks like this is mostly about boundaries, motte building, Wat—and of course, Ari uses three words where one would do. This will take me a little. Go bedevil your wife, and I will tell you if there is anything you need to know tonight."

Bedevil his wife. Now there was a pleasant idea.

Ivo left Brand to Ari's scratchings and wandered back to where Alaida and Geoffrey were setting the chessmen on the board. He motioned the steward away and took over the black, watching Alaida to make certain he placed his men correctly. He had played enough with the monks who had taught him French thirty years before to know the general outlines of the game, but he tended to reverse the bishops and castles. In his mind, it made little sense to place churchmen closer to the throne than knights and castellans, but that was the game. The world was changing.

"'Tis a handsome set," he said as he settled the last of the black pawns into the front rank.

"It was my grandfather's." She picked up one of the knights and traced the simple bend across the plain shield, Tyson's sign. Her face, so full of light a moment before, faded into sadness.

Ivo walked around the table, gently uncurled her fingers, and put the knight in its place. "If he repents his treason and is accepted back into the king's good graces, he may have it back." It was an easy promise to make: when word reached London of how the new lord of Alnwick had vanished under strange circumstances, the king would likely find himself more forgiving of Tyson's poor judgment and restore him to his lands. "In fact, it may pass that you can return it to him yourself."

"I fear that will never happen. If the king were willing to forgive a second time, you would not be here."

He still held her hand, and when he lifted it to place a kiss where the knight had been, her palm smelled faintly of the cedar that lined the chess box. "Then I hope you are more merciful than the king, my lady, for I need your forgiveness."

"Why?"

"Because I find myself glad for the king's intolerance. It has given me you."

He could tell by the way she squeezed her eyes shut that he had confused her again, and that pleased him, as did the battle evident on her face. He placed another kiss in her palm, and then one on her wrist, this time raking his teeth gently over the sensitive skin. The tiny curves that appeared at the corners of her mouth told him when the battle turned in his favor. He wondered if she ached the way he did, if she would be ready for him or if he would have to woo her a little more.

She sighed deeply and opened her eyes. "I am ready, my lord."

He couldn't help grinning. "Are you now?"

Fierce color spotted her cheeks as she realized what she'd said. "I didn't mean . . . That is . . ." She took a deep breath and started over. "The *board* is ready, my lord, if you will tell Sir Brand."

He liked her flustered, he decided. He might try to fluster her again later, when she was naked, just to see how low he could make that rosy bloom spread. Still grinning, he turned to motion Brand over.

Brand was staring at him, Ari's message hanging loosely between two fingers and an expression on his face that made Ivo's stomach twist. Smile fading, he released Alaida's hand and started across the room. "What?"

The question startled Brand out of his daze. He shook himself, then strode past Ivo with a curt, "Not here."

"Is there trouble, *messire*?" asked Alaida as Brand passed her and started up the stairs. He didn't answer.

"We will be a moment," said Ivo grimly, following him.

When they reached the solar, Brand pushed the door shut and held the message out to Ivo. "Near the bottom. There." He indicated the spot with his thumb.

It took Ivo a moment to work through the runes. Ari had received a vision, it seemed. No, two—and he had called the second of them. That explained the raven's injured wing. Ivo had seen Ari slice his hand open before, pouring blood from his palm as though it were a laut-bowl as he tried to persuade the gods to talk to him. Sometimes it worked; often it did not.

Today, apparently, it had. He had seen the same images in both visions, he claimed: Alaida, a bird, a babe. A babe. That last made Ivo smile. It would be good to bring a son into the world, even if he could not be present to raise him. But the next words tore the smile off his lips and made the gorge rise in his throat, for in the second vision, Ari had seen an eagle rise from the infant's cradle and fly out the open window of the solar. He had seen Alaida screaming. And he had seen Cwen smile in triumph.

He crumpled the parchment without finishing. "This is absurd. Even as an eagle, I would not harm my own child."

"That is not what he sees, Ivar. Read the last of it." Brand laid a steadying hand on his shoulder. "He says it was the babe itself who changed. He says . . . It seems the curse passes to our children."

"No." Ivo grated out the word between jaws locked to keep from heaving his supper onto the floor. "No."

"I am sorry, my friend."

"No," repeated Ivo. He jerked away from Brand, paced a few steps away and back in agitation. "This cannot be right. Ari must not have seen clearly."

"Clear enough for him to write of it."

"He writes to write, you know that," Ivo countered. His mind, his being, rejected this abomination. "He is wrong about this, just as he is wrong about Cwen."

"She is alive."

"She is not, and since she is not, he cannot have seen her,

and this vision cannot be true." Ivo grew more confident of his argument. "Ari is wrong. Again."

"Ivar . . ."

"He is wrong! Why do you even want to believe him?"

"Want? You think I *want* this to be true?" The words exploded out of Brand in a howl of fury and anguish. "This is on my head. I led us into Cwen's grasp. I killed her son. To know I brought this on us, on my men, was bad enough, but now to find that our children—" Choking on the words, he stood there shaking as he struggled to bring himself back under control. "These two days had given me more hope than I have had since it happened. To see you in your own hall, with a wife . . . You have a *life*, Ivar, the first of us to get one. I don't want Ari to be right any more than you do. But he has seen it."

"He's seen something," conceded Ivo. "Perhaps he reads it wrong, or . . . or perhaps the gods play games with him."

"Perhaps you play games with yourself." Brand shook his head heavily. "You must not lie with her again."

"Not lie . . . ? I have had one night with her, man. One night! And she . . ." Ivo could not find the words to explain what that one night had meant, or how much he needed more like it. How he had needed nights like that for year after cursed year without ever realizing it. For Brand it was simple; he had not had a woman in his bed since they sailed from home. Suddenly, Ivo knew the words. "Would one night have been enough with Ylfa?"

Brand sucked in his breath as though he'd been struck. Calling up the memory of his long-dead wife was a gut blow, Ivo knew, but he wanted to remind him. Brand's ardor for his young bride had been the talk of Vass—they had barely left the bed for the first month. When Brand finally spoke, his voice was tight with emotion. "No. But it must be for you."

"It isn't."

"It must be," repeated Brand more firmly. "Think, Ivar. If there is even a small chance that Ari is right, you cannot risk getting her with child."

Ivo's building certainty shattered on that simple argument and left him hollow and sick. "She could already be."

Brand considered a moment, but dismissed the idea. "It has only been the one night, and the moon is wrong. Few women breed so quickly when the moon is not with them."

Few, but enough, thought Ivo.

"We must leave," Brand continued quietly. "Now. Tonight. It will be easier for her and for you. Ari can stay behind, watch over her from nearby. He will let you know if she's—"

"No."

"But he can—"

"No!" How could he leave her? Leave all that heat before he got his fill of it. Leave that skin, that hair, that scent. To *Ari.* "She is my wife. If anyone watches over her, it will be me."

"If you stay, you will want her."

There was nothing Ivo could say to that. It was true. He already wanted her. He turned away and went to stand before the fire, where he didn't have to look Brand in the eye. "There are ways to enjoy a woman without making a child. Frey knows, I've used them often enough."

"Spilling into the sheets doesn't always work," said Brand bluntly.

"Then I'll teach her to use her hands and mouth."

"And how long before that palls? Before you're on top of her, thinking just once won't hurt?"

"That won't happen."

"Listen to yourself! It will. It's in your voice already. This is mad."

"It's been mad from the beginning. Our entire lives are mad." An ember popped off a log and rolled toward Ivo's foot. He ground it out on the hearthstone, leaving a smudge of ash the color of a raven's wing. "I didn't ask for a wife, but the gods gave her to me. There must be some reason beyond one night's pleasure."

"Take the one night and walk away. She's just a woman, after all, and you knew this would be a short venture."

"Not this short. No. I intend to keep her and this hall for as long as I can. If you cannot support me in it, then go."

"I go nowhere 'til you do. But as your friend and your war-leader, I must counsel you against this. You cannot lie with her."

Ivo drew himself up and turned to meet Brand's eyes with a level gaze. "You have counseled me; your duty is done. Now go downstairs. My wife waits to teach you chess. Tell her I will join you shortly."

Brand's eyes narrowed angrily at Ivo's tone. He yanked the door open, pausing in the frame just long enough to make one final, terse warning. "Do not do this."

Ivo stood in the empty solar, the blood pounding in his head as he fought down the urge to put an arrow through that damnable raven. Curse Ari and his visions. He couldn't be right. The gods would never permit an infant to be cursed just to torture a few unimportant warriors—even Ran and Loki were not that malicious. This had to be false.

He was still wrestling with his anger when Alaida's voice drifted up from below. She had started to explain the pieces and their movements. In a little while she would do as he'd asked, come up to the bed, shed her gown and kirtle, and lie back, ready to gift him with her body, and then . . . he would tell her what? That he could never accept that gift again? It was his due. He was her husband.

With a snarl, he turned and drove a fist into the wall. The thin plaster cracked, and dust swirled around him like smoke from the priest's censer. The pain cleared his mind, gave him something to hold on to beyond the rage. After a time, he pulled himself together, slapped off the film of white that had settled on his clothes, and headed downstairs, avoiding so much as a glance toward the perch where the raven sat.

Brand had already made his opening move. Rather than playing against him, Alaida had recruited Father Theobald to do so, while she sat by to advise Brand of moves and strategy. Ivo ignored the empty chair beside her and stood across the table, where he could pretend to watch the play as he sipped at the horn of ale someone pressed on him. In truth, he saw nothing but Alaida.

As the play progressed, more men clustered around to watch, and soon the air around them grew close. Alaida raised a hand to stifle a yawn. "My pardon."

She continued with the game, tutoring Brand with a patience and good humor she had yet to practice with Ivo, but a little later there came another yawn, broader, and another apology, this one accompanied by a glance toward Ivo that made him understand that this was her way of leaving the hall without embarrassment. Her modesty in this reminded him of how immodest he had made her be the night before, and desire lurched within him. Every move she made began to speak to him of sex, from the sway of her breasts as she leaned across the board to point out a move to the way her fingers curved around a captured rook. Even watching her take a sip of wine inflamed him—her hand cupping the bowl; her tongue flickering across her lips after a stray droplet. *I'll teach her to use her hands and her mouth,* he'd told Brand. That mouth. That quick tongue. He gripped his drink so hard he heard the horn crack. He drained it and called for another.

Finally, she yawned a third time. "Forgive me. I do not seem to be able to keep my eyes open." She rose and glanced around at those watching, and her eyes lit on the marshal. "Oswald, your game is good. Come tutor Sir Brand for me."

"With pleasure, my lady," said Oswald, stepping forward to take her place.

"Beware the Church," she warned as she started toward the stairs. "Father Theobald loves his bishops. Hadwisa, Bôte, attend."

Her retiring was the signal for the other women to quit the hall. Within moments, only men remained, and the noise both increased and grew ruder as they relaxed. In an effort to convince himself not to go to her, Ivo tried to apply his mind to the game.

After a little, Alaida's body women came back down and

went off to join the other women, leaving her up there, alone, waiting for him. The knowledge of it called to him, and suddenly the game could no longer hold him at all.

"I will retire now." He stared over Brand's head so as not to see his look of warning. "The rest of you do as you will."

Father Theobald rose. "Will I see you at Mass in the morning, my lord?"

"I have business which takes me away early."

"But you failed to attend this morning, my lord, and—"

"It cannot be helped, Father." Ivo had been expecting this, but he didn't want to deal with it tonight. Early on, he had realized the power that the Church held with the Normans. He'd learned to mimic the Christian words and ways in order to move among them, and eventually, he'd even come to appreciate the religion and the way their god and his dead son fit neatly at the table with Odin and Baldur. But their priests were a different matter. They were womanish and grim and they talked too much, especially this one. Especially now. "Sir Brand and I ride out before dawn each day. It is impossible for us to attend Mass with the others."

"But you must recognize the importance of attendance for your souls, my lord."

Frey's pillock. The priest wasn't going to be put off, and Alaida was up there, waiting. Ready. "Of course, Father. You come to Alnwick each Sunday to do services, is that correct?"

"Yes, my lord. After I say the Mass in Lesbury."

"Then you will stay and say Mass especially for Brand and me each Sunday evening." Brand glanced up sharply at this, but Ivo glared him into silence. "Also on the evening of every day you visit Alnwick on other duties."

"Mass at night? That is most irregular, my lord."

"You will have payment for the additional services, and bed and board for the nights you must rest here."

The promise of silver and food worked wonders for the irregularities. "Well . . . I suppose nights are better than not at all. If you will give me a moment, my lord, I will prepare—"

"Not tonight," said Ivo, already regretting this. "You have your bread and pallet for tonight. Sunday will be soon enough."

The priest looked unhappy, but he bowed his head. "As you will, my lord."

"Sit down, priest," muttered Brand sullenly, clearly disgusted with Ivo on all counts this evening. "'Tis your move."

"Hmm? Oh." Father Theobald glanced down at the board and moved his bishop to take a knight. "You are in check, *messire*."

"Eh?" Brand's face clouded as he studied the board. "How did you do that? Oswald, explain."

As the marshal laughed and leaned forward, Ivo turned on his heel and climbed the stair to his wife.

She was waiting for him, as she should have been the night before, sitting in the center of the bed with her unbraided hair spread around her like a copper mantle. The way she clutched the furs she held over her nakedness showed there was yet a little nervousness in her, but as she met his eyes, he saw that there was desire as well, and the willingness that had been missing at the outset last night. Suddenly, he burned.

Ari must be wrong.

He stripped out of his clothes as though they would char away—his tunic and shirt yanked off there by the door, his boots kicked away as he crossed the room, his hose peeled off by the bed.

Do not do this. The echo of Brand's warning stopped him. He stood there, aching, his hand at the tie of his braies, unable to move.

"My lord?" Her brows knit in concern. "Are you unwell?"

He shook his head slowly. "I was only thinking how very beautiful you are, Alaida of Alnwick."

Even in the shadows of the bed he could see her glow. "You flatter, my lord."

"Truth is not flattery." He reached out to cup her cheek,

intending to draw her to him for a kiss, a long, drunken kiss that would leave her wet and wanting—

It's in your voice already. His hand froze in midair.

Brand was right. He couldn't do this. If he touched her now, tonight, if he let her touch him, he would have to have her. He would not be able to stop himself from pushing into her, spilling into her, any more than he had last night. Better to wait a few days, until he had himself under control, until his knowledge of her wasn't so fresh and he wasn't so crazed with wanting. With a groan, he pulled his hand back.

"You are *not* well," she said firmly. She came up onto her knees and reached out to press a hand to his forehead, and that simple touch alone was nearly enough to make him push her down and take her. "You have no fever. Perhaps something at dinner did not agree."

"No, I am fine. I just . . ." He cast about for some excuse. "It is too soon. You will be sore."

"Oh." She blinked twice, taken aback. "I do not . . . That is, I . . ." Her blush washed down to the edge of the fur.

Pull it away, urged the part of him that didn't believe the visions. *See how pink her breasts are. Press her back. Taste her. Take her. Ari's wrong.*

"You will be sore," he repeated gruffly. "I demanded too much of you last night. Lie down, Alaida. Go to sleep. I will not bed you tonight." As he retied the waist cord of his braies, she stared at him, her lips pressed into a thin, angry line. "What?"

"Nothing," she said tightly.

"God's legs, woman, what?" Frustration made him yell, and she flinched. He reefed in his temper and tried again, a little more calmly. "Why are you unhappy with me now?"

Her eyes narrowed as she studied him. "You truly do not know? By the saints, you are . . . If you leave me now, after this morning, my humiliation will be complete."

"I'm not leaving," he lied. He'd been intending to go downstairs, to get as far from her as he could for the night, so he would not be tempted, but she was right—there would only be more talk, and neither of them needed that, least of all him, if he intended to keep Alnwick for any length of time. For that, he needed the men's goodwill and trust even more than he needed hers. He would just have to be disciplined. "I only keep my braies as armor against your enticements, wife, lest I wake to find that I have been overcome with lust and taken you in my sleep. Move over."

Ivo took a moment to put out the candles, leaving only the oil lamp for light. He made a quick, silent prayer to Freyja to relieve him of desire for the night, then slid between the sheets, trying to ignore the warmth that wafted over from Alaida's side of the bed carrying her scent. He punched at his pillow, taking out some of his frustration as he worked it into a serviceable shape before he flopped down on his back. If she would just lie there . . .

Wordlessly, she edged over next to him.

"Alaida."

"The room is chill. I grew cold, waiting for you." She tried to pillow her head on his shoulder, but it wasn't comfortable for either of them. With a sigh, he snaked his arm around her and pulled her close.

She cuddled against his flank. "Thank you, my lord."

"Ivo," he said without thinking, and the heat crackled between them. He curled his fingers into the blanket and stared at the draperies overhead. "Go to sleep, Alaida."

"You're hurt," she said suddenly, touching the hand that rested on her shoulder.

Ivo lifted the hand to look. It was bruised and swollen, and a thin line of blood showed where he'd split one knuckle against the wall. "'Tis nothing."

"It does not look like nothing." She twisted to press her lips to the battered knuckle, and as she did, her bare breast fell free of the blanket. Desire surged through his body like a bore tide through a fjord, and in one motion he was on her, pinning her to the mattress. He hovered there above her, ready, and her eyes said she would welcome him into her softness. *Just once more,* he told himself. He could have her one more time without worry. Ari was wrong anyway.

He lowered his head to kiss her. Her mouth opened to him, and in his mind the soft exhalation of her breath turned to a scream as she watched her child fly away. With a curse, he flung himself back onto his pillow.

"My lord?" There was shock in her voice, almost a tear.

"I told you, we cannot do this." He managed to say it without sounding angry, though he wasn't sure how. How could he even have thought . . . ? "Go to sleep, sweet leaf."

She was silent long enough that he thought she might actually be obeying him, but then her voice came out of the dark. "You will be gone in the morning?"

"Before dawn," he said, his hold on himself so fragile now that if she so much as moved, he could not be certain what he'd do. He took a deep breath and said as gently as he could, "Sleep now, sweet leaf."

Please, Freyja, make her sleep.

CHAPTER 9

IVO LEFT THE solar well before dawn, carrying his clothes and boots, unwilling to linger long enough within range of Alaida's temptations even to dress. Below, while the others slept, Brand still occupied the table, studying the chessmen as though they would reveal some secret if he stared at them intently enough.

He glanced up at Ivo, and disapproval roiled off him like steam off a cauldron. Ignoring it, Ivo tossed his clothes onto an empty chair. Before he could pull on his shirt, Brand abruptly rose, collected the raven off his perch, and stalked out. His reaction only stoked Ivo's anger, and he yanked on the rest of his things, managing to break one lace and jab himself in the shoulder with his cloak pin in the process. By the time he stepped outside, his mood had gone from foul to murderous.

A fog had rolled in overnight, and Brand stood there in it with Ari on his shoulder, a solid, hulking shadow of man and bird against the misty glow of the torches by the gate. Ivo's fists curled and uncurled of their own accord. He needed to hit something, something more alive than the wall and bigger than a bird. Brand would serve.

Before he could do much about it, though, a man stumbled around the corner and smacked into him.

"Wha—?" The man jumped back with a start as the raven leapt off Brand's shoulder and fluttered up to the safety of the eaves. "Christ's toes, my lord! 'Tis a good thing I just pissed, or for certs, I'd be wet now. By the saints, you two do wake early. I don't have the steel for it unless I must use—"

Wat. Steel. Ivo's anger crystallized. In the breath between words, he whirled and drove his fist into the reeve's flapping mouth. Wat hit the ground with a whoof.

Ivo loomed over him. "Now you can tell them my fist is steel as well."

"Aye, my lord," Wat mumbled, pushing himself up on one elbow. He spat out a mouthful of blood and touched a tentative finger to his lip. "Aye, my lord. I can, that."

"Trouble, my lord?" One of the men on the gate approached with a torch.

"No," said Brand. He stepped between Ivo and Wat, grabbed the latter by his shirt, and hauled him to his feet. "Return to bed, Reeve, and be grateful he chose his fist and not his blade." Wat took the good advice and lurched off toward the hall. Brand waited until the door closed behind him, then rounded on Ivo. "Try me. You'll find I'm harder to knock down."

Ivo squared off with him, but the violence had found its release on Wat's jaw. With a snort of disgust, he turned and stalked away.

Brand gave him a few yards, then caught up and fell in beside him. They walked in tense silence to the stable.

As they approached, they could see the glow of a candle stub, left burning in a crude holder on the top of a barrel. Ivo frowned at this carelessness, and more so when he looked into Fax's stall. "I'll have that boy's hide. He left Fax saddled all night."

"I did not," protested a voice. A shock of flaxen hair appeared over the top of the stall that housed Brand's roan, followed by eyes that grew round when he saw who it was. "Your pardon, my lord, but he was cared for well and proper. They both were."

Ivo unlatched the gate and stepped into the stall to feel beneath Fax's saddle blanket. The hair was smooth and dry, not sweaty or matted. He checked over the horse thoroughly. Sure enough, he'd been brushed and his hooves had been picked. Even the tack had been cleaned.

"Who told you to have our mounts ready at this hour?" demanded Ivo.

"No one, m'lord. I saw that you took them before I woke this morning, and I thought to have them ready should you want them again—though you are earlier than I expected."

Ivo grunted and led Fax out into the yard.

"What's your name, boy?" asked Brand.

"Tom, *messire*."

"It was a good thought, Tom. We will want them every morning before dawn."

"They will be ready, *messire*." He opened the gate and led Brand's roan out. "Your pardon, m'lord. Did you call your animal Fax?"

"Mmm."

"It's for Hrimfaxi," said Brand when Ivo didn't go on, then explained to the boy, "It's from an old tale. Hrimfaxi is the great horse of the night and they say the rime drops fall from his mane. Mine's Kraken. A monster. Watch out for him—he bites."

"Aye. He nipped me last night." Tom pulled up his sleeve to show a wicked-looking bruise on his forearm, but he seemed to hold no grudge against the animal.

"Bad habit," said Brand. "But he can run forever, and carrying me, that's saying a lot."

"Aye, *messire*." The boy held Kraken as Brand checked his girth and mounted, then shifted over to hold Fax for Ivo. "Godspeed, my lord."

"Mmm," grunted Ivo again. He glowered as the raven sailed down to take his place on Brand's shoulder—on the far side, out of reach of an angry hand. "Gate!"

They headed west and south as they left the village, sticking to the moors and meadows to avoid the tangle of forest undergrowth for as long as possible in the fog.

Brand waited until they were well away, then said quietly, "You didn't, did you? With her, I mean. That's why you're in such a wrath."

"I didn't," said Ivo between gritted teeth. "And I won't."

"Good."

"We're still not leaving."

Brand chewed on this for a moment. "You choose a difficult path for yourself, Graycloak."

"It will be easier tomorrow, and easier yet the day after."

"No, it won't. But you'd better get yourself back in hand if you intend to stay. You're going to make enemies of your men if you continue like this."

"I will take myself 'in hand'"—Ivo jerked his hand in a crude gesture that made his meaning clear—"at first opportunity. As you said, she's just a woman. I've lived without them before."

"Aye. As we all have and now must." Brand sighed deeply. "Balls. Some of the others have taken your lead and are beginning to venture out. How can I tell them they can never have a woman again?"

"The same way you told me," said Ivo, and he thought of his wife, alone in bed, and turned his horse toward the forest that was both shelter and prison.

HE HAD NOT wanted to cause her pain, Alaida reminded herself as she went about her work the next day. A considerate husband was a rare thing. A good thing.

So why was she so put out over his not lying with her? She hadn't even wanted him as husband, after all. She wasn't certain she did even now, especially if the only time she would see him was at night when he used her for his pleasure. But no, that wasn't fair: he had seen to her pleasure, too—by the saints, he surely had done that—and he didn't seem nearly as heavy-handed as she'd expected. But his refusal to tell her why he must leave so early every day grated, and his strange behavior last evening had left her out of kilter. But he had not wanted to hurt her.

But, but, but.

Her feelings toward Ivo swung wildly back and forth all day, as though buffeted by the gusty wind outside. The day was a miserable one, the wind having brought an icy rain with it, and as it grew colder and wetter, Alaida ordered the fires kept blazing against the dankness and had enough torches and candles lit for the men to work indoors.

During a lull in the downpour, she bundled herself against the wind and set out to the kitchen to see that the evening meal was under way and that the cook had all the spices she needed. As she came back, she met Wat crossing the yard. He held his head down against the wind, and his cowl drooped so far forward she nearly didn't recognize him.

"Good day, Wat."

"Gdaymlady," he mumbled from beneath his hood as he hurried past. His voice sounded oddly thick, as though he spoke around a mouthful of bread. Something was amiss.

"A moment, Reeve."

He stopped but didn't turn. "Yeth, m'lady?"

Alaida frowned. "What's wrong with you, Wat?"

"Naught, m'lady."

"Then turn around and face me properly when you speak to me."

"My lady, I—" he began.

"Look at me!" she commanded. Slowly, Wat turned and raised his head. His hood fell back and Alaida gasped. The left side of his face looked like it belonged to another, larger man, so swollen was it, and a dark, ugly bruise spread from his chin across his split lip and up his cheek. "Who did this to you?"

"I, uh, ran into thomething in the fog latht night, m'lady."

Apparently his tongue was swollen, as well—and his brain, too, if he thought she would believe such twattle. "Do not lie to me, Reeve."

"I would not dare, my lady. Godthtruth, I ran into thome-thing. Thomething hard," he added, a bit darkly.

"What?" she demanded. He had no ready answer. "Tell me who hit you. I shall see that he is—"

"It wath my own fault, m'lady. Truly. I wath clumthy and my fathe bearth the mark of it, that ith all. I'll mend. Do not trouble yourthelf. Pleathe, my lady." He backed away, bowing, as he spoke, then turned and scurried off before she could say more.

Alaida watched after him, shaking her head. She tolerated neither fighting nor drunkenness among the men—likely his bruises were the result of both and that's why he lied. Well, she would find out soon enough and deal with it; anything of note that happened around the manor or village found its way to Bôte's ears soon enough, and thence to her own. She scurried inside as the wind blew in a fresh sheet of rain.

Those women without kitchen work had clustered near the fire in the solar with their spinning and sewing. Alaida joined them, and as she removed her needle from her little lordling's crotch and returned to the problem of the chevron on the altar cloth, Bôte plopped down next to her with a basket of mending.

An outbreak of snickering made Alaida glance up. Her cheeks went hot as she saw the first garment Bôte had pulled out of her basket: the torn chainse from her wedding night.

"I could put in a seam, my lady, with a bit of stitchery to hide it." Bôte's innocent expression belied the mischief under her words. "Or shall I make eyelets for laces?"

The women all looked to Alaida expectantly. She hesitated only a moment: Bôte had caught her at a moment when she was feeling more kindly toward Ivo, and an imp took possession of her tongue.

"Eyelets. Although my lord's lack of patience may prove too much even for laces."

The laughter was hearty and the jest brought her firmly into the fold of married women. Hadwisa and the other maidens were quickly shunted off to the far corner, and the chatter took a swift turn from village gossip—no mention of Wat—to talk of men and bedding, and thence to babies and birthing. By the time the servants put away their handwork and headed down to prepare for supper, she sat wide-eyed with new knowledge and fresh fear.

"Do not let them frighten you, my lady," said Bôte as she slipped her needle into its wooden case and tucked it safely away. "You are made for childbearing. Good, wide hips you have, and a husband with strong seed to plant in your womb. You will drop a healthy babe when the time comes."

"It worries me, Bôte."

"It worries all women. But you will do well at it, lamb, I promise."

Her certainty was a balm, and Alaida let it ease the fear. She slipped her needle into the wool and rose. "Shall we see what trouble the men have gotten into today?"

None, as it turned out, and in fact, good work had been done. Between them, Edric and the others handed over a dozen new horn spoons, a bone knife handle, and a fine wooden spindle whorl to replace one that had broken before Christmas, while the stable master carried two mended bridles and a newly braided girth strap when he headed out with Tom to see to the horses for the night.

There was no sign of Ivo and Brand by the time the stable master returned, nor by the time the hall was ready and every hand washed. They all stood by, Alaida absently fiddling with her keys, as the food grew cold. She was about to give the order to go ahead when the door finally burst open on a gust of wind and Ivo and Brand blew in, looking like wild men as they shook the water from their hair.

"Bring dry linens and gowns," Alaida ordered. A servant hurried off and she motioned to another. "The cook was to warm some mead for after supper. Fetch some now, and be quick about it."

Ivo and Brand strode toward the fire, tossing their sodden cloaks and gloves to the nearest maids to be hung. The bedraggled raven was set on its perch, and the two men began peeling off clothing.

She knew that handsome flesh, Alaida realized with a sudden stab of possessiveness as she watched her husband strip down to his braies; she recognized those muscles and the scars she'd traced in the night. The varlet returned with dry clothing, and as Ivo tugged on a clean, white chainse, it struck her that she was licking her lips as though he were a well-basted shank of mutton.

Flushing, she tore her eyes away, grabbed two of the washing-up towels, and hurried over. "Here. Dry your heads before you take a chill."

"Too late for that, my lady," said Brand, taking a cloth. "I'm wet to the bone. 'Tis brutal out there."

"I wonder that you stayed out all day." She knew as the words came out of her mouth that they sounded more critical than she had intended, and when Ivo turned to take the second towel, his expression said he'd taken them badly.

"Wife." He put both greeting and warning in the word.

"Welcome home, my lord." She set a smile on her face, but that imp from earlier came back, now irritated by his tone. "Did you enjoy good . . . hunting, was it?"

He stopped toweling his head and assessed her. "No."

"Ah. Well. I imagine most wild creatures have . . ." Have the sense, she started to say, but did manage to rein in the imp a little. "A place to stay out of the rain." She gestured at the raven that squatted miserably there on the iron branch that had once held her grandfather's hawk. "Unlike that poor bird, who looks like he roosted under a waterfall."

Brand poked his head out of the tunic he was pulling on. "I promise, my lady, he had good shelter most of the day."

"Better than we did," added Ivo sourly, dropping his towel into a servant's waiting hand. "Where the devil is that mead you sent for?"

The mead arrived in short order, but it turned out to be the only truly warm thing about the whole meal—including, to Alaida's consternation, her husband. The warrior who had burned his way past her defenses the last two nights was as chill as the weather, spending much of the meal in conversation with Brand and directing barely enough attention toward her for politeness. There were none of the random touches that kept her senses tingling, none of the hungry looks that made her go all liquid, none of the sweet words and wicked jests that set her mind spinning wildly off onto thoughts of flesh against flesh. There was only a courteous, somewhat dour nobleman who might have been a visiting stranger. By the time the gingerbread was brought out to end the meal, she was ready to pitch it at him.

Eventually, however, Sir Brand excused himself for a little, and Ivo leaned toward her. *Finally*, she thought—then he spoke.

"I have explained my absences as much as I intend to, Alaida." He kept his voice low, so his words were for her ears alone. "Do not challenge me on it again, especially not in front of others."

"You mistook what I first said, my lord."

"Perhaps, but not what came after."

She opened her mouth to protest, but found she had no good argument. "Granted. Though I did try to soften my words."

"Not very successfully."

"No, I suppose not." From the low tables, they probably appeared to be whispering endearments to one another. Alaida encouraged that mistaken belief with a half smile as she reminded him, "You have laughed at worse from me."

"What amuses me in private and what I will tolerate before my men are two different matters."

"Well, then, perhaps you should list out your rules, my lord, so I may commit them to memory." She broke off a piece of gingerbread and started to pop it into her mouth.

He stopped her, staying her hand as easily as she might stay a young child's. "You were doing well until that last bit."

She looked up and found amusement sparking in those

flint eyes of his. A curious flutter of pleasure quashed much of the irritation she'd felt a moment earlier. "My lady grandmother, God rest her, oft pointed out my inability to stop at the proper moment."

"So it is not just me."

"No, my lord—though you do seem to make it worse."

"Do I?" Before she could answer, he turned her hand and guided the gingerbread into his mouth. His lips brushed the tips of her fingers, and like that, the heat was there between them.

"I missed some," he murmured, and dipped his head to lap off a morsel with the tip of his tongue. There must have been another crumb, because he went back again, this time slowly drawing the tip of her thumb into his mouth in search of the elusive speck. He sucked, and sensation burst through Alaida, streaking from her hand throughout her body. He was readying her, she knew, telling her he would do this later, in the great bed, but not to her thumb, and the parts of her that had felt the plunder of his mouth throbbed with want.

She blushed at the wicked impatience of her lust, unable to take her eyes off the hand that held hers so firmly, so gently. Poor hand. Here in the light, it looked much worse than it had last night, all bruised and battered. She leaned forward to touch a kiss to the swollen knuckles.

"My lord." Brand's voice cut between them like a broadax. "A reminder—you wished to speak with Oswald."

For a breath, perhaps two, Ivo might have been stone. He sat motionless, distant, some strange, frightening battle going on behind his eyes. Then his face cleared and he rose.

"Your pardon, my lady. I have business to attend to. You will want to retire." He still had her hand, and he tugged gently to bring her to her feet and led her to the foot of the stairs.

The swiftness of the change stunned Alaida, as did the abrupt way she was being dismissed—like a child being sent to bed. She stood there in a haze of arousal, trying to figure out what had happened, her eyes searching his face, his manner, for some clue. Her gaze landed once more on the hand that held hers.

The damage actually *was* worse, she realized. That split across his knuckles was much longer, the bruising deeper. A row of bloody cuts marched along the tops of his fingers, as evenly spaced as teeth—those hadn't been there at all last night. He'd hit something else since then, and hard, by the look of it. Something hard . . . Suddenly the whole thing fell together. "Wat."

When she looked up, the truth was in his eyes. He shifted his hold to his other hand, and flexed the injured one slowly, deliberately, before her.

The center of her went cold. "No wonder he would not say who hit him."

"It is not your concern."

"It is. These are my people."

"They are mine now, just as you are. No one offends my wife without consequence."

"I took no offense."

"I did. The matter is finished, Alaida. Go to bed. My business with Oswald will keep me awhile. I will be up later."

"Do not trouble yourself, *monseigneur*." She jerked her hand free. "You will surely rest more comfortably in the hall."

Her foot had barely touched the first step when he grabbed her and spun her back into his arms. The kiss he pressed on her was brief and ruthless, a show of power that held no trace of affection. When he finished, he put his mouth next to her ear. His low growl echoed the rage that shook them both.

"Never think to ban me from your bed, *madame*. That choice is mine, not yours. Do you understand?"

She nodded.

"Now go, and stop on the landing where all can see to bid me a pretty good night. I will not have the entire hall know what passes between us."

He released her and stepped back. Alaida lifted her chin and swept up the stairs, her anger carrying her to the landing. Her hand touched the door as she considered disobeying, but she was not ready for a full-out battle with him, so she pulled it back and turned to look back down at him. By the saints, look how he stood there, pretending nothing was amiss.

As if possessed, she found herself asking sweetly, "Are you sure you will not come up *now*, husband?"

His eyes narrowed, and she could see his fist flex and open again, as if he wanted to come up and thrash her. Let him. He would lose every man in the hall.

"Later," he promised. Vowed. *Threatened.*

"Ah, well." She forced a smile to her lips. She suspected she would become quite good at these smiles with no joy to prop up their corners. She made a pretty courtesy, even as her eyes told him to burn in Hell. "God bid you good night then, husband."

"And you, wife. Keep well." He turned away, on to other things.

"Bôte. Hadwisa. Attend." As she waited for her women, she watched Ivo beckon Oswald over to join him at the fire. There had been no stranger at table after all, only Lord Ivo de Vassy—truly the king's man after all, with William's heavy hand and his willingness to use it. She should have kept her first sense of him in mind, should never have let him dupe her with his false charm and skillful seduction.

She would not make that mistake again.

But she didn't bar the door.

CHAPTER 10

NEARLY A WEEK passed before Ivo came face-to-face with Wat again. By then, his hand bore only a single faint line to show he'd ever been marked, swift healing being one of the few blessings to come with Cwen's curse.

Wat hadn't fared as well. When he finally slunk back into the hall at Ivo's express command, his jaw glowed purple and green with the bruise, and an ugly scab still clung to his lip. He watched Ivo warily from the low table during supper, keeping his head down and his mouth shut while laughter and jokes flew around him and occasionally at him. The change in Wat's demeanor made Ivo wince inside. He should have handled the reeve differently, and would have if the man hadn't stumbled out of the fog at the wrong moment. It was unfortunate, but perhaps Wat had learned a lesson that would save him trouble later. There were nobles in William's court who would happily take Wat's tongue over less.

Alaida sat like a stone maiden on Ivo's left. She'd been like that every night—distant, polite to a flaw, and quieter than he'd thought possible—and though the steely chill in her every word and gesture made it easier to resist the urge to follow her up to bed, it was beginning to wear. He had himself back under control now. It was time to see if he could set things right with Wat and put an end to at least the worst of his bride's anger.

She'd barely put the last bite of food in her mouth when she rose and motioned to her women. "I will retire now, *monseigneur.*"

"Excellent. Brand and I will join you in the solar." Ignoring her cross frown, he beckoned the steward over. "Geoffrey, have our chairs carried up, and then you, Oswald, and Wat join us."

Alaida glanced toward the reeve with such sympathy in her eyes that Ivo wanted to shake her. Nodding for her servants to follow, he took her hand. "Come, wife. We will pass a pleasant evening together."

She let him lead her upstairs without comment, but went to her sewing frame instead of taking her place next to him by the fire. Her women sat near her while Brand, Geoff, and Oswald gathered around Ivo. Wat hung back by the door.

"Take a seat, Reeve," said Ivo.

"Yes, my lord." He found a stool, placing it, Ivo noted, slightly behind Oswald, and nearer to Alaida than himself.

"You all know the king commands a castle at Alnwick," began Ivo. "The question becomes where to build it. Ari tells me there is some disagreement between you three on the best place."

"Aye, we differ," said Oswald. "Geoffrey says the hilltop. I say right here, as does Wat."

"Why?"

"The well, my lord. 'Tis—"

"The well?" exclaimed Alaida, looking up from her needlework. "Surely you don't believe that old tale, Oswald."

"But he does, my lady," said Geoffrey, giving Oswald a smug look.

The marshal's ruddy cheeks turned brighter red. "It may be an old tale, but I have seen and heard enough to know there's something to it. And there're the villagers to consider as well."

Geoffrey snorted. "Why should Lord Ivo make his decision based on stories spun by cottars?"

"Because he knows cottars can be as wise as stewards," said Ivo, provoked by Geoffrey's tone. "They most often spin their tales for good reason."

"Here the reason is to frighten children, *monseigneur*, so they stay away from the well and do not drown themselves." Alaida looked to Bôte and smiled. "The same reason my nurse told the story to me."

"So you know this tale, too, Bôte?"

"Aye, my lord. Everyone in Alnwick knows it, and many put great store in it."

"Then I would do well to hear it before I make my decision. Tell me about the well."

He directed the last to no one in particular. Oswald and Geoffrey looked at each other. Geoff held up his hands and shook his head. "I will not give credence to this nonsense."

"'Tisn't nonsense," blurted Wat, adding, "My lord."

"You are a believer, Reeve?" asked Ivo, and at his nod, "Then you tell it."

"But my lord . . ." began Geoffrey.

"No hurt can come from listening," said Ivo. "Go on, Wat."

Looking as though he wished he'd kept his mouth shut once more, Wat glanced toward Oswald, who gave him a nod. The reeve still hesitated. "I do not like to tell it, my lord. My pap would hardly speak of it, for fear that speaking would raise the evil."

"It never rose when Bôte told me the story," said Alaida. "Pray, tell it for my amusement, Wat, if for nothing else. It is a good tale, and I have not heard it in years."

"But my lady . . ."

Ivo leaned back in his chair and stretched his legs out, hooking one foot over the other. "*This* would be the time to talk, Reeve."

Wat turned red beneath his bruises, making him look like an overripe plum. "Aye, my lord." Giving a nod to Alaida, he began. "There was a great and awful beast, my lord, in the old days before the time of King Alfred."

"What sort of beast?"

"I do not know, my lord, but it was said to be fearsome, a she-beast that wrought its evil over the whole of the kingdom, until a hero, a brave knight named Sir Egbert, came riding out of the north upon a winged horse. He found the beast and did battle with it and struck it down. Aye, he ripped the heart from its very chest—and yet the beast lived."

Despite his reticence, Wat had quickly fallen into the rhythm of his story. Ivo was reminded of the old days, listening to Ari spin tales around the fire. He caught Brand glancing up at the raven on its perch and saw the same memory reflected in his friend's eyes.

"The beast rose up and ran off, and Sir Egbert chased it up hill and down dene, all over the land, until it found a great hole and hid itself," continued Wat. "When Sir Egbert saw he had the beast trapped, he pushed a great rock into the hole, so huge that no other man would ever be able to move it, and he marked it with signs so that no man would ever try."

"The standing stone," volunteered Alaida. "I have seen the markings myself." Eyes dancing with enjoyment, she put aside her needle and came to take her chair, and even though Ivo knew she did so only to better hear, having her by his side of her own will pleased him. "I have long thought the beast must have been a great dragon. An immense red dragon with eyes of amber fire. Beautiful, but deadly, as a she-beast should be."

She was having fun with Wat, who responded in kind.

"Perhaps it was, my lady, or perhaps not, but whatever sort of creature it was, its heart still beat in Sir Egbert's hand. He threw it, intending to hurl it into the sea for the fishes to eat." Here, Wat acted out his words, heaving an invisible heart toward a distant ocean. "But it fell short and landed in Alnwick, which was barely a vill then. Where it landed, it left a deep hole, and at the bottom of the hole, a spring rose up, so sweet and pure that a well was built to catch its waters. Sir Egbert was named champion and the people heaped gold and silver on him, and the lord hereabouts, whose name was Bisbright, gave him his daughter for wife. Sir Egbert put her before him on his winged horse and carried her away to his own land."

"Man after my own heart," said Brand. "Slay the enemy, ride off with the woman."

Everyone laughed at this, and Wat waited for the merriment to die down before he went on.

"All was well until the next new moon. Then the hill of Alnwick began to tremble and the well to make strange noises. The people cowered in terror and cried out for their lord to save them. When Lord Bisbright saw what was happening, he sent a priest up the hill to pray for relief, but the priest was a craven man without true faith, and he came down white with fear and ran away.

"Then Lord Bisbright sent for a wise woman, a healer of the old ways who lived in the forest nearby. She stayed upon the hill for three days and three nights, and when at last she came back down, she told Lord Bisbright that the beast had crawled through the earth in search of its heart, all the way from the hole where it had gone to ground, and had come up within the hill. The woman said Alnwick would be safe only if Lord Bisbright built his manor on the place where she touched her staff to the ground—here, that is—to defend the well and keep the beast at bay. She warned that if the beast ever joined with its heart again, it would come back to life more powerful and evil than ever.

"So Lord Bisbright founded his hall upon the very spot, and he made a covenant with the villagers to keep the well and to protect them from the beast, and they promised to serve him faithfully so long as he did so. When the beast found she could not reach her heart, she settled down to wait.

"And there she still lies," finished Wat, "curled up within the hill, sleeping until the day when men forget and she can awaken and reclaim what is hers."

The room was silent for a long moment, even Alaida subdued by the dark magic of the ending.

"Well told, Wat," said Ivo finally. "Well told, indeed— but how much is truth?"

"It is what my father told me, and his father told him, and his father before that."

"A peasant's tale," scoffed Geoff.

"We already know your thoughts, Steward," said Ivo. "What of you, Oswald? You say you've seen and heard enough to make you believe."

"Perhaps *believe* is too strong a word, my lord, but I wonder, at the least. I heard the story years ago and never gave it weight, but then one midnight, I grew thirsty and went out to draw myself a drink, and . . ." The marshal hesitated, scratching at his grizzled chin.

"What?"

"I am unsure, my lord. I heard something in the well—a deep drumming, like. *Shh-thump . . . Shh-thump . . .*" He sounded the beats slowly, dragging out the long pauses between, then shook his head. "I would not credit it, had I not heard it for myself."

"And do not forget the hill," said Wat. "There's certain places on it as you can hear the beast breathing."

Ivo looked to Oswald.

"I have heard that as well," admitted the marshal a little sheepishly. "Or at the least some noise that sounds like a great animal breathing. I'm no longer certain."

"What of the rest of the villagers?" Ivo asked Wat.

"They are like those of us here, my lord: some believe, some do not, some are unsure," said Wat. "Those who do believe fear that building on the hilltop might waken the beast, and that there would then be no manor to stand guard on the well. And even those who don't believe ask if the new lord of Alnwick intends to break the ancient covenant."

"There is no record of such a covenant, my lord," said Geoffrey.

"Just because it is not written in your Latin letters does not mean it doesn't exist," said Brand. "I have heard stranger tales than this that proved true."

"As have we all," said Bôte, echoing Ivo's thought.

"Build here, my lord," urged Oswald. "Use the manor yard as bailey. Guard the well and keep the freemen of Alnwick content. 'Tis a simple enough thing."

"How content would they be if the castle were built only to fall to Donald Bane or whoever comes after him?" asked Ivo. "Malcolm was killed barely a league from Alnwick's gate. The Scots will be back sooner or later, and building on this spot leaves the highest ground to the enemy."

"In all the years the Scots have ridden on Alnwick, not once have they kept to the hill past one day," said Oswald. "They ride up, but when the next morning comes, they've abandoned it. Something drives them off during the night."

"The beast's foul breath," muttered Bôte. Alaida hushed her.

"No, let her speak," said Ivo. "You're the oldest here, Bôte. What do you know of the monster?"

"No more than Wat, my lord. As my lady said, I told the story to keep her away from the well as a bairn—but I do believe it."

"Then what of this covenant between manor and village?"

"I have heard that Lord Gilbert affirmed it when he first took lordship of Alnwick, but I wasn't there to see it."

"Because it did not happen," said Geoffrey.

"Your sureness confounds me, Steward, considering you weren't present either," said Alaida. "You are neither that old nor Alnwick-born—even I recall when you first came to us."

"True, my lady, but over the years I have examined every record. There is no mention of any covenant regarding the well."

"Perhaps the previous stewards were not as careful as

you." Ivo turned to Wat. "Who are the oldest men of the village?"

"Céolsige, who lives by the meadow, my lord, and Drogo the Blind."

"Bring them on the morrow to speak with the seneschal about what happened in Lord Gilbert's day. They will swear on the Gospel book and you and two other freemen of your choice will be witness to what they say." Ivo gave Geoff a hard look. "And this time it *will* be recorded, whatever is said."

"Yes, my lord," said Geoffrey and Wat together.

"I must consider all of this. It is not a decision to be made lightly or without all the facts." Ivo pushed to his feet and the manor men rose with him. "For tonight, though, I give you all thanks for speaking your thoughts. Geoffrey, what do we usually pay to a *jongleur* for an evening's entertainment?"

"Board and bed and two deniers, my lord."

"Then see similar value is given to the reeve in seed of his choice, for tonight he played *jongleur* and did it well."

"No need for that, my lord," said Wat.

"Take it, Wat, for you not only gave me valuable information, you made my lady smile. That is worth a great deal to me, as is a good reeve."

"Then my thanks, my lord. I am not entirely a fool." Wat grinned so wide his lip split afresh. He dabbed the blood off on his sleeve, but the grin remained as he headed downstairs behind Geoff. As the door shut behind them, Ivo glimpsed Oswald clapping him on the shoulder. There was one mistake repaired.

The other was watching him in that guarded way of hers. He chose to ignore her for the moment. "Some chess, Brand?"

"Only if your lady will aid me. I'm still no good at the game."

"Of course, *messire*." Alaida rose and signaled Bôte and Hadwisa to move the chess table into position. "Though Oswald told me you beat him all on your own last night."

"Only by chance, my lady. I blundered into his king without realizing it."

"Then let us see if we can improve your blundering." She began setting up the game. Ivo didn't help: seeing her handle the pieces was already enough to throw him back into that foul night, both the good and the bad of it. He studied the toes of his boots until she had finished, then took his place as Alaida settled in near Brand.

They were well into the game before Ivo broached the subject. "So, what do you think?"

"It goes against all I know of war to set a fortress at the base of a hill," said Brand.

"Aye." Ivo touched a finger to his queen's knight, then reconsidered and moved the neighboring rook instead. "And yet the manor has long survived here. What about you, my lady? You've said nothing about the castle, though I suspect your interest runs deeper than bloodred dragons with eyes of amber fire."

His attempt to make her smile failed miserably. She nodded to Brand as he reached for a pawn, then looked up at Ivo with infuriating blandness. "'Tis your decision to make, *monseigneur*, not mine."

"It may come down to you to defend the castle in my absence. Where would you rather it be?"

"The hilltop would be easier to defend but it is too far from the village. If the Scots came on us suddenly, the people would not make the safety of the walls. And there is the problem of water."

"Ari suggests a cistern to catch rain."

"Even in our wettest years, it would run dry with the village and an army and all its horses drinking from it. The Scots could wait us out, drinking from our good well as we shrivel up like last year's apples."

"There are no springs or seeps on the mount at all?"

"None that I know. Bôte once said the dragon's fire must have dried up all the water."

The nurse chuckled over her stitching. "You had barely

four years on you when I said that, my lady. How do you recall such things?"

"My lady wife is quick, Nurse, as you should well know."

"Aye, m'lord, quick to learn, quick to anger, and to all our fortune, quick to forgive—except when she isn't. Then she is stubborn and slow to forget what you wish she would."

"So I'm learning." Ignoring yet another sour look from his wife, Ivo jumped his knight onto the bishop Brand had brought out. "Check and mate."

Alaida sat up, startled out of her snit. She studied the board with Brand. "My apologies, *messire*. I fear I have been the one to blunder this time. I should have seen that knight riding down on you."

Grunting, Brand tipped his king on its side and reached for his ale. "As should I. Perhaps I should play merels instead."

"And perhaps I should join you," said Alaida. "I clearly have no head for chess tonight."

"Do not give up so quickly, wife," said Ivo. He began resetting the board. "Take Brand's place. He can play merels with Bôte."

"I would prefer not, *monseigneur*."

Ivo merely smiled and motioned for her to take the white. Her huff was audible and Brand's warning look dour as he moved her chair into position.

"You cannot force me to play," she muttered when Brand moved off to challenge Bôte.

"True. Here." He handed her the white bishop he'd taken.

"I will lose quickly and go back to my stitching." She set the bishop in place and handed him the black pawns Brand had captured.

"All right." He lined up his pawns. "You start."

She pursed her lips stubbornly and pushed a pawn out. He did the same, then proceded to mirror every move she made, refusing to take a single piece, even when she offered her queen for sacrifice.

She glared at his similarly proffered queen as though it were an insult. "You play better than this, my lord."

"God's toes, I do hope so."

Arching one eyebrow, she looked him over like a horse she was buying. "What are you up to?"

"Making the game last longer."

"Why do you want it to?"

"I have made peace with Wat. I wish to do the same with you."

"I do not trade my goodwill for a measure of seed." She realized the double meaning of what she'd said and clarified, "Grain."

"Neither does Wat." Ivo let her mistake pass without comment—difficult when she was blushing so temptingly—and started moving the chessmen back to their starting positions. "We both exceeded our bounds. He paid with his lip. I paid tonight with seed and a good word before the steward who is his superior and the marshal who is his friend. We are back to a proper balance as lord and reeve. Now we will set about earning each other's trust once more."

"I doubt it is that simple, my lord."

"It is, and it must be, lest every misstep bring down all. Wat and I understand that. He's content with how things now lie. You saw his smile."

"He smiled because you gave him seed."

"He smiled because I gave him his *due*." Something he owed her as well, though he couldn't yet see how to give it. "Your move."

She looked at him thoughtfully, then pushed out the same pawn she had the last game. He responded with more reasoned tactics, and they played in silence for a while. It quickly became clear she was playing seriously this time—she soon captured both of his castles and threatened his queen. Ivo put his full attention on the game and managed to fend her off for a dozen moves, but she eventually backed his king into a corner.

"Check and mate, my lord." She rose, done with him now that she'd beaten him.

"One more," he insisted. "Sit."

With a purpose in mind, Ivo played the third game even more deliberately, dragging it out until her eyelids drooped and she began to stifle yawns behind her hand. Then he kept her at the board a little longer yet, making sure she was truly exhausted and ready for sleep—and that he was ready as well.

Finally a man came in to bank the fire. As he left, Ivo rose and stepped around the table to take Alaida's hand. "We will finish tomorrow. It is time to retire."

Her eyes flared at this, whether from anticipation or anger, Ivo wasn't certain—not that it mattered. He was not bedding her—and so he reminded himself several times as he handed her over to her women.

Brand rose and took the raven off his perch. At the door, he turned and gave Ivo a hard look. "Are you certain of this?" he mouthed in Norse.

Ivo nodded once, and answered aloud in French. "I will see you in the morning."

"Mmm," said Brand doubtfully. He dipped his head to Alaida, "Good night, my lady."

"God's rest, *messire*."

The door shut, leaving Ivo to deal with the sight of Bôte and Hadwisa stripping his wife. It conjured up his wedding night, but this time he could not permit himself to grow excited.

He did all right, too, until they started brushing out her plaits. Then the sudden memory of how her hair felt spread over his skin sent blood pounding into his groin with such fury, he near groaned. He dropped into his chair, fighting to get his body under control before his reaction became evident to all.

Curse it, he needed to do this, to pass an occasional night with Alaida in order to keep the talk down. Brand had warned him once more on the way home that it wouldn't be easy, but no, he'd been sure of himself, confident that all the times he'd found release by his own hand during the past week had blunted his desire. But here he was, the front of his clothes sticking out like he'd shoved a marrowbone down his breeks. He leaned forward to further disguise his state while the women finished with Alaida. The bed creaked as she crawled in, setting off visions of her naked in the bed, followed by another rush of arousal.

Her women left, and it was just him and Alaida and a mad desire to bury himself in her no matter what the consequences. She lay in bed staring up at the draperies as if she were trying to decide something, then rolled to her side and rose up on one elbow.

"I will be along in a moment," he said quickly, before she had a chance to say something that might make this situation even more difficult. "I have much to think about before I sleep."

She pressed her lips together against whatever it was that went through her mind, flopped back down on her pillow, and lay there, silent, watching him. He waited her out, studying the board until the location of each piece was burned into his mind, until he wasn't hard anymore, until her eyes closed and she finally, blessedly, began to snore.

The sound made him smile, half with relief, half with amusement. His lady wife snored. It wasn't much of a snore, not to a man who had spent a lifetime sleeping next to men whose snores could frighten horses in the next village, and he suspected she would deny she snored at all, but he rather liked it. He sat there listening as she slipped more deeply into sleep.

When he finally knew he could handle lying next to her, he put out the candles, kicked off his boots, and crawled into bed fully clothed.

"*Mmmpf,*" she said, and rolled against his side, warm and soft and smelling of Alaida. He took a deep breath, checked his intentions, then slipped his arms around her. Yes, that worked. He could permit himself that much pleasure, at least, from this pretense of marriage, so he took what he could, holding her while her breath slowed and she began to snore once more, and then longer, until she finally rolled away and the warm imprint of her body against his cooled.

When he left the bed sometime later, the mattress and pillow bore the mark of his body for others to find the next morning. If he was very lucky, Alaida might even recall that she'd lain in his arms. He pulled on his boots, collected his cloak and sword, and went down to the hall.

He found Brand outside, hanging over the well, head cocked, listening intently. He glanced up as Ivo walked over. "You all right?"

Ivo nodded. "Hear anything?"

"Listen for yourself."

Ivo listened for a moment. "I don't—"

A low boom, barely heard, interrupted him. The hairs on his neck rose. He leaned far over the edge, risking a broken neck to get his head in as far as possible, and waited. *Shh-thump,* like thunder, or a tree falling far away—except it came from beneath him. He hung there, holding his breath. *Shh-thump.*

"The dragon's heart," whispered Ivo.

"No. Listen."

Shh-thump. He closed his eyes and listened as the beats echoed in the well shaft, faint and slow, but steady. *Shh-thump.* Pause. *Shh-thump.* And then he recognized it, a rhythm that had been his life for so many years. "'Tis the sea. Waves."

"Aye. That's what I thought." Brand pulled himself out of the well with a grunt. "Waves against rock. You can only hear it when it's dead calm. The breeze was up a little bit ago, and I didn't hear a sound. When it died . . ."

"The shore is only a few leagues from here," said Ivo, also straightening. "Some trick must make the sound carry through the land and come up here. No wonder the villagers fear it. Most of them have never traveled beyond Lesbury to hear the sea."

"Are you going to tell them?" asked Brand.

Ivo shook his head. "Not unless I must. I want to see what the elders have to say."

"If there is no beast and no covenant, you can put your castle where you want."

Ivo whipped his cloak around his shoulders and jammed the pin into place. "Covenant or not, I will put it where it will do Alaida the greatest good when I'm gone."

"Mmm." Brand gave him another of those hard, dubious looks, then shrugged and nodded. "Do you really want to head out this early? I doubt Tom has the horses ready yet."

"Probably not," said Ivo, but they turned toward the stables anyway.

A FEW MORNINGS later, Alaida hung out the window, watching a gang of men scribe a great circle on the field behind the manor. They used a rope stretched from a post driven into the center to measure, and marked the line with stakes and powdered chalk. Another gang traced a second circle some five yards inside the first, marking, she assumed, the ditch, while Sir Ari and Oswald watched from horseback. Wat was one of the men scribing the line. She couldn't spy Geoffrey.

"I thought the noise would have you up, my lady," said Bôte, coming into the room bearing a tray of bread and cold meats. A little boy with a ewer and another with an armload of firewood followed on her heels. "Saint Peter's knees, 'tis freezing in here."

"The fire died," said Alaida. "So, they begin the castle. I did not realize the plans were set already."

"Set enough, it seems." Bôte took up the poker and jabbed at the coals a little. "Aye, 'tis dead. Get a flame and kindling from the hall, Hugh. And Ralph, you go tell Hadwisa she's late, that my lady is already awake. Be quick, both of you."

The boys dashed off, and Bôte pulled a fur off the bed and came over to wrap it around Alaida's shoulders. "Come away from the window, lamb, before you catch a chill."

"It is warmer outside than in." She leaned on the sill and tried to envision a drawbridge connecting the yard—soon to be a castle bailey, it seemed—to the motte and tower that would rise within the ringing ditch. "I expected he would build here, after what Drogo and Céolsige said, but I did not know they planned to start this morning."

"They decided last night, after you came up to bed. Are you sure you feel well, lamb? You fell asleep so early."

"I was just a little tired. I feel fine this morning."

"Still, I will make you a posset, to be sure. As I said, my lord decided last night, and this morning Wat called out everyone in the village who does not have other work. They began as soon as the priest gave the blessing."

"Father Theobald is here?" She scanned the crowd, and sure enough, there was his black among those watching.

"Aye, Sir Ari brought him along when he came back this morning."

Young Hugh trotted back in carrying a lit rush in one hand and a basket of dry moss and twigs in the other. Alaida held her tongue while Bôte relieved him of his load and dispatched him to other duties. "So Sir Ari was gone all night again, just as the other two are gone all day. What do you suppose they're about, that none of them stay within the manor a full day 'round?"

"Has Lord Ivo not told you what he does, my lady?"

"Only that he must be gone on business."

"Men and their business. Well, 'tis nothing of mystery, I'm sure. They have their habits, is all."

"I would change his habits," muttered Alaida to the air.

"You will not make yourself loved trying to do so, my lady." Bôte finished laying the fire, took up the burning rush from its clamp, and bent to touch it to the moss. "Men do not take kindly to a woman's meddling with their habits, and men of their sort, even less."

"And what sort would that be?"

"The sort that hunt all day or whore all night, I venture. Be glad your lord husband is one of the hunters, my lady, for Sir Ari, I fear, is not."

Alaida's eyes widened. "You think he spends his nights whoring?"

"What else would a man be about at night? Probably has bastards scattered all over England, fair as he is."

"Hmm." Alaida took another look out the window at Ari, sitting there on his horse looking like an angel come to earth as he directed the villagers forward to break ground. *Whoring. One never knew.* "Is that what occupies my husband as well?"

"Whoring? Lord Ivo?" Bôte sounded shocked at the idea. "Whatever would make you ask that?"

"He and Sir Brand bring home precious little meat for men who hunt every day."

"Hunting is not always about meat. Grown men like to play in the woods as much as boys do." Bôte's searching gaze brought a rush of color to Alaida's cheeks. "Lord Ivo lies only with you, lamb. 'Tis in the very way he looks at you. Do not trouble your heart with such things."

"I won't," said Alaida as though reassured, but the thought settled more deeply into the back of her mind. If her husband were taking his pleasure elsewhere, it would explain much. She hadn't told Bôte about his lack of desire, letting the old woman think, along with the rest of the manor, that the nights he passed in her bed were passionate. It was strange, since she'd told the old woman everything for so many years, but this was too close, too tender. Besides, she hadn't yet decided what she thought of it, any more than she'd decided what to think of him. Perhaps it would be good to have a husband who made few demands on her. Or perhaps not.

The fire took, and Alaida padded over and held the fur open like butterfly wings to catch the first heat. "How long will it take to raise the motte?"

"Wat claims it will be built before harvest, and the tower will come as soon as it settles." Bôte selected a gown and hose from the cupboard. "Of course, that's if more men are hired in, so Geoffrey is off to Durham to see to that."

"Has he gone already?"

"Aye, left at dawn, with guards and four men in wagons to bring more supplies along with the workers."

"It is all happening so quickly."

"'Tis that. You will surely celebrate Christmas as lady of Alnwick Castle."

"That will be merry, indeed," said Alaida. She sighed. "A castle proper. I wish Grandfather were here for it."

"If Lord Gilbert were here, you would not be lady of a castle," said Bôte in her practical way. "Here is Hadwisa at last. Let us get you dressed. Father Theobald must return to Lesbury today without doing Lord Ivo's Mass, but he would see you in chapel before he goes."

Alaida rolled her eyes heavenward, but she laid aside the fur and raised her arms for the gown. Here, at least, was one good thing about a husband who did not desire her: she would have nothing new to blush about with Father Theobald.

CHAPTER 11

IT WAS ALWAYS this way, this agony that ripped through him each dawn and dusk, but even after so many long years, Brand fought it. It did no good—it never did—and he finally submitted, as he did every night, waiting for the twisting pain to finish with him. Long, wrenching moments later, it subsided enough to let him catch his breath, then further, so he could begin to think again.

It took him a time to decipher where he was, to remember what he was doing, to recall what the noises around him meant. This den he lay in was strange, not the usual hollow under a fallen tree. He fingered soft grass beneath him, looked up to find a sort of roof, made of more grass tangled in the brush overhead. The bear had clearly taken some other creature's burrow. Something large, that smelled bad . . . like a pig.

Pig. No, wild boar. His heart began to thud wildly.

Still half in the bear's thrall, Brand scrambled out and staggered to his feet. The wind whipped over his bare skin, chilling him as he tried to make out which way to go in the twilight. Something rustled in the brush and he whirled, snarling.

The boar hit him like a boulder, knocking him sideways. Brand rolled, trying to escape, but the boar had ten stone on him plus the rage of an animal defending its home. Spear-sharp tusks tore into Brand's hip. He screamed.

The sound only excited the boar. Shrilling, it swung its head back and forth, savaging Brand and ripping a long gash down his thigh. Desperate, Brand grappled blindly for some weapon. His hand landed on a branch and he swung hard. The wood was old and brittle, and it broke across the beast's skull. The boar backed away, stood there a moment, panting and squealing, then charged forward again, aiming at Brand's head. With a shouted plea to Skadi, Brand thrust the splintered end of the branch toward the creature's open mouth. The boar's weight carried it forward. Brand shoved with all his strength, pushing the point home as the tusks tore into his arm.

The boar's battle squeal turned into a death scream that drowned in the arc of hot blood that spattered over Brand. The boar collapsed, Brand's hand still within its jaws, still trying to gore him even as it died. Brand yanked free and scrabbled away, finding shelter in the roots of a tree while the boar lay twitching, pouring out the last of its lifeblood into the forest litter.

He was pouring out blood of his own, Brand realized. Battle-heat was keeping him warm and pain-free for now, but that would fade quickly. The injuries wouldn't kill him— the witch had seen to that—but he needed help nonetheless.

"Ari?" Some small animal skittered away at the sound of his voice. He heard wings, but too small for the raven's. "Balls, Ari, where are you?"

With Ivo and the horses, no doubt, wherever they were. Brand lifted his head and peered around. He recognized nothing, had no idea which way to go in the fading light. He was likely bleeding like the great pig that lay a few yards away, though he couldn't tell with so much of the beast's gore on him. Without even his clothes to shred for bandages, he scraped a handful of moss from between the roots of the tree and jammed it into what felt like the worst of the wounds. This was going to be grim.

Jaw clenched, he used the tree to haul himself upright. As he put his foot down, warm, fresh blood poured down his leg and the first inklings of the pain he would suffer seared through his body. Even with the magic, if he didn't find help soon, he would pass out and spend the next several nights lying in the forest naked and freezing while his body fought to heal.

"I can do this," he muttered aloud. "Walk."

He walked. It was slow going and got slower with each step. He found a clearing, spotted stars enough to orient himself, and turned east, toward Alnwick. "Walk."

Forever passed, one step at a time, his strength fading as he bled his way through the forest. His leg blazed with pain that threatened to curl him into a ball on the forest floor. Sheer will kept him moving.

When he caught the first flicker of light between the trunks of the trees, he thought it was his mind playing tricks. He shouldn't be able to see the village yet; he was still too deep in the forest. But there it was again, barely a glimpse of soft yellow. If it was a mind-trick, it was a good one, one he wanted. He angled toward the light, pushing himself toward whatever it was. The effort and pain raised sweat on his skin that froze in the cold night air.

Not a trick. A hut. A hut with light escaping around the edge of a shuttered window. People. He forced himself across the tiny clearing, found the door, raised his hand to knock.

His arm wouldn't come up. He tried to call out, but he had no voice left to call with. He began to fall. He hit the door and it burst open, and he kept falling, falling, into light and warmth. Into nothing.

IVO HEARD THE screams just as he finished changing, the faintest of sounds mingled with the other forest noises, carried by a fitful wind and heard through ears no longer eagle nor yet human. They could have been anything—a wolf, a dying rabbit, even a pig squealing on a distant croft—but he'd waited here with the horses far too long now, and the sick feeling in his gut told him what had screamed: a man. Brand.

He looped Kraken's reins in his fist and mounted Fax. Above him, the raven chattered noisily, and Ivo stuck his arm out. "Get down here. I'll need you to find him."

The raven settled on his wrist like a falcon. Beady black eyes met Ivo's as the bird spread his wings and lowered his head in a strange bow of apology.

"I know," said Ivo. "You can't help what the gods tell you. Come, let's find him. I think he's hurt."

Chittering softly, the raven sidestepped up to his shoulder, and Ivo turned the horses in the direction from which he thought the screams had come.

MEREWYN HAD BEEN waiting for him all day.

For weeks now, since just after the winter solstice, her dreams had been of a swimming gander—that meant a male visitor—and only this morning when she'd dropped her knife, it had stuck straight up in the dirt floor, a sure sign he would arrive within the day. Sadly, a wren had fluttered in the open door a few moments later and landed on the exact spot where the knife had pierced the ground. That's when she knew her visitor would be accompanied by death.

Still, when a giant of a man crashed through her door, naked and bloody, Merewyn shrieked and snatched up the same knife to defend herself.

No danger followed him, however, and after she got her racing heart back under control, she realized this poor, wounded soul could harm no one. Feeling foolish, she laid the blade aside and stepped around the bloody hulk of his body to push the door shut against the cold, slipping the iron fire poker into the cleats to replace the bar he'd broken in his falling. Her home secure once more, she turned to examine this strange visitor the night winds had brought her, kneeling to lay her hand over his heart. It was, to her surprise, steady.

"By the Mother, you *are* still alive," she whispered. "Let us see if I can help you stay that way."

She set to work.

A HAND. COOL and calm, it reached through the blaze of pain to draw Brand toward consciousness, giving him that one thing he could hold on to, put a name to, beyond the hurting.

Slowly, he found others. Bed. Blanket. Fire. A voice, talking nonsense. Help. He'd found help. Why had he needed it?

The hand went away. He wanted it back and tried to say so, but his throat was full of sand. "Ho . . ."

There was a squeak, like a puppy's yelp, and then the voice again, female and gentle, saying something he couldn't quite understand.

"*Endr,*" he managed. Again.

The female repeated herself, not in Norse but in Saxon English. His ear made the shift as she finished. " . . . still, my lord."

Someone seemed to have tied anchors to his eyelids. He prized them open a crack and caught a glimpse of blue sleeve before they slammed shut again.

He wanted something. It took him a moment to think of the word. "Drink."

"Of course."

He listened to her move around, then the hand came back, this time to lift his head. A cup touched his lips, and he let her pour whatever it was down his throat, barely tasting it as he swallowed greedily. Warmth eddied through him, and the sand began to dissolve.

"What is?" *That wasn't right.*

"Watered wine with herbs to give you ease, my lord."

He nodded that he understood, or at least he thought he nodded. His head didn't seem to move much. "Name."

"Merewyn, my lord. And you?"

"*Brandr.* Brand."

"You are sore hurt, Lord Brand. You must lie still."

He lay there a little, listening to her move around until her herbs began to work. Slowly, he located one hand, far, far away at the end of an arm that went on forever, and touched the places where the pain came from. He found bandages, first on his thigh, then his hip, then, after he worked out how to bring his other hand into play, on his forearm.

He tried his eyes once more and found them slightly less weighty. The room spun before it settled into thatch and beams, thickly hung with bundles of herbs and strings of dried apples and a small bacon, thick with salt. Pig. Ah, yes, the boar. That's what had left him in this state.

It must be getting on toward dawn. He needed to get away before the sun found him and the bear found her—wherever she was. He gathered his strength, rolled onto his good side, and pushed himself up. Her herbs weren't *that* good. "*Nnn,* balls that hurts."

"What are you doing?" She flew across the room to block him from rising, holding her blue skirts wide before him, as though she were herding ducks. "Stop that. You'll tear yourself open."

"Probably." He sat there on the edge of the little bed, so wobbly he couldn't even look up at her. Ducks would likely give her more trouble than he could just now. Ducklings. "Come down here where I can see you."

When she knelt, she wore an expression nearly as sour as Lady Alaida at her worst. As jennet-stubborn as the lady, too, he sensed, but there the similarity ended: where the lady's coloring ran to copper and gold, this woman had walnut hair and eyes that set off skin as pale and creamy as new ivory. He'd have to be more hurt than this not to notice how fair she was.

"Merewyn, is it? Where am I and how long is it until dawn?"

"You're in my cottage in the Aln woods, my lord. Dawn is a little while yet. The sky has not yet begun to lighten."

"Good. Help me up."

"No, my lord. You must rest here a few days."

"You would not like me as a guest. Help me up, I say."

"No, my lord."

He put his hands on her shoulders and used her to lever himself into a better position, in preparation for rising. "It is not for discussion, Merewyn. I must leave."

She looked him like he was a madman and waved a hand over him. "Will you go off naked, then?"

Brand looked down at the blanket, which had puddled across his lap precariously. "This will do."

"No, my lord, it will not."

He tried to rise, but she put a finger in the center of his chest and pushed him back down as easily as he would have stopped his old grandmother.

"I don't have time for this," he protested. "Help me up."

Instead, she darted across the room, flipped open an iron-bound chest, and began sifting through its contents.

"I'll never fit into one of your kirtles," he grumbled.

"But you will fit my husband's old things."

So, she was married. Where was her husband, that he would leave her to tend a naked stranger alone?

She turned, holding out a short tunic of thick wool, a baggy pair of linen breeks, and a worn pair of stockings. "They will be tight, but better than naught. And you can take the blanket as a cloak."

It shamed him, taking the clothes of a poor man, but there was no way to refuse them without insulting her. Besides, if he didn't find Ivar, he might need them at sunset. He let her dress him. "My thanks. I will return them as soon as I'm able."

"Keep them," she said. "I would not have you die with no clothes on."

Brand snorted. "I'm not going to die."

"I would not wager on that, my lord."

"I would," he said. He held his hand out. "Help me up."

"No, my lord. If you cannot rise alone, you have no business out in the woods alone."

Brand glowered, but in truth, he couldn't fault her. She was only trying to help an injured man and didn't realize what danger she was in. With a grunt he pushed to his feet, swayed and swore a bit, then found his balance.

"There. That's not so bad," he said as he tugged his borrowed breeks up the rest of the way and knotted the ties.

"You are a terrible liar, my lord. I think I will follow you a little, until you fall over and—"

"No!"

She jumped back, startled by his vehemence. "I only mean to be there to help you, my lord."

"No," he repeated. "You are *not* to follow me. In fact, you will block your door and stay inside until I am well away, and if you hear any strange noises at all, you will remain inside all day. Do you understand me?"

"No, my lord, I do not."

"Then obey me without understanding." He cast about for some way to make her do what he said. "I command this in the name of the lord of Alnwick. You will stay inside. You will not follow me. Swear it." He took two steps toward her and roared the order as if he were on the deck of his ship. "Swear it!"

She flinched as though he'd slapped her, and her dark brows knit in bewilderment, but she nodded. "I swear, my lord. I will do as you say."

"Good." He escaped out the door while he still had legs. "Which way to Alnwick?"

"Follow the path, my lord. There by the birch."

He spotted where the track led off to the east. "You have my thanks for all you have done, Merewyn of Alnwood. Now bar the door." She hesitated, and he growled at her over his shoulder. "Keep to your word, woman."

"Yes, my lord." With a last, confounded look, she pushed the door shut. The iron bar rang as it dropped into place.

"Your word," he repeated one last time, loudly enough for her to hear though the door. Then he turned west, away from Alnwick and into the woods, driven by thoughts of good Merewyn and what would happen if the injured bear wandered back to her.

The sky had begun to take on the charcoal tinge of night verging on dawn. A single bird chirruped tentatively on a high branch; he had very little time.

He pushed as fast as his legs would carry him, but it wasn't fast enough. The sky gradually lightened, more birds sang, and still he was within bear's-reach of the cottage. Suddenly, a chattering black shape dove at him from between trees.

"About time," he muttered, hobbling after the raven. Moments later, he heard horses, and relief flooded through him. "Ivar! Here."

"You look like you've been eaten by something and shat out the other end," said Ivo as he rode up. He leaned down to hand over Kraken's reins and sniffed the air. "Smell like it, too."

"Good to see you, too." Brand started to mount up but realized he would never get his foot into the stirrup. He led Kraken over to a fallen log, hoisted himself up clumsily as Ivo watched with a bemused expression, and slid into the saddle with an *oof* and a groan. "Come. We haven't much time."

Riding proved barely less painful than walking, but definitely quicker. Brand gritted his teeth and clung to Kraken's mane like an infant as the horses picked their way through the forest.

"I found a dead boar a little while ago," said Ivo after Brand had a chance to catch his breath. "Was that your doing?"

"Aye." Brand gave him a brief version of the night's events as they rode. "She tried to clean me up, but even I can still smell the beast's filth on me. I think it's in my beard."

"Perhaps it is time for the beard to go."

"And look like a Norman?" sneered Brand.

Ivo rolled his eyes, but let the subject drop. "You know, it's cold enough that the carcass should be good still. If the wolves haven't found it yet, Ari can dress it out and we'll drag it in tonight."

"I will eat its heart," vowed Brand. He glanced at the threads of gold beginning to paint the clouds. "Let me off here and get the horses well away. The bear will be cross with pain today."

Ivo nodded as he looked around for landmarks. "I'll meet you back here tonight. Don't wander off."

Dismounting brought tears to Brand's eyes and made the breath catch in his lungs. He shook it off before he looked up at Ivo. "I'll try, but the bear does what he does."

As Ivo disappeared into the forest with the horses, Brand stripped off the loaned clothes and stuffed them into a hollow tree so he could return them to Merewyn's husband later. He found a good den under a nearby log and crawled in, in the hope the bear would simply stay there, sleeping. He lay there aching and shivering in the cold, happy to be far enough from Merewyn's cottage, until the sun broke the horizon and the other pain caught him and he roared his agony into the rose-pearl sky.

CHAPTER 12

ALAIDA SAT WITH her women after dinner, stewing as she sewed. Her husband hadn't come home at all last night, not even to ignore her and rest in the hall. She had been trying hard not to think of what that might mean, but such discipline was difficult when her hands were busy and her mind was not, and unfortunately, none of the women seemed very talkative today.

Left free to wander, her mind followed its most disturbing paths. The longer she stitched, the more disgusted she grew and the more mistakes she made, which made her more disgusted still. She was picking out a seam for the third time when a voice at the door begged her pardon.

Alaida looked up from her seam and smiled. Here, at last, was something to think of other than *him*. "Yes, Oswald. What is it? "

"Did Lord Ivo say anything about going off on a journey?"

Smile fading, she wove the needle into the cloth and laid the garment aside. "He did not. I assumed he had spoken to you."

The marshal shook his head. "I fear not, my lady."

"Ah. Well, likely they found themselves nearer to one of the vills than to Alnwick and decided to pass the night." *Pass the night whoring,* her mind added, unbidden.

"That was my first thought, but Sir Ari did not return this morning either."

"Really?" The revelation served only to deepen her suspicions. She tried to maintain a dispassionate tone. "I didn't see him at dinner, but I thought he must have duties elsewhere."

"None that he told us, and that is what unsettles me. I would like to send out a rider or two, with your leave."

Alaida studied the worried wrinkles between Oswald's brows, and in them, found her something else to think of. "You are concerned about the Scots."

"They are always a concern, my lady."

"Aye, but there's been no word of raids. Truly, I doubt our friends to the north have anything to do with this." However, Oswald's caution had served them more than once. "Very well. Send whomever you think best. But I wager they will find my lord and his men sitting comfortably in some hall, with a jar of ale each and nary a Scot in sight." *A jar of ale and a woman each. Or would they simply share one woman among them?* The thought made her ill.

"That is my hope, my lady." Oswald dipped his head once more and left.

"I'm sure they are well, my lady," said Hadwisa.

"I'm sure," echoed Alaida, barely managing to avoid a note of scorn. She picked up her sewing again. "Hunting, most likely. I wonder what sort of game they will bring."

BRAND HAD ON the clothes the healer had given him when Ivo rode up that evening, and his face showed some color.

"You look better," said Ivo as he dismounted. He took a sniff. "You smell just as bad, though."

"You're not so sweet yourself." Brand pointed at the front of Ivo's tunic. "What happened to you?"

Ivo looked down at the blood that stained his clothes. "Ari. Apparently he decided we looked too clean for men who had killed a boar." He untied the bundle of clothes from behind Kraken's saddle and handed them to Brand. "Let's see what he did to yours."

"Balls," said Brand a moment later as he held up his tunic and breeks. Not only had Ari soaked them with the boar's blood, he'd also hacked ragged holes in places that roughly matched Brand's wounds and given those places an extra coating of gore. "This was a good, warm tunic! Best I've had in years. Give me that bird. I'm going to pluck every feather on his scrawny arse."

Ivo chuckled as the raven fluttered off out of Brand's reach. "Don't be too angry. He's right about the clothes. They wouldn't have looked right, with you that torn up and a dead boar behind us."

"Well, I'm not going to put the stinking things on," vowed Brand. "I'll keep to what the woman gave me."

"We'll find you something that fits better when we get back. At least put on your boots. Ari didn't foul them too badly."

"Bad enough. Look at this." Brand pointed to a nasty smear of muck down the side of one boot. "I'll never get it all off."

"If it's any comfort, he ruined some of his things, too."

"Bet he didn't get blood on his boots."

"No, but then, he doesn't get to boast of killing a boar with his bare hands and a branch."

"No, he doesn't." Brand cheered visibly. He eased himself down on a nearby stump and began pulling his stained boots on, grunting in pain with each tug.

Ivo watched a moment, glad he wasn't the one the boar had found, then scooped up Brand's ruined clothes, bundled them up, and tied them back on Kraken.

"Lead him over here," said Brand as he clambered stiffly onto his stump. It took him nearly as long to maneuver himself into the saddle as it had the previous night, and his grunts and groans made it sound nearly as painful.

"Are you sure you're good to ride that far?" asked Ivo.

"Of course." Brand thumped himself on the chest with a heartiness that belied the pain Ivo had just seen in his face. "I killed a boar with my bare hands and a stick, didn't I?"

"That you did, my friend," said Ivo, and turned Fax toward thicket where the dead boar awaited them.

ALAIDA HELD SUPPER again that evening, waiting to see if Ivo and Brand would turn up. Their usual time for returning came and went once more, however, with no sign of them, and she reluctantly gave the signal to bring in the food. People were just filling their trenchers when the door burst open on young Tom.

"They come, my lady. Edric just spied them crossing the orchard, and he says they have large game and that one of them looks to be hurt."

He flew back out without waiting. Oswald was up and after him, calling for men and a litter before Alaida could even get to her feet.

"Bôte," she began, but the nurse was already snapping instructions. The household scrambled to obey, the meal forgotten, and Alaida was left with nothing to do but hurry outside.

The gate swung wide as two horses walked out of the dark. Ivo's mount labored hard, but as it neared, she could see that was only because it dragged a rough sled with some large animal on it. Relief washed over her as Ivo swung easily off his horse. Sir Brand, however, wobbled dangerously in the saddle, and Oswald moved quickly to his aide, calling for the litter-bearers to hurry.

"I'm not that hurt," growled Brand. "I just need a hand down and a jar of good ale."

"Be careful of his right side," directed Ivo as Oswald reached up to help him down.

Brand swayed a bit as his feet touched the ground, but he straightened and shrugged off Oswald's steadying hand. "I'm fine, I tell you."

"Oh, yes, you look quite fine. Since you're so well, in fact, you may help *me* inside." Alaida slipped her arm into Brand's, and they started slowly off toward the hall. "What happened?"

Brand jerked his head toward the carcass. "That boar caught me on foot."

"A boar!"

"A huge brute of a boar, my lady," called Tom from the group clustering around the carcass. "'Twill feed us for days."

"Aye, and he killed it with his bare hands and a twig," said Ivo. His words drew a snort of pained laughter from Brand and a stir of admiration among the men. He fell in beside Alaida, calling back to the men. "Summon the butcher, and tell the cook Sir Brand wants the heart for supper tomorrow."

Brand took one look at Bôte's makeshift sickroom and shook his head. "No bed. A sturdy chair will do me better."

Ivo picked up the lord's chair and plunked it down before the fire. "Here. Sit."

Brand gingerly lowered himself down. "Aaah. At last, something with steady legs. I never before realized how often that horse of mine stumbles."

"Perhaps you were never before so unsteady to carry, *messire*," Alaida pointed out. "Where are you hurt?"

"Thigh and arm, but the worst is here." He touched his right side.

Bôte lifted his shirt and tugged down his braies enough to show the horrific gash that marred his hip, as long as Alaida's palm was wide and fully two fingers deep, even with the powdered herbs and cobwebs packed into the gap where flesh was missing.

"Who stitched you?" asked Alaida.

"Some woman in the woods. Merewyn, she said her name was."

"Good. You were far better off with her than you would have been here. In fact, I likely would have sent for her myself."

"That's good to know." Brand jerked as Bôte probed the edges of the wound with one pudgy finger. "Be gentle there, old woman."

Bôte poked another time or two, then laid her palm over the area. "There's no fever in it. Fortune favored you, Knight, putting you in Merewyn's hands."

"Aye. She did well by me."

Alaida studied the wound from over Bôte's shoulder. She pointed. "I wonder why she put stitches clear out here, where the flesh is barely torn?"

"There was much blood and it was night," said Brand, tugging his shirt down. "Likely she couldn't make out the edges."

"Still, 'tis strange she didn't bind such a deep wound," said Alaida.

"She did. It came loose."

Alaida pushed up his sleeve and found that gash open to the air as well. "This one, too?"

"He tore the bandages off," said Ivo. "Said they itched—and you see how pigheaded he is."

"Aye," said Alaida sympathetically. "Well, you are lucky indeed, *messire*. This one is healing as cleanly as the other. I do not know what herbs Merewyn used, but if you were not here to tell me otherwise, I would think your wounds were a week old, at the least. Let us dress these, and then we will see to the one on your leg."

"He needs a bath first," said Ivo. "He reeks of the boar's filth."

Alaida shook her head. "'Tis unwise to bathe an ill man."

"I'm not ill," said Brand.

"You will be if you have a bath," said Bôte. "A chill will set in."

"Bah, I dunk myself in rivers when there's snow on the ground," argued Brand. "Fetch me water and soap. I will scrub the stink off myself if I have to."

"And tear your wounds open?" Alaida shook her head. "No, *messire*. If you must have a washing, you will get it—

but from gentler hands than yours. Then your wounds will be dressed and you will be put to bed. And that is my order as your lady."

"But I . . ." he began, but Ivo cleared his throat and Brand finished without enthusiasm, "At your command, my lady."

"Wash his hair, too, and trim his beard while you're about it. In fact, shave him, if he'll stand for it," said Alaida in an aside to Bôte as servants came forward with soap and toweling. "And ensure he stays warm."

"We will, my lady."

"He needs fresh clothing," said Ivo. "His are beyond repair. Merewyn loaned those."

"We shall see they get back to her and—"

"I'll take them back," interrupted Brand. "I need to say a proper thank-you."

"As you say, *messire*. And as I was saying, we will provide new for you. For both of you," she said, noting for the first time the blood staining her husband's tunic. "Hadwisa and Eadgyth, help Bôte while I see to dressing our hunters."

Alaida took up a candle and headed for the wardrobe as the others began easing Brand out of his clothes. Few on the manor had shoulders so broad, and it took some searching to find a chainse and winter gown she thought would fit. Then there was the matter of braies. She quickly found the patched ones meant for the servants as part of their yearly boon, but hunted through the cupboards without finding any of the better quality that would go to a noble knight. If Geoffrey were here, he'd know just where to lay his hands on them, but he hadn't yet returned with the extra men. Perhaps they were in with the women's things. She unlocked the other chest and began sorting through the contents, digging deeper and deeper in her search.

"Was your mother frightened by a badger while you were in the womb?" asked Ivo from behind her just as she located the braies. Alaida straightened to find him leaning in the doorframe. He had shed the stained gown and wore only his linens and a crooked smile. "Every time I turn around, I find you tail up, tunneling your way into something."

She was in no mood for his teasing. "Then your mother must have been frightened by an ass. Hunting boar with just two men!"

"The disposition of a badger as well," said Ivo, his smile gone. "We were not hunting the boar, it was hunting us—or Brand, at least, since I was not with him. Do not make that face at me, woman."

"What face?"

"That one." He jerked his chin toward her. "The one that says you don't believe me, and that if you did, you would see me whipped. Yes, that one."

She snorted and began replacing the items she'd pulled out of the chest. "Very well. Tell me the rest, my lord, and I will try to mind my face."

"There's little more to tell. We were separated. I heard the fight, but by the time I reached the spot, the boar was dead and Brand had stumbled off, bleeding. I spent most of the night trying to find him in the dark."

"And then chose to dress out the boar rather than bring him home," she said without masking her disgust.

"Ah. The face," he chided. "Ari dealt with the carcass while Brand rested, as he much needed to do."

"One of you might have come for help. We could have sent a wagon for him and—"

"It would have been worth my life to try to load him in a wagon," said Ivo with certainty.

"I suppose it would have," she granted after considering a moment how Brand would view such treatment. "But could you not have sent Sir Ari to tell us what had happened?"

"It wasn't possible."

She waited for him to explain why, but he didn't, and when she glanced up, he wore that closed look that came over his face every time he spoke of his and his men's odd absences. Well, piss on him. She rose, dropped the lid of the chest with a loud clunk, and picked up the clothing she had chosen for Brand. She started around Ivo, but he shifted so he blocked her more completely.

Exasperated, she backed up a step or two and glared up at him. "Is there something you need, *monseigneur*?"

Amusement flickered across his face. "To have my curiosity satisfied."

He was doing it again. She knew she shouldn't ask, but she did. "Curiosity about what?"

"You. As we rode in, I thought I saw some . . . concern on your face."

"Tom said a man was injured."

"And you worried it was me?"

"I worried it was anyone. We are sore short of knights and cannot afford to lose one. Even one who only appears after dark."

"So it was concern for Alnwick." He stepped closer. "And that is why you wished for Ari to tell you where we were?"

"We were inconvenienced. We waited supper on you both nights."

Another step. "But you weren't worried."

"No."

"Are you certain? You weren't worried about . . ." He was on her now, a handspan away, looming over her, his eyes dark and mysterious in the dim light. "Anything at all?"

Yes, she wanted to say. *Yes, I was worried about you, that you were hurt, that I would be widow before I am hardly wife.* She wanted him to kiss her and carry her upstairs and release this desperate ache that rose up in her every time he came near, and in the same thought she wanted to beat her fists against his chest in frustration and rail at him never to touch her again. As his head came slowly, slowly down to her, she chose neither course. "Actually, you are right, my lord. I was worried. About my silver thymel."

That brought him up short. He reared back. "Your what?"

"My thymel. For sewing," she added when he looked

blank. "I wagered it today. The women were guessing what game you would bring home from your *hunting.* As you rode in, I realized I had lost it to one of the spinsters—Rohesia guessed a boar—and I was thinking how I shall miss it."

"Your thymel," he repeated.

"My thymel," she said firmly. "Sir Brand will be needing these."

She sidestepped around him, but his hand shot out and curled around her arm to stop her. "What was your guess?"

"That you were not hunting at all." His hand burned through the cloth, as warm as if it lay against bare skin, and suddenly the choice was open again and she took the risk, offering herself up. "Your things are upstairs, my lord. Will you come up with me?"

The noise from the hall filled the silence that stretched out between them. Finally, he gave his answer. "I think I had better make use of the soap and hot water as well. Send them down, if you will."

She did so, and by the time she went back down the next morning to break her fast and pray, he and Brand were long gone.

CHAPTER 13

FIVE DAYS HAD passed since Sir Brand vanished into the dawn when Merewyn once more knocked her knife off the table. It stuck itself in the same spot.

Thus, it was no surprise when she rounded the corner of her little cottage that evening after feeding her chickens and saw him there, a shadow man on a shadow horse against the dark trunks of the trees. Beside him sat another man on horseback—a friend, from the ease she felt between them. She started toward them, and they nudged their horses out into the clearing and met her halfway.

She smiled up at the face she had come to know so well in a single night. "You shaved your beard."

He stroked his chin, chuckling ruefully. "Not by choice."

"It looks well, my lord. I hope you find yourself better than when you left here last."

"Much better, thanks to you, Merewyn, but stop calling me 'lord.' I'm only a knight." He indicated his friend. "Him, you can 'm'lord' as you please. He is the new lord of Alnwick."

"Lord Ivo," she said as she knelt to the pale-haired nobleman. "I've heard your name in the village. You wed Lady Alaida when you took the hall."

"You are at the advantage, Healer. All I know of you is your name and that my wife was pleased when she heard who had cared for Brand. She said she would have sent for you herself."

"I have often carried my herbs to the manor and will gladly do so again if your lady asks, my lord. But what has brought you both to me this evening?"

"I came to thank you properly and to return the clothes you loaned me," said Sir Brand, twisting to untie the bundle behind his saddle.

"You thanked me well enough, my"—she caught his glance and made the shift at the last instant—"*messire*. It is my work to heal."

"Nonetheless, I do thank you again, and I bring you a gift." He handed the clothes down to her, then unhooked a brace of hares from the pommel and held them out. "I set a snare today, thinking you might find some use for fresh meat."

"They are most welcome, my—Sir Brand." This time all three of them smiled at her near slip. She took the hares with pleasure. Fresh meat was rare in her pot, and the skins would make warm mitts for next winter. "Will you stay a little? I would see how you are healing."

"We cannot stop long," said Sir Brand. "They wait supper on us at the manor."

"It will take only a moment. Please, *messire*."

He looked to Lord Ivo, who shrugged. "Let her look. Then I can tell Alaida her healer has seen your scars and perhaps she will stop grumbling about you riding out each day."

"All right." Sir Brand swung easily off his horse— remarkably easily, considering the hole in his side. Merewyn took a moment to set the clothes on a bench by the door and hang the hares on a peg beside it, then turned back to the knight. "Arm first, *messire*, if you please."

She had thought Lord Ivo exaggerated when he spoke of

scars, but when Sir Brand pulled up his sleeve, that was all that remained of the wound on his arm—a rough, red scar that looked to be perhaps a month old. She turned his hand up and touched his palm where the tears and scrapes had faded to mere lines. A shiver ran up her spine, and she glanced up to find eyes the color of a summer sky sparkling down at her.

"I told you I heal quickly," he said.

Cheeks heating, she dropped his hand and stepped back a pace. "You will have to loose your braies for me to see the others."

"I've had more women asking me to drop my breeks this week than in many a year," Brand said to Lord Ivo, who laughed. He lifted his shirt and put his hands to his ties. "Does your husband not mind you having men, uh, bare themselves?"

"I have no husband, sir."

His brows knitted together in puzzlement. "My mind was clouded, but I would wager a good horse that you said those were your husband's old clothes."

"So I did. But my husband is dead some five years since."

"I am sorry for that, but grateful you still had his clothes. They got me back to Alnwick without freezing my . . . without freezing."

She smiled at his quick change of direction. "Someday you must tell me how you came to be naked in the woods."

"Someday." He eased his braies down just enough to show her his hip and her smile faded. This wound, too, was healed far beyond expectation. The bruise, which should have been just beginning to fade, was nearly gone, and the edges of the wound had completely closed and healed, though a thick scab still clung to the part she had not been able to stitch. "This is . . . most strange. And most remarkable. Where are all my stitches?"

"I plucked most of them out. They pulled as it healed."

She nodded absently. "I had no silk to use. Now the thigh, sir."

He dropped his braies lower, gave her barely a moment to see the angry red scar, then tugged them back up hastily.

"Quick healing is one thing, *messire*, but this is . . ." Magic, she wanted to say, but she knew too little of these men and where they stood with the Church to use the word. She repeated, "Remarkable."

"My wife's old nurse spread a poultice of honey and comfrey over the wounds each time she rebound them," explained Lord Ivo. "She said it would speed the healing."

Merewyn nodded, still absorbed by what she had seen. "Bôte is wise. I had no honey left, else I might have done the same." Not that honey had done this, nor all the comfrey in England. There was something most strange about this man and his healing. "Tell your lady that Sir Brand is fit to do what he pleases, my lord, and that I say she may stop grumbling at him."

"'Tis me she grumbles at," he said, his eyes flashing with good humor, and she took a sudden liking to this new lord, despite the mystery surrounding his friend. He pulled his purse from his belt and drew out several coins, which he held out to her. "I wish to reward you for the aid you gave him."

Merewyn shook her head. "I cannot take your coin, my lord. My family long ago pledged to aid the lords of Alnwick in return for free range of the woods. If I take your silver, the pledge is broken."

"You took Brand's hares," he pointed out.

"He offered them as a gift, my lord, as I offered my care to him." Her cheeks grew warm as Sir Brand smiled down on her.

"And I offer these coins as thanks," said Lord Ivo.

"You may call it thanks, but I fear you mean it as payment."

"'Tis a fine point."

"On such fine points are pledges made and kept."

"True enough," he conceded. "But what if Brand had offered his hares as payment?"

"I would have taken them," she said matter-of-factly. "For *he* is not lord of Alnwick."

"And thankful for it," said Sir Brand, chuckling. "By the saints, Ivo, this land of yours comes with more covenants and pledges than the throne of England."

"This pledge goes back further than the throne, sir. The women of my family have been healers in these woods to a woman, back to a time before my grandmother's grandmother's grandmother. Before Alnwick was a vill, or England united, we were bound here to help those who need us."

"Well, I for one am glad you were here, whatever pledges are behind it," said Brand.

"As am I, even if you will not take my coin," said Lord Ivo.

Sir Brand made moves to get back on his horse, and disappointment surged through Merewyn. "Would you not come in before you ride on, my lords? My table is poor, but I am a good cook with what I have. And I have ale and a little wine to share. You would be most welcome."

"'Tis a kind offer, Merewyn, but we cannot," said Lord Ivo. "My lady awaits, and it would not do to stop her grumbling about Brand only to have her start up again because we are late for supper."

"Blame me, my lord. Tell her I insisted on poking and prodding to see why your knight heals so well, so that I may use his secret on others."

"You may not want to do that," said the nobleman. "It might make the others as stubborn as he. We will share your hospitality another time perhaps."

The edges of the clouds still glowed as Sir Brand swung up onto his roan horse. Merewyn stood by her door watching them away.

"I will keep a pot of ale waiting for you, my lords," she called out.

"And I will come to drink it one day," promised Brand as they turned onto the path to Alnwick. "Fare you well,

Merewyn of Alnwood, and once more, my thanks." Just before the forest dark swallowed them, he whistled, and a large raven sailed down off a branch and landed on his shoulder.

The breath caught in Merewyn's throat: the Father's sacred bird, companion to a knight who healed far too quickly. No wonder the omens had been so clear. The seriousness of his wounds and the strange hurry in which he'd left had distracted her from the signs, but now that she turned her mind to it, there was little doubt—magic swirled around Sir Brand and his lord like gnats around a flame. It would be interesting to see why the gods had sent him into her life.

Other than to bring her meat, of course.

She looked at the hares, and her mouth watered with the thought of such a treat. One whole hare to roast, and another for the pot. She sent a silent blessing sailing off down the path where the two knights had disappeared and took up her knife to skin her meal before it grew too dark.

CHAPTER 14

UNDER ARI'S STEWARDSHIP, the motte gradually bulged upward behind the bailey like the cap of a sprouting toadstool. Geoff returned from Durham with nearly two score men, which pushed things along more quickly and freed the village men, under Wat, to expand the bailey ditches and strengthen the paling wall.

Ivo and Brand got into the habit of checking the progress each night as they rode out of the forest, circling the growing mound before they headed in and handed the horses over to the ever-ready Tom. After supper they read the day's message from Ari and scribbled instructions back to him before settling in for games or other entertainment. Most nights, Alaida sat nearby, silently stitching away on some project or other, then retired early, seemingly exhausted by the presence of the extra men and the work they entailed. Her fatigue worked in Ivo's favor; she went to sleep so quickly and slept so deeply that he felt no jeopardy at all in slipping into her bed every few nights.

The gossips stayed quiet, and January lapsed into February, more quickly than Ivo would have thought possible.

First plowing started at Candlemas, the furrows as regular as the passing days, and the motte continued to creep higher. There was comfort in the rhythm of it all, a pleasure in having a home to return to and familiar faces to see each night, which blunted both the constant fear of discovery and that other dread which hung over them. Whether it would last, only the gods knew, but for now, at least, life had a cadence that felt almost normal.

Thus it was unsettling to ride into the yard one night near the ides of February without Brand, who had announced a desire to sample Merewyn's ale, and find, for the first time, no Tom. Frowning, Ivo rode around to the stable and handed Fax over to a boy he barely recognized. "Where's Tom?"

"In the hall, m'lord. Lady Alaida asked for him."

"Ah. Well, take care with my horse."

"Aye, my lord. I help with Fax sometimes. I'll see to him."

What Ivo found in the hall only added to his sense of disquiet. Usually all was ready for supper when they arrived, with everyone present and washed and waiting. Tonight nothing was in place. People scurried around like ants, the tables were just being set up, and a jumble of kegs and boxes sat stacked near the door. A maid noticed him and hurried over to take his cloak.

"What the devil is going on? Where's Geoffrey?"

"In the solar, my lord, with Lady Alaida. Shall I fetch him?"

"No. I'll go." Still frowning, he trotted upstairs, where he found Alaida holding court over a knot of servants that included both Geoffrey and the missing Tom.

The latter glanced up and saw Ivo, and his eyes went round and wide. "My lord. Forgive me. I didn't realize the hour."

"Clearly," said Ivo. "I was—"

"The fault is mine, my lord," interrupted Alaida, quickly putting herself between Ivo and Tom, as though she thought he might take his fist to the boy like he had to Wat. Ivo's gut churned at this evidence of her continuing mistrust. Nearly a month now, and he still hadn't found the way to correct his many mistakes with her. "I have distracted everyone for my own purposes, and Tom was caught up in it. Go, Tom."

"What purposes could you have that put the entire manor in an uproar?" he asked as Tom dashed out the door.

She ignored him and smiled at the steward. "I believe we are finished here, Geoffrey. 'Tis time we sup."

As Geoffrey and the others cleared the room, the bed came into view. At the foot, stacks of folded clothing sat next to her jewel casket, looking all too familiar. "The convent again?"

Either she missed the humor or she was in no mood for it. "Chatton and Houton. I have yet to take proper possession of my lands."

"Nor have you mentioned this little progress to me," he pointed out.

"It was not a deliberate omission, my lord. It only occurred to me today that I must make the trip now if I wish to return before Shrove Tuesday. I intended to tell you at supper."

Tell, not ask, he noted. "This is a poor time of year to travel."

"The weather looks to hold a little, and 'tis only a short day's ride, even to Chatton." She picked up a pair of hose and refolded them unnecessarily. "I do this for you, my lord."

"Indeed."

"With the extra expense of the castle, it is doubly important that all the fiefs contribute fully to Alnwick's coffers. As your wife as well as your vassal, I wish my own holdings to set a good example."

"And to line your own purse, I hope. That was the point of the gift."

"If all goes well. I leave on the morrow. I assume you have no objection to my going."

Of course he had objections—several—but Ivo found himself floundering as she stood there looking up at him with calm expectation. At the time he'd given her the lands, he'd thought it likely he'd be discovered and gone before she needed to visit them, and that if by chance he weren't, she would be more securely his wife. The idea of her riding off on her own when they barely spoke to each other from evening to evening made him uneasy. Yet she was right—as his vassal, it was her duty to see to her properties. And this was the time to do it, before sowing, so she could make whatever adjustments to her crops she saw fit.

"None at all," he lied with a smile. "Who will you take with you?"

"Bôte and Hadwisa, of course, and Oswald has chosen several good men as guards and one to drive the cart. And I thought to take a steward with me as well, to help me check the accounts this first time. With your leave, perhaps Sir Ari could—"

"No."

"But the motte is well started now and I will be but a fortnight, perhaps less. If I could have him—"

"Impossible." He turned toward the fire, hoping its flicker would mask the jealousy that must show in his eyes. "He has pressing duties here. You may have Geoffrey."

"Geoffrey has duties here also, my lord, perhaps more vital. The marling must be done and—"

"He will leave instructions," said Ivo impatiently. She was right about who was most needed at Alnwick over the next weeks, but Ari could never go with her, even if Ivo had wanted him to—which he didn't. It was bad enough knowing he was here with her all day, every day. "Ari will manage both his duties and Geoff's. As you say, it will only be a fortnight."

He braced himself for more argument, but she merely dipped her head in unexpected acquiescence. "As you wish, my lord. Geoffrey will serve well enough, and in truth, he already knows the lands and the men on it. I only thought Sir Ari would be less missed."

The envy eating at him demanded to know, "Was there no other reason you wanted Ari?"

"I did think to collect a story he owes me as forfeit. He has been avoiding me for some weeks because of it."

"Avoiding you?"

"I've barely seen him, even at dinner. He takes a peasant's meal in the field with the men most days and seldom comes into the hall at all unless he must. Even then he spends his time stooped over his parchments like a monk. I think he has no dragon story in him and does not wish to admit it."

"He must be distracted by his work," said Ivo as he absorbed this news. His ugly jealousy dissolved into uglier shame. Of course Ari wasn't sniffing around Alaida. He had more honor than that, and Ivo should have known it—had known it, until the gods had offered up their vision and everything had gone so foul. Besides, Ari's days of tumbling women for sport were over as surely as everyone else's.

They headed down for supper, and as they took their places at table, Alaida noted Brand's absence. "I hope he has not gone boar-baiting with his twig again."

"He'll be along later," said Ivo, chuckling.

The meal was a good one—boiled beef and cabbage root with fresh bread, as that day had been baking day—but it was hardly peaceful. Alaida kept calling servants up as she thought of various chores to be done before her departure or in her absence. Already uneasy about her leaving, Ivo found the whole process irritating, and was relieved when she finally settled in to enjoy the last bites of her meal.

"What did you need of Tom?" he asked by way of conversation when the silence between them dragged.

"He took Lark out for me, to get her accustomed to the bit again. She hasn't been ridden since before Christmas."

"You have a mount of your own?" He frowned. He should have known this. Would have, if he were a proper husband.

"A fine black mare. She was a gift from my lord grandfather on my betrothal." She spooned a stewed apricot into her mouth.

"And you're taking her to Chatton?"

She was still chewing, so she nodded.

"Who will ride her?"

"She is my horse, my lord. *I* will ride her."

"Behind a groom, you mean."

"No, my lord, nor with a man leading her. I *ride* her." She dipped another plump apricot off the trencher and held it out to him. "These are very good. Would you care for one?"

The gesture caught him off guard. In the weeks they'd been married, not once had she offered him a taste of anything. Wanting to encourage this small intimacy before he questioned her further about her riding, he smiled and leaned forward, intending to take a bite. Instead, she shoveled the entire fruit into his mouth. It was swollen with honey and wine, and as he bit down, it spurted so much spiced liquor down his throat that it made his eyes water.

As he choked and gasped, she leaned forward. His heart scuttered a beat or two as she smiled up at him.

"You may as well hear it now, my lord," she said more sweetly than she'd spoken to him in weeks. "Not only do I ride without a groom, I ride astride. Wearing a pair of braies beneath my gown. Ah, look, here is Sir Brand."

She rose and sailed off to greet Brand as Ivo choked down the apricot. By the time she ventured back to the table, Ivo had no choice but to laugh.

Brand eyed him curiously. "What is so funny?"

"My wife. We will discuss the matter later," he told her before he asked Brand, "How was Merewyn's ale?"

"So that is where you went," said Alaida. "Our healer is fair, is she not?"

"Aye, she is, but that is not why I went, my lady. I took her a skin of wine, to replace what she used on me."

"Ah," said Alaida, in that woman's way that tells a man she knows the truth no matter what he says. Brand made the appropriate "*phfft*" and poked a piece of beef into his mouth.

They were still dancing around the subject of Merewyn

and ale when Tom slipped quietly into the hall a little later. He slid into his place at the low table and began stuffing down food as quickly as possible, trying to fill himself before the tables were cleared.

Brand pointed to him with the rib bone he'd been sucking on. "That boy has a spirit to him. He has yet to miss a morning, and he was still waiting for me tonight, as late as I was."

"Making up for loitering around the hall all afternoon, no doubt." Ivo intended it as a joke, but Alaida's eyes widened in panic.

"Truly, my lord, it was my fault. Don't blame the boy when I'm the one who made him late."

"God's knees, woman. What is it you . . ." And then it hit him: the solution to two—no, three—problems, right in front of him. He pushed to his feet and bellowed, "Tom, get up here."

The boy scrambled up to the front of the hall, swiping his mouth on his sleeve as he came. "Yes, my lord?"

"My lord, please," begged Alaida.

"You were not at your post this evening, boy, and my lady seems to think I should beat you for it."

Tom went red as a currant, and gasps echoed around the hall, the loudest from Alaida, who came to her feet ready to do battle. "I think no such thing, *monseigneur*, and you know it well!"

Unsure what was happening, Tom looked first to Alaida, then to Ivo, then lifted his chin bravely. "If Lady Alaida says it, then I surely earned it. It was my duty to attend you at the proper hour, and I failed."

Ivo tried to maintain his glare, but failed in the face of such straightforward courage. Snorting back a laugh, he glanced toward Brand, who watched the boy intently, nodding to himself, then at Alaida, who stood there with her fists clenched, ready to take his kneecaps off rather than let him touch Tom. Ivo winked at her just for the fun of watching her jaw drop open.

"Good lad. You're loyal to your lady, I see."

"I . . . I would die for her, my lord," Tom said with pride and more than a little confusion.

"Then you should know that she did not tell me to beat you. 'Twas only a poor jest on my part. She does tell me you ride, though, well enough that she lets you exercise her mare."

The relief on the boy's face was almost comical. "Aye, my lord."

"And how old are you?"

Tom chewed his lip, thinking. "I'm not certain, my lord."

"Your mother birthed you about when I won my horse in battle," offered Oswald from his seat. "That would give you near three and ten years."

"As the marshal says then, my lord. Near three and ten."

"That's the right age," said Brand from his seat. He'd caught on to where Ivo was going with this.

"Oswald, what's your opinion of Tom here?"

The marshal rose and came to stand next to Tom. "He is quick, honest, and a hard worker, my lord. He sees things that need to be done and he does them. I wish I had a dozen like him."

"Would he make a good squire?"

Oswald's face split in a wide grin. "He would, my lord, excepting he's not of noble blood."

"Many a squire is low-born, and even some knights. Tom, do you want to try your hand as my squire?"

The boy gaped at him like a dullard. Not an auspicious start.

"Say yes, boy," urged Brand, laughing.

"Yes. Yes, my lord! I do want to be your squire, and I will be a good one. I swear it."

"It will be difficult. Most squires spend their early years as pages, learning how to serve at table, to carve, to read, to speak properly. You have none of that, so before you become squire, you will be my lady's page for a little."

Ivo resisted the urge to glance down at Alaida again and

stepped around the table to stand before Tom. "Accompany her to Chatton and Houton and learn as much as you can in a fortnight. When you return, you will train with Oswald, but you will also be page for a part of each day, at my lady's will, until she says you will not embarrass me, even at court. And you will learn to read and write. French and Latin."

"I will do whatever I must, my lord." Tom fell to his knees and held up his clasped hands for Ivo to enfold. "I am your man in all things and give you my pledge of homage."

"I accept your pledge and hereby make you mine. Learn well, Thomas, and you will be a squire and a serjeant. Prove yourself brave and bold, and you may even win your spurs one day." He hauled the boy to his feet and gave him a friendly shove toward his seat. "Now go, finish your supper, and be ready to ride with Lady Alaida on the morrow. Oswald, pick a good mount for him and replace him in the stables. Geoffrey, he needs clothes more suited to his new station."

"Yes, my lord," said both men, and Tom half stumbled, half floated back to the low table, where the others began pounding him on the back and giving him a bad time.

Ivo watched with satisfaction for a moment, then returned to his chair. Alaida sank into her seat beside him, her face a mask of emotion so mixed he couldn't sort it out. The only thing certain was the glitter of tears on her lashes. He touched the corner of her eye. "What's this? I thought making Tom squire would please you."

"It did, my lord. But I thought . . . You are . . ." She stopped, her voice thick with emotion, and collected herself, blotting the tears away with the corner of her head rail. "Do you enjoy torturing me?"

"Only a little. Do you enjoy thinking the worst of me?"

She flushed crimson and looked down at her folded hands, but there was a tiny glint of humor in her eyes when she looked up again. "Only a little."

Ah. There. The weight of a bruised reeve fell off Ivo's shoulders at last. He smiled down at her. "Perhaps we can find better ways to amuse ourselves."

"I would be in favor of that, my lord. Do you have any suggestions?"

The way she asked the question might have been an invitation to her bed—or it might not. Even as his body stirred, he put the idea to rest. "For now, a game of chess, I think, while your women finish with your packing."

Disappointment flickered over her face, but she nodded with good grace. "We will have to play in the solar, then, so I may supervise. Sir Brand, perhaps you can tell us a story while we play."

They were soon ensconced before the fire upstairs, the board between them, and Brand spinning a tale that Ari used to tell often around the fire. Ivo sat back, satisfied. This was how it was supposed to be—except that Bôte and Hadwisa were busy putting the last of Alaida's clothes into a chest. If things were truly right, he would be going with her, ensuring her safety, keeping her close each night. But instead she was going to ride off on her own. Which reminded him. "We must settle this matter of your riding."

"There's nothing to settle, *monseigneur*."

"There is. I wish for Tom to lead you."

Her lips set in a stubborn line. "You may wish it, my lord, but it will not happen. I ride, as do many noble ladies here in the north—except that I ride better than most of them."

"If you will have no groom, there is a wagon—"

"For baggage and Bôte, not for me," she said mulishly. "I no more like to bounce around in a wagon than Sir Brand does."

"Hold, my lady." Brand laughed and held up his hands. "Do not put me in the middle of this."

Ivo glared at his wife. "Bôte, summon Oswald for me."

"Yes, do," said Alaida, glaring back.

The nurse bustled off. A few moments later she returned with Oswald.

"Marshal, tell me true," began Ivo with no preliminaries. "Does my lady wife ride well enough to make this journey to Chatton without a groom?"

"She does, my lord." He beamed at Alaida like a doting

uncle. "Better than half my men. And her Lark is as steady as any animal I have seen in my life."

"And do these braies she wears show while she's riding?"

"*Monseigneur!*" said Alaida indignantly.

Brand snorted in surprise, but Oswald only laughed. "Not that I've seen, my lord, but in truth, I would not say if I had, for I think it would mean my skin."

"You can be assured," she hissed under her breath.

"You are wise and honorable, Marshal," said Ivo. "See that the men you send with my lady are equally so. She is the greatest treasure Alnwick possesses and I would have her safely back."

"You will, my lord. My vow."

"Good then. You may go."

"Hold, Oswald. I will go down with you." Brand stretched to his feet. "How about you, my lord? Join us for a round of merels and another horn of ale?"

Alaida flushed under the intensity of Ivo's gaze, and desire unexpectedly curled up within him like smoke, kindled by the bronze fire in her eyes. "Aye. I think I'd better."

"But you . . ." she began.

"*Shh.*" Ivo reached across to touch a fingertip to her lips, so warm and soft. Against his skin, they would be like . . . Ivo cut short his wanderings before they stripped him of good sense entirely. Sheer will carried him to his feet. "It is not for discussion, sweet leaf. You have a long ride ahead of you tomorrow, and I would see you well rested for your safety."

That odd mix of emotions played over her face again, still unreadable and made more so by the way she lowered her lashes.

"Very well, my lord." As he moved to leave, she took his hand between hers and pressed a kiss to his knuckles, on the same place she had kissed after the incident with Wat. In the touch of her lips, he felt forgiveness and apology and seduction all wrapped together. "I have not thanked you properly for what you did for Tom tonight."

"Alaida," he began, but stumbled to a stop as she finally met his eyes.

"I am glad you did it before I left, my lord. I will think better of you while I am gone, and perhaps when I return, we can begin afresh."

He could think of nothing to say to her that would be neither false promise nor lie.

"God give you a safe journey, wife," he managed finally, and made his escape.

As they went down the stairs, Brand shook his head. "It would have been easier to keep her angry with you and leave Tom in the stable."

"Aye," said Ivo. But in his soul, he knew that the look in her eyes was worth every aching throb of unsated desire he was going to suffer over the next weeks. "Aye, probably."

THE NEXT DAY dawned clear and mild, and Geoffrey had everyone ready to ride immediately after early morning prayers. They crossed the Aln and headed northwest along the track that followed the river.

As they reached the open moorlands, Lark whinnied her excitement. Alaida held her back just long enough to remind her who held the reins, then gave the mare her head and let her gallop off the boredom of the winter pasture. Tom, riding the dun rouncey Oswald had selected for him, felt the responsibility of his new position and raced along with the two guards trying to keep up, while Geoffrey, who had ridden with Alaida too many times before and knew her habits, merely urged his little group of servants—Hadwisa rode pillion behind one groom—up to a canter so as to keep her in sight.

When Lark began to slow of her own accord, Alaida brought her around in a big circle, so that she came back in line with her guards and her new page.

"She runs wondrous well, my lady," said Tom as she rejoined the group.

Alaida laughed and patted Lark's neck. "The stableboy

admires you, love. But you're a page now, Thomas, and very soon a squire. Your compliments should always go to the lady, not to the horse—unless it is a new horse, of course, and even then, 'tis wise to find a way to turn it to the lady."

Tom colored a little, then offered, "You ride wondrous well, my lady."

The guards snickered at his clumsy shift, but Alaida nodded graciously, as though it were a fresh thought. "Thank you, Thomas. Ride back and tell Geoffrey I wish to see the standing stone, and to send the others ahead and join us."

"Yes, my lady," he said, and galloped off on his first official task as page.

The stone, which sat in a wooded area near the bottom of a hill, was as Alaida remembered it but for a little more moss. She dismounted and traced the markings with new interest. A large spiral marked one flat side, while a menagerie of rudely carved beasts romped on the other: a wolf or dog, a stag, a bird or two, and others partly obscured by the moss that grew up from the base. She took her knife from her waist and scraped away a bit of the green to uncover the toothsome snout of some beast of indistinguishable form.

"'Tis the monster, my lady," said Thomas.

"It is only a lion," said Geoffrey, his voice thick with disdain.

"If it is a lion, it is a fat one with no tail," pointed out Alaida as she scraped a bit more. She indicated a jagged line that lay over the creature's back. "Thomas, what do you make of this?"

"Lightning, my lady, striking the beast. And there is an arrow."

"That looks like a hayfork," said Geoffrey, finally joining in to point at a mark off to the side. "And there is the Holy Cross."

"And here are three lines together. For the Trinity, do you suppose?" wondered Alaida. She crossed herself as foreboding rippled down her spine. To mix Christian symbols with pagan was a sign of the Devil's own work. Suddenly, she wanted nothing more than to be away from this place.

"Give me a leg up, Thomas."

"A moment, my lady. I think you had it right about the monster." Tom was still brushing away moss on the stone, this time on the side below the spiral. "Look. Here is your dragon."

Sure enough, there, with flames streaking from its mouth, lay an age-worn carving of a dragon she had never noticed before.

"A leg up, Tom," repeated Alaida firmly, her apprehension growing more intense. As soon as she was in the saddle, she urged Lark away, leaving the stone and its evil signs behind. They had gone only a little way when she noticed Geoffrey glancing skyward. She followed his gaze and found what he saw, soaring high overhead. "Is that an eagle?"

"Aye, my lady. The same bird that followed us the day Sir Ari rode the bounds."

"And how would you know one eagle from the other?" she asked, laughing.

"By his tail, my lady. See the crooked feather? Today he seems to be following you."

Alaida checked Geoff's face to see if he was serious. He was, which made her laugh again. "I have never known you to be so full of fancy, Steward."

"It is not fancy, my lady," he said, not taking his eyes off the bird. "I've been watching him since we crossed the river. He's flown along with you the entire way."

"Surely not," said Alaida.

"But he has, my lady," said Edric, who was playing guard for the journey. "I noted him when you first galloped ahead. He soars along above you as we ride, and he stopped with us at the stone, on a tree nearby."

"Nonsense. It is just a bird." Alaida brushed the idea away, but it added to the sense of foreboding that haunted her. "Let us move more quickly. I find myself growing hungry." She kicked Lark into a canter.

"We dine along Eglingham burn, my lady," said Geoffrey as he caught up. A wagon carrying Bôte and their gear had rumbled off before dawn, so that dinner could be waiting when the riders caught up. "I instructed them to have your cloth laid in good time."

It was, and the meal was all the tastier for being eaten outdoors. As they started off afterward, Alaida couldn't resist sneaking a glance skyward. There, circling overhead, was the eagle.

He kept near through most of the afternoon, until the sun started to sink in the west, when he suddenly wheeled off to the south, headed back toward Alnwick. She watched until he vanished from sight, and foolish as it was, she wished he had flown with her all the way to Chatton.

CHAPTER 15

"BASTARD KING." IVO ground Ari's note into the mud in disgust.

"Is there another kind?" asked Brand, chuckling as he bent to check Kraken's hoof. "What did this one do?"

"He sent one of his men to check on me. Robert de Jeune and a dozen of his knights sit in my hall as we speak. They arrived after Nones today."

"Balls," said Brand, every trace of amusement gone. "How will we come and go if your hall is full of the king's men?"

"We won't. Ari told everyone I left today for Durham on sudden business. We can't return until they leave."

"'Tis poor timing, with your lady due back tomorrow."

"Aye, but there's worse. One of the men riding with de Jeune is that mongrel Neville."

"The oily one we had to throw out when we first came? See? You should have let me gut him." Brand sliced a phantom sword out and up, and Neville's guts spilled invisibly onto the leaves at his feet. "That's what you get for turning Norman. What do we do?"

"Stay out of sight. Ari will have to deal with them unless I think of something."

Brand looked over at the raven perched on a nearby snag, feathers fluffed against the misting rain that had hung in the air all day. "And how will *he* stay out of their way?"

"I don't know, but he says he can. It helps that everyone thinks he goes off whoring every night."

"You could send a message for him to join us in Durham," suggested Brand. "Provided he isn't caught first . . . If he is, it will mean the end of your time at Alnwick."

Anger bubbled up again, bitter as wormwood. Ivo whipped out his sword and in one stroke took off a nearby sapling, the closest substitute for William's thick neck. "Bastard king." Feeling slightly better, he shook off the tingle in his palm. "Come. If we must lurk in the woods, we'll need that gear we cached."

Out of habit, they had hidden extra supplies deep in the woods against the sudden need to escape. Now they could use them to stay comfortable while they lay low.

"I have a better idea," said Brand. "I was going to visit Merewyn this evening anyway, to give her a mortar and pestle I picked up off that tinker yesterday, and we—"

"What are you doing buying her a mortar and pestle?" asked Ivo.

"Who said *I* bought it? You're the rich man. I thought this would be a way to pay her without violating the terms of that pledge of hers."

"Fine." He eyed Brand over Fax's back. "You're not getting sweet on the woman, are you?"

Brand snorted. "As I *said*, I was going to take her the mortar. If you come, too, we can pass the evening in her warm little cottage instead of out here in the rain."

"We're supposed to be in Durham, remember? If word gets to de Jeune that we're near, he'll have me strung up by the thumbs, and then it'll be over for certain."

"And how would he hear? Merewyn has no neighbors to see."

"Word travels. She may live alone, but she goes in to trade with the villagers, and they come to her for healing."

"We'll say we're leaving in the morning. She'll keep her tongue if you tell her to. She's bound to you."

"Still . . ."

"Come on. It'll be hard to find the cache tonight anyway," said Brand. He swung up on Kraken and reined him around to face toward Merewyn's. "We'll dig up our things and have a proper camp tomorrow. For tonight, we'll give Merewyn her mortar and eat her pottage—"

"And drink her ale," said Ivo, chuckling.

"Of course. And while we sit by her fire, we'll think of some way to be rid of this de Jeune."

"That," said Ivo, thinking of his wife and Neville in the same hall together, "would be a good thing."

THE JOURNEY HOME from Houton lacked the fine weather of the ride to Chatton but still managed to be mild. The clouds lay over the land, thick and heavy, but their blanket kept the chill air out of their bones. Alaida passed the miles playing a rhyming game with the others. Geoffrey had just won for the third time, when the lead man suddenly called out.

"Riders."

Edric galloped ahead, the better to see the two figures who topped a rise in the distance, while Alaida's escort closed ranks around her, hands to weapons. She shifted, seating herself more securely in preparation for flight if necessary. Sensing the tension, Lark danced and pulled at the reins.

It all seemed foolish a moment later when Edric announced, "'Tis only Sir Ari and Penda."

"Do not sound so disappointed," said Alaida, laughing with relief. "I would rather not spend the afternoon running from Scots. Come, let us go to meet them."

She gave Lark a kick, taking this as a good excuse for one last gallop.

"Why have you ridden out so far, *messire*?" she asked as they neared. "Is there trouble?"

"Not trouble precisely, my lady," said Ari as he and Penda wheeled in to join her party. "Guests. Lord Robert de Jeune comes from the king to see the progress of the castle, and he brings twelve knights with him."

"Twelve!" With squires and grooms and hangers-on, that meant thirty or more extra bodies to house and mouths to feed, on top of the men hired for the castle. They would be stacked in the hall like cordwood, and the food . . . She started running through the stores in her mind, wondering where the food was to come from with the Easter fast on them. Geoffrey frowned, apparently doing the same. Ari cleared his throat, and she realized he had more to say. She sighed. "Tell me the rest."

Before he could, Penda blurted out, "Sir Neville is among the knights, my lady."

"Neville? What is that little stoat doing riding for the king?"

"For now, licking noble boots," said Ari. "Though I have no confidence he will keep to such useful duty."

Alaida smiled at the seneschal's forthright assessment. "You must have met Neville before."

"No, but I've met men like him. He's the reason I came to meet you. Oswald suggested you would not want to ride in unawares."

"If I had known, I would still be at Houton," she confessed. "I do not like Neville."

"Nor does Oswald. He remained behind to ensure neither Neville nor the others take too many liberties in your absence."

"Wise marshal. Shall we give him relief from this siege?"

"The wagon is some way behind, my lady," said Geoffrey. "Perhaps you should take shelter at Denwick until it comes. That would put Bôte at your side, as well as Hadwisa."

"I will not cower in a cottar's hut with my own hall a league away," said Alaida firmly. "Bôte will be along soon enough, and I will keep all of you at hand until my lord husband presents himself this evening. And there is that look again, Seneschal. What now?"

"I fear Lord Ivo had unexpected business in Durham."

"Ah."

"He left yesterday, before we knew Lord Robert was coming."

But he knew I was coming. Farewell to that fresh start. A large rock formed in the center of Alaida's breast, but she forced herself to ignore its cold weight for the moment. There was more important business at hand than the state of her marriage.

"Well, then. Still more reason I must get back to Alnwick."

"My lady, there are twelve strange knights present. Your safety . . ."

"Is guaranteed by a noble lord who is loyal to the king who ordered my marriage," she said with a good deal more surety than she felt. "I must represent Alnwick in my husband's absence. Geoffrey, ride ahead with Penda and make preparations. I think . . . I think a show of affection from my people would please me today. Nothing too grand, but enough that Lord Robert and his knights will see I have the support—and close eye—of both village and manor."

She was graced with one of Geoffrey's rare smiles of approval. "Of course, my lady, and you will want all of the women in the yard, to greet you and escort you to the solar."

"*Bien sûr!*" she laughed. "Preferably all talking at once."

Ari shook his head. "Lord Robert occupies the solar."

"As well he should, with neither my husband nor I in residence. But now I am home, and he will yield my own chamber to me."

"And the saints help him if he does not," said Ari.

Alaida smiled serenely. "Exactly."

"I will have the wardrobe cleared and the small bed set there for him, my lady," said Geoffrey.

"With a freshly stuffed mattress and our best linens and furs. He is the king's emissary, after all." She considered a moment. "Offer him a bath as well."

"See if one of the, um, friendlier women would like to wash him," added Ari in an aside to Geoffrey, who nodded, and muttered, "Perhaps two."

The guards covered their laugh with coughing, and Alaida pretended she didn't hear as embarrassment turned her ears to flame beneath her wimple.

"Go on, then, Geoff, and ride quickly. We will delay here a little, but the mist grows heavier. I do not wish to stay out longer than need be."

"I will have the church bell rung thrice when all is ready, my lady." He and Penda galloped off.

As she watched them vanish over a hill, Ari watched her in turn. "You play this game well, my lady."

"I had much practice at it when my grandfather was off warring," she said. "I do not like it, but it is too often necessary. Do the ladies of Guelders not have to play the game as well?"

His face went blank, then cleared. "Our women prefer knives and poisons to games, I fear. That's why I left. Too many of them unhappy with me."

"The ladies, or their fathers and husbands?"

He shrugged, but the mischief in his eyes said he was hardly sorry, either way.

"You should have settled into marriage long ago," said Alaida. "You and Sir Brand, both."

"Brand was married, my lady. His wife died many years ago."

"I did not know." She absorbed this news and nodded. "That would explain the sadness I sometimes glimpse behind his laughter. He loved her, I think."

"*Inn makti mur,*" said Ari. When she raised an eyebrow in question, he explained. "An old saying in Guelders. It means the grand passion—the kind of love that turns a tale boring once the couple are wed—though Brand would never admit to the passion or to being boring."

"His lady was fortunate to know such love." Alaida pressed her lips together against a sob that suddenly welled up from nowhere.

Feeling ridiculous, she struggled to swallow back the tears that burned her throat. She had never been the crying sort, but tears had crept up on her several times in the fort-night since she'd cried about Ivo's kindness to Tom. And over the oddest things. This time she understood—Brand's lost happiness contrasted so sharply with her own marriage that she was bound to feel the ache—but only yesterday it had been the sight of men sowing her new fields at Houton that had made the tears come. And a few days earlier at Chatton, a sunbeam falling on the cross in the chapel had made her think of the Holy Mother's sorrow for her Son and had brought on such sadness she had nearly sobbed during Mass.

Today, she covered her distress by fiddling with her cloak and chape, and by good fortune the mood passed as quickly it had come on. She soon had herself under control enough to fill the silence with the first thing that came to mind. "You were speaking of tales, sir. I believe you still owe me a dragon."

"You will have it soon, my lady."

"I will have it now," she said firmly, not about to miss this chance. "It will distract me from this drizzle." *And from these ridiculous tears.*

"At your command, my lady." He glanced up and she fol-lowed his gaze to see a black shadow cutting in and out of the wisps of low-hanging cloud.

"Look, Thomas, my eagle is back. He flew along as I rode to Chatton," she explained to Sir Ari.

"Did he?"

"Aye, he circled over Lady Alaida near all the way, *mes-sire.*" Tom stuck his arms out like a soaring bird and pretended to swoop from his saddle, so that Hadwisa, who rode pillion behind him today, squeaked and clutched at him in a panic. "See his crooked tail?"

"Sit still, Thomas." Alaida turned to Ari. "Geoff said it is the same bird that followed you along the bounds."

"Perhaps." Ari stared upward for a long moment. When he turned back to Alaida, his face had shuttered over as though a storm were brewing. "Well. A dragon. Let me see. Once there was a princess by the name of Alaida . . ."

He spun out his tale until they forded the Aln and heard Geoff's bell ring.

Alaida groaned. "He is too quick. Now I suppose I must wait another month to hear the ending."

"Only until you are safely in your solar, my lady. Come, everyone." Ari organized the group to his satisfaction while Alaida arranged her skirts and mantle to hang more gracefully—difficult, since they were so sodden from the mist.

"You do look like a princess, my lady," said Tom.

"A very damp princess, I'm sure. Come, let us make this royal progress." She led the way out across the field, her back straight, her chin high, and a confident, if false, smile on her lips. She was, after all, the lady of a castle. A lady with an eagle, for she caught another glimpse of the bird winging through the clouds. Her smile turned real.

Geoff had done his job well. The villagers greeted her with enthusiasm, and some of them, but not too many for the effect, followed her along to the manor. She slipped her purse to Ari, so he could pass out alms at the gate, and rode in to be greeted by the manor servants, nearly all of whom turned out wearing smiles and chattering like jackdaws. The stir pulled Lord Robert and most of his men out into the yard—precisely where she wanted them.

"Greetings, Lady Alaida," called Lord Robert over the din. He was a lean man of dark complexion and thickly sensual features. She remembered thinking him handsome years ago when he had visited Bamburgh during her fostering, but he was past his prime now and looked tired and worn despite his fine clothes and heavy rings. He stood by as a groom helped her down from Lark.

As the man led the mare off, Alaida glanced around at her noisy servants and held up a finger. The yard immediately dropped silent. *Excellent.*

"It is I who should have been here to greet you, Lord Robert." She dipped graciously low in her courtesy. "Forgive my absence, and my lord husband's. Had we known you were coming . . ." She let the thought trail off, a subtle reminder that a messenger should have been sent ahead.

But of course he hadn't wanted to send a messenger. He had wanted to come on them unawares, to see what they were up to. There would be much mistrust of the marcher lords after last year's rebellion, even of the new, loyal ones like her husband. She expected they would have many unannounced visits over the next years, even after the castle was built. Perhaps especially after the castle was built.

"Never fear, my lady," said Lord Robert. "Your officers have made us welcome."

"I am glad to hear it. Now, if you will excuse me, my lord, my journey has been damp and chill, and I find myself exhausted. I believe I will sup in chamber tonight. This is Alnwick's steward, Geoffrey, who was with me. He will see to your needs now, so our seneschal may return to building the castle the king so desires. Hadwisa, come."

"Of course, my lady, but I hope . . ." Lord Robert's words were lost in the chatter as her women surrounded her and swept her inside and up the stairs.

By the time she stuck her nose out to go to prayer the next morning, the solar was firmly hers.

CHAPTER 16

NEVILLE BEHAVED BETTER than Alaida had expected. A week into Lord Robert's stay, and he had not approached her, nor even spoken to her, other than a polite greeting if they happened to pass. Geoff and Oswald said he was even gentle with the servants. Perhaps he had repented his vileness on Ash Wednesday.

Or perhaps he was up to something.

In her experience, Neville fitz Hubert turned courteous only when it served his purpose, so she watched him out of the corner of her eye during dinner, trying to discern what that purpose might be while Lord Robert regaled her with tales of his recent boar hunt in Nottinghamshire. The king's emissary had proven pleasant company, by and large, except when he talked about hunting. And he did love to talk about hunting.

"Our Sir Brand recently killed a boar with his bare hands," she commented when he slowed.

Lord Robert smiled the kind of tolerant smile one used with boastful children. "No doubt he embellished the tale to impress you. A boar would tear an unarmed man to shreds."

"It very nearly did. Sir Ari, you were present. Tell Lord Robert what happened."

"Well, he did have a small branch, my lord, barely a twig," began Ari, who had been spending more time in the hall since their guests' arrival. He spun the story out, keeping Lord Robert and his men well diverted—excepting Neville, whose jaw clenched more tightly with every mention of either Brand or Ivo. True colors showing at last, thought Alaida.

As Ari finished, de Jeune and his knights thumped the tables. "Well told, *messire*. You would make a *jongleur* if you were not a knight."

"*Jongleurs* contrive their tales from mist and smoke, my lord. This tale is the truth."

"I would like to meet this Brand for myself," said Lord Robert.

"Unfortunately, he travels with my husband. We do have the tusks, however," said Alaida. "He hasn't yet decided what to have made of them. Thomas, fetch them."

The boar's thick, curved tusks were produced in short order and passed from Lord Robert to his knights with much commenting on their size and on the bloodstains that darkened them. De Jeune turned to Alaida. "I'm sorry I questioned your word, my lady. Let me make amends by taking you riding. 'Tis a fine day."

"That is not necessary, my lord."

"Ah, come, my lady. You have barely left your solar since we arrived. You will be well escorted and safe."

"I have no doubt, my lord, but I—"

"I could tell you it is the king's command," he interrupted, his eyes full of mischief.

"But that would be a lie, *monseigneur*."

"Alas, it would," he admitted. "But I would happily tell it to pry you out of your chamber for a little. Please your guest, Lady Alaida. Ride with me."

Alaida hesitated. She had assured Geoff and Ari she was safe, and until this moment she'd thought she was. But why was he so insistent? What if this was no simple ride, but an attempt to lure her out where she could be seized? William had been known to take a wife hostage to ensure her husband's behavior. On the other hand, what if her imagination was running away with her? She had a duty to Alnwick and her husband to keep the king's representative happy. She silently cursed Ivo for leaving her in the situation, but conjured up a gracious smile.

"Of course, my lord. Give us a moment to ready ourselves. Oswald, see to everything."

"Yes, my lady." The marshal selected a few men to follow him, and Alaida headed for the solar with Bôte and Hadwisa. As she topped the stairs, she couldn't help noticing that Neville looked pleased with himself. The hairs on her neck prickled. The little stoat truly was up to something.

"ARE YOU CERTAIN of this? I have noticed no interest at all."

"Positive, my lord." Neville fitz Hubert kept his voice low lest any of the manor servants hear. "You were too absorbed in Sir Ari's tale to notice, but I watched Lady Alaida—and she watched you with great longing in her eyes. She tries to hide it, but she warms to you."

Lord Robert fiddled with the tab of his belt. "She is so very tempting."

"You have left yourself the perfect opportunity." Neville sidled closer and dropped his voice even lower. "The lady rides astride which, as you know, my lord, leaves a woman well stimulated. Add to that the fact that she has been nearly a month without her husband . . ."

"I have heard talk that de Vassy disappears every day from dawn 'til dusk when he is here," said Robert. "Is that true?"

"So I have heard as well, my lord. Such constant absence of her husband must surely leave the lady wanting. Add a good gallop to the wine she just had for dinner . . ." Neville stopped to let his lordship absorb the idea.

Lord Robert looked to where Alaida spoke with her men. Seven of them had brought out horses, one Alnwick man for each of Lord Robert's men who would be going, plus her page and a groom to carry a maidservant pillion. Neville, of course, was not riding with them. She would never tolerate it, and it would not do to have her angry.

"But I tell you, she has revealed none of this interest to me."

"She hardly would, before others," said Neville. "She would not want word to get back to de Vassy."

"Nor would I, though she would be worth the risk." Robert studied her like he would a castle he wished to capture. "I will find a way to get her alone today, and see whether you are right about this."

"Do not be diverted by feigned reluctance, my lord."

Robert looked at Alaida again. "You are certain she wants me?"

"Like a bitch wants a dog, my lord."

"Perhaps I will oblige her by taking her that way, eh?" Robert snickered and nudged Neville, then groaned as Sir Ari gave Alaida a leg up. "God's knees, would I were that saddle."

Neville nodded at the sentiment. He had often wished to have Alaida that way. "Imagine what a good gallop will do to that quaint, my lord. How tender it will be. How ready."

Robert's ragged sigh said he imagined precisely that. "And to think I was aggrieved when de Vassy was not here to welcome me. I think I will forgive him if she proves as willing as you say."

His tongue flickered over his lips, as though he were tasting her, and jealous bile filled Neville's throat. Alaida should have been his—would have been if he hadn't made the mistake of trying to persuade her to marriage instead of simply forcing her. Would have been anyway, if de Vassy hadn't turned up with the king's writ before he could wear her down.

She would never have him now, but setting de Jeune on

her would serve its purpose. He would have the pleasure of seeing de Vassy cuckolded, while buying himself a powerful man's goodwill. And knowing she'd been bedded at his suggestion, if not by his body, would merely add to the sweetness of the revenge. Perhaps he could even find some way to watch de Jeune with her. He hardened, just thinking of it.

"You have my thanks, fitz Hubert," said Lord Robert as he pulled on his gloves.

Neville bowed. "At your service, my lord."

Lord Robert mounted and took his place beside Alaida as they rode out the gate, leaning close to say something to her that made her smile. Good, he was starting to work on her already. Neville watched them away, then went off and found a dark corner of the barn. There he spilled into the hay after only a few quick strokes, imagining how she would look when Robert put her on her knees and took her from behind, like the bitch she was.

DE JEUNE VEERED north and west out the gate, headed toward the Aln woods. Ari immediately caught Alaida's eye. "Your pardon, my lady, but did you not say you wished to ride Swinlees soon? Perhaps today would do."

She had said no such thing, but there was a tautness beneath Ari's words that made the hair rise on the back of her neck. He didn't want her in the woods with Lord Robert and his men—and if Ari didn't want it, that was reason enough.

"You're good to remind me, *messire*. My lord, may we ride south instead?"

Without waiting for de Jeune's agreement, she turned Lark toward Swinlees, with Ari and her men following in close order. Lord Robert shot an irritated glance at Ari as he and his knights came about to rejoin her. "Of course, my lady. The outing is for you, after all."

The problem then became finding some purpose for this visit to what was, after all, nothing more than pasture. She asked Ari to remind her of the bounds, which he did with impressive accuracy for one so new to Alnwick, discussed the number of sheep the field could support, and was trying to come up with some other pressing reason she had wanted to see it when Edric pointed out a small herd of deer grazing far to the south.

"Shall we give chase?" asked Lord Robert.

"We are in the Easter fast, my lord," said Alaida. "'Tis wasteful to hunt game we may not eat."

"Not hunt, my lady, merely chase." He reached across to lay a hand over hers. "For the sport of it."

She could find no fault with that, so she nodded and they were off, running the deer until they finally bounded off into a thicket of furze. Alaida pulled up, unwilling to shred her gown on the thorns.

"Well done, my lady," said Lord Robert as he reined in beside her. "You have a good seat and ride fearlessly. Shall we continue on?" He motioned south.

"Much farther and we will be in the mire."

"Then you lead. We will go where you wish."

She hadn't realized how tightly she'd been holding her shoulders until they turned back toward Alnwick. It really was just a ride with a well-mannered nobleman—though he was riding a bit too closely, she noted when his calf brushed hers for a second time. He proffered a charming smile. "Your pardon, my lady."

"Of course. Have you had a chance to look down on the castle, my lord?"

"With the weather, I have not."

"Then I know the place. You can see how the land lies."

She led him to the wide clearing at its crest, where they could see village below with its half-plowed fields all around. The hall and its outbuildings squatted like giants among the tiny cottages and huts, but from this vantage it was clear the tower and motte would soon dwarf them all.

"I still think it foolish to leave the high ground to the enemy." Lord Robert gestured toward the ancient hill fort that lay ruined nearby. "They knew that even in the old days."

"But this fortress fell or was abandoned, my lord, and those who came after settled below for good reason," said Ari. "Lord Ivo elects to follow their lead."

"The manor has survived a good many years in its spot, Lord Robert," added Alaida. "A well-built castle with a strong force to defend it will stand a good many years more."

She hoped for Lord Robert to answer in some way that would let her broach the subject of that force, so much of which moldered in the king's dungeons, but he merely nodded. "Perhaps."

He studied the land a little longer, until Alaida finally pointed out the fading afternoon. "We should return before it grows chill."

"Mmm." He straightened and gave her a brilliant smile, one that made him look twenty years younger. "I propose a race to take us back. My men against yours, from here to the edge of that first field, with the winner having a prize from each of us. What say you, my lady? "

She looked to Ari, who shrugged as though he didn't care, though she knew he had a fast horse. "Excellent. It will be good entertainment."

"For judges, I suggest your serving woman and groom, and my Sir Wakelin here," said Lord Robert.

Again, Alaida nodded, and the three of them cantered off.

"Now, for prizes," said Lord Robert. He twisted a heavy silver ring off his forefinger and held it up. "This ring from me. And from Lady Alaida . . . ?"

She thought quickly what she might have of similar value. "A sturdy belt, with a bronze buckle and strap end."

"May I race, too, my lady?" asked Tom, who had managed to keep quiet all afternoon.

"Let the boy try his luck," said Lord Robert, so she nodded assent.

The judges reached their spot, the riders lined up, and with the drop of Lord Robert's arm, they were off. Laughing, Alaida made to go after them, but Lord Robert cut her off and grabbed Lark's bridle.

"Loiter here with me a little, my lady. We have not made a wager between ourselves."

Alaida looked after the racers vanishing down the hill, Ari well in the lead. "Hurry then. What would you have?"

"If my man wins, a kiss. And if your man wins . . . a kiss."

Alaida felt a sudden chill that had nothing to do with the breeze. "I am married, my lord."

"You are lonely." He tugged Lark closer, so his leg pressed the length of Alaida's, powerful and lean. "You're barely a bride, and have been apart from your husband as much as you have been with him. It has been in your eyes all week, how you long for a man's company."

"I long only for my husband."

"In his absence, another man may suffice. It is the way of the world."

"Not my world."

He smiled as though she'd said something amusing. "You need not pretend here, sweeting. We are alone. I desire you, and you desire me."

"You are mistaken, my lord. I do not."

"You will find me a considerate lover, Alaida. I will give you great pleasure, as you will me. Say yes."

Alaida's heart raced in alarm. If she angered this man, he could destroy her, her grandfather, her uncle, her husband, Alnwick, all with one word to the king. Lord Robert read her hesitation as consent and quickly snaked his free hand behind her head. She pulled back, but he was fit and strong, and short of falling out of the saddle, there was nowhere to go. He drew her to him easily. His lips touched her cheek, cool and dry.

"Imagine lying beneath me, feeling our bodies meld," he murmured against her skin. "Send your women elsewhere tonight. I will come to you in that lonely bed of yours and make your body sing."

"I am a faithful wife and will remain so, *monseigneur*." Her voice was low and even as she gathered herself to fight if she must. "Release me."

"One kiss first, to show you how it can be."

His mouth covered hers, greedy and hard, his tongue stabbing into her lips as he sought entrance to her mouth. She brought her crop back, ready to lash his face, king's emissary or no.

Something fell from the sky before she had to make that choice, a screaming storm of wings and talons that shrieked past them inches overhead. Lord Robert was jerked away, cursing, as his horse reared in fright. Freed, Lark skittered backward, Alaida clutching at the saddle for balance. The eagle streaked past her again to hit Lord Robert like an arrow. Robert howled in pain as the bird pounded off with his coif and a chunk of his scalp. Blood poured down his face.

Alaida put her heels to Lark and left Robert to bleed, pelting down the hill before he could regain his wits. Below, Edric or one of the others saw her flight, and the Alnwick men raced back with Lord Robert's men hard on their heels. Ari was first to her.

"Lord Robert is injured. See to him," she shouted, barely slowing. Ari snapped a few quick orders and the other men closed around her. They pushed the horses hard, whipping into the village past startled cottagers, not stopping until she was safe within Alnwick walls.

"UGLY WOUND THAT," said Bôte as she entered the solar carrying her box of salves and herbs. "'Tis clean, so it will heal well, but he'll not grow hair there again."

"How unfortunate," said Alaida, thinking the opposite. She had not said a word about their guest's attempt at seduction, not even to Bôte, instead letting them all think she had fled from the eagle. Unless he was a fool, Lord Robert would tell the same lie, at least in front of others—and there would be others every moment from here forward, Alaida vowed to herself, if she had to order the entire village into the hall to ensure it. She had no less than ten women with her right now.

"I wonder what demon got into that eagle, to make him go after Lord Robert like that," said Bôte as she busied herself lighting more candles.

"No demon but the fur on his lordship's coif," said Alaida, blessing the coif, the fur, and the eagle all in one silent prayer between words. "The poor creature likely thought he was getting an easy meal."

"Poor creature?" said Hadwisa doubtfully.

"How would you feel, if you thought you were to have squirrel for supper and got only boiled wool and hair?"

They all laughed, but Bôte said, "Well, he had better enjoy whatever meal he finds today, for Lord Robert vows to put an arrow through him on the morrow."

"He cannot. He has no right to hunt on Alnwick land without leave."

"But the bird attacked him, my lady."

"It attacked a *cap*. I will not have it killed for that."

"I thought you were frightened of it, my lady," said Rohesia, in for another day's spinning. "Edric says you rode like Satan himself was after you."

"The suddenness of the attack startled me, that's all. And all that blood."

That last made Bôte turn and give her a hard look. Blood had never bothered Alaida, even as a child, and Bôte well knew it. Her lips pursed and unpursed thoughtfully. "Thomas, go tell Lord Robert that my lady does not want the eagle killed."

Tom popped up from his stool in the corner and disappeared. He slipped back in a few moments later. "Lord Robert says he would hear your reasons from your own lips, my lady, and that he will sup with you in the solar in order to discuss it."

"He will not," said Alaida, so firmly that Bôte gave her another hard look. "Call Sir Ari to attend me."

"He's gone, my lady," said Tom.

"Is it so late already?"

"Aye, they carry out the trestles for supper now. Geoffrey calls for Mildryth and the others to come."

The women who had duty in the hall rose to go, but Alaida held up a hand to keep them. "Geoffrey will have to do without you tonight. Thomas, how many of Alnwick's men are in the hall so far, and how many of Lord Robert's?"

"All of Lord Robert's knights and their squires, plus his two pages. Of ours, Oswald, Geoffrey, Penda, Daegmund . . ." He continued listing, ticking them off on his fingers. When he had gone through all his fingers twice, she stopped him.

"And all the hired men," he added, but she couldn't count on them.

"Run and tell anyone still in the yard or stables to come in for supper."

Bôte gave her another piercing look as Tom dashed out. "What are you about, my lady?"

"Seeing that everyone is fed." She gave Tom a little time to do as she bid, then rose. "Bôte, ask Oswald and Penda to wait on the stairs."

She waited in the doorway until the two men were in place, then took a deep breath and stepped out on the landing. Below her, the Alnwick men sat scattered around the hall, with more drifting in the door. The visiting knights filled the upper tables, and on the dais, de Jeune occupied the lord's chair as though it were his own, while Neville bent to whisper in his ear. *Neville.* Her lip curled as she watched Lord Robert murmur something back. She should have known. If Sir Brand were here, she would ask him to gut the little stoat as a favor.

But he wasn't, and neither was her husband. She would have to do her best without them. "Oh, Lord Robert."

She made her voice high and sweet, so it tinkled out over the hall like a bell, calling every man to silence. De Jeune came to his feet eagerly. "My lady. I am at your service."

"I wish to speak to you about the eagle," she said, keeping the same agreeable tone.

A smile spread over his face and he started for the stair. The fool actually believed he could win her, bandage and all.

"There is no need for you to come up, *monseigneur*. It is more convenient to speak to you there." She heard Oswald and Penda shift to better block the stair as de Jeune's smile faded. "I come only to repeat the message I sent with my page. The eagle is not to be harmed."

"You have a tender heart, my lady, but the bird is dangerous. Lord Ivo will thank me for dealing with it in his absence."

"He will not. Especially if you do so against my wishes." She sighed as if the whole thing could not be helped, keeping her eyes fixed firmly on de Jeune despite some sort of stir at the door. "Have you not noticed, *monseigneur*? The eagle is my husband's sign. And that particular eagle is . . . a sort of pet of mine."

"Then you should control your pets better, my lady," he said, which drew snickers from Neville and some of the others.

"I said a sort of pet, *monseigneur*, though a wild one, I grant. He flies along sometimes when I ride. It pleases me."

His eyes narrowed. "Surely it did not please you to see my head laid open."

"No, but it will please me even less to see the creature die for being true to its nature. As I told my women, he likely mistook the fur on your chape for a . . . a wood rat." This time it was the Alnwick men who snickered. She smiled grimly as she added, "Or perhaps he thought to protect me."

Alnwick's laughter shifted to an angry mutter that rippled around the hall. Several of de Jeune's knights came uneasily to their feet, and Oswald's fingers curled around the hilt of his sword.

"From what? You well know I would not harm you, my lady," Lord Robert said smoothly.

"Of course. You are the king's emissary and a gentleman and would never do anything untoward." She let her smile ease. "Which is why I know you will hear me now. Do not harm that eagle."

"I cannot promise you that, my lady."

"Then perhaps you can promise me," said a voice from the back of the hall.

CHAPTER 17

IVO STEPPED OUT of a knot of men, wearing a smile that fell short of his eyes. "Or is it your habit to hunt on another man's land, Robert?"

The missing title implied either familiarity or contempt. The blood in de Jeune's cheeks said it was the latter.

"Only when a dangerous beast needs killing," he said tightly. "I was explaining that to your lady."

"Indeed. Come." Ivo turned toward the stairs and his smile vanished. "You can explain it to me."

He knew. She didn't know how, but he did. It was in the glint in his eye and the stony set of his jaw as he passed Oswald and Penda on his way up. Suddenly the situation became both less dangerous and more so.

She stepped forward to greet him. "Welcome home, husband. I am *most* glad to see you."

His bearing softened and he reached for her. "I have missed you, too, sweet leaf."

His kiss was more about marking her as his before de Jeune than about passion. Alaida understood, but it had been so long, and he tasted so good, that for a heartbeat she lost track of everything else. Then Lord Robert's boots sounded on the steps below them, and Ivo set her back on her feet, the moment gone. His jaw hardened again and he led her into the solar.

He frowned at the women who had clustered near the door to eavesdrop. "Out."

Their rush to obey clogged the stairs and delayed Lord Robert. Alaida grabbed the moment to explain, "I did nothing to—"

"I know. Stay out of harm's way."

He sent her to stand by the fire and was filling a horn with ale when Lord Robert entered. Ivo took a sip, then stood, holding the horn without offering any to his guest, another insult.

Lord Robert's gaze flickered from Ivo to the horn, to Alaida, and back to Ivo. "Your journey to Durham was quick, Lord Ivo," he said with unnatural heartiness. "Did you accomplish your business?"

"Yes."

Clearly Ivo would not be distracted by common conversation. Lord Robert scratched his palm nervously and tried a new sally. "It is good you returned early."

"Is it?"

Lord Robert flushed. "Uh, yes. Of course. I had thought I would not see you at all before I left."

Ivo assessed him over the top of the horn as he took another deliberate draught of ale. "Apparently."

He was playing de Jeune the way he played chess, Alaida realized: lying back, relaxed, offering little, saying less, just waiting to see if the other player could stand it. She had watched Brand give up game after game to him, trying to force something to happen, and she had lost a few of her own by making the same mistake. It would be interesting to see how de Jeune fared.

"The king asked for a report on your progress," he said. "*Mmm.*"

"I have the silver he promised." He waited for Ivo to say something, and barreled on when he didn't. "He said I should release it only if I'm satisfied."

"And are you? *Satisfied?*"

Lord Robert glanced toward Alaida and flung himself into the trap. "Whatever she told you is a lie."

"Told me?" Ivo's voice turned to steel. "What would she have had to tell me, *Robert*?"

Panic widened de Jeune's eyes as he saw his misstep. "I meant . . . about the eagle. It attacked me, but your lady insists it was an accident and forbids me to kill it."

"You take issue with that."

"Y-Yes, I do."

"*Mmm.*" Ivo drained the horn and set it aside, his eyes never leaving de Jeune's. "I, on the other hand, take issue with a man who refuses to hear when my wife says no, as you have done twice today."

"I have no idea—" de Jeune began.

Ivo took a step forward to loom over the smaller man, his voice sizzling with anger. "You were *seen*."

De Jeune's mouth worked soundlessly. His eyes pivoted once more to Alaida, and the breath froze in her throat. If he tried to shift blame to her, she had no doubt Ivo would kill him.

She saw the instant he chose life, watched the effort it took him to yank himself back from the edge. When he finally spoke, he was contrite. "I offer my deepest apologies, my lord. I had been led to believe the lady would be open to my attentions.

"Not by her," he added quickly as Ivo's face darkened. "Lady Alaida never . . . As you say, she told me no, and clearly. My own vanity stopped my ears." He suddenly dropped to one knee. "Forgive me, my lady. How can I make amends?"

His regret seemed sincere, but whether it was or not, she wanted this over before they found themselves in a fresh war. "I accept your apology, my lord. As to amends, in truth, all I wish is for you and your knights to ride on in peace."

"We will depart at first light."

"You will depart now," said Ivo. "I have already sent a man ahead to Lesbury. It is but three miles and the weather and road are good. My bailiff there will accommodate you, and you can ride on in the morning."

De Jeune's lips thinned at this third affront, but he swallowed his pride and rose, grunting as his knees popped. Suddenly looking much older, he turned stiffly and walked out to call down to his second.

"Wakelin, make ready. We start for Bamburgh tonight."

Ivo had followed him out onto the landing, and as the men below rose and began collecting their equipment, said, "'Tis unfortunate you must leave so soon, my lord. I had hoped to seek your advice on the tower."

Lord Robert's expression went from startled to suspicious to grateful as he realized Ivo was letting him save face before his men. He dipped his head slightly in acknowledgment. "We have enjoyed Alnwick's hospitality too long already, my lord. Your offer of lodging in Lesbury is welcome. It will make for a shorter ride on the morrow."

He turned to where Alaida had come to the doorway to spy, and bent his head respectfully. "My lady."

"*Monseigneur*. God speed." She took her place beside Ivo, who echoed her farewell, adding, "I will see to that eagle."

A tentative smile touched Lord Robert's lips. "And I will pass your greeting to the king when I see him. Speaking of which, you will want this." He opened his purse and pulled out a bronze key. "The casket is in your treasury, to which your lady holds the key, I believe. I will remove my guard, of course."

The two of them nodded to each other and Lord Robert started downstairs. "Fitz Hubert!"

Sir Wakelin scanned the hall. "I do not see him, my lord. He was standing next to Lord Ivo's big man there." He pointed to Brand.

"By me?" Brand touched his chest as if unsure Wakelin meant him. He twisted, looking all around himself. "Oh, you mean Neville. He left. Looked a bit green for some reason."

"Find him," snapped Lord Robert. He strode out, his men hurrying behind him. Brand grinned up at Ivo. "I'll go help them look."

"Take Oswald—and anyone else who would enjoy the sport." Half the hall emptied, leaving the rest laughing and looking up to Ivo and Alaida for what came next.

"What do you think Brand said to him?" asked Alaida under her breath.

"Something about braiding his guts for a belt, I believe." He raised his voice. "Geoffrey, Lesbury will not have baked for so many. See Lord Robert's men get bread enough to carry them to Bamburgh." Ivo spun Alaida around to face him. "And you, wife. Challenging a hall full of armed men over a bird?"

"Not a mere bird, my lord. My eagle. He helped me, and I was bound to return the favor."

His brow pinched a little, then smoothed. "You are either a madwoman or a brave one."

"Not so brave, my lord." She held out her hands, shaking now that it was all over. "I cannot seem to stop them."

He curled his fingers around hers. "Even warriors shake after battle. I have a cure for it." He tugged her into his arms.

"We are watched, my lord," she admonished.

"Let them learn." This time the kiss they shared was as real as the shouts of delight that rose up from the hall below, and her heart soared with the possibilities of this new beginning.

By dawn the next morning, Alaida knew it had been a false hope. She lay in the dark, listening to Ivo's footsteps fade and fighting a loosing battle with the tears that scalded her throat. She gave in to them finally, after she heard his distant call for the gate to be opened.

They spilled out of her, drenching her pillow and the linens beneath, tears like she had never cried in her entire life, even when her mother had died. She cried until her eyes ached and her mouth felt like sawdust, until at last there was no more liquid in her and the sheets had grown chill with the dampness.

She rolled away from the cold, hiccupping out the last dry sobs as she sat up on the edge of the bed. What a fool she was, weeping over a man who didn't want her.

But Ivo *did* want her; that was what made this so incomprehensible. Sometimes he looked at her with eyes so full of craving, she felt his ache like it was her own. Sometimes, he even grew hard as he held her. But always he would just lie there, and if she didn't do the same, if she tried to touch him or to entice him to touch her, he would make some feeble excuse and tell her to sleep, and yet she could feel him shaking as he fought back his desire, and oh, God, why did he not *want* to want her? She swallowed back a wail of despair and sprang to her feet, determined to get this ridiculous sniveling under control so she could think.

Before she could, the room tilted wildly, and her stomach tilted with it, and a moment later she was crouched over the chamber pot, heaving up what little was in her stomach. When the retching stopped, she rinsed her mouth with the dregs of ale left in a cup and crawled back in bed, so empty there was nothing she could do but find a dry corner and sleep.

She awoke much later, fuzzy-headed but otherwise fine, and all she could think was that her foolish crying had made her ill—yet another reason she needed to figure out what had suddenly made her so prone to tears and make it go away.

ALAIDA LOST HER stomach a few more times over the next fortnight, always for different reasons. Mostly it was smells that set her off—the scent of fish cooking, a measure of wine gone musty, a too-strong whiff of the pigsty when the wind changed. But once she got dizzy looking out the window, and a time or two she simply woke up feeling queasy. Fortunately, she managed to find some privacy each time,

so her illness, whatever it was, remained her business and
not the entire hall's . . . until one Sunday at Ivo's evening
Mass.

She was kneeling for prayer when the incense began to
overpower her. She held out 'til the "Amen," but suddenly
the odor went foul, and before she could do more than push
to her feet, she vomited onto the stone floor, barely missing
Father Theobald's toes and sending everyone scattering
back against the walls.

All she could do was stand there after, covering her face
and repeating, "I'm sorry. I'm so sorry."

"Hush," said Ivo. He scooped her up and started back for
the house as Bôte fretted along behind. "Illness is nothing to
be sorry for."

Mortified, Alaida clung to him, her face buried against
his chest. "But in church . . ."

"Hush. The chapel can be cleaned. I will get you to bed,
and Bôte will take care of you. Everything will be fine."

He took the stairs as though she weighed no more than a
scrap, then lingered long enough to press a kiss to her forehead and see her tucked in.

The odd thing was, she felt fine by the time he left, just as
she had felt fine soon after the other incidents. However,
Bôte was already heating water and fussing with her herbs
and ordering everyone else away, so Alaida let her fuss, and
soon she had a stack of pillows to prop her up and a cup of
some posset or other in her hand.

Alaida sniffed at the liquid. "Mint and chamomile?"

"Aye, and other things to ease a sick stomach. Drink
slowly. Tiny sips." Bôte sat on the edge of the bed and
smoothed back Alaida's hair. "I've seldom brewed that for
you, lamb. You never were one to lose your supper."

"Fortunately, I had no supper to lose tonight."

"For which Father Theobald should be grateful. I'd no
idea the man could dance."

Bôte's wicked chuckle drew Alaida along. She recalled
Father Theobald in that first instant, aghast and disgusted,

and despite her part in it, the chuckle quickly grew into a giggle, then to a full-bellied laugh that ran on too long.

"'Tis not that funny, my lady," scolded Bôte.

"I know," gasped Alaida, and she tried to stop, but the laugh had taken on a life of its own. It possessed her, feeding on her efforts to quit, which tickled her more, until her sides ached and tears ran down her cheeks and Bôte took away the cup for fear she'd spill it, and still it went on. Then suddenly, when Alaida could bear it no longer, the tears became real tears, stupid tears for no reason at all, and she was sobbing.

"Ah, lamb." Bôte gathered Alaida into the comfort of her familiar arms. "Hush. *Shh.*"

"It was so hu-humiliating." Her voice caught on the word and broke through as a half-sob. "W-what is w-wrong with me? V-vomiting. Crying. I n-never cry, you know that."

"Aye. Aye."

"Yet now I c-cry all the time. I feel like I'm going mad. Or d-dying."

"Nonsense." Bôte laughed gently. "You are no more mad than I. Tears and laughter and even your sick stomach are signs of life, lamb, not death."

Alaida wiped away tears with the edge of the sheet. "What are you t-talking about?"

Bôte took Alaida by the shoulders and held her out at arm's length. "Think, lamb. When were your last courses?"

"I don't know. About . . ." She thought back, and the tears dried instantly as what Bôte was saying hit her. "No. I cannot be. I had a flow after we wed. About the time Sir Brand was hurt."

"Only a tiny one that would hardly signify, and more than a month has passed since that."

"But we never . . ." Alaida stopped herself. She still had yet to tell Bôte that her husband never touched her, keeping the secret as the only thing she and Ivo truly shared. "I mean, I have never been moon-steady. I skip months now and again, or it comes late."

"Aye, but as you say, you've been getting sick."

"Not in the mornings, though. Not always."

"Some have trouble at other times. But it makes no mind. I've known for a while now."

"How?" Alaida challenged.

"Have you not looked at your own teats?"

Alaida crossed her arms over her chest self-consciously. "You told me a woman's breasts bloom after she's wed."

"Aye, but not that much, nor with such veins. Even Hadwisa noted it, though thick as she is, she has no idea what it means. They'll be hard and sore for a time as well."

Like rocks with bruises, and they had been for weeks, but Alaida shook her head. "I'm not breeding. I cannot be." *Not from one night.*

"With a husband like Lord Ivo, you could hardly not be."

A husband like Lord Ivo, Alaida thought. And what was that? One who left her every day and avoided her every night? Surely this was why he kept himself from her—because he didn't want her to bear children. How would he respond if she came up breeding from just that one night?

"Do you not see, lamb?" continued Bôte, apparently crediting the look on Alaida's face to her sick stomach. "The teats, the sickness, the missed flow. It all leads to the same place."

Alaida shook her head, not wanting to admit the possibility. "The crying and laughing do not."

"But they do, my lady. The babe takes over your heart with its spirit. Many a woman spills tears like the child she carries, and some cannot stop laughing once they begin. Be glad you are one of those—it means the babe will be merry."

Alaida hugged herself more tightly. "There is no babe."

"But there is, my lady. Ah, lamb, I know you are frightened of birthing, but that will fade as the time nears." Bôte stood up and began tidying up her herbs. "I will fetch Lord Ivo so you can tell him. He will be greatly pleased."

Panic shot through Alaida. "No!"

"My lady . . ."

"Not yet. None of this is certain. All these . . . ailments can have other cause."

"Aye, apart. Together they mean but one thing." Bôte reached over and curved her hand low over Alaida's belly. "You will see soon enough."

"Until I do, my lord need not hear. No one need hear."

"But, lamb . . ."

"No one," repeated Alaida. "I mean this, Bôte. Swear to me you will tell no one 'til I'm certain."

Bôte's lips went as tight as an oyster, but she nodded. "I swear it. And I will see that Hadwisa keeps her tongue as well, if she works it out."

"Good," said Alaida, and then she saw the disappointment in her nurse's eyes and softened a little. "Just 'til I'm certain, and then you may cry the news from the wall if you wish. *After* I tell Lord Ivo."

Bôte sighed, mollified.

"Now, hand back that posset and go have your supper," said Alaida. "I would be alone a little."

"Yes, my lady. I will bring you something when I return. You should not go hungry now, sick stomach or not." Bôte put away the last of her herbs, handed Alaida her cup, and started for the door. "And if Lord Ivo asks to see you?"

He would not; Alaida knew. Even if her illness had not given him an excuse, he had already made it clear he intended to abide by the Church's ban on relations during the forty Holy days before Easter—an odd shift for a man who had argued that there was no sin in what passed between man and wife.

"Tell him I fell asleep, and will see him tomorrow if I am well."

Alaida waited long enough to be sure Bôte was settled at table, then set aside the posset and tugged off her chainse. She cupped her breasts in her hands, gently because they ached, and studied them. They were half-again bigger than they had been, taut as gooseberries, and so covered with blue tracery they looked like vines had grown over them. But did that mean she was breeding?

As she counted back the days once more, her hands slipped down to her belly. It felt no different, but she wasn't sure whether it would after only two months. If only that flow didn't confuse things, she might be certain, but as it was, there was really only thing to do: wait to see if her belly swelled and the babe quickened. The third or fourth month, she thought it happened. She counted forward this time. Easter, perhaps, or a little past.

At Easter she would know.

And she would have her husband back then, too, by the saints, and a father for this child if there was one. If Ivo would not lie with her of his own accord, she would find some way to make him. He had overcome her reluctance on their wedding night—her body still flushed with the memory of how thoroughly—and she could surely overcome his.

Seduce her own husband. She wondered why she hadn't made the decision before.

She wasn't sure how, but she had a bit over a month to figure it out. Until Easter.

CHAPTER 18

THE CHURCH'S BAN against swiving extended through the week after Easter, but it did eventually end, and as every man with a wife headed off to make up for lost time, Ivo was forced back into Alaida's bed. She snuggled up to him with an expressive "*Aaaah.*"

"You sound content, sweet leaf," he commented as he wrapped his arms around her.

"I am. Egg custard for dinner, and cheese tart for supper." She sighed again and rested her hand on his chest. "It was a very long forty days this year. It seemed we would never see eggs and cheese again, and now they are back, I cannot have enough of them."

"'Twas the pork for me." Ivo had tired of pease and beans and nuts in all their forms within the first week. He wasn't sure how these Christians did it every year. "Give me meat any day."

She rose up on one elbow and studied him carefully. Her fingers drifted lazily across his bare skin. "Was meat all you missed, my lord?"

His entire being narrowed to the path she traced.

"What do you mean?" he asked carefully. His gaze wandered to the curve of her breasts, rising so temptingly within reach. He'd forgotten how full they were. How ripe for his mouth.

"There is so much forbidden during the season." She shifted, and when the covers slipped, he nearly groaned. "Surely there are other pleasures you wish to enjoy, now it is ended."

She wasn't trying to seduce him, he told himself. She probably didn't even realize what she was doing to him. She was, after all, innocent, save that one night.

"I have not thought on it," he lied.

She leaned over him, just enough that her breasts grazed his ribs. The contact made him close his eyes as he sought the will to keep his hands to himself. *Frey's pillock.* It was difficult enough to withstand this torture at the best of times. If she suddenly mastered the art of seduction, he wasn't certain, even after these several months, that he could keep himself from her.

"You should, husband," she murmured, and when he opened his eyes, she was right there, her gaze mysterious and shrewd as it met his, not innocent at all. "You should think on it in great detail."

Then she rolled away from him to go to sleep, leaving him alone on his side of the bed to do exactly that.

In great detail.

ALAIDA'S EFFORTS TO seduce her husband were a failure.

After that first night, Ivo went back to his old ways, dragging Brand along each night he bothered to come up, and lingering over chess until Alaida all but collapsed in exhaustion. On the single occasion he came to bed while she was still awake, naught she did had any effect.

"All I have to do is lie down and he's on me," one of the village women said when Alaida turned conversation toward men. "Just let him catch a peek of my teats and he's ready in a trice," said another. A third had mentioned that,

"Bawdy talk stiffens my Deagmund's pole faster than anything."

Phfft. She had been practically lying *on* him last night, dangling her breasts in his face, speaking so suggestively she barely kept from blushing. He'd been so hard that it might have been a tent pole in bed with them—and still he'd pushed her away. Surely no priest was more dedicated to keeping himself from women than her husband was to keeping himself from her. She clearly needed more than bosoms and bold speech.

So after dinner one day, she distracted Bôte with some mending, borrowed Tom from Oswald, and set out with him and Hadwisa for a walk that led, after some meandering, to Merewyn's.

They found the healer in her clearing, speaking to the rowan bush growing near her door. Without turning, she held up a finger to still them. It took Alaida a moment to spot the missel-dick sitting in the branches, its brown head cocked.

"She talks to a bird!" exclaimed Hadwisa.

"Hush," said Alaida, but it was too late. The bird rattled its irritation and flitted off. Merewyn turned, smiling.

"I fear we frightened it," said Alaida.

"He will come back. Welcome, my lady. You want to come in, I think."

Alaida nodded and turned to Tom and Hadwisa. "Find something useful to do and stay well away from the cottage so I may speak in private. "

Merewyn led her inside and offered her a scat at the table, where a jar of ale sat next to a board of bread and cheese, already cut.

Alaida smiled. "You always seem to know I am coming."

"I hear you on the path, my lady."

"Am I so noisy?"

"You speak with your servants, and I am always pleased to hear your voice. I was coming to meet you when the storm-cock called."

"And what did he have to tell you today?"

Merewyn's smile spoke of a secret held close. "Something I already knew. The true question is, what do *you* have to tell me, my lady? Or rather, to ask me?"

"I ..." Now the moment was here, Alaida found herself hesitant. "I came to thank you for caring for Sir Brand."

"I have been thanked already, my lady, so well I grow embarrassed by it."

"Still, I wish to add my own."

"And they are welcome, but you are not truly here about Sir Brand."

"No." Alaida studied the crumbs on the breadboard until Merewyn said, "My lady?"

"I do not know where to begin."

"Then let us begin with the babe."

Alaida started. Surely it couldn't be seen yet. "How ... ?"

Merewyn only laughed. "Your face glows with it, my lady. I have had signs for some weeks now and only waited to see which woman had been blessed. When I heard you on the path, I knew. What I do not know is why you come to me when you have Bôte."

"To be certain, and to ..." *A babe!* Hearing it from Merewyn made the news fresh. The tears ambushed her again and she choked them back and took a moment to compose herself. "To find out what to do about *that*, for one thing. The tears."

"Cry them, my lady. That is all I know."

"I would be crying all day some days, even when I am happy. Unless I start laughing, which is nearly as bad."

"Both will ease as your body grows accustomed to the child, as will the sickness."

The child! Alaida nodded, still fighting the lump in her throat. "That, at least, has begun to fade."

"Good. Having it means the babe is strong, but 'tis a relief when it goes. And now the other thing," prodded Merewyn, and when Alaida looked confused, she said, "You said, 'For one thing, the tears.' What is the other thing?"

The other thing. Embarrassment pushed Alaida to her feet and set her circling the tiny room, touching clay pots and dry herbs, looking for anything to distract her from what she needed to ask.

"My lady, whatever it is, you will not find the answer on my shelves."

"In truth, I might, though I would not know it." With a sigh, Alaida returned to the table. "I . . . I do not know how to ask this. I need a . . . something to make my husband love me. Or at least to lie with me."

Merewyn glanced to her belly. "Surely you have accomplished that, my lady."

"Only once," said Alaida, and the entire story poured out, from her husband's strange absences to his stranger disinclination to bed her again. It was a relief to tell someone at last, to have Merewyn nod and ask questions and listen with sympathy.

"I do not wish to distress you, my lady, but does he perhaps take his pleasure elsewhere?"

"I once thought so, but now . . . All I am certain of is that he does not take it with me." Alaida rose and paced the room again. "As the nights grow shorter, he spends less and less time at home. Summer is nearly on us, and the sun will barely set before it rises again. If I do not capture his affections soon, I will have no chance at all until I am so far gone with child I can do nothing. And by the time I am able afterwards, I fear it will be too late."

"By the Church's law, my lady, it already is. The priests teach abstinence while with child."

"And on feast days and fast days and Sundays and Wednesdays and Fridays and Quadrigessima and Advent and and and. Even last week was forbidden, though we just had forty days without. If I bow completely to the Church's teachings, I will never lie with my husband again. It cannot *all* be sin."

"None of it is sin in my mind, my lady," said Merewyn, calling up bitter memory of Ivo's words. "I only warn you of what Father Theobald will say when you confess."

"Then I will do penance, but at least I will have a husband," snapped Alaida, and immediately regretted it. "I'm sorry, Merewyn. This has become a sore subject. Can you help me?"

"Perhaps." Merewyn traced some unknown figure on the table with her fingertip as she considered. "How do you feel about Lord Ivo, my lady? Do you care for him?"

"He is my husband."

"Aye. But do you care for him beyond that? If he were not your husband . . . ?"

Alaida closed her eyes and tried to imagine it. "At first, I would have told you I could never have affection for him. I was convinced he was King William's man through and through. But I have come to see the good in him. Strange as his habits are, he is a worthy lord for Alnwick and even-handed with the men. Most of the time," she amended, thinking of Wat. "And when he does err with them, he makes it up somehow so they end up even more loyal to him. He even made an ally of Lord Robert."

"And with you?"

"He is gentle, even when I perhaps do not deserve gentleness. He made Tom squire to please me, though I was thinking ill of him at the time. In fact, every time I think ill of him, he proves me wrong. Even our wedding night," she added, blushing.

"You enjoy his touch, then?"

"Aye, what little of it I have had." Alaida sighed and blushed some more. "He is very . . . pleasant to lie with."

"Do you love him, my lady?"

"I . . . I do not know," she said honestly. "I do know he makes me laugh, even when I think I do not wish to. And sometimes he kisses me, and I think now, finally, all will be well if he will just keep his arms around me. I am so lost in this, Merewyn. I ask again, can you help me? Will you?"

Merwyn studied her a long while, then slowly nodded. "I may have something."

She dragged her stool over and stepped on it to reach a high shelf, from which she took down a tiny clay vial, thick with dust and cobwebs. She carefully wiped it on her sleeve, then opened it to sniff the contents. "Yes, this will do."

"What is it?" asked Alaida.

"A very special potion, my lady, made of the rarest herbs and roots, and brewed under a blue moon. Put a single drop in your bath, and wash yourself well in it, then persuade your husband to bathe in the same water. He will not be able to deny you."

Alaida reached for the vial greedily, but Merewyn held it back.

"This is powerful magic, my lady. You must use it carefully. And you must tell him you are with child."

Alaida colored ferociously. "What makes you think I have not?"

"You have barely admitted it to yourself. Am I wrong?"

"No. I will, I promise. It is time anyway." She accepted the vial from Merewyn and clutched it to her breast. "What if I cannot lure him into the same water?"

"Then bathe yourself and go to him still damp. The moisture on your skin will carry enough of the magic, and if you approach him with certainty, you will find success."

Nodding, Alaida slipped the vial carefully into her purse, making sure it stayed upright as she returned the pouch to her belt.

She followed Merewyn to the door. Outside, Tom was pulling weeds in Merewyn's little garden, while Hadwisa stood by watching, lazy thing. She turned back to Merewyn. "My thanks, Healer. You have once again done good service to Alnwick."

"'Tis my pleasure, my lady, as always." Her calm voice belied the sparkle of humor in her eyes. "And your pleasure, I hope."

"We shall see," said Alaida, smiling at the thought, and she called her servants to go home.

"AGAIN?"

Ignoring Ivo's tone, Brand reached into his purse to bring

out a silver ring that barely fit over the tip of his little finger. "I won this from the smith at dice last night. 'Tis far too small to be of use to me, so I thought to give it to the healer."

"Why would she want a ring that ugly?"

"Isn't a ring, you ass. 'Tis a thymel. For sewing."

My thymel. For sewing. Ivo heard Alaida's voice, tart and just a bit amused as she'd told him of her wager. That was probably hers, traded from Rohesia to the smith, and now gambled away to end up in Brand's hand. Going to *Merewyn.*

"'Tis still ugly," he grumbled, angry that he couldn't return it to Alaida. "Just sell it."

Brand shrugged as he put the ring away. "Merewyn can sell it if she likes. She needs the coin more than I."

"And *you* need an excuse to go a-wooing."

"A little conversation and a cup of ale are not wooing."

"Whatever it is, 'tis foolish." A branch hung over the trail, and Ivo growled and swatted it aside as though its offense were personal. Brand gave him an odd look, but said nothing, which irritated Ivo more. "You have repaid Merewyn many times over. Stop now, before you find yourself wanting what you cannot have."

"That will not happen," said Brand, not succumbing to Ivo's foul mood. "I know I bear the same curse. But I have been in the woods far too long to deny myself a few evenings in a woman's company, whether I can bed her or not, if for no other reason than that she smells good. You surely understand, for you are still here with your lady, for all the torment you claim to suffer."

"The torment is real enough," muttered Ivo, thinking of how Alaida smelled, how she tasted, how her legs felt wrapped around him. How he couldn't have any of what she offered—just as Brand couldn't have Merewyn and needed to remember that.

Brand shook his head in sympathy. "I warned you it would not get easier."

"And yet you put yourself in the same position. You should heed your own warning."

"I am heeding it. Merewyn is not my woman and I will not make her so."

Ivo's snort of disbelief made both horses lay their ears back. "Don't tell me you never think of how she would feel beneath you."

"I'm not dead and I still have my balls. Of course I do," said Brand. "But that is mere dream, and I have lived all these years with nothing more than dreams and my hand. Your problem is, you've been with women. You've been with Alaida. You *know* her. I will never know Merewyn."

"See you don't," snapped Ivo.

Brand gave him another hard look. "By the gods, you're a prick tonight. What's wrong with you?"

"Nothing," Ivo growled, then, "I don't know. Something's in the air. Can't you feel it?"

Brand cocked his head, as if trying to sense whatever it was Ivo felt. "A storm, perhaps."

"No. 'Tis more than that. 'Tis . . . Aargh. I don't know. She just . . ."

"Balls," said Brand. "She is getting to you. You'd better stay away from her tonight."

"I stay away from her every night." *While Brand trotted off to enjoy his time with Merewyn.* He'd seen them together, so easy with each other while he and Alaida . . . Ivo gestured ahead to the narrow track that veered off toward the little cottage. "There is your path to madness. Give her my greetings and enjoy your wooing."

"I'm *not* wooing her," repeated Brand testily, and then, because Ivo had tweaked him, "Enjoy not bedding your wife."

"Impossible," said Ivo as he wheeled Fax toward Alnwick. "As I suspect you will soon discover."

Brand watched Ivo go with a sense of foreboding. There was trouble brewing there. He should probably ride back with him, as much to keep him from thrashing one of the men again as to stand between him and Alaida.

But it was just a little way to Merewyn's, and he'd been looking forward to this visit all day—all that he'd been human anyway. Besides, he didn't want to deal with Ivo right now, any more than Ivo wanted to deal with him.

He would stop by just for a little, give Merewyn the thymel, share that cup of ale with her, then go see to his friend. Supper always dragged out at the manor. There would be plenty of time to get back before they would be alone. Before they could get into trouble.

He turned toward Merewyn's hut, smiling. *Aye. Plenty of time.*

CHAPTER 19

BRAND WAS RIGHT, Ivo concluded by the time he handed Fax over to the new boy. He was being a prick, and no wonder, considering his was so constantly on his mind.

It was this ache, there every night, even when he stayed away from her, even when he took care of himself. It had eased for a time, but worsened in the last week, since Alaida had learned she could bedevil him. He had grown to both anticipate and dread her little forays into seduction. There was nothing quite so enchanting as a woman offering herself, nor quite so torturous as not being able to take her offer.

But just because Alaida enjoyed torturing him didn't mean Merewyn was out to seduce Brand. And certainly, if he could keep his hands off Alaida all this time, Brand could keep his off Merewyn during his occasional, brief visits.

Aye, he'd been a prick, and he must make amends—but later. For now, he had to get through another evening with his lady wife. He wondered what painful joy she would have for him tonight.

He went inside, spoke briefly to Geoff, and found a corner where he could read Ari's message. He'd just finished it when Tom approached. "*Monseigneur.*"

Ivo tossed the scrap of parchment into the fire. "Thomas. Did Oswald work you hard today?"

"I do ache, my lord. Lady Alaida said when you had read your message to ask you please to come to the solar. She wishes a word."

And so the torture began. "Very well. See my mail is sanded and oiled tomorrow."

"Yes, my lord."

He gathered his fortitude before heading up, but when he pushed the door open, the sight of Alaida sitting in an oblong wooden tub before the fire brought him to a stunned halt.

"Ah, my lord. I did not think you would be so quick. Bôte." She rose, water streaming over those rich curves he so longed to touch, and in the instant before the nurse wrapped a towel around her, he glimpsed every damp, naked inch of her, from the coil of coppery braids on her head to the matching curls between her legs. "Shut the door, if you please, my lord."

He slammed the door and turned away, his blood pounding. "Your pardon. I should have knocked."

"Nonsense. My body is yours, husband."

Frey's pillock. She should be working for William of Eu. He took a couple of deep breaths to settle himself. "What was it you wished to see me about?"

"This and that. One moment."

He tried staring at the door, but that didn't work, so he closed his eyes, and that was even worse. She was naked and someone was rubbing a towel all over her. The fact that it was her old nurse didn't make much difference to his imagination or to his desire to take over the duty. Definitely the hall for him tonight.

"There we are," said Bôte at last. "You may turn around, my lord."

As he did, Alaida put a knot in the belt to a heavy green

robe and stepped into a pair of matching slippers. "Have the tub taken away, Bôte."

"Perhaps his lordship would like a bath before we empty it," suggested the nurse. She turned to Ivo. "'Twould be a shame to waste the water, my lord."

It sounded good, but hardly wise, considering Alaida's recent mood and his current state. He shook his head. "My wife has business with me."

"I can talk while you bathe, my lord," offered Alaida. "Or it can wait if you would rather."

"The laundress is below," said Bôte. "She can wash you while we tend my lady."

The two of them looked at him expectantly. He needed a bath, and they all three knew it. A normal husband would accept the offer—and why shouldn't he? The laundress would be there, plus Alaida's women. Three people in the room besides him and his wife would surely be enough.

"Fine, then. A bath."

Orders were given and the laundress and fresh hot water summoned, and a little later Ivo had managed to calm down enough to strip and was having his back scrubbed by a practiced hand. A strong hand. "God's knees, woman, leave the skin."

The laundress's laugh matched her hands, rough and hearty. "Sorry, my lord. Is that better?"

"Aye. Much." He sighed as the tension seeped out of his shoulders and looked to where Alaida sat, having her hair taken down. *Like a normal husband,* he told himself. "Now, what was it you wanted to discuss, sweet leaf?"

"May Day, my lord. As you know, it—Hadwisa, pour me some wine. Would you like some, my lord?"

"Fine," he said, and a cup was placed in his hand. He took a deep drink and hunched forward for the laundress to scrub his lower back. "What about May Day?"

"We have certain traditions here at Alnwick, and I was wondering if you—" She stopped again, interrupted by a knock at the door. "Get that, Hadwisa."

The maid cracked the door. "Your supper, my lady."

"Ah, good. Have them bring it in."

Servants started filing in, carrying chairs and cloths and bowls and trenchers and arranging things for a meal. Ivo dropped a small towel over his crotch to cover himself. "What the devil is going on?"

"I am supping in chamber tonight, my lord," said Alaida.

Ivo eyed the table doubtfully. "That's a great deal of food for one woman."

"I took the liberty of having them bring your meal as well." She waved one of the servants over and tore a leg off the chicken the man carried. "Pardon if I begin without you, my lord. I am starving. Would you like more wine?"

He hesitated, but she didn't look too dangerous, sitting there clutching a chicken leg with her braids half-undone, so he said yes. A little later, when the laundress asked if she should wash his head now, he drained his cup, leaned back, and said, "I expect to have some hair left when you finish," and enjoyed the woman's chuckle.

It truly was bliss, Ivo thought, having his hair washed in a warm bath in a warm room instead of shoving his head in a horse trough. He relaxed into it, easing back against the padded edge of the tub and closing his eyes against dripping soap as servants continued to move around the room. He really was just a normal husband taking a normal bath.

"Rinse, my lord."

He tipped forward while the woman ladled water over his head, then leaned back for a second soaping. She took longer with this one, massaging him into a stupor with those strong laundress hands. The murmur of conversation between Alaida and her women as they groomed her lulled him like a song, and the wine wended its way through his blood. He began to drift.

He didn't notice when things changed, just, slowly, that they had. The conversation had trailed off to nothing, the room gone silent, the hands grown gentler. Smaller. Oh, no. "Alaida?"

"Here, my lord," she whispered at his ear, and he knew

even before her soapy hands slid around his neck that he was lost.

HE WILL NOT be able to deny you.

And he couldn't. From before the first touch, he was hers.

Alaida held the power of that promise in her heart as Ivo's muscles went taut beneath her hands. Before he could think to escape, she curled over his shoulder and kissed him, not demanding anything yet, just reminding him. He could not deny her.

He tugged his towel over his lap. "Where are your women?"

"Gone. You taste of soap," she said softly. "Rinse."

He ducked under the water once, then again, and when he came up, she shifted around to the side of the tub and kissed him through the streaming water, another reminder. "Better."

"Call them back," he said. His hands curled over the edge of the tub as he fought, but it was no use.

"No." Meeting his eyes, she untied her robe and let it fall open. She had nothing beneath, and she knew the power of her ripening body. The power of Eve. "Touch me."

The tub groaned as he tensed, pulling against the wooden staves as if they could save him. Foolish man. She was the only thing that could save him, and she was Temptation. She leaned forward to drag one nipple over the backs of his fingers until it puckered, then shifted for the other simply because it felt good.

This time the groan that rose up was his. She leaned forward and caught the sound in a kiss, taking in its power and adding it to her own. "Touch me."

He shook his head. "No. God's knees, Alaida, I—"

She reminded him again, this time more firmly, demanding that he part his lips to her. She swept her tongue into his mouth, using every skill she had to show him how much she wanted him, to make him recall how much he wanted her.

He cupped her head between both hands and pulled her away. "I said no, Alaida."

"And I say yes. You have avoided me too long, husband." She shrugged away the robe, accepting the harsh intake of his breath as tribute. He moved to rise, and she put her hands in the middle of his chest and pushed him back. She dipped one hand down into the water, pushed his towel aside, and curved her fingers around his hardness. "You want me, and here is my proof. You cannot deny it. You cannot deny me."

"You don't understand," he began.

She moved her hand and felt him jump as his breath hissed. "I understand this. Kiss me." A stroke. "Kiss me." Another stroke. "Kiss—"

And suddenly he was there, his lips on hers, his hands wandering over her shoulders and arms. One found her breast, thumbing across the tip she had already made sensitive until she gasped. The other slid down to where her hand held him, curled around her fingers, and began guiding her motions.

He began to buck and tense, and suddenly she understood what he was doing. "No." She jerked her hand away angrily. "No. Not that way. In me."

His eyes were wild, his voice stark. "Alaida, I cannot."

"You can." In one swift motion she slipped over the edge of the tub and onto his lap, straddling him there, trapping him with her body. His hardness called to the rising wildness within her. She moved and he groaned.

"Take me." A whispered command.

"Ah, woman, you do not know what you ask." He gripped her waist, but he didn't push her away though she knew that he could have easily. He would have, too, any other time, but tonight Merewyn's magic stayed him.

"I ask only for what is mine." She moved, just a little, not wanting to push him over the edge, but needing the feel of him against her, all heat and man and soap-slick water. "I ask for you."

She leaned forward to brush her breasts against his pale

skin and he pulsed against her. Enthralled, she began to kiss
him and touch him, running her hands over every inch of
skin she could reach, just to learn what else would make
him do that: a tonguing kiss. Touching his nipples, as small
and flat as they were. Brushing the skin low on his belly
with her fingertips. Reaching back to cup him. Slowly, she
discovered his weaknesses and used them to demand his
surrender the way he'd once demanded hers.

"Touch me," she whispered once more when she thought
he was ready, and with a harsh sigh, he yielded. His hands
glided over her wet skin, gathered her breasts to bring them
to his lips. Her breath caught on a moan, and he slipped one
hand between their bodies to stroke her. The first spasm
swelled within her. She pulled his hand away. "No. I told
you. In me. *In* me."

He tried one last time to refuse, but she was too far gone
to listen. With a moan, she rose up, shifted over him, and
slid home. She broke as he entered her, the pleasure he'd
started with his hand catching her before she was even full
with him. Ivo groaned again, lifting into her and holding
himself deep within while she pulsed and shook over him.
But even as the shuddering peaked, she knew he still held
himself back, that he hadn't joined her and that there was
more for her as well. She began to move, riding him, taking
him as he refused to take her. The tension climbed in her
again, even sharper. He began to shake beneath her.

"Stop. Alaida. *Please.*"

She knew that plea. She recognized it from their wedding night, when she hadn't known better. Now she understood, and it excited her, pushed her closer to that place
again. His fingers bit into her hips with a final effort to control her, perhaps to stop her, but she bore down, searching
for the pleasure, and finally, he gave in and met her. His hips
bucked and lifted as he pulled her down onto him, muscles
tightening in rhythm. *Almost. Almost. Almost.* And then she
was there and he was with her, and she closed her eyes and
gave herself over to the magic.

* * *

NOT YET. NOT yet. Alaida's heat enveloped Ivo like a wave, and she shattered in his hands, arching back and curling forward, her body pulling in on itself, tightening senselessly around him as she gasped out her pleasure. He held back as long as he could, but his own release surged up to follow hers. With a shout of desperation, he found one last fragment of control and lifted her up and off, setting her away to spend himself into the water.

"No. No. You weren't to deny me." She collapsed against him, shaking, as he finished. "You weren't."

"*Shh*, sweet leaf. I find I can deny you very little. Give me this." He gathered her close and pressed kisses to her hair, her neck, whatever he could reach, as he murmured, "If only you could understand."

She found herself more quickly than he thought possible and pushed upright to meet his eyes. "I tire of hearing that. I tire of all of it. And I understand more than you think, my lord." The flush of pleasure on her cheeks deepened into the red of anger. "I understand you wasted your seed for no good reason."

"It was not a waste, sweet leaf. I took as much pleasure as you." And protected her in the bargain, he thought, grateful to whatever god had lent him that final bit of strength. "And I have reason enough."

"*Phfft.* Your reason is an ass, m'lord, and blind to boot." She struggled to her feet, wobbly from using him, and stood over him streaming water from her naked body like one of Ægir's daughters. "Look at me."

He could hardly do otherwise, considering how she straddled him. By the gods, he could dive into that quaint and not come up for a year.

"You have not enjoyed my body for some months, *monseigneur,* but is this truly what you remember of it?" She cupped her hands over her breasts. "Do you recall me being so big here?" She ran them down over her waist. "Or here?"

Lower, cradling her belly. "Or here? Or do you think I merely grow fat?"

His stomach twisted into a cold knot as he saw what he'd missed in the blindness of his lust. Breasts swelled, waist gone thick, belly just beginning to round. *Odin, help us both.* "You're with child."

"So I am. Here you played monk when you could have used me without further risk." She stepped out of the tub and found a towel. "As I said, I understand well enough." Snatching up her robe, she stalked off someplace out of his sight, muttering evilness against him.

Ivo sank down in the water, his hands pressed to his head to keep it from bursting. He'd told Brand she might be breeding, but he'd never truly believed it. When the weeks had passed with no word from her, he'd been sure they'd escaped the threat.

But they hadn't. There was a child, and somehow he had to help it and Alaida—especially Alaida—survive. Silently, he began to call on every god and goddess he knew who might help her, even the Christian one and his son and their thousand saints. Please. *Please.*

After a long while, quiet footsteps drew him out of his prayers. He cracked his eyelids to find Alaida standing beside the tub. She unfolded a towel and held it wide for him. "Come out before you catch a chill."

A chill. She likely carried a monster in her belly and she was worried about his chill. With a sigh, he levered himself up. She wrapped the towel around his shoulders and began patting him dry. "Forgive me, *monseigneur*. That is not how I intended to tell you."

"There is nothing to forgive. It was . . ." He stroked a wisp of hair off her forehead, and she jerked her head away. "You should have told me sooner."

"I only grew certain in the last fortnight. It had just been the one night, and I didn't think . . ." She handed him the towel to dry his hair and went to fetch his fresh linens. "I doubt even Bôte realizes I caught so quickly." She paused,

staring at the bed. "She still believes we have been lying together as man and wife. As do the others, I think."

Balls. *She* was trying to reassure *him*. It should be the
other way around; he was the husband here, though a poor
one. He twisted the towel around his hips and went to stand
behind her. Tentatively, he brushed her hair off the nape of
her neck and, when she didn't draw away this time, kissed
her there.

"For what little it is worth, I sought only to protect you."

"From a babe?" She turned and smiled up to him, innocent of what was to come, and rested a hand on her belly. "A
child is a blessing, my lord, not something to fear—though
I know you do not want it." Her smiled faded. "What I am
unsure of is whether it is a child you do not want, or only a
child from *me*."

By the gods, there was too much on this woman's slim
shoulders, and every stone of it his fault. He could at least
ease part of her burden, and best of all, he could do it with
the truth. "There is no woman I would rather have a child
with, Alaida. Not in the whole of England."

He pressed kisses over her face, tasting salt as tears began to leak from beneath her closed eyelids. "Ah, sweet leaf.
Don't cry."

"I'm sorry, my lord. I know you don't like tears," she
sniffled, swiping at her cheeks with her palm. "At least these
are glad ones."

With a rueful laugh, he wrapped his arms around her.
"Then cry them, for I would have you glad of something, at
least."

"Glad or sad, I have little choice." She wiped her cheeks
again and heaved a shuddering sigh against his chest. "I
have been crying for weeks now. Blame your son, and feel
fortunate you have missed most of them."

His heart leapt despite himself. "A son? You know this?"

"No, but surely it must be, to crawl into my womb so
willingly." She grinned crookedly, still weeping a little. "I
am told men like it there."

"*I* do," he assured her, not certain if she was joking but

not willing to upset her if she was not. If he could help it, he would never needlessly upset her again. She would have enough to face without him adding to her pain.

"I am also told that a boy child turns a woman more lustful with each passing day." Now that *was* mischief in her eye, bright behind the remains of the tears.

"And is that true of you?" he asked carefully.

"Aye, unfortunately," she said, threading her arms around his waist. "Or perhaps not so unfortunately?"

God's knees. Perhaps it *was* a boy. "When did you grow so bold, wife?"

"It was necessity, my lord. I have had a reluctant husband, though I hope that ends now." She pressed a kiss to his chest. "You no longer need avoid me, my lord. What is done, is done, and we may as well take our pleasure with each other."

Ivo looked down at her, unsure how to respond. The horror of what might be coming sat heavily on him, but there was naught he could do right now but keep Alaida happy and make the next few months pass easily for her so she might have the strength to deal with what came after. Apparently, it would make her happy to have him in her bed—and truly, there was no more damage to be done. But could he do it?

"Do not deny me." She leaned back to look up at him and fitted her hips to his groin, as bold as any dockside whore. His body jumped beneath the towel. He could do it.

"A man would have to be a eunuch to deny you. Or mad."

"Which are you, my lord?"

"Neither." *For her*, he told himself. He pulled away the towel and backed her onto the bed, determined to do his best by his lady wife. He owed her that much and more. "And 'tis Ivo."

IVO SLIPPED OUT of the hall a bit later than usual. He'd barely rounded the corner headed for the stable when something picked him up, slammed him against the adjacent wall, and held him there, his toes a good foot off the ground.

"Are you mad?" Brand's voice was a savage growl in Ivo's ear. "By the gods, I ought to cut it off and nail it to her door to remind you." He bounced Ivo against the wall once more, just to knock the rest of the air out of him, then dropped him in a heap.

"Heh," said Ivo, lacking wind for more.

"I *saw* you," Brand hissed down at him between clenched teeth. "I came up and started to push the door open, and there you were on top of her. It was all I could do not to walk in and pour a bucket of water over you like the dog you are. And you had the balls to warn me off Merewyn."

"She ..." Ivo gulped down another breath and pushed himself up. "She's with child."

Brand froze, the same look on his face that Ivo knew had been on his own. "She what?"

"She's with child. Now come. We will discuss this where there aren't so many ears."

They retrieved their horses and rode out in silence, and when they were far enough from the wall, Brand said, "After so long, I didn't think . . ."

"Nor did I. Apparently the moon was with her after all."

"Balls. What are we going to do?"

"I don't know." Ivo had forced the whole mess out of his mind while he'd lain with Alaida; now it came rushing back. If Ari was right, in a few months they would have to figure out how to care for an infant who could fly. He remembered one day early on when sunset had caught him a hundred feet off the ground. He'd snagged a branch on the way down, but the vision of a child tumbling that far nearly made him vomit from the saddle. "Maybe we can find another witch, a white witch, to remove—"

"I've tried other witches. None of them are white," said Brand curtly. "They all have souls black as this bird. What about one of their priests?"

"Who, Theobald?" Ivo asked, and Brand snorted. "Exactly. Besides, they burn what they see as evil, and I have no desire to see if we can die by fire." He glared at the bird, "Call another vision. Ask for guidance this time."

"They don't always come when he calls them," reminded Brand. "What will we do while we wait?"

"What choice do we have? We will live our cursed lives as best we can, and I'll do what I can to keep Alaida safe and happy."

There was a pause before Brand asked, "Keeping her safe tonight, were you?"

Ivo glanced at him, saw the glint of a smile, and felt a wash of gratitude at his understanding and forgiveness. "No. That was the happy part."

"Well, it can't do any harm at this point. You may as well enjoy her while you can."

They rode on in silence. The forest grew thicker around them, dimming the gray light of the approaching dawn, though the birds chirruped and trilled around them.

"Have you ever heard that a male child makes a woman more . . . willing?" asked Ivo as they neared the spot where he would leave Brand.

"No." His friend twisted in his saddle and studied him keenly. "Balls. I think a part of you is happy for this."

"After three months denying myself? Aye, a part of me is *very* happy." Ivo reined Fax to a halt at the edge of the grove where the bear would prowl that day. "But I would gladly let you cut that part off if it would make things right for her."

Brand slid off Kraken, quickly stripped, and tied his clothes behind the saddle. As Ivo rode away, he called after him, "If it would make things right for her, I'd cut off my own."

"I know," said Ivo, grateful that he had such a friend.

CHAPTER 20

"NO MORE."

Exhausted, Ari plunged his hand into the blood-reddened water and held it there as he looked to the eagle sitting on the dead tree across the pond.

"I cannot do this more. I'm spilling too much blood." He groaned as the sting of the water worked its way past the numbness brought by his entreaties. "I'm sorry, my friend, they will not speak, and I'm no use to either of you if I cannot stay upright. It ends for now."

The eagle stared with those golden-brown eyes, so unlike Ivo's, blinked that strange front-to-back blink, then leapt into the sky and streaked toward Alnwick. Wincing, Ari reached for the clean strip of cloth he'd laid nearby. He had called the visions every day for nearly a month now, and his palm was striped with fresh cuts and fading scars. His constant bandage was raising questions in the hall, and the drain of bleeding so much and so often had turned his limbs to lead. He needed time to rest and regain his strength before he approached the gods again.

He struggled to his feet and went to his horse. The animal seemed to have grown immense while he bled. Swearing, he lifted his leaden foot into the stirrup, took a deep breath, and hoisted himself up, grunting as he had to pull with his bad hand. A nap, that's what he needed. A long nap, a good meal, and a sennight without laying his veins open. With a sigh, he turned his mount toward Alnwick.

THIS ONE HAD even more magic about him than his friends.

Merewyn stood in the thick shelter of a willow and watched the seneschal ride away. She knew Sir Ari from the village, having seen him from a distance as he oversaw the building of the castle mound. Today, she had come upon him as he'd knelt, bleeding and calling to the gods, and watched silently from the green shadows as his efforts failed. *A seer who could not see, and who spoke to an eagle as to a friend. Very strange.*

She added these new tidbits to what she knew of Sir Brand and his friends. Their odd comings and goings continued, despite the ever-shorter nights and the child, which was now common knowledge. A few well-placed questions had told her that none in the village or manor had seen Lord Ivo or Brand by day, nor this Sir Ari by night.

Nearly as strange, though, was how few seemed troubled by that. The village was thriving, the folk were happy at the prospect of a strong castle to defend them, and all three men were known as generous and fair-handed. Most believed that Lord Ivo and Brand hunted a great deal—though seldom successfully—and that Sir Ari's nightly absence could be attributed to some whore in Lesbury. So long as things continued well and Lady Alaida stood by her husband, there would be little reason to question those beliefs.

Yet what Merewyn had seen today spoke of some deep trouble. The seneschal's efforts had bordered on desperation; he had poured so much blood into the water that she would not want to harvest herbs from the pool's edge for a good while.

And who was the "she" he was trying to help? Surely

some Lesbury whore was not worth the expenditure of all that blood-magic. But who? And why?

Her morning's picking ruined and her mind awhirl, Merewyn turned back toward home. As she walked, images floated past her inner eye: knife, blood, eagle, Lord Ivo, raven, Brand, the lady, love potion, Sir Ari, pond . . . They jumbled together, dark and troubling. And over them, the lady's voice asked, "Can you help me? Will you?"

Here might be the purpose she'd been seeking all this time, the reason the gods had led Sir Brand to her door. They had surely set her in Sir Ari's way today to put her more firmly on that path, as clear a message as they could give without pouring a true vision into her mind. As Merewyn absorbed this possibility, the clouds overhead suddenly parted, shooting a beam of light down through the tall trees to gild a woodland rowan, its branches thick with still-green berries.

"Yes, Mother," said Merewyn. She dropped to her knees in the patch of gold before the sacred tree and raised her palms into the light, surrendering. "As always, I obey. But first, if you please, show me the rest, that I may understand and better follow your will. So mote it be."

". . . AND THE DUKE married the washerwoman, though she was not of noble blood, and she bore him a son who grew to be even greater than his father. But that is a tale for another day."

"Well done, Thomas!" Alaida and the others clapped appreciatively as Tom finished. "If I had known you were such a fine storyteller, I would have claimed your services long ago, and my lord would not have a squire."

"Hey," protested Ivo from where he sat shirtless on a cushion at her feet.

"Then I'm glad you did not know, my lady," said Tom, flushing with pleasure. "I fear 'tis not my own tale, though. I got it from Sir Ari."

"Wherever it comes from, you told it well," said Alaida.

"You haven't been hounding the seneschal, have you, boy?" asked Oswald. He moved a stone on the Morris board.

"No, Marshal. I merely listen when he's about. He is nearly always telling some tale or other."

"Nearly always talking, you mean." Ivo countered Oswald's move and took a piece. "Keep listening to him, Tom. I like a good tale nearly as well as your lady does."

"'Twas only to please her that I learned that one, my lord," he confessed. "But I learn other things from listening. And not only to Sir Ari."

"As you should. Marshal, what work do you have planned for young Tom tomorrow?"

"He'll be running the hill, my lord." Oswald looked Tom up and down. "Twice. In mail."

Tom's groan was barely audible, but Ivo laughed. "Go on to bed, then. You'll need the rest." He glanced up at Alaida. "As do you, my lady wife."

"Come along, you lot." Oswald scooped up the Morris board and stones, and he and the others followed Tom out, offering their "God's rests" as they went. Only Bôte lingered to turn back the furs and fuss over the tray that Hadwisa had carried up earlier, slicing bread and spreading butter.

"Ach. That lazy thing." She lifted a clay jar and clattered around in it with a spoon. "The honey's gone hard as stone, and Hadwisa did naught about it. I'll tell her to bring up better."

"Just put it by the fire," said Alaida. "It will soften long before Hadwisa straggles back upstairs."

"Aye, I suppose it will, at that." Bôte set the little clay jar at the edge of the coals and straightened with a grunt. "Don't leave it too long, lamb, lest it boil."

"We won't," said Alaida. "God's rest, Nurse."

"And you, my lady. My lord."

As the door shut behind her, Ivo shifted up onto his knees, so his eyes were nearly even with Alaida's.

"You're doing well with Tom," he said. "There's less of the stable in him every day."

"He would still embarrass you at court," said Alaida. "But given time, he'll serve. He's as quick as his father, and if you're lucky, he'll prove just as brave."

Ivo's brow creased. "Oswald said he's a bastard and an orphan."

"He is. But 'tis clear who his father is. Was, I mean."

"Oh? And who is—*was* that?" he teased.

"Merewyn's husband. Aelfwine." She pursed her lips at Ivo's dubious expression. "Tom is the very image of him, down to the way he walks. Even Merewyn sees it—perhaps especially her."

"What do you mean?"

"She never had a child of her own. I was too young to know, but Bôte said that's why Aelfwine turned to other women. Tom's mother was one of them."

"Merewyn mentioned her husband dying, once when I stopped with Brand. What happened?"

"It was four, no, five years ago. I had just come back from fostering at Bamburgh. A dog attacked a flock of our sheep on Swinlees. Aelfwine heard and ran to help the shepherd. Both were bitten, not badly, but . . ."

"It was mad," said Ivo quietly.

She nodded, lost in the memory. "Bôte and Merewyn worked so hard, and we all prayed, of course, but they both died of the mad fever within the month."

"A terrible death."

"And a terrible loss for the village: Merewyn and Ebba widowed, six children left with no father—and young Tom left with no one at all. His mother was already gone. Grandfather took pity."

"That's how he came to work in the stable?"

She nodded. "And how I ended up with Hadwisa. She was the oldest of Will Shepherd's children. They needed her wage to eat."

Ivo's eyes brightened. "Aah. *That* explains much."

"About what?"

"About why you're so easy on the girl. She needs a firmer hand. You tolerate from her what you do not from the others, even from Bôte."

Alaida sat back, frowning at him. "Perhaps you are correct."

"Perhaps?"

"Oh, all right. You are correct. But I do tolerate much from Bôte as well."

"Too much, even if she was your nurse."

"How can I scold the woman who wiped my tears?" she demanded. "And what about you? You tolerate just as much from Sir Ari. He vanishes every night to go off whoring and you say nothing."

"Whoring? Is that what he's doing?" Amusement twinkled in his eyes as he said with all innocence, "I did not know there were whores among the good women of Alnwick."

"Why? Are you looking for one?"

"I am not," he said firmly. "Besides, when would I have time for one? Or energy?"

"*Phfft.*" She pushed away the hand he'd slid up to cup her breast. "He has a woman in Lesbury, Bôte says."

"Ah, Lesbury. I knew it couldn't be Alnwick." His hand slipped back and she left it, enjoying the warmth.

"You should make him stay here, my lord, to amuse you, if nothing else. He does tell good tales, the few times I've been able to corner him into telling one."

"I've heard them all." He tugged at the edge of her robe to expose the upper curve of one breast and leaned forward to place a lingering kiss there. "Besides, I prefer the amusements *you* offer."

"But he—"

"Enough, Alaida." His voice was calm, but when he raised his head, his eyes sparked with warning. "Ari's nights are his own."

"Ah, yes. Like your days, *monseigneur*." Angry, she pushed to her feet and stepped around him.

Behind her, he sighed. "Do not do this, Alaida. Things are as they are."

She turned, ready to snap at him, but stopped. He suddenly looked so worn, so alone, staring off into the fire like that. "If you would just tell me why, perhaps I could . . ."

"It would not make things different. Leave it. Please."

Please? In all this time, he had never once said *please*, not about this, and her anger softened at the hopeless sound of the word. "I will leave it for now, my lord, but I cannot promise it will not come to mind again."

"Then 'for now' will have to do." He glanced up, some small measure of his humor back. "For now."

She ruffled his hair gently. "Pax? I would come down and offer a kiss as pledge, my lord, but I fear you would find too much merriment in watching me get back up again."

He sprang up before she finished the sentence and held his arms wide. "Never let it be said I make it hard for my wife to kiss me."

She went to him willingly, so happy his strange melancholy had vanished that she didn't even remind him that, not so long ago, he had made it very difficult indeed. But that was the past and this was the present, and the kiss they shared was tender and undemanding and full of forgiveness that flowed in both directions.

"You do look tired," he said a long moment later as he held her.

"No more than I am any night." She leaned back in his arms to look up at him and caught the smell of the warming honey, drifting up from the hearth. "But I am hungrier."

"Go to bed. I'll bring you your bread."

She had taken to having a slice of bread with honey every night before retiring. It kept her from waking at midnight, ravenous, and seemed to ease the sick stomach. As Ivo retrieved the honey from the hearth, she laid aside her robe and slipped into bed, pulling the covers up to hide her ever-growing belly.

"I think we left it too long," he said, holding up the spoon. The warm honey ran off in a thin stream.

"It will be fine. Two slices, please."

"Two? You *are* hungry." He quickly spread the honey over three slices and carried them over, offering her one, keeping one for himself, and holding the extra. As he ate, the second piece tilted a little, and honey ran over his fingers.

"Here." Alaida gobbled down her first piece and reached for the second before Ivo was half done. She licked off the edges and took a bite. "You're getting all sticky."

"So are you." He gestured as a drizzle she'd missed landed in a warm stream on her breast, just above the covers. "We're going to have to wash again."

They sat there, finishing their bread, holding their sticky hands up to keep the linens clean. As Alaida came to the last bites, the imp that so frequently got her in trouble poked her with his fork.

"You know," she said lightly, "the best way to get honey off skin is to lick it away."

"Is it?" A slow, wicked grin spread over his face. He held out his honey-covered fingers. "Show me."

Suddenly embarrassed by her brazenness, she took only a tentative lick.

"You'll have to do better than that," he challenged.

She drew his finger into her mouth, sucking it like a sweet. He groaned, and her embarrassment melted away in the heat that flamed up between them. She moved to the next finger, then the next, finishing one hand, then the other, taking her time over each finger until the honey was gone, even lapping the last traces off his palm before she sat back.

"See? All clean."

She raised the last bit to finish it, but he curled his still-damp fingers around her wrist and drew her hand toward him. Instead of stealing the bite, though, he dragged it down and touched it to his chest, so that a streak of honey spilled over his nipple. "I'm not convinced. Show me again."

She leaned forward, obediently, hungrily, and tongued away the sweetness, hearing him suck in his breath as she rasped over the tightening circle. By the time she sat back the second time, his arousal was evident. She popped the last bite of bread in her mouth and held out her hand. "Now clean me, if you please, *monseigneur*."

He obliged, taking even more time over her fingers than she had over his, until she could feel every suckle, every flicker of his tongue, in the center of her. Then he leaned forward to the drop on her breast. It had apparently run lower, as he worked the covers down to follow it over her nipple, cleaning it quite thoroughly before he finally stopped.

When she opened her eyes, he was smiling down at her in that hungry way of his. How that look had ever frightened her, she couldn't comprehend. Now it only summoned her own rising appetites, wanton that she was. Wickedness lay in that smile. Sin that called her to sin with him.

Without a word, he rose and stripped out of his braies, then walked over to the table to pick up the pot of honey.

"What are you doing?"

He didn't answer, but he came back and crawled up on the bed beside her, the honey in one hand. He stirred the honey, the spoon making a soft stutter across the bottom of the pot. "Lie back."

She did, but asked again, "What *are* you doing?"

"I wish to discover something," he said.

"What?"

"Uncover yourself, sweet leaf. I want to see all of you."

She obeyed once more. He shifted to kneel between her legs, nudging them wide apart, and she felt herself blush at the way he devoured her with his eyes. Stirring the honey once more, he held the jar over her belly and lifted the spoon.

Honey, still warm and thin from the fire, cascaded down over her belly. She gasped as he trailed it up, tracing slow, liquid spirals around her breasts. He took another spoonful and worked his way down this time, and she gasped again as the warm honey spilled between her legs. She trembled there before him, already on the edge of pleasure even without him touching her.

"I wish to discover," he finally explained as he set the jar aside and bent over her, "which is sweeter. You, or the honey."

"Oh," she said as he began to taste her. "*Oh.*"

It was a long time before he decided, and by then she was very, very clean.

The sheets, however, were not.

CHAPTER 21

SIR ARI WAS scribbling again.

Alaida stood on the landing and watched him hunch over the bound book that held his attention. He added to the volume often, but it wasn't the only writing he did. She often spied him late in the afternoon scratching furiously on a fragment of used parchment or a scrap of plain leather, or even, a few times, on a bit of wood or bark. Frequently, she spotted the same oddments later in her husband's hand or Sir Brand's, or saw one curling to ash in the fire—the only evidence she'd seen that Ari ever crossed paths with them at all.

She grew more curious about his writing by the day. It might, she suspected, have something to do with why her husband still was hers only during darkness—time which grew so short as summer neared that she barely saw him.

Not that Ivo didn't put their limited time to good use. She flushed just thinking of what he'd taught her over the last weeks—what he had done with that honey, for example, would likely send them both to Hell, and she would never be absolved because she had every intention of asking him to do it again someday. Someday soon, she resolved as she went all liquid just thinking of it.

She was still immersed in thoughts of honey when Ari noticed her. He immediately came to his feet. "Do you require something, my lady?"

"Mmm?" It took her a moment to come back from the heat, and she was sure Ari must see her high color from where he stood. "Oh, no, *messire*. I merely grow tired of the chatter." She motioned vaguely toward the solar, where a burst of derisive laughter interrupted Mildryth's complaints about her husband. "My head begins to ache from the noise. What do you write, *messire*?"

"A chronicle." He leaned down and blew gently over the lettering to encourage the ink to dry.

"A monk's duty."

He chuckled. "I assure you, I am no monk, my lady."

"So I've heard." She started down the stairs. "Read me a little and let me hear what you write."

Laying a square of fine kidskin over the page to protect the new ink, he closed the book firmly and pulled the straps tight before she could catch more than a glimpse of the text. "No, my lady. I would be ashamed, for you would see that I have no skill with words at all."

"*Phfft.* I hear you speak every day, sir, and you use words like a goldsmith uses his tools." That made him color, and she pressed on, teasing. "I could always *order* you to read."

He looked down at his book and back up at her, his face growing grave. "Please do not, my lady, for I would have to disobey."

His reluctance only increased her wish to see what he wrote, but it was clearly not going to happen today. "I only intended to persuade, *messire*, not command," she said lightly, pretending it was altogether unimportant. "If your story is so clumsy, you *should* keep it to yourself. Give me another in its place, though, for I grow bored with those the women tell."

His face eased, though he still rested one hand on his book as though he thought she might snatch it up. "Another dragon, my lady?"

"No, this time I think I would like some other monster. Perhaps a—"

"M'lady!" Tom came crashing through the door, wooden practice sword in hand, face flush with excitement. "There's a man at the gate. He says he's brought a message from the king!"

"Well, my lady," said Ari evenly as he scooped up his book to put it away. "It seems you will not need my story to ease your boredom after all."

WITH A MIX of curiosity and foreboding, Ivo took the folded parchment from the king's messenger and motioned for Brand to follow him upstairs.

Alaida rose as he entered, showing a belly that he could swear was bigger than it had been just that morning.

"Have you—?" She stopped as she saw the message in his hand. Her hands twisted together anxiously. "You have. He arrived just after dinner. What does it say?"

Ivo pressed a kiss to her cheek and smiled at her fretfulness. "And greetings to you, too, wife. Don't frown so. 'Tis only a message."

"From the king," she said with distaste. "Little good has ever come from that direction."

"I have had both good and bad from William," said Ivo. "Let me see which this is before you assume the worst. Go, begin supper. I will be down in a little."

He waited until the door closed behind her and her women before he popped the wax on the seal. The text inside was plainly written and direct, and Ivo frowned as he read it, hearing William's choleric stutter in each word. However, there were possibilities in what the king asked as well, and he considered them quickly. "Hmm."

"What?" asked Brand.

"Good and bad, as I told Alaida. There is more trouble in

Wales, plus he suspects that Roger of Poitou plans treason in Cumbria and orders me to look into it."

"Is that the good or the bad?"

"Both, I think. On the bad side, it will take me away now, just when Alaida and I finally have a true marriage. On the good, it will take us away *now* when the nights are so cursed short. She has begun questioning my habits again."

"Wonders why you barely get your clothes off before you start putting them on again, eh?"

"Something like that. I suppose Merewyn never questions why *you* visit at such odd hours."

"In truth, no. She just seems to . . . accept it, as she accepts everything."

Ivo thought that strange, but the healer was a little strange, so he let it drop.

"It solves another problem as well," he pointed out. "These woods are too small for a bear in summer."

Brand nodded. Summer had always been the worst time. The long warm hours brought mortals both common and noble streaming into the forest for timber and beeswax, game and berries, charcoal and wattling, and there were far too many hours of daylight in which to be seen. For Ivo the only real risk lay in being caught changing; for Brand, it was in being seen at all—there were no more bears in England.

"Cumbria has forests thick enough to lose entire armies," Ivo pointed out. "You will be safe there while I do my spying for the king, and by the time we get back, harvest will have started and only swineherds will be in the woods. I can keep them away from you."

"That would be good. But what about the third problem?" Brand curved his hand out over his gut to shape Alaida's belly. "You don't want to be away when the child comes. It will need you. *She* will need you."

"She is only"—Ivo ticked it off on his fingers—"a bit over four months gone now. We will be back in plenty of time, and maybe while we're gone, we will find something, learn something, have some new thought. I don't know. But it will be better than sitting here, useless, watching her swell."

Brand nodded in sympathy. "Aye. I watch her, too, and she isn't even mine. All the same, you'll find it difficult to tell her you're leaving. I remember how Ylfa used to look at me when I'd say we were going *a-viking* again—like I was either mad or already dead. And she'd cry."

"Alaida understands that I have a duty to the king. She expects it. She was raised with it."

"Ylfa understood, too. She still cried." Brand's brow furrowed momentarily with the recollection, but he shook it off. "What about Ari?"

Ivo glanced at the raven on his perch. "He stays here. This is his time to be most human. He may as well use it.

"Take care of her," he told the bird, glad that foolish jealousy no longer bubbled up at the idea of leaving him with Alaida. "Get the castle finished. I want her well protected when I truly must go."

The raven tipped his head and chortled softly.

"That's yes, I think," said Brand. "Balls. I'm not looking forward to a strange forest without even him for company. When do we need to leave?"

Ivo glanced back down at the message, at the urgency hidden beneath William's blunt words. "Before dawn."

"Which means we actually ride at sunset tomorrow. I will say my farewells to Merewyn then."

"Aye." Ivo nodded, wishing he had another day before he had to say his own farewells, before he had to make Alaida cry.

Then he started downstairs, because he didn't.

CHAPTER 22

IT WAS STRANGE how little the days had changed with Ivo gone, reflected Alaida as she watched Tom attack a straw man under Oswald's observant eye. The servants still went about their duties. The motte still climbed skyward. Her belly still swelled. And Ari still scribbled, though only in his book now, since there was no need to pass messages. Except that the manor's schedule had shifted back toward normal, every day simply rolled along the same as when Ivo was here.

Every *day*.

The nights were a different matter. It was then she felt his absence. The hall seemed empty with no lord at the table; her bed grew cold with no husband in it. But it was more than that. She missed him with an ache that went beyond Alnwick's need for a lord, and beyond her body's cravings for a husband's touch.

It had been nearly three months now, and she wanted Ivo home. She wanted to play chess with him, to share morsels at supper, to murmur nonsense back and forth in the dark, to fight with him, to hear him laugh with Brand. Anything. She wanted to know he was near, even if he was out doing his mysterious business all day and she could only see him by night.

Her hand rested on her belly, and she felt a tiny flutter, like a hummingbird beneath her palm. *That* was something that had changed. The babe had quickened not long after Ivo left, and every time it had moved since, she'd wished he were here to feel it with her. She wanted to watch his face when he did, to see if he wanted this child or not. The babe moved again, more restlessly, as though it read her thoughts.

"*I* want you, little bird," she soothed. "And your papa will, too, once he knows you. Never fear."

Alaida made her way to the *garderobe*, where she'd been headed on one of her ever-more-frequent visits before she'd let herself be distracted. Afterward, she stopped at the kitchen to check that the cook had the day's spices and to relieve the stores of an apple, then wandered back to the hall. Tom and Oswald had disappeared, and when she entered the hall, she was surprised to find Ari gone, too. His book, however, sat on the table.

She drifted over to look at it. The cover was plain but substantial—boiled leather tacked over boards, with sturdy straps to hold it closed—straps that weren't fastened right now. Tempting, to just ease it open . . . but she wouldn't.

"Where is Sir Ari?" she asked a passing varlet.

"Word came of a fight between two crews at the motte. Sir Ari and Oswald ran to see to it."

The man went on about his business, but the book whispered to her. A fight. They would be gone awhile.

She shouldn't, but . . . With a quick glance around, she lifted the cover.

She couldn't read a word.

Whatever Ari wrote, he did it in some strange hand, with spiky letters that looked vaguely familiar though they bore no resemblance to the Latin and French she knew. Disappointed, she turned another few pages to be sure, but found only the same odd markings.

Why he bothered to hide the book, she didn't know, for

surely no one here at Alnwick would be able to decipher it. The only thing she could comprehend at all were the tiny animals decorating the margins: a bear, a wolf, a raven—Brand's bird, she supposed—and what must be a lion. She found a stag on another page, along with a fearsome hound, a bull, and an eagle. Her eagle, perhaps, if this was a chronicle, or the one from Ivo's shield. She looked for her dragon.

Approaching voices drifted in the door. Guilt jolted her, and she flipped the book shut and hurried upstairs. Sir Ari was right to keep his chronicle in that strange script, she decided, to keep people like her from prying.

What she'd seen niggled at her, though, through supper and chess and right into bed. She was lying there behind the draperies, half-asleep, when her mind finally drifted to where she'd seen those animals before: some were the same as the beasts on the standing stone. Perhaps Ari had drawn what he'd seen, then added the others for his own amusement. Aye, that must be it.

Except for two things, her sleepy mind whispered: some of his letters were on the stone, too—the lightning bolt, the odd cross, the pitchfork.

And Ari hadn't been at the standing stone.

Suddenly she wasn't sleepy anymore.

ALAIDA WAS STILL mulling over what she'd seen some days later as she strolled through the tiny village market—not a proper market, for that would have to be chartered and taxed by the king, but the simple local trade of extra food and goods that sprung up at the crossroads like a *dent-de-lion* each year at the Feast of the Magdalen and again in the fall after harvest. She was hoping a clever hand had created some small token she could buy as a gift for Ivo on his return, to add to the new cloak she was embroidering for him. Nothing immediately drew her eye, but she laid down a half-penny for a bone flute and handed it to Tom.

"My thanks, my lady, but I do not play."

"Then learn," she ordered. "We need more music in the hall, and you need some way to entertain the ladies when you begin to travel with your knight. Esmund here can teach you—for a penny?"

"He'll be playing a simple tune by the end of the day, my lady," said Esmund, beaming. "Here, boy, let me show you."

She left Tom to his lesson and drifted along to where the next man had brought out what he'd carved over winter. She was admiring a cloak pin when she heard a familiar voice.

Alaida turned, smiling. "Merewyn. You've come to market."

"Aye, my lady. To see what I might get in trade for my cheeses." She tilted the basket at her hip to show off several wrapped and salted rounds. "I've still a few for the manor if you want them."

"I do, and we will have them all," said Alaida, motioning for one of the servants who followed her to collect the cheeses and for Geoff, who carried the manor purse, to pay. "Do we have leeks for a tart?"

"Yes, my lady."

"Good. That's what I want for supper. See to it, then you and the others may do as you will for a time. I wish to walk with Merewyn."

Merewyn slipped her coins into her purse and followed Alaida along the row until they left the market and its crowd behind.

"I have not seen you to thank you," said Alaida when they were alone. "Your potion worked as you said, and afterward all was easy between us."

"I am glad of it, my lady, but sad your lord husband had to leave so soon after."

"'Service to the king is the price of land'—or so I tell myself, little as it gladdens me."

"Lord Ivo will return well before the child comes," said Merewyn. "Did you have some question, my lady?"

Alaida sighed. "Many, but for today I wish to learn about the standing stone. What do you know of it?"

"'Tis very old, my lady, from the days when a monster roamed these lands."

"I know the story. What interests me is the marks on the stone. What are they?"

"Runes—a kind of writing the old ones used."

Alaida's hopes flared. "Can you read them?"

"Alas, no, though I do know their names and meanings in magic. In proper hands, they can reveal much of a man's fate. I use them, at times, though with less skill than my mother."

"Do you know anyone who *can* read them?"

Merewyn pondered a moment, then shook her head. Disappointed, Alaida pressed on. "What about the creatures carved with the runes?"

"My grandmother said they betoken the souls of those the monster destroyed. My lady, what brings this sudden curiosity?"

"I rode past the stone sometime back and it has been in my head. In my dreams. I thought perhaps you could settle my mind about it."

Merewyn frowned, clearly disturbed. "Beware, my lady. The stone possesses great binding magic—it must, to hold back a monster all these years. Do not let it touch you, lest it do you great harm."

Merewyn looked so worried that Alaida confessed. "In truth, 'tis not the stone that absorbs me, but Sir Ari's book." She glanced about to make certain no one was within hearing, then told the story quickly.

"Tell me the animals again, my lady," said Merewyn, and Alaida listed them off. "Are you certain he has never been to the stone?"

"No, but he did not go with me, and when I mentioned it, he said nothing."

"'Tis said the seneschal is a great storyteller. Perhaps he chronicles the tales he spins."

"I had not thought of that." Alaida considered a moment. "But you said the rune-writing was only used in the olden times."

"In England, my lady. I know nothing of how they write in other lands. I think you have let your imagination fly with you."

"Perhaps you are right. I felt such evil at the stone, and then to see the same marks in Sir Ari's writing . . ."

"'Tis natural enough, but truly, my lady, you cannot let yourself dwell on such dark matters. They will do you ill. Turn your mind to other, happier things, for the sake of yourself and your child." She set her basket on the grass and extended her open palms toward Alaida. "May I?"

Alaida nodded and stood while Merewyn's hands traveled over her taut belly. A profound peacefulness flowed into Alaida and sent the babe tumbling and thumping as if dancing, and a slow smile lit Merewyn's face.

"All is well." She gave Alaida a keen look. "Keep it so, my lady, I pray you."

"I shall," said Alaida, properly chided. "You have, indeed, given me ease. Now I must go, for I have much to do today before I sit down to my leek tart. Farewell, Healer."

"Farewell, my lady." Merewyn scooped up her basket and headed off toward her cottage.

Alaida turned toward the hall and the various duties that occupied the rest of her day, ate her leek tart for supper, and slept that night for the first time in several nights without thoughts of book or stone.

CHAPTER 23

ONE LAST TASK, Ivo told himself. One last message to deliver, and he could go home.

He approached the isolated hall carefully, his skin prickling with caution as he presented himself at the gate shortly after full dark. The guard quickly passed him into the yard, where he was greeted by a sow-bellied old knight whose legs bowed like they'd been formed 'round a barrel.

"Welcome to Ribbleswood, my lord. I am Godfrith, and this is my hall. Come. There is someone who wishes to meet you." He led the way around the hall proper to a second, smaller building and pushed the door open. "This is our chamber bower—a wedding gift to my young bride. You will have better privacy here. Join us in the hall when you finish." Godfrith backed out and pulled the door shut.

The man inside knelt. "Lord Ivo. I am Wakelin. You may remember me."

"You ride for de Jeune," said Ivo, motioning him to his feet.

Wakelin nodded. "My lord sends his greetings and asks if you ever killed that eagle."

"A wise man does not kill his wife's pet lightly."

"No, my lord," Wakelin said soberly.

Ivo pulled off his gloves. "You're married, I take it."

"I am, my lord, though I see her seldom. Do you have news for Lord Robert? He told me to say the redwing lost his voice."

"And the wren lost her wings," said Ivo, completing the pass code. He pulled the prepared message from his sleeve. After nearly two months in Wales leading William's forces to the hidden camps of outlaw lords, he'd spent a third month here watching Roger of Poitou, with no sign the man was doing anything other than minding his lands. William's suspicions that Roger and Dolfin Dunbar were plotting to restore Cumberland to the Scots had proved unfounded.

Wakelin tucked the message securely into his boot. "Lord Robert waits in London to carry this to the king in Normandy. Now, Sir Godfrith has held supper for us. We should join him."

"How is it this Godfrith provides refuge for us?" wondered Ivo aloud as he pulled open the door. "Doesn't he owe his lands to the Poitevin?"

"Aye, but his new wife is Lord Robert's niece."

"Ah. So, does he lay a good table?" asked Ivo.

"Not as good as yours, my lord, but better than most."

"Then it will be far better than what I've had these past months."

Godfrith's wife bore an unfortunate resemblance to her uncle, but her smile was genuine and her husband's table generous, as his belly should have made evident. By the time the bones were thrown to the dogs, Ivo had managed to fill a hollow under his belt that hadn't been filled since he left home. He leaned back, sated, and studied the men around him. They were a mixed bunch, some Norman, some English, and some few who looked like their fathers must have been raiding Scots or Danes.

Suddenly, he saw a familiar face, lurking at the back of the hall. "What's fitz Hubert doing here?"

Wakelin followed his eyes. "Lord Robert loaned him as part of Lady Ivetta's escort."

"Aye. Said I could keep him if I want," said Godfrith. "I haven't made up my mind yet."

With all three of them staring his way, Neville quickly realized they were talking about him. He glared at Ivo, eyes narrowed and lips drawn thin as a sword edge.

Godfrith was too pleasant a man—and his new wife too young a woman—to have Neville fitz Hubert poisoning his hall. Smiling evenly, Ivo pronounced each word so the weasel could read them over the chatter in the hall. "If you do keep him, *messire*, watch him closely and do not expect much in the way of courage."

Godfrith crinkled his brow into three deep furrows that made him look like a new-plowed field. "And you, Sir Wakelin. What say you on this?"

"That Lord Ivo gives good advice."

Godfrith's furrows deepened, then cleared as he made his decision. "Sir Neville, attend me."

Neville came to kneel before the high table. "Yes, my lord."

"I have decided to do without your services. You are free to leave with Sir Wakelin when he goes."

Ears flaming, Neville bowed his head. "Yes, my lord." When he rose, the venom in his look was not for Godfrith, but for Ivo.

It bothered Ivo not at all, and after a pleasant evening at Godfrith's table, he made his farewells, mounted Fax, and headed north and east. By dawn, Ribbleswood and Neville were far behind, and at sunset he continued onward, toward Brand and Alaida and home.

A SENNIGHT LATER, Ivo and Brand sat on the northern bank of the Aln looking at the stockaded motte across the way.

"You have a castle," said Brand.

"It still needs a tower, but Ari's done well." Ivo scanned

the night, seeking the black bird against the stars. "I wonder where he is. 'Twill look strange if you turn up without him."

"Probably hiding from owls." Brand stuck two fingers in his mouth and whistled, and a cry went up on the wall. "Your gatemen are awake."

"They'd better be."

They skirted the motte to see what they could by moonlight and were headed toward the gate when a flurry of wingbeats announced the raven. Brand stuck out his arm, and the bird soared down to a landing and sidestepped up onto his shoulder.

"Nice work," said Brand under his breath then louder, "God's beard, 'tis good to be back."

"Name yourselves," barked Oswald from the gate.

"What? Gone three month and forgotten already?" asked Ivo.

"My lord? Open the gate. Open the gate for Lord Ivo. Someone wake Lady Alaida."

"No, let her be," ordered Ivo.

The greetings in the yard were enthusiastic notwithstanding the late hour—well past midnight, despite the hard riding they'd done from their last camp. Geoffrey came stumbling out of the hall, groggy and disheveled, followed by Tom and a few others, but most of the men remained asleep. Ivo accepted brief accounts from his officers about what had happened during his absence, told them to hold the rest until the next evening, and excused himself. As he climbed the stairs, Tom handed Brand a horn of ale and everyone headed back to their blankets.

Pallets and sleeping women cluttered the solar floor where Alaida had surrounded herself again in his absence. Ivo picked his way through by the light of the little lamp on the table, stripped off all but his breeks, and tugged aside the bed curtains. The shadowy mound that was his wife moved restlessly in the bed, and her scent rose up and wrapped around him like silken ropes to pull him down next to her. She mumbled something, and he slipped his arm around her.

By the gods, she was huge! Her girth shocked him 'til he counted the time: over seven months gone now. Grown round with child, she was all soft and warm and sleepy in his arms. "Alaida?"

"*Mmm*. Ivo," she breathed.

Not 'my lord.' Ivo. Finally, Ivo. He pressed a tender kiss to the curve where her neck met her shoulder. "Yes, sweet leaf. Ivo. I've come home to you."

She sighed, a bone-deep sigh that echoed in Ivo's soul. Her hand found his and tugged it around, locking it between her breasts as if she would never let him go again, and he grew dizzy with the longing that had piled up on him the past weeks.

"I like this dream." She sounded intoxicated.

He *was* intoxicated, drunk on the scent and the feel and the heat that burned off her. "Not a dream. I am here with you."

He kissed her again, this time higher, behind her ear, and felt the shiver that ran down her spine. She stirred, curled down to kiss his fingertips there where she had his hand trapped, and as she did, her hips pressed back to touch him.

"*Mmm*." She squirmed a little, moving her bottom against him as she shifted her hand—his hand—over her breast. Bigger there, too, but not just bigger. More womanly. Even the peak felt different. He strummed over it until it puckered. Sudden awareness tensed her muscles as she came fully awake.

"You're home!" She twisted and flung herself on him, peppering kisses over his cheeks, his eyes, his chin before she settled on his mouth and their tongues tangled in greeting. Another of those soul-easing sighs warmed his face. "You are safe? Unhurt?"

"I am," he said. As if she didn't believe him, she ran her hands over him, checking: face, arms, thighs, belly, then boldly, his cock. "All of me," he said, muffling his laugh against her hair as he pulled her hand away. "Stop that. Your women are here."

She reached over him to yank the curtain shut, plunging them into darkness and muffling the sounds of snores from beyond. Her whisper was pure wickedness as she tongued the curve of his ear, "Then be quiet lest you wake them, for I will not stop 'til I am satisfied you are truly with me."

"Nor will I." With her. *In* her. That's all he wanted, to bury himself in her and know he was truly home. He drew his hands over her, learning her new shape.

"Now I *am* fat," she whispered against his ear. "You will never want me."

For answer, he took her hand and guided it back to his cock, straining against his breeks. With a tiny sound of delight, she explored him through the cloth, tracing the ridge with a fingernail. He choked back a groan and steered her fingers to his laces. Moments later he was free, the breeks lost somewhere at the bottom of the bed in the franticness of need.

She was too round for the usual way, so he stayed on his side and dragged her legs over his hips, drawing her close. He slipped his fingers down, found her slick and ready, and made her more so, until he couldn't bear it any longer. She understood, reached for him and shifted, and suddenly he was in her.

When they were locked together, the need eased and time slowed. She was his, laid out in the blackness where he could see her only with his hands. He explored her slowly, discovering this strange-yet-familiar body by feel alone, learning, remembering, reminding her what he had taught her on other nights.

She began to move, to stir like a restless sea, surging against him in waves of heat and scent that ripped him from his last moorings. He touched her again, found that favorite spot, and felt her tighten, tighten. The swift intake of her breath in the darkness told him she was there even before she arched beneath his hand. He pressed into her, letting her pleasure embrace him, until he spilled into her, his release as silent as hers as she welcomed him home.

A long time later, when he thought she slept, he reached down to find his breeks and worked them on beneath the covers.

"Where are you going?"

"Nothing has changed, sweet leaf. I still must be away by dawn."

Her accusing silence stung worse than words—he could have argued with words. As he worked the cloth around his laces, she reached over to tug the curtains open. A single wedge of light from the lamp fell across the bed.

"What are you doing?"

"I wish to see your face a moment," she whispered. "Move a little. Perfect." With him organized to her liking, she found his hand and drew it to her belly. "There. Now wait."

A chill settled over Ivo. He'd dreaded this moment and had been hoping he could somehow avoid it. But this was Alaida; she never let him avoid anything. It was all he could do not to pull away, in fear of what he might feel, but as he lay there with his hand curved over her, he schooled himself once again to respond as she needed.

"Wait. Ah, here." She moved his hand a few inches and pressed it flat. "Feel?"

Something round moved beneath his palm, shifting and rolling, alive. Even the threat of the curse faded in the wonder of such a thing, to feel a child move within a woman's womb. *His child.* The mound rolled past his palm again. He pressed a little harder, trying to discern what it was. "Is that the head?"

"Buttocks, I think," she said, and the smile he had thought would be difficult came to his face with ease at the idea of a bum so small. She reached over and stroked Ivo's cheek. "Ah, you do smile at him. I am glad."

"And I am glad you're glad," he said, speaking pure truth.

"Here." She guided his hand up near her ribs, where a harder oval stood out against the taut skin. "His foot."

He traced the outline. "'Tis so tiny. Are you sure?"

"Aye. He thinks my ribs exist solely for him to scratch his toe against." She yawned and slid around to settle her head on his shoulder, and he pulled her close. "Please stay, just this once. I would show you the tiny shirts I've made."

"Show me tonight. I'll be here as quickly as I can."

"I still do not understand these strange comings and goings."

"It is not important you understand them." That sounded harsher than he had intended, so he yielded what he could. "I can stay a moment longer, if it will please you."

"It will," she said with a sigh and wrapped her arms around him. "But only because it must."

THE EASTERN SKY was already brightening as Brand walked down into the dene where the bear would spend its day. The early morning was warm but damp, clear overhead but with ground fog that curled around his knees like sea foam. *Mugga*, they would have called the weather back home. He didn't know what they called it here, even after all this time.

He closed his eyes and let the morning noises wash over him. Before he'd sailed to this cursed land, this hour before dawn had been his favorite time, when he would lie listening to Ylfa mumble in her dreams and sometimes wake her for loving. He wondered what Merewyn was like in the night, whether she snored or muttered or just lay there, as peaceful in sleep as she was awake. He had spent many hours thinking about such things over the past hundred days, a pleasant, if futile, way to pass the time. He would have to stop now. It would be too tempting, now that he would be seeing her again. Tonight. He smiled.

Only moments now. The sun's disk sat just below the horizon. Brand was making his final preparations when he heard the crack of a twig on the bank above.

"Who's there?" He spun toward the sound, searching the underbrush but seeing no one. His heart pounded as the panic rose up. "Show yourself."

The first wave of pain ground down on him just as a figure stepped out from a thicket near the top of the ravine. "You're back, *messire!*"

Merewyn. *Merewyn!*

She got a good look at him and her smile gave way to confusion. "You have no clothes."

"Run," he shouted as the second wave ripped across his back and claws split the end of his fingers. "Run!"

But she stood there as if in a trance, watching as he was slammed to the ground with the pain of changing. He tried to shout again, but the word swelled into a roar. The sound shook her, woke her. The last thing he saw before the bear took him was her eyes, wide with shock and terror. Then the haze rolled over his mind and the bear began to hunt.

CHAPTER 24

THE BEAR CAUGHT Merewyn's scent and reared up, standing like the man he had been moments before.

"Mother, protect me!"

Her plea followed the bear's roar skyward. In her heart, she knew that she was about to die, that she could never outrun such a beast.

She ran anyway, tearing back the way she'd come as she bought a few precious moments of life. The bear crashed to the ground behind her, a thunderous sound, and she ran harder, her breath growing as ragged as the mist that tore and feathered around her.

The mist. Perhaps. "Mother, please!"

Looking around wildly, she spotted a great tree a few yards away, half-dead but still standing, its bark split to reveal the hollowness within. She threw herself into the crack, knowing it was slim shelter, but needing someplace, anyplace. Wedging herself back as far as the tree would let her, Merewyn closed her eyes, found the quiet within, and reached out with her mind.

She called the mist, barely breathing the words, summoning, summoning. The dampness swirled around her; darkness enfolded her. The bear roared again, only feet away, but she continued calling, gathering, weaving until the mist hung so thick around the old tree that it muffled everything beyond and made her shiver in the summer warmth.

The bear paced around the tree, snuffling and snorting as he tried to find what he could no longer see. He passed by the crack, and his scent wafted in, musky and rank. Certain he could smell her, too, Merewyn pressed back and squeezed her eyes more tightly, like a child trying to hide behind closed lids. If she let herself see, the bear would have her, for she would be too frightened and the magic would fall away.

An animal cried out in pain nearby, and the bear moved off, seeking easier game. His footsteps slowly faded. Still Merewyn clung to the mist, certain every crack and rustle was the beast returning. Only when the sun breached the branches overhead did she release the mist to burn away. Tentatively, she crept out into the sunlight, half expecting claws to rip into her.

Instead, Sir Ari was there, sitting on his horse a little way off, his beautiful face ablaze with anger and concern. He rode over to her and extended his hand. "Come, Healer, before it returns."

Shaking with exhaustion and the aftermath of fear, she let him pull her up behind him. "I was gathering dew for . . . I did not know. I must help him."

"You cannot help," he said bitterly as he turned his mount toward her cottage.

"The Mother thinks I can," she said, sure that must be what the gods intended. "What evil laid this curse on him?"

"It is not my place to tell you."

"But you . . ." Her mind flashed over the things she knew. "Are you the raven?"

His back turned to stone before her. "I will take you home and see to your safety. Ask your questions of Brand."

He did as he said, leaving her at her door then standing

watch at the edge of the clearing as the sun traveled across the sky and down, until finally he had to ride away.

MEREWYN.

Half-crazed with the knowledge of what the bear must have done, Brand started searching even before the last of the beast left him. There was nothing—no body, no blood, no stench of death—but as his mind cleared more, he realized this wasn't where he'd last seen her. The bear had wandered. Still twisted with pain, he stumbled toward the dene. He found nothing there either, and the nothing gave him hope, for even if the bear had devoured her, he would have left scraps. Nothing meant she might be safe. *Please, Thor, let her be safe.*

He was still laboring to return to himself when Ivo came tearing through the woods leading Kraken.

"She saw me. The bear . . ." said Brand as he wheeled to a stop.

"I know. She's fine."

Brand's knees nearly went out from under him with relief. He grabbed at Kraken's mane to steady himself. *Thank you, Thor.* "Where is she?"

"Ari took her home. Brand, she knows what we are." Anger mixed with the anguish in Ivo's voice, the prospect of having to abandon Alaida clearly at the front of his mind.

"Only me. I'll . . . I don't know." Brand began yanking on clothes. "I'll take care of it. I'll figure it out."

Jaw working, Ivo stared off into the trees, as though he searched them for the means to control himself. "You never said she was a witch."

"She's not."

"She used magic to save herself—she called up a mist."

That brought Brand up short, but he cast off the idea. "No. She's like Ari, touched by it, but no more."

"Ari can't call a mist," growled Ivo. "He can barely call his visions."

"She's *not* a witch, and she doesn't know about you. We

can salvage this." Brand threw himself onto Kraken and tore off, leaving Ivo behind as he raced toward Merewyn's cottage.

The helplessness crashed back down on him again as he saw her standing in the doorway, waiting for him as she always did. He slid out of the saddle and threw his arms around her, but not until she sighed into his chest and he felt her breath, warm and alive, was he convinced. *Safe. She was safe.*

"I thought . . . I could not stop it. If it had . . ."

"*Shh.*" She lifted a hand to hush him, her fingertips grazing his lips like a kiss. "I know that creature is not you."

Thank the gods, her face contained no fear. He couldn't stand it if she were afraid of him. The bear, yes, he understood that, but not him. Please, never him.

Ivo galloped up just then, and Merewyn drew away to meet his seething fury directly and without apology. "The gods put me there, my lord. I had to know."

"Know what?" demanded Ivo.

"Why they sent you all to me. A knight who is a bear. Another who is a raven. And a lord who is"—she glanced to Ivo, with a lifted brow—"an eagle?"

Ivo swore violently and flung himself off Fax to loom over Merewyn, his face white with rage. His hand went to his sword. "Swear you will never speak of this, *Witch*, or die now."

"Ivar!" Brand shoved Ivo back and stepped between him and Merewyn.

"She will swear!" blazed Ivo. "I will not have her talking. I must be here when Alaida has the child!"

"We will be. She won't talk."

"The babe," breathed Merewyn, yanking them both around. She dropped to her knees and raised her clasped hands to Ivo. "I swear on my life, to all three of you, your secret is my own. May I die if I reveal it to anyone."

"Are you satisfied?" demanded Brand, furious, as he helped Merewyn to her feet. "Or must she swear in blood to please you?"

"He only seeks to protect his own," she said, more forgiving than Brand was inclined to be. "Do not fear me, my lord. The gods intend me to help you."

Ivo's eyes narrowed. "How?"

"I don't know yet, but they must. Why else would they have set our paths to cross? They brought you to Alnwick, led Sir Brand to my door, showed me Sir Ari calling to them and speaking to the eagle. The Mother even drew me into the woods this morning so I might understand."

"And risked your life," fumed Brand, incensed that she'd been put in harm's way, even by a goddess.

"She sent the mist to protect me," she reminded, laying a calming hand on his forearm. "There must be some purpose in all this beyond me becoming your . . ." She hesitated, then a hint of a smile curved her lips as she finished. "Alewife."

"Are you a witch?" asked Ivo bluntly.

"I told you, no," snapped Brand.

She gave him a searching look, and when she spoke, it was to him, not Ivo. "The gods speak to me. They use me to heal and give me what skill I need to do it, as they have all the women in my family since time began."

"Healers don't call the mist," said Ivo.

"No. That is something I could always do. As a child, I used it to hide from my mother. A game."

"'Twas no game that saved you from the bear. I ask again, are you a witch?"

"A small one."

"No," said Brand, his disgust for Cwen and her kind boiling up. "You cannot be."

"But, *messire*, I . . ." She stopped, her dark eyes widening with understanding. "A witch did this terrible thing to you."

Brand couldn't bring himself to answer, but Ivo spat it out. "Aye. One called Cwen."

"Why?"

"We killed her son," said Ivo.

"*I* killed him," said Brand heavily. "And I'll tell the tale. Go, Ivo. Your lady will be wondering where you are."

Ivo started, as if he'd been so concerned with the future that he'd forgotten that Alaida awaited him in the present.

"Go to her, my lord," urged Merewyn. "You have barely returned and she needs you."

"I will be back before dawn to see if you do indeed have any help for us," Ivo said, threatening her without actually voicing the threat.

They watched him ride off into the dusk then went inside, where Merewyn drew Brand some ale. "The fear is so thick on Lord Ivo, I could smell it."

"He has much to fear." He took the cup, brushing her fingertips on purpose, just to touch her. "But he shouldn't have threatened you."

"You would have done the same for Ylfa."

"Aye." As he would for Merewyn, even if she didn't know it. He turned to stare into the fire. He would have fought Ivo tonight for the sake of this woman—this *witch*, he told himself, though everything in him rejected that name—yet today he had nearly killed her. The gods taunted him at every step.

"Tell me of this Cwen," she said softly behind him.

"Evil made flesh," said Brand, forcing the words out past the acrid taste that filled his mouth, metallic as the blood spilled that long-ago night. "There were two full crews of us. Five score and ten. Now there are but nine, all cursed, and all of it is on me."

MEN WHO BECAME *animals and lived to be tortured for eternity. Visions of a curse that carried to their children.*

Merewyn stood staring into the fiery red heart of the embers as she tried to absorb it all. She and Brand had traded places several times as he'd talked, one moving to the hearth as the first took a place at the table, as though neither could stand to look into the eyes of the other as the story unfolded. He leaned on the table now, his head heavy in his hands. She'd poured a fair amount of ale into him, trying to make the words come more easily, but he'd struggled all the way through, still weighed down, after all these years, with the knowledge that he'd led his men into the witch's trap.

No. Not witch. Cwen was more than a witch, more than a mixer of potions and spinner of spells. She was a true sorceress, and one of great power—perhaps even a priestess of the dark gods—and her centuries-old vengeance still glowed as hot as these coals. To do this to a single man, the one responsible for her son's death, that, on some level, Merewyn could comprehend. But to all of them? And their offspring? A curse fueled by such hate might never be broken.

Mother, why bring me these men? she prayed silently. *I am a healer. My magic is not that kind, not that strong. I cannot possibly help them.*

Tears of frustration and sorrow welled up. She should never have raised their hopes. It had been foolish. Cruel. But there had been so many signs . . . Perhaps she'd missed something, some tiny detail that would tell her what to do.

She scrubbed the tears out of her eyes and turned to ask Brand to tell her again. The words died on her tongue. He looked so tired, bowed by the weight of all those dead men. She crossed and rested a hand on his shoulder. The tightness there flowed up into her arm. "How long has it been since you truly slept? Lie down for a little."

He shook his head. "I cannot. The bear . . ."

"I will sit up, and Lord Ivo will come. We will wake you in time." She took his hand and tugged him the few feet to the bed, where he eased himself down with a sigh. Merewyn sat beside him and made him turn so she could rub his shoulders.

He sighed again. "That's good."

Slowly he relaxed, and when she felt him start to fade, she slid to the end of the bed and pulled him down so his head lay cradled in her lap. He was asleep in moments, his breath regular, his head heavy and warm on her thighs. After a time, when she was sure he slept soundly, she gently brushed the hair off his forehead and traced a sign of protection there with one fingertip, then rested her palm on his chest and began to pray to the Mother. In his sleep, he covered her hand with his.

They were still like that when Ivo returned near dawn. Merewyn raised a finger to her lips as he pushed open the unbarred door. He stood there in the frame, staring at them—at her—then closed the door quietly and went to sit at her table.

"You *are* a witch, to make him sleep so." His voice barely carried over the song of the crickets outside.

"'Tis no spell, my lord. The telling exhausted him." She stroked a lock of Brand's hair where it curled over her thigh. "He carries too much guilt, as you carry too much worry."

"There are reasons for both," said Ivo, stomach twisting as thoughts of Alaida and the child tumbled through his skull. "Have you good news for me?"

She shook her head. "I fear such dark magic is beyond my ken, my lord. I will keep my mind to it, and perhaps the Mother will reveal something."

"I will have Brand bring you Ari's book. Perhaps it will show you a way."

"Perhaps." She hesitated, then raised the issue that most concerned him. "He told me of Sir Ari's visions."

The angry fear boiled up again, but this time he was able to stay in control. "Then you understand why I must be here."

"Aye. But what if you're not? If the child comes by day . . ."

No. Please, Odin, no. "That has been on my mind since Alaida told me. Even if it comes at night, I must leave before dawn. I cannot carry a newborn into the woods if it does not change, yet I cannot leave an eaglet in Alaida's arms if it does. I need someone there who understands, who can stay when I must leave, who can care for them both no matter what. Someone like you."

"Then I will be there, my lord, though I am not sure what you wish me to do."

"We will figure it out together." He studied her through

narrowed eyes. She said yes so easily. Could it truly be that simple? "You are a strange one, Healer. How is it you hold me no ill will?"

"You did me no harm."

"Nonetheless, I should not have been so . . ." He sought a word, but didn't find it. "You have my apology."

She nodded in acceptance. "What has changed, my lord? Why have you decided to trust me?"

He nodded toward Brand. "Him. He despises everything witch, yet he sleeps in your lap." He rose and went to the door to check the sky.

Behind him, Merewyn exclaimed in understanding. Ivo turned to look at her.

"I have watched Sir Brand do that so many times," she explained.

"And now you know why."

"Aye. I will guard your secret well, my lord," she promised again.

"I know." Ivo squeezed his eyes shut against the emotion that welled up at the simple acceptance contained in Merewyn's words. Brand was right: this was a good woman. It was hard to believe she was witch. "Wake him, Merewyn, lest we are still here when the bear returns. I would keep you safe."

CHAPTER 25

A FEW EVENINGS later, Ivo pushed his bishop into position and said, "Checkmate."

"Already?" With a sigh, Alaida flicked over her king with one finger. "I do think my head grows softer as my belly grows larger."

"It does, my lady," said Bôte, from her place in the corner. "The babe sucks the wits out of you now, just as he will suck the milk out of you after, and leave your paps as flat as a poor man's purse."

"Bôte!"

"'Tis one of the reasons you should hire a wet nurse," continued Bôte, unabashed. "As I have told you many times."

"I, uh, think I'll see what Oswald is up to," muttered Brand, rising.

"And I have told you I do not want a wet nurse," said Alaida, ignoring him and his abrupt retreat. "What are my breasts for, if not to feed my own child?"

"I have occasional use for them," volunteered Ivo.

Alaida made a face at him and started setting up her men for the next game. "*Your* enjoyment is not at issue."

"And why not?" demanded Bôte. "You will want him to desire you enough to get another child on you." She turned to Ivo. "If she suckles this one, 'twill be longer before she can have another."

"Is that true?" Ivo asked Alaida.

"I don't know. 'Tis what she says, but she tells me all sorts of things I *know* are wrong. And it makes no difference." Alaida turned back to Bôte. "I'm not having a wet nurse, and you will stop hounding me about it, lest I send you away and have Merewyn midwife me."

"I'd like you to have Merewyn anyway," said Ivo, seizing the opening she'd so nicely left him.

"I deliver all the manor babes, my lord," said Bôte.

"As you will this one. However, I want Merewyn to help as well."

Angry red spotted Bôte's cheeks. "I have no need of her help and I—"

Alaida held up a hand to still her. "My lord, I only teased Bôte. I did not intend you to take me seriously."

"Your words only reminded me I had not told you my wishes." He tried to sound like it wasn't important, so she wouldn't fight him. "I know you don't need her, but humor me."

For just a moment, her hackles went up in the old way, but happily, she only huffed a little before she assented. "Oh, all right, then. We will welcome her aid—won't we, Bôte?"

"As you will, my lady." Bôte's voice was sweet enough, but her look for Ivo was pure venom.

"Go tell Brand 'tis safe to come back," said Ivo, wanting her gone. "Then see if there is more of that apple tart. I'm still hungry."

As she left, Alaida opened the new game with her usual pawn. "We have other things to discuss, my lord, like a name."

A name. Ivo's hand hesitated over the board. He didn't

want to pick a name. A name made the child real. A person. "We have time."

"Waiting only ensures he will come early—or so Bôte says."

"Ah. Well, then, pick something."

"Have you no preferences?"

"No."

"Your father's name, perhaps, or your grandfather's."

Thorli, or Bjarnlaugr? "They would not suit."

"Then a friend. Would you name him for Brand or Ari or some other companion?"

"No." If he didn't answer, perhaps she'd drop the matter. But her badger side came out again, digging at it. "I am sure of those I do *not* want," she continued, trying to engage him. "Robert, Neville, Vital, Eustace."

"Eustace? Was that the short, timid one?"

"No, that was Vital. But I do not want a child of mine sharing a name with any of them. Nor William," she added. "Even if he is your liege."

"And yours. Whether you love him or not, you owe him allegiance as king."

"He will have my allegiance when I have my grandfather, but I will never name a son for him."

"Then pick something else."

"But what?" she prodded, clearly vexed by this lack of interest in what should be—was—an important decision. "Hugh? Fulk? Alaric? Guy? Martin? Stephen? And what of names for a girl, in case I'm wrong? Do you like Isabel? Matilda? Herleve? Jehanne?"

"God's knees, Alaida, name it whatever you wish."

"I shall," she snapped. "Why do I bother? You did not want this child, and 'tis clear you still do not. I daresay you put more thought into naming your horse. Perhaps I should call him Hrimfaxi. At least I know you like the name." Eyes bright with tears, she shoved her stool back, knocking over chessmen in her anger.

Before she could struggle to her feet, Ivo was on his

knees before her, contrite. "Forgive me, Alaida." He caught her hands between his and brought them to his lips. "I did not mean to upset you. I know this is important to you."

"As it should be to you." She closed her eyes and took a deep breath, and when she opened them again, the tears were gone. "Names are important. They have meaning and weight, and our son's name must be carefully chosen—if for no other reason than that he is not known as *le petit oisel*."

His fingers tightened mindlessly around hers. "What?"

"It is what I call him sometimes," she explained, smiling happily down at her belly. "As he first quickened, the little flutters felt like tiny wings beating. So, *mon petit oisel*."

Odin, no. Her voice, the crackling of the fire, the sounds of the hall—all were drowned out by the thunder of his heart in his ears. Alaida cocked her head, looking at him strangely, and he realized all the blood had drained from his face, perhaps from his entire body, so that his heart pumped only dry air, loud as a rowing drum.

"What is wrong?" she asked, her voice full of concern. "You look as if you have seen a ghost."

His tongue felt thick, but he managed a "No."

"Did I say something wrong?"

"No." He shot to his feet. "No. I, uh, I just remembered . . . something I must do." Leave. He must leave. "I will return shortly," he said, barging past Brand as he reentered.

He made it to the stable before his knees buckled. Foundering, he caught himself on the wall of Fax's stall and hung there, unable to stand and unwilling to fall down into the dreck where he belonged for doing this to Alaida. Heavy footsteps crossed the yard coming after him.

"What's wrong with you?" demanded Brand. "You looked like you were staring into the mouth of *Hel* as you passed me."

"I was," said Ivo. "Alaida called . . . She calls the child *mon petit oisel*."

"Ba . . ." Brand couldn't even manage a proper curse,

but after a moment, he nodded. "Maybe 'tis not as bad as you think."

"Brand, it means her little *bird*."

"I know what it means, but women do that," said Brand. "They give them pet names, almost before they stop bleeding. Ylfa called our first Flotnar because she puked so much—like being seasick all the time, she said, so he must be a seafarer. And my sister, Runa, called all of hers Egg, right up to the day they were born and named."

Ivo looked up, trying to see if Brand was serious or just trying to reassure him. "Really?"

"Don't you remember? Egg this. Egg that. 'Egg's making me sick,' she would say, or, 'Stop kicking, Egg.'"

Ivo nodded, recalling, and Brand thumped him on the back. "Alaida's doing the same thing, that's all. It doesn't mean anything, other than that she talks to it."

"Ah, by the gods, I hope not." Ivo pounded his skull against the edge of the stall until the pain drew the blood back to his head. "I feel like a whale's been chewing on me ever since we got back, and it's only been a week. How will I make it through two more months?"

"By doing what you must. Smile, shut your mouth, and keep her happy for as long as you can."

Ivo straightened and pulled himself together. "Keeping her happy seemed easier when it mostly involved swiving."

"It would," said Brand. He thumped him on the back again. "Come. That nurse of hers was on her way up. Your lady will be crying in her arms."

"Oh, good, another excuse for the old sow to hate me. She's almost worse than the rest of it."

"They always are," said Brand, and walked him back to do battle with demons and nurses.

THIS WAS GOING to be easier than he'd thought, Neville fitz Hubert concluded as he perched in the concealing branches of a yew, watching Sir Ari approach one crisp evening a few days before Michaelmas.

He'd spotted the seneschal two days earlier, riding into the forest just before sunset, then seen de Vassy along the same trail the following evening. A little backtracking had brought him to a thicket where he'd found two horses—Lord Ivo's and Sir Brand's—in a rough enclosure, but no sign of either man. Today, Neville had hidden his horse well away and come back to climb this tree and wait. As he'd waited, he'd counted once again the humiliations he'd suffered at de Vassy's hands: Four. Five, if he counted his father's reaction. Neville ran his tongue over the scar on his lip where the old *bricon* had backhanded him before ordering him away until he "made some good of" himself.

He'd drifted around for a few weeks, looking futilely for a lord who needed another lance and would have him, nursing a desire for revenge until it grew teeth. Eventually he'd found himself at Morpeth, still without a lord, so close he had just ridden on to Alnwick. He wasn't even yet sure how he would satisfy the desire—murder seemed both too easy on de Vassy and too dangerous to his own neck—but he would. That he knew for certs.

Below him, Sir Ari looked around carefully, then dismounted. He wasted no time in unsaddling his horse and putting it in the pen with the other two. He shoved his gear beneath a fallen log, then, to Neville's shock, began to undress.

So that's what brought de Vassy and his men to the woods every day—sodomy. Neville smiled to himself. Even if the whispers were right about the king, the same perversion would hardly be tolerated in a lesser lord. It was just a matter of witnessing the two of them together—or would it be the three of them? A sudden shriek from above made him start, and he caught himself just short of falling.

"There you are," said Sir Ari as the eagle came swooping down from overhead and settled onto the ground. "I thought you were going to be late."

An agonized groan rose from below just as the sun settled below the horizon. It grew into a scream, changed, went higher and less human. Sir Ari began to crumple, to shrink and darken, even as the eagle grew bigger and lighter. *Mother of God, what was this?* The figures pulsed and shifted in the twilight, one figure growing more human as the other became more birdlike, as though they traded souls. The eagle's shriek grew more human. Neville started shaking, and it was all he could do to keep still and not piss himself.

Impossible. Horrible.

Yet real. Terrified, Neville clutched at the tree trunk, his fingers digging into the bark until they bled as he listened to the cries of agony from below. And then it was over as abruptly as it had begun, and there was silence except for the thud of his own racing heart.

De Vassy huddled naked where the eagle had landed, while a large black raven tried its wings on the spot where Sir Ari had stood. The raven hopped and fluttered, then rose up and circled lazily over the thicket as de Vassy struggled to his feet and began retrieving his gear from various hiding places. Neville flattened to the tree trunk, willing himself invisible, praying for protection from these demons.

Below, de Vassy finished dressing and quickly saddled his horse and Brand's. A few moments later, he called the raven down to his shoulder and rode off toward Alnwick, passing within yards of the tree where Neville clung.

Neville's mind raced over what he'd seen, trying to make sense of it, but there was no sense to be made. They were monsters, both of them, half beast and half man, and no doubt Sir Brand was like them. Pure evil, this was; devilry of the worst sort. They should be killed, burned like the demons they were.

That's when he saw it. His revenge, handed to him by de Vassy himself. He wouldn't have to kill the man—the Church would do it for him, or the Crown, and one or both would reward him for bringing the abomination at Alnwick to light. Excited by the prospect of watching de Vassy burn, Neville checked to be sure he was alone in the woods and clambered down out of the tree.

That's it. He would go to Durham and tell the Archbishop. Oh, that's right, the old buzzard had died. He would tell the king then, personally, and when William asked him to name a reward, he would say Alaida and Alnwick.

Alaida . . . He was lost in the fantasy of possessing her at last when a nearby twig cracked. With a yelp, he bolted off, crashing through the underbrush in his frantic rush to escape whatever other monsters lived in the Aln Wood. When he was lord here, he vowed, he would kill everything that moved and have the woods restocked with beasts he knew were beasts.

But for now, he just wanted to be gone. He found his horse, quickly returned to his camp to gather what gear he could find in the gloom, then rode like the Devil himself until he left Alnwick behind. Once safely away, he took shelter for the night at the first cottage he found, and at dawn the next morning, he started for London and the king.

CHAPTER 26

BY THE TWINGES in her back, she'd been sitting too long, and on a stool too low. Alaida pressed both hands to the ache and shifted to get up, but her belly made her unwieldy.

"A hand, if you please, Thomas." Tom sprang up and hurried over, and she took his arm to rise. "'Tis good Oswald makes you work so hard. Your strength keeps up with my girth."

"You are as slender as a reed, even now, my lady."

"Nicely done, Squire. However, if I look like a reed, you have walked along strange rivers. This reed has a very large . . . *unnh*." The twinge came back suddenly, so hard it took her breath away.

"What, my lady?"

"A large—*nyaah*. Oh, God." Water gushed down her legs and pooled around her feet. "Oh."

"Bôte, help! M'lady's sprung a leak."

In a trice, five women shoved a wide-eyed Tom aside and hustled Alaida toward the bed, all talking at once.

"Not the bed," said Alaida, convinced it would hurt to lie down. "My chair."

"But my lady, you—"

"The chair." She veered away from the bed, dragging the others along. "Tom, come back here. Do you know where Lord Ivo hunts today?"

"No, my lady."

"Ask Sir Ari. Perhaps he knows. He should be here. I *want* him here."

"Yes, my lady. I'll fetch Merewyn, too."

"We have no need for her," grumbled Bôte, still aggrieved by Ivo's decision. "She will be in the way."

"Then make room for her," ordered Alaida, out of patience. "Lord Ivo made his wishes clear, and I find now that *I* want her, too."

Bôte snorted her disgust. "She's no better midwife than I."

"No, but she calms me. You do want me calm?"

"Aye," Bôte allowed. "Ah, well, get her, Tom, and while you're about it, tell Geoffrey to send for the priest. And we'll want the birthing stool, the linens I put aside, and plenty of water and wood for the fire. And no men are to come up."

"Except Lord Ivo," said Alaida.

"Not even him," said Bôte.

"It will be amusing to watch you try to stop him–*m– maaaah*." She clutched at Bôte as a cramp arched her back. Tom blanched and shot out of the room, calling for the steward and Sir Ari. The pain crested and passed quickly, thank the saints, and Alaida folded down onto her chair. "I thought this started more slowly. Why are they so close so soon?"

"Has your back been hurting, lamb?"

"Aye. All day."

"Some women labor in their back instead of their belly. Likely you are further on than you think, and with your water broken, the babe should come quickly." Bôte's words encouraged Alaida. "Come, let's get that wet gown off you."

With so many hands to help, they had her stripped and into the soft old chainse Bôte had set aside before the next pain hit. Alaida was ready for it now, and tolerated it without so much as a groan. Perhaps she could manage this with some grace after all. Women started parading in with the things Bôte had ordered, and soon the room was ready and all there was to do was wait and labor and wait some more.

IVO DIDN'T NEED to read Ari's note to know the time had arrived: the eagle had seen Tom pelting toward Merewyn's and the recollection was clear in Ivo's mind as he climbed to his feet after changing. There was only one reason for the boy to ride for the healer.

Hands shaking, he began throwing on clothes. He barely took time to tighten the girths on both horses before he was on Fax and headed toward the rendezvous with Brand.

"It comes," he said tersely as he reined to a stop at the edge of the dene. Brand looked blank for a moment, then understanding dawned. He swung up on Kraken and they took off, the dread so thick between them they couldn't speak.

He couldn't let Alaida see that dread, Ivo told himself. He had to pretend all was well, keep her calm through her labor and until morning, when they would know one way or the other.

They reached the gate well before dark. Ivo tossed Fax's reins to the nearest man and ran for the solar.

"You cannot go up, my lord," warned Geoffrey as Ivo hit the bottom step.

"Yes he can," said Brand.

"But the Church forbids ..." The steward's voice trailed off under Brand's baleful glare, and Ivo continued upstairs. He met similar resistance from the woman at the door, but Alaida groaned, and he shouldered past, not caring what they thought.

She was standing before the fire, gripping Merewyn's shoulders while Bôte rubbed her lower back. Her face was a mask of pain as she panted and moaned.

Ivo's stomach twisted with concern beyond his fear for the child. "Why isn't she abed?"

"Walking helps things go faster," said Bôte from her side.

He looked to Merewyn, who nodded. "Bôte is right, my lord."

"Of course I am," grumbled Bôte. "Is that better, lamb?"

"Aaah. Much." Alaida looked up to Ivo and smiled, but the skin around her mouth was taut and pale. "I'm glad you're here."

He drew on all his discipline to return her smile, and bent to kiss her as though nothing were wrong. "I came as soon as I was able. How is it?"

"Painful, but Father Theobald says it must be, as punishment for the sins of Eve."

He was going to rip Theobald's liver out through his mouth for that, but for now, he held on to the smile and pushed a lock of sweat-soaked hair off her cheek. "If I could bear this for you, I would, sweet leaf."

"Unfortunately, you cannot, but knowing you would will give me strength."

"You're already strong. You'll do fine."

"You sound like Bôte," she said. She grimaced as another pain beset her, dragging a moan out of her that made Ivo want to hit something to make it stop.

"You must go, my lord," said Bôte.

"No. I want him here," said Alaida. "Rub harder, Bôte."

"He cannot stay." The nurse pressed into her back, working the muscles.

"Harder!" said Alaida.

"I can do it no harder, lamb."

Merewyn caught Ivo's eye and motioned him toward Alaida. "A stronger hand will give her ease, my lord, and more so if it is yours."

Grateful, Ivo nudged Bôte out of the way and fit his hands to Alaida's back. Huge as she was, she seemed suddenly tiny. He'd never thought her fragile until this moment. How would she stand this, the labor and then . . . ?

"God's knees, husband, I will not break. Harder!" cried Alaida. Ivo leaned into her so hard he thought he would crack her spine, but she only grunted and pushed back. "Ah, yes. That's it. Better."

She sighed as the spasm passed, and Ivo cocked an eyebrow at Merewyn over her shoulder. "Is this usual?"

"I see it enough to call it common, if not usual. She is fine."

"Stop talking as though I'm not here," said Alaida.

"Forgive us, sweet leaf." He pressed a kiss to the nape of her neck and asked Merewyn, "How long can I stay?"

"You should be gone already," said Bôte. "'Tis sin, and you shame my lady."

Ignoring her, Merewyn spread her fingers over Alaida's belly. "Not long. You'll know when you should leave, my lord."

He helped Alaida through a half-dozen more pains, each coming faster than the last, each twisting him more than it did her. Then another one struck, worse than the others. Her groan grew louder, more animal, and would have become a scream if she hadn't pressed her lips together so stubbornly. He rubbed as hard as he possibly could without hurting her. "Be at ease, sweet. Be at ease."

She snarled and smacked his hands away. "At ease? Let me stick a pair of knives in your back and see if *you* are at ease. *God's knees*, that you were having this thing! Get away from me."

The women laughed, but Ivo drew back, stunned at this viciousness that had come out of nowhere. Merewyn shook her head and smiled sympathetically. "She does not mean it, my lord."

"I do, too," said Alaida earnestly. "He did this to me. I

never wanted him." She doubled over, clutching at her belly. Her eyes widened in panic. "Oh, God. Help me."

"What is wrong?" demanded Ivo. "Why does it hurt her so much?"

"Because it is time," said Bôte in a tone of impatient disgust. She bumped him out of the way with her wide hips and put her arm around Alaida. "Come, lamb, let's get you settled."

"I, uh, guess I should go," said Ivo, and Merewyn nodded.

"Should never have been here," grumbled Bôte as she coaxed Alaida over to the birthing stool.

He would have kissed Alaida once more, but neither she nor her nurse would have any part of it. As he backed out of the room, Merewyn reassured him. "This is what happens as the time nears, my lord. She will push now, and be done."

"Take care of her," he begged. "Both of them."

He caught a glimpse of Bôte and Hadwisa stripping the gown over Alaida's head as the door was slammed in his face, and then all he could do was go downstairs and make silent prayer to Frigga for Alaida's well-being, and to Odin, to help him with what he must do after.

WHEN IT WAS all over, a little after midnight, Ivo had a daughter, a red-faced, copper-haired, slightly wrinkled miniature of Alaida, the terrifying result of her mother's pain.

Ivo stared down at the infant in Merewyn's arms with more fear than he'd ever felt in battle. He'd expected a boy, and that would have been bad enough, but a girl? How was he to raise a girl child in the forest? Half beast, half human, never to live among either kind. Impossible. It would be a blessing if the child died now, tonight, but if Ari's vision were true, it could no more die than the rest of them.

"She is healthy and strong, my lord," said Merewyn softly, news which should have been good. "Would you like to hold her?"

"I . . ." *I cannot.* He couldn't even bring himself to touch it. He stepped past Merewyn. "I wish to see my wife first."

"She is tired, my lord," said Bôte, tucking the furs around Alaida. "Do not try her."

"You fuss too much, old woman," said Alaida. "I'm not tired at all."

"She is," said Bôte firmly. She looked at Ivo with meaning. "She just doesn't know it yet."

"I understand. I will only stay a little while." It was like battle-heat, he guessed, all that effort and the elation of victory, then the sudden exhaustion after. He bent to kiss Alaida. "You taste of tears. Was it so terrible?"

"Not nearly as bad as I feared. The tears came only when I saw her. Isn't she perfect?" Alaida beamed up at him, her happiness a golden glow around her that made Ivo suddenly understand the halos in paintings of the Christian Mother.

"I know little of infants."

"You will learn. Now that I've discovered how easy it is, I intend to have many more," said Alaida, twisting the knife in his heart without knowing it. "Merewyn, bring her, please."

Merewyn came and laid the bundled child in Alaida's arms. Gentle as she was, the shift woke the babe, and it mewed and opened eyes that startled Ivo with their paleness.

"They're not brown." He sat on the edge of the bed and bent to look more closely. "With that hair, I thought they would be brown like yours."

"They all have blue eyes at first, my lord," said Merewyn. "The true color comes later. Hers are so light, they may stay blue."

"No, they will go gray, like her father's, and she will have ten hundred freckles," said Alaida, talking to the babe. She stroked a fingertip lightly across the baby's nose and over her cheeks. "Right here, and here, and here, won't you, sweeting? But we will worry about that later. Right now, it is time to meet your *papa.*" She tilted the babe a little and held her out to Ivo. "My lord, your daughter. Beatrice."

Beatrice. He stared at the infant, who blinked solemnly at some invisible thing a dozen feet behind him and burped.

"Go on, my lord," urged Merewyn. "Hold her."

"I . . . I will break her."

"You won't," said Alaida. "Help him, Merewyn."

"Like this." Merewyn took his arms and curved them into a cradle, and he felt the calmness that Brand spoke of in her touch, a blessing just now. Alaida leaned forward and nestled Beatrice into the crook of his arm. She began to squall, and Ivo instinctively pulled her closer and jiggled her, just a little. She fussed a bit more, then quieted and settled against his chest, and something in him altered and it was as though he'd known all along how to hold a daughter.

A daughter. His daughter, for better or worse. He stood and carried her nearer the fire, partly to keep her warm and partly to hide how hard he fought the tears wadding up in his throat. When he thought the women weren't looking, he dipped his fingers into a bowl of water on the table and touched the liquid to the babe's forehead as he whispered her name, welcoming her to the world in the old way.

"Hello, little one." He brought Beatrice up to press a kiss to her forehead, and as his lips touched her soft, damp skin, he caught a whiff of something delicately salty. He turned in wonder. "Do they all smell like broth?"

Merewyn wore an amused look. "Only for a little. Until they begin to smell of something else."

"What? Oh."

"'Tis your fortune not to deal with that, my lord," said Bôte.

But he would have to deal with it, and the panic as he realized he didn't know how must have shown on his face, for Merewyn came over and touched his arm again to calm him. "I will show you, my lord, if you like. 'Tis good for a father to know."

Bôte and Alaida both looked at her strangely, but Ivo said with relief, "I would appreciate the lesson, Healer. Now, if you please."

"But I just swaddled her," said Bôte.

"Then you will swaddle her again. I am her father and will know how to care for her even if I do not do it." He held Beatrice out to Merewyn. "Show me."

As Alaida watched, bemused, Merewyn laid the babe on the foot of the bed and unwrapped her. "This is her tail clout. It goes so." She set the cloth in place and tucked the ends under to hold them around the ridiculously tiny bottom. "'Tis not difficult, but the cloths must be changed often to keep sores from forming, and she and them washed well between. The wrappings keep everything in place, like so."

"Again," said Ivo.

Merewyn obliged, unwrapping her again and stepping him through the process with no regard for Bôte's huffing disapproval. "Those who have no clean cloths often use dry moss or handfuls of wool," she said, anticipating his next question. "And be sure that when you pin the wrappings, the pins do not poke her."

"Of course," he said numbly. "My thanks." He could never do this. Never. *Please, Odin, do not make me do this. Release my child from this horror that lies on me. I will do anything. Anything.*

"My thanks also, Merewyn," said Alaida. "I didn't know either. I suspect Bôte would keep it all a secret, to assure her place for another year or two, because we all know how anxious I am to be rid of her."

Bôte snorted and scooped up the babe. "'Tis no secret, but you will never have to do it, my lady, so there is no reason for you to know."

"If I listened to you, there would be no reason to know anything about her at all, even to her name." Alaida sighed heavily, almost a yawn.

"See, you do tire," said Bôte, but she tucked the baby into Alaida's arms. "Before you sleep, you must let her suckle a little, to help start your milk. Time for you to be gone, my lord. This is not a man's business."

"He'll see nothing he hasn't seen before," said Alaida.

"No, she's right. I'll go. A moment," he said to Bôte and Merewyn, and they stepped away, giving them a little privacy.

When he turned back to Alaida, it was with the painful knowledge that this might be the last time he saw her. If Ari's vision came to pass, tomorrow at sunset he would be fleeing with the child, leaving Alaida to face the aftermath of what he had done to her.

As he stood there, she opened her gown and eased Beatrice to the breast that had been his alone until now. The baby nuzzled openmouthed, then found the teat and latched on, sucking as noisily as a cottar's piglet.

"Good girl," whispered Alaida. "See, we don't need Bôte after all. She will just have to spend her time sewing for you and telling you stories."

How was he to do this, when Alaida so clearly loved Beatrice already? How could she bear losing husband and child in one blow? How could he bear losing her?

"My lord?" she said, glancing up. "Are you unwell?"

"No." He sat beside her and gently touched her cheek, remembering another time when she had asked that. "I was only thinking how very beautiful you are, Alaida of Alnwick."

Her brow wrinkled. "You frighten me when you look at me so. 'Tis like you would take what you see into your very soul."

"I would, to carry with me all my days." With bitter awareness of what he was doing, he kissed her good-bye.

"Sleep well, sweet leaf. Dream of me," he said when he finally pulled back. He stroked Beatrice's cheek. "You, too, little one. Drink deeply, then sleep, for your mother's sake.

"Bôte, see to them," he said, and left, pausing on the landing to stare down into the hall and wait for Merewyn to follow.

"Ari rests nearby," he said under his breath as she stepped out beside him. "He will be here just after sunrise."

She nodded. "If things go foul, you will find me where we agreed, but in truth, my lord, I sense nothing strange. I think tomorrow you will be here with your wife and child."

"I hope you are right, Healer." *Odin, Frigga, Thor, Freyja, all of you—let her be right, I beg you. Please, let her be right.*

CHAPTER 27

IT WAS TIME. Heart pounding, Merewyn stood over the cradle and waited for the sun to rise.

Behind her, Lady Alaida and the others slept soundly, lulled by a potion slipped into the ale shared in celebration of a child brought safely into the world. Those below lay in a similar stupor—Brand's doing—and Sir Ari would divert the guards outside. All was in readiness.

As the moment approached, she quickly loosened the swaddling bands and traced a sign of protection on the babe's chest. She pushed aside the tapestries and opened the shutter in case the eagle made its appearance fully fledged and ready to fly. She began mouthing the same prayer she'd repeated throughout the night, for the Mother to shield little Beatrice from this horrible curse, or if she could not, to aid those who worked to keep her safe and to ease Lady Alaida's heart in what would be a terrible sadness.

The first ray of light breached the horizon and froze the breath in Merewyn's chest. She scanned Beatrice, searching for the first sign of feather or claw, expecting screams as

the pain of changing tore through her tiny body. *Anytime.*
Anytime.

Beatrice stirred, whining. Her little arms, free of the
swaddling, flailed, flapping like wings. Tears filled Merewyn's eyes. *Please, Mother, no.* The light grew brighter,
the sky bluer, the clouds pinker. The child blinked a few
times and drew her arms in. Her fists bunched and flexed
by her chin, she snuffled twice, then, with a soft exhalation,
drifted back to sleep, at peace. No pain, no feathers, no
claws.

Stunned, Merewyn knelt by the cradle and quickly examined her. Fingers, toes, belly, back, head—nothing. Beatrice was a fine, healthy child with no mark of evil on her,
and she stayed so, even as the sun gilded the land outside
and the roosters crowed the morn. Words of thanks came to
Merewyn's lips as her tears, now full of joy, dropped onto
the baby like rain.

She was still there on her knees when the sound of Sir
Ari's voice outside startled her from her thanksgiving. She
rewrapped Beatrice and hurried to meet him on the stairs.
He saw her tears and blanched before she could say, "All is
well."

"Are you certain?"

"Yes. See?" She showed him the babe, and he blinked
several times as if fighting tears of his own. "Can you tell
him?"

"You show him, at the window. He comes as we speak."

Merewyn hurried back to the solar just as a dark shape
whisked past outside. The eagle made a slow turn and lit on
the paling wall barely a dozen yards away. Merewyn pulled
aside the baby's wrappings just enough to show her chest
and arms and carefully held her up in the frame of the window. The eagle stared, blinked, then spread his wings and
leapt into the air, sweeping past the window once more, his
wing tip just inches away. The rush of chill air over her
bared skin startled Beatrice awake and she wailed, the sound
of a newborn, not an eaglet. Outside, the great bird rose up,

soaring higher and higher, wheeling and spinning, joy evident in every wingbeat as he danced the sky.

"Bôte?" came a groggy voice behind her.

"Merewyn, my lady." Merewyn hugged Beatrice to her chest and quickly rearranged her wrappings.

"Why is she crying?"

"We were greeting her first dawn, my lady." Merewyn closed the shutter, wiped the last of the tears from her cheeks, and turned with a smile to carry the baby to her mother. "Your eagle came to visit, and Lady Beatrice was bidding him welcome."

"ARE YOU NEARLY done, m'lady? Lady Beatrice sucks at her fist and 'twould be better for your milk if she sucked at you."

"Fetch her here." Alaida choked down the last of the bland oat gruel that was her supper and set the bowl aside as Bôte brought her daughter.

"Here we are, lamb." Bôte perched on the edge of the bed, grinning broadly as Alaida put Beatrice to the breast. "Look at her. She knows what she wants. Suckles like a calf."

"And me the cow," said Alaida, wincing as Beatrice worked hard for milk not yet there. "What makes you smile so, Bôte?"

"You with a bairn, lamb. I always thought you would go off to marry and that would be the end of me. But here you are, lady and mother, and me still here to help. 'Tis a miracle."

"Aye, that it is, Nurse," said a low voice from the door.

"Ivo!" said Alaida, relieved beyond reason.

Bôte popped to her feet and stepped forward to block him from coming closer. "The lying-in room is forbidden to men, my lord, as the birthing room was last night—or should have been."

"Rules invented by men without wives or children."

Bôte crossed herself. "Sacrilege."

"Truth." He bypassed her and bent to kiss Alaida's cheek.

"Good evening, wife." He bent further, to kiss Beatrice's head. "And you, too, daughter."

His breath warmed Alaida's breast, and tears leapt to her eyes. She tried to hide them by ducking her head, but he was too quick.

"What's this?" He lifted her chin and frowned. "Is Bôte right? Should I leave?"

"No." She pressed a kiss to his fingers. "I just . . . I wondered all day if I would see you tonight."

"You should *not* be seeing him," said Bôte. "Not until you've been churched. You cannot stay, my lord."

Ivo straightened, a smile on his lips but an angry glint in his eyes. "Nurse, would you like to find a new lady to serve?"

Bôte's expression went flat. "No, my lord."

"Then close that mouth. I will submit myself to the priest and do whatever penance he demands, but I will *not* wait forty days to see my wife and child. Now leave us. I will only stay a little. I know they both need rest."

"Yes, my lord." Bôte backed toward the door. "Of course you do, my lord."

"She seeks only to protect me," said Alaida when she'd gone.

Ivo came to sit on the edge of the bed. "Do you need protection from me?"

"Only on occasion." She slipped one hand along his jaw and drew him back to kiss her properly. "You're sweating. Is it warm out?"

"No, I rushed. I could not reach you quickly enough."

She swallowed back a lump in her throat as more tears dribbled down her cheeks.

"Again? If I am going to make you weep at every turn, I will go and send the old woman back."

"No!" She clutched at his sleeve. "Every time I dozed today, I dreamed of searching for you. I tire of it. I want you here."

"And why did you hunt, in these dreams of yours?" he teased gently.

"To find you for Beatrice's christening. I made Father Theobald wait for your return, you know, since she is so hale."

"Ah."

"And because your kiss last night felt like a farewell," she added, accusation shading her voice.

Some strong emotion flickered behind his eyes as he stroked her cheek. "Well, it was not. I am here, lady wife, and here I will remain so long as Heaven permits." He worked his finger into Beatrice's balled fist, letting her tiny fingers curl around his joint as she suckled. "I have not attended a christening in many a year and paid little attention when I did. Remind me, what must I do?"

BEATRICE SNORED LIKE her mother, Ivo discovered later that night.

The next night, he learned that if he stroked gently down the bridge of her nose, her eyes would close despite herself and she would fall asleep, even if she was fussing. On the third, he realized that the nail on her smallest finger was no bigger than a barleycorn.

These discoveries all came in the silence after midnight, after Beatrice had woken to nurse and been put back in her cradle. Ivo would listen from the hall, wait to give Alaida time to fall asleep and for Bôte to crawl into her cot, then slip into the solar to hang over the child until dawn approached, marveling at what the gods and his lady wife had given him.

On the fourth night, a stool waited for him there by the cradle, beside a table with a cup of ale, freshly poured. When he glanced over to where Bôte lay, her narrow eyes glittered in the lamp light, watching him. He nodded his thanks, and wonder of wonders, she smiled, giving her blessing to his vigil.

So watching Beatrice became his whole night, just as watching the manor from a nearby tree had become the entirety of the eagle's day. Each night, he would see what new thing he could discover about his daughter. The speed at which she grew and changed stunned him—he could see the differences day by day—and the more she grew, the more she looked like her mother.

Except those eyes were definitely not going to be brown, he decided as she stared at his ring one night nearly a month after her birth. He moved his hand and chuckled at her determination as she tracked the gleam from side to side with eyes somewhere between light blue and gray. It was good, he thought, that he'd left his mark on her somehow, but he was glad she looked like her mother in everything else—especially the nose. She began to whine a little, so he stroked that tiny Alaida-nose to put her to sleep before she could wake her mother again. He yawned as she yawned, exhausted from all these nights and days of watching her but unable to keep himself from it even for a little.

He reached for the spiced wine Bôte had left him that night and drained the bowl, relishing the pleasant warmth that flowed through him. Beatrice snuffled again in her sleep, and Ivo set aside the cup and knelt by the cradle to see if she was waking. She wasn't, but he stayed there anyway, his chin resting on his folded arms, and watched her sleep.

The next thing he knew, roosters were crowing outside and his head felt thick as pease pottage. Trying to shake off the cobwebs, he struggled to his feet and opened the shutter. The fog outside glowed faintly pink. *Was dawn so close?* Panic rose just as the first pain of changing hit him.

Odin, no! He started for the door then realized he had no time to escape. With little else he could do, he pushed the shutter fully open and peeled out of his clothes, kicking them and his sword beneath the bed where they might not be noticed. The second wave of pain ripped through him, tearing a groan up from his gut.

"Ivo?"

He whirled as Alaida sat up in the bed.

"No," he begged the gods as pain ripped down his arms where feathers sprouted. Alaida stared, her face a mask of confusion that twisted into horror as his feet cramped into

claws and he buckled to the floor, shrinking, drawing in to
fit the eagle's form. He clamped his mouth against the tearing pain, only his lips were no longer lips but a beak, and the
eagle's piercing cry covered Alaida's gasp of shock.

This was what Ari had seen, the last vestige of Ivo realized as the sky beyond the open window beckoned. This
was the vision the gods had given. *Him*, not Beatrice.

Hands clutching over her open mouth, Alaida tried to
scream and failed, too terrified to make a sound. With another screech, the eagle leapt to the sill to test his wings,
flapping them powerfully above the sleeping infant, then
sailed out into the mist, away from the terrible silence.

SCREAMING. SHE WAS screaming but there was no sound and
she couldn't move and it was *him*.

Then Bôte was there, her familiar, safe arms gathering
her close, and Alaida's scream finally came out, muffled
against the old woman's bosom.

"Hush, my lady. Stop. Quiet yourself. Lady Beatrice is
fine. She's fine."

"But it was *him*," sobbed Alaida, trying to tell her. "It
was *him*."

Bôte hugged her tighter, half smothering her. "Aye, it
was, but he flew away. He's gone. All is well."

No. It wasn't well. Nothing was well. Alaida tore away
from Bôte and scrambled over to the cradle where her
daughter slept as though nothing had happened. Outside,
the fog had swallowed any sign of the bird, and for a heartbeat Alaida doubted herself. *A nightmare,* she thought. *A
trick of the eyes*. She slammed the shutter and latched it and
stood there, breathing so hard her lungs burned.

Oh, God. It was *him*. He had changed into a bird. An *eagle*. A moan welled up, building toward another scream.

Bôte grabbed her by the shoulders, her fingers digging
into Alaida's flesh as she shook her. "Silence, you fool, before someone hears you," she hissed. "Where will you be if

the others learn your husband is a demon? Where will Lady Beatrice be? They will burn you both."

Her words cut Alaida's scream short with an even deeper terror.

"A man who becomes a bird," continued Bôte, her disgust clear. "'Tis no wonder he leaves you each dawn."

"Then you saw it, too," Alaida breathed, almost relieved, because it meant she wasn't mad.

"Aye, I saw it, but 'tis our fortune no one else did, else they would be here even now, dragging all three of us off, to put you and me to torture and Lady Beatrice to death."

"No. Oh, God, please no." Alaida fell to her knees next to Beatrice's cradle and crossed herself.

"Prayer will do you no good," said Bôte. She poured a cup of wine and pressed it into Alaida's hands. "Drink this. All of it." She waited until Alaida obeyed. "Now listen to me. Lord Ivo is more danger to us than the Church. We know what he is, a devil who took a man's form so he could get a child on you. He will take Lady Beatrice and kill you and me."

"No. He wouldn't hurt us."

"He would. He must, for so long as we live, we are a threat to him, and to those friends of his, too, for surely they come and go so strangely for the same reason. They are all three of them demons."

"I asked him and asked him why. 'Trust me,' he said," Alaida whispered. She rocked back and forth, holding herself as she tried not to shriek. "And I did. Oh, God, I did, and he is this . . . thing." She grabbed Bôte. "What can we do?"

"Run, my lady. We have no choice. We must be away before he returns."

"But . . ." This didn't seem right. Ivo had always been gentle, and he adored Beatrice—but even Satan would love his own spawn. Her head felt so thick. "I don't know. Oh, God. What do I do?"

"Run, I tell you, fast and far, so that no one ever knows what Lady Beatrice is, or that you lay with a devil."

"But I didn't know," protested Alaida. "Surely I cannot be blamed. Nor Beatrice."

"No one will hear your innocence, my lady, they will be too busy burning you and your half-devil child. We must run." Without waiting for Alaida's decision, Bôte began gathering warm clothing. She tugged Alaida to her feet. "Dress yourself, my lady, and find as much gold and silver as you can. We will need it to make our way to Scotland. Aye, he'll not find us there."

Still numb with shock, Alaida let Bôte's sureness guide her. She donned thick hose and boots and layered on two heavy woolen kirtles beneath her warmest gown and cloak. She dumped out the money in the casket, filled her purse and Bôte's, and wrapped what was left into the bundle of clothes along with her jewels. As Bôte tied up the remains of the previous evening's supper in a cloth, Alaida tucked a few more jewels into Beatrice's swaddling and wrapped her more heavily against the cold. The baby began to whine and fret.

"I should nurse her first, to keep her quiet."

"Later. I will not burn for that demon." Bôte leaned over the cradle, did something Alaida couldn't see, and Beatrice stopped crying. "That will hold her. I know a safe place where you can suckle her once we're away. Hurry, my lady. Sir Ari will be back. He's one of them. He will never let us go."

"What about Oswald and the others? How will we explain . . . ?"

"I will see to it. Stay here." Bôte slipped out. A few moments later, she was back, carrying a skin of wine and a cheese, which she pressed into Alaida's hands along with the bundle of clothes. "Fortune is truly with us, my lady. They all still sleep. Come. Quietly."

Bôte scooped up Beatrice, and they passed down the stairs and across the hall in silence, surrounded only by random snores and grunts. Outside, the fog hung so thick it muffled all sound and turned everything to specters. No one challenged them in the yard, and the man who should have been on duty at the postern gate seemed to have stepped away. Bôte quickly raised the bar and pushed the gate open enough to slip through. She motioned for Alaida to follow.

This didn't seem right, that faint voice whispered again, as if through the fog. Alaida glanced back toward the hall, but it had all but disappeared in the mist, just as Ivo had disappeared, an eagle. Her eagle, she suddenly realized, and that made it worse.

"Come, lamb," urged Bôte. "I will keep you safe."

A muffled footstep sounded somewhere nearby. Panicking, Alaida stepped quickly through the gate and Bôte shut it behind them with nary a squeak. Unable to see more than a few feet in the fog, they made their way toward the river almost by feel, found the bridge, and crossed noiselessly. On the far bank, they hurried west, away from Alnwick and the evil that was its lord and her husband.

And all the while, Beatrice slept peacefully in Bôte's arms.

CHAPTER 28

"GATE," SHOUTED ARI for a second time, and for the second time no one answered. Strange. The yard should be bustling with activity by now—he'd gotten turned around in the sudden fog and it had taken him forever to find his horse and get back. It was nearly time for dinner.

He pushed against the gate and found it barred. He shouted again, louder, and pounded against the iron strapping, but the only answer was the neighing of horses from the stables. A chill ran down his spine, and with a curse, he whipped his mount around and rode for Wat's cottage.

He found the reeve digging beetroots in his croft. "Something's wrong at the manor. Muster as many armed men as you can find quickly and come."

By the time the villagers turned out, Ari had discovered the postern gate was unbarred. He drew his sword and silently pulled it open. The others slipped in behind him, huddling with their weapons as he and Wat, armed with a broadax, edged forward through the mist.

As they neared the well, Ari spotted what looked like a body. He crept closer, saw no blood, and noticed the man's chest rise and fall. He prodded him with the tip of his sword. Edric rolled over and yawned.

"Ass! Get up! Get up!" Furious, Ari hauled him to his feet. "Sleeping on watch, and with a gate unbarred. I'll have your hide for this. Fifty lashes."

"Wha—?" Edric gaped at him. "But I . . . But I—"

"Where are the others?"

Edric shook his head thickly, but Wat called, "Here, sir."

The two men who should have been guarding the main gate lay sprawled against the posts like drunkards. Uneasiness rapidly replacing his anger, Ari left Wat to wake them and dashed for the hall.

He shoved the door open to find every man in a similar stupor, even Oswald. Ari yanked him up and shouted into his face. "Wake yourself, Marshal. What goes on here? The wall is unguarded and every man asleep."

Oswald scrubbed his eyes with his hands and struggled to comprehend as Wat came in and starting waking the others. "I . . . I do not know, *messire*. All was well." He thought hard, clearly confounded. "Lord Ivo came as usual, but not Sir Brand. We played chess, I went to bed, and the next thing, you were shaking me."

"Where are the women?"

"Uh . . ."

"The pantry, *messire*," said Tom, yawning wide. "Bôte sent them all down late. She said Lady Alaida was too tired to have anyone about."

Alaida. Without bothering to ask, Ari flew up the stairs.

The utter silence of the solar confirmed the worst. Signs of hurried departure were everywhere, from the night linens on the floor to Alaida's jewel casket lying open and empty on the bed.

"Ah, God," said Oswald behind him. He pushed past Ari and ransacked the room, ripping aside draperies and opening cupboards and chests as though he might find them inside. His bellow of helpless rage echoed through the hall as he collapsed to his knees. "God help me, I have failed her. I have failed my lady."

"We've all failed her, Marshal, but regret will do her no good." He scanned the room, taking in what was there and what wasn't. "Whoever carried them off took warm clothes for the women and things for the child. They intend to keep them alive. For ransom, perhaps. I want everyone awake and in the hall. Hold them there. I want no one disturbing the tracks."

Oswald stormed downstairs barking orders, and Ari took one more look around the solar. This time, a gleam of metal beneath the bed caught his eye. He crossed to pull the object out: Ivo's sword and, hooked on it, his gray tunic. With a sick feeling, he reached under the bed and discovered the rest of Ivo's clothes.

Balls. This was bad. Ivo had clearly turned eagle here . . . With a groan, Ari looked toward the window. He could see it: the eagle rising over the cradle, Alaida screaming, just as in his visions. But it had been Ivo, not Beatrice. Alaida had seen Ivo change. No one had taken them. She had run in terror.

He sagged against the bedpost and pounded his skull with his fists. "Odin, what have I done?"

He would carve the visions out of his head if he could, but as he'd told Oswald, regret was no use. What was needed now was to fix this. They were going to have to flee, that was certain, but first they must get Alaida and Beatrice safely back, without further exposing Ivo. Working quickly, he rolled Ivo's clothes inside his linen shirt, then tied the bundle with a strip torn from the bottom of Alaida's discarded kirtle, checking to be sure none of Ivo's gray showed. He stepped to the door and called for Tom.

The boy trotted upstairs still yawning. "*Messire*, have Lady Alaida and Lady Beatrice truly been stolen away?"

"So it seems." Ari considered how best to say this. "I have a task for you, Squire, but no one must know what you do. Will you swear your silence in service of your lord and lady?"

Wide eyes grave, the boy nodded. "Of course, *messire*."

"Go to the stable and saddle Fax."

"Did Lord Ivo not take him this morning?"

"No. He . . . had something to do on foot. Take Fax to Merewyn's cottage and wait there for him. And take these things with you." Ari indicated the clothes and sword.

"His sword! *Messire*, he goes nowhere without his sword."

"He did this morning—but again, no one must know, so I will drop them out the window to you. Can you get out the gate without anyone knowing you go?"

"The guards will see me pass."

"I'll call them inside. Get Fax, then whistle when you're ready. Make sure no one sees you leave, Tom. This is important."

"I understand, *messire*. My lord will need his armor, too."

Ari hesitated. Ivo's mail would be costly to replace, but . . . "No. He'll need to ride light. Run, Tom."

Tom sped from the room. Ari went to the landing and called for Oswald to bring the guards in, then went back to wait by the window and consider his plan for flaws. It seemed like only moments had passed when Tom whistled. He had both Fax and his dun horse ready to ride. Ari dropped the clothes, then the sword and belt, and the boy quickly fastened them to Fax's saddle.

"Use the postern gate," Ari called down. "Make sure the yard is clear."

Tom nodded and started off, and Ari went downstairs. Every voice dropped silent as he strode to the front of the hall.

"Lady Alaida has been taken, along with her child and maid. We do not know who took them or why, so Alnwick is to prepare as if for war." He waited while worry murmured through the room and settled into a grim determination. "I will carry word to Lord Ivo and Brand, and we will ride down whoever has done this, and get the women back."

"Please, *messire*, let me go with you," pleaded Edric, clearly wanting to redeem himself. "You know I have a good eye."

Ari shook his head. "Every man is needed here until we know who and what we face. Oswald, you have command. Be ready for anything."

"Yes, *messire*, and we will be ready to ride as well, if needed."

"Good." Ari looked out over the men and women he had known and laughed with for nearly a year, silently bade them farewell, and left.

Starting at the postern gate, he rode arcs back and forth in the fog until he spotted marks in the soft earth. He wasn't surprised by what he found: two sets of footprints, both women's, one light and one heavy, headed toward the bridge. He picked the trail up again on the other side of the river, and saw where they veered west. There were a few hoofprints nearby, but they looked older, and surely if someone was taking them and had mounts, the women would have been put on horseback to make the escape quicker.

No. Alaida was going of her own will and, for whatever reason, on foot. He could easily ride her down, but what then? She was clever and might have figured out he was the raven that rode Brand's shoulder each night. If so, she would never willingly return with him.

But he could track her at least, and let Ivo know where she'd gone.

Then *he* could decide what to do.

IN ITS PANIC, the eagle flew fast and far, and by the time Ivo regained a piece of himself and turned the bird back toward the village, the fog had boiled up so thick it hid the land for miles. Disoriented, the bird circled between blue sky and a sea of white, searching for some sign—a familiar tree, the top of the tower—until the exhaustion that had caught Ivo in the solar overcame even the eagle's strength. Unable to fly more, he sailed down into the mist until he found a tall tree, lit on a sheltered branch, and slept.

When he woke, the fog had burned off and the tower

showed in the far distance. He flew toward Alnwick, but it was late and he barely had time to skim past the walls before the approach of sunset forced him toward the woods.

As he passed over Merewyn's cottage, Fax's familiar whinny drew him down. He found Tom standing between Fax and his dun, watching the woods as though expecting someone. The boy spotted the bird overhead and called out.

Merewyn came out wiping her hands on a cloth. She looked up and said something to Tom about pottage. The boy vanished into the house, and Merewyn picked up a bundle from the stool by her door and headed into the woods. The eagle followed her to a clearing, where she laid the bundle on the ground, cut the bindings, and stepped away. He sailed down to land nearby, and as the sun slid below the horizon, the pain hit.

Merewyn watched until he started to become more man than eagle, then turned away, giving him privacy while he lay there naked and agonized on the ground. The pain still twisted him as he crawled to his clothes.

"She saw me," said Ivo between pain-clenched teeth.

"Yes, my lord. I guessed when Tom came with Fax, and then Sir Ari came a little while ago and told me all. My lord . . ." She hesitated, and even from behind her, Ivo could tell she was unhappy about what she had to say. "Lady Alaida is gone, and Lady Beatrice and Bôte with her."

He froze with one foot in his breeks. "Gone? Gone where?"

"Run from you, my lord. From the eagle."

Ivo groaned. "Alaida . . . Why didn't Ari and Oswald bring them back?"

"Your men think they were stolen away for ransom, and Sir Ari let them believe it, to protect both you and her. But he tracked them. They're on foot. The raven will show you their path—he comes with Brand."

"They're all right, though?"

"Yes, my lord, but there is much troubling about what passed this morning."

He continued dressing while she told him of how Ari had been delayed in reaching the manor and of what he'd found there.

"I also slept too hard," said Ivo, dread slithering up his spine like a viper. "That's how I was caught. I thought I was merely tired."

"'Twas more than that, my lord." She turned, her brow furrowed with concern. "The morning mist was strange. I was milking my goats when it came up. It rose suddenly, from everywhere at once, and I could taste the evil in it. The birds felt it as well. They've not sung all day."

Ivo shook his head. "I sensed nothing."

"Perhaps because the eagle is not truly a bird, my lord."

"Tell my wife that." Bile scalded his throat.

Her eyes filled with sympathy. "I will if you wish, my lord. I can come with you and explain it to her, soothe her fears."

Ivo shook his head. He'd seen the terror, the repulsion, on Alaida's face. "She has seen too much magic already to be soothed by more, even from you. Anyway, Bôte saw me as well. Things are too far gone." He fastened his boots and rose. "My sword?"

"With Tom. He knows none of this, my lord. Just that someone stole them away. I left it for you to tell him if you choose." She led him back toward the cottage.

Tom met them at the edge of the clearing. "My lord! I heard screams, like an injured man. I thought—"

"'Twas the eagle," said Merewyn, making Ivo's heart skip a beat. "On a squirrel."

"I find myself without weapon, Squire," said Ivo, anxious to get Tom on to something else and take that doubt off his face.

Tom retrieved the sword and belt. "'Tis sharp, my lord. I honed it while I waited."

"Good lad." As Ivo buckled his belt, Merewyn slipped into the cottage and returned bearing a bowl and spoon.

"Eat, my lord, while you wait for Sir Brand."

Ivo took the bowl gratefully and began shoveling the hot

pottage in as fast as he could. Merewyn made another trip inside, this time reappearing with a skin of ale, a loaf of bread, and a plump cheese. Tom stowed them on Fax while Ivo finished his meal.

The sound of heavy horses crashing through the underbrush told them Brand was coming. Ivo handed the bowl to Merewyn and swung up on Fax. Tom went to his dun.

"Where are you going, Squire?"

"With you, my lord."

Ivo shook his head. "I want you at the castle. Oswald needs men for the wall."

"But, my lord, I—"

"The wall, Thomas."

He bowed his head, however unwillingly. "Yes, my lord."

Brand rode up, leading Ari's bay. "What is this damnable bird trying to tell me? Where were you this morning? What's Tom doing here?"

"I'll tell you on the way," said Ivo. "My thanks, Healer."

She stepped forward. "Take me with you, my lord. Lady Alaida will need—"

"No. I won't put you in danger as well."

"Danger?" said Brand. "Who's in danger?"

"Later," snapped Ivo. "Leave Ari's horse and come." He put the spurs to Fax and headed for the river.

BRAND HESITATED A moment, then gave Merewyn a smile and a shrug, tossed the bay's reins to Tom, and tore off after his friend.

Merewyn watched him go, burning the memory of how he looked into her heart. She might see him again, for a little, but once he and Lord Ivo brought the women back safely, they would be gone forever. Every memory became suddenly precious.

Behind her, Tom cursed softly. She blinked back the tears and turned to find him wearing a sullen frown. "Why are you so angry?"

"Lord Ivo made me squire," he grumbled. "But he never lets me ride with him."

"He wants you better trained first, so you'll be safe."

"But he doesn't even take me hunting! I'm good with a bow."

"Your time will come, Tom. Patience." He would need a great deal of that now, to find another knight willing to have a bastard stableboy as squire. "Come inside and finish your meal before you go."

She refilled his bowl and cut him a thick slab of cheese, then left him while she went to care for her animals. When she had finished, she found him standing in the doorway, still aggrieved, fiddling with some small charm that hung on a thin chain around his neck and looking so much like his father that her heart squeezed tight.

"What have you there?" she asked, trying to distract him from his disappointment.

"Hmm? Oh, this." He held the bit of silver up. "'Tis my good luck piece."

Merewyn looked closer, and the hairs rose on her arms. "Where did you get that?"

"My—A man found it in the well the last time they cleaned it. He gave it to me."

A man. Aelfwine, he meant—he'd been the one lowered into the well five years ago to scoop out the muck, the only one who'd been willing to go down. This was probably the last gift he'd ever given the boy. But that wasn't what chilled her. "Has Lord Ivo ever seen it?"

He looked at her oddly. "I don't think so. I keep it under my shirt most times. But I think its luck made him choose me for squire. See?" He tilted the token in the fading light. "'Tis an eagle, like his shield."

No, like the one Brand had shown her in Ari's book—Lord Ivo's amulet. *Well. Curse. Token. Monster. Sleeping men.* Her mind spun over it all at dizzying speed, and suddenly her cottage vanished and she was sailing over the land north of the river, watching Bôte lay Lady Beatrice before the standing stone.

"Merewyn?"

She thumped back to earth and, without pausing to think, ran inside and grabbed her rune sticks off the shelf. "Mother, what must I do?"

She dropped the sticks on the table by Tom's empty bowl. Only three fell face up: Guide, Lover, Death. Her breath caught in her throat, but she nodded, obedient to the Goddess even in this. "I understand, Mother. So mote it be."

Tom stared at her from the door. "I had heard you were a witch."

"Only a small one. Squire, are you willing to disobey your lord to help save his lady and daughter?"

He jerked his head toward the runes. "Do your sticks say I must?"

"No. They say *I* must, but I have no way to follow them. Will you help me?"

He stared at her, then nodded and started toward the horses. "The bay is faster. Sir Ari will forgive us, I think."

When he put a hand down to help her up, his strength surprised her. "You're becoming a man, Tom."

"Aye." He gave her a wise look over his shoulder. "As good a one as my father, I hope."

So he did know. Merewyn wrapped her arms around his waist and gave him the hug she would never give a son of her own body. "If you are, you will surely become the knight Lord Ivo wants you to be. Can we catch them?"

"Aye. Hold tight." He dug his toes into the bay's ribs and they were off.

CHAPTER 29

TO AVOID THE bridge and the eyes of Alnwick's guards, Brand and Ivo forded the river above the upper weir, then turned west. As they followed the raven over the moors, Ivo explained the situation as best he could.

"So we are through here," said Brand heavily. "Once we see them safely home, we must go."

To hear it put so bluntly made Ivo's gut knot, but he nodded. "Aye."

"I had finally . . . Merewyn." Brand's groan came from so deep it seemed to rise from the soil beneath them. "I didn't even tell her farewell."

"I could say nothing before the boy. I'm sorry."

"She knows, though?"

"Aye. She'll understand." Unlike Alaida, who would never understand why he'd done what he had, how badly he had wanted her and all she represented. The only good thing in all this was that he hadn't had to take Beatrice from her— Beatrice, whom he would never hear laugh or see walk. "I should have stayed in the woods."

"No. You were right to come out. We cannot hide forever. You've shown us we can live among men again."

"Only to leave. No matter what we do, no matter how long we make it last, we will always have to leave." Leave wives and daughters and friends and eager young squires.

"'Tis no worse than other men face when they go to war," said Brand.

"Other men go to war hoping to come home. We leave with no hope at all." He thought of Beatrice again, and of Alaida, who had warmed him clear through and now would teach his daughter to fear and despise him. "We can never return."

"Perhaps you can find a way," countered Brand. "But even if you cannot, at least you've tasted a man's life once more."

"And found it bitter."

"No, Ivar. You've had a wife and a child. That is as sweet as life ever gets."

Ivo had nothing to say to that truth. They rode on in silence until the raven veered south from the track. The land seemed familiar from the day the eagle had followed Alaida. Suddenly, he knew where they must be going. "The standing stone."

"From Wat's story?"

Ivo nodded. "'Tis just ahead, in the wood near the bottom of that hill. What would they be doing at the stone? They haven't come very far."

"I'm more curious about the fog," said Brand. "There's something odd about it."

He was right. The fog that wove through the trees in moonlit ribbons lay only on the north flank of the hillock, around where the stone stood. Ivo thought of what Merewyn had told him about the morning mist. In his need to get to Alaida, he'd passed off her concerns, but now . . .

They rode to the foot of the rise, then skirted the edge of the enshrouded woods till they came to a narrow path. Down it, the fog glowed dimly yellow, as if from a fire. Brand nodded toward the glow and touched his ear. Ivo cocked his head to listen.

The sound rose faint and sweet—a distant lullaby, crooned by a familiar voice. Ivo's concern eased. If Bôte was singing lullabies by the fire, surely all was well. He motioned for Brand to dismount, and they secured their horses and stepped into the fog, leaving the raven perched nearby.

From within, the pall of mist swallowed the moonlight and obscured anything more than a foot away. As they felt their way between tree trunks, Ivo inhaled deeply, drawing the damp air over his tongue. Bitter, it was, and clay-cold, and his wife and daughter were somewhere in the middle of it. He should have listened to Merewyn. He should have brought her to help.

The path abruptly widened, leaving not even the ghostly trees as guides. Ivo groped his way forward, certain the stone was near and anxious to find Alaida and Beatrice and get them away from this place. Bôte's song swelled around them and the mist glowed more brightly, seemingly on fire.

In the next step, the ground vanished.

Ivo plunged down some unseen slope and slammed to a stop at the bottom. Brand smashed into him an instant later. They scrambled up, winded, swords in hand.

Before them lay a wide, low cavern, glowing with the light of an uncanny fire that blazed in the center. At the edge of the flames stood Bôte, swaying gently side to side, singing to the infant cradled in her arms. Alaida lay unmoving on a pile of fresh-cut heather off to one side.

Bôte's song faded away, and she looked up with a strange, pleased smile. "You have found us. Good. I have waited a long time for you to come. A very long time."

Uneasy, Ivo stepped farther into the cave. "Nurse. Is all well?"

"Very well." She stroked Beatrice's cheek. "Such a good bairn. She's not cried this whole time."

"And my wife?"

"Asleep, as you see," said Bôte.

Brand's gaze traveled the rock walls. "What is this place?"

"The place beneath the stone," said Bôte, continuing to sway. "The place where Sir Egbert chased the dragon to ground. But of course, that is only an old tale. There was no dragon."

"And no heart," said Brand. "The sound in the well is but the echo of distant waves."

"Only men who spent time with the sea would know that." She spoke as if to herself. "Aye, 'tis waves, but the heart cut out was real enough."

Ivo sheathed his sword and went to kneel by his wife. "Alaida?"

"Are you certain you want her awake?" asked Bôte. "She will not be pleased to see you."

The old woman was probably right. He shook Alaida anyway. "Wake yourself, sweet leaf."

"Ivo?" Alaida stirred and slowly opened her eyes, a smile on her lips until she woke enough to remember. The smile vanished, and she sat bolt upright and scrabbled back, flattening against the rock wall. "Why are you here? Go away."

Ivo held his empty hands out so she could see he meant no harm. "I've come to take you and Beatrice home."

"No. I know what you are." The fear in her eyes soured Ivo's stomach. "I saw you turn into that . . . that thing."

"An eagle. The same eagle you claimed as your pet, who watched over you and protected you from de Jeune. Come, let me see you safely home."

"We cannot go home. The Church . . ."

"No one will know. Once you're safe, I'll vanish, I swear. You can say I was killed. No one will know."

"But Beatrice . . ." She bit back a sob. "Her father is a demon."

"No. I'm no demon. I'm a man, Alaida. A cursed man, but only a man."

"Only a man," echoed Bôte, chucking Beatrice under the chin. "Men do not have feathers and fur, do they, sweeting?"

"Eagles have no fur," said Brand.

"No, no, no, of course not. What has fur, sweeting?" Bôte cooed. "Lions and horses and wolves and stags and dogs and bulls."

Cold fear rippled down Ivo's spine as Bôte named the animals the others became.

She glanced to Brand, her face lit by that peculiar smile. "And bears, little one. Let's not forget big, brown bears that would eat a tender bairn like you."

"Who are you, old woman?" demanded Brand, but Ivo already knew. He drew his sword again and put himself between Alaida and evil.

"You know me. I'm Bôte. Old Bôte, who raised Lady Alaida for your friend to breed on. Bôte, who pulled the eagle's child from her womb and breathed the life into it." She rubbed Beatrice's belly, and smiled when the child gurgled happily. "You know me, don't you, sweeting. And you know me, too, Bear. I made you."

Snarling, Brand raised his sword and charged.

"Brand, no!" Ivo stepped in front of Cwen and caught Brand's descending blade across his own. In his fury, Brand swung again, the brutal force of his blow driving Ivo to his knees. "Brand, stop! Beatrice. You'll hurt Beatrice."

His words penetrated Brand's blood rage and stopped his sword at the top of its deadly arc. Brand's arms shook with the effort of controlling himself as he slowly lowered his weapon and took himself back from the bear's savagery.

The old woman laughed with delight. "Good, Eagle. You stopped him this time. You should have stopped him before he killed my Sigeweard."

Ivo spun to face the witch. "What do you want, Cwen?"

"Who is Cwen?" asked Alaida.

"The witch who cursed us," said Brand. "Her."

"What do you mean? That's Bôte." Alaida clambered to her feet. "Bôte, tell them, before they hurt you."

"Be at ease, lamb. They cannot harm me." The witch

passed one hand over the fire and stepped into its center. The flames licked up, curling around her skirts, embracing her without burning. Alaida screamed as the nurse's plump form melted away, leaving Beatrice unharmed in the arms of a thinner, younger, taller woman whose only resemblance to Bôte was the satisfied smile. "You see, I *am* Cwen."

"Beatrice!" Alaida lunged toward the fire. Ivo caught her around the waist and spun her back. "Let me go." Alaida flailed at him, frantic to save her child. "Beatrice."

"Alaida, stop. She's fine. Don't make Cwen drop her." Ivo trapped her against his chest and held her until his words penetrated her frenzy and she stilled. "I will put her back in your arms," he whispered against her ear. "Let us do this."

She stared up at him, the reality of this new fear overcoming some of the old. She nodded, and he slowly released her and pushed her behind him.

"I raised you for this, you know," said Cwen. "I foresaw he would win your hand, years ago, and I came to wait, to ready you, to see that you desired him and bore his child."

"The posset," whispered Alaida, suddenly comprehending the strange desire that had swept over her that night.

"Aye. It made you want him. It made his seed catch, so this little one was born at the right time. She's a month today. You know what today is, don't you, lamb?"

The air caught in Alaida's lungs. *The eve of Allhallowmass.* A day of dark magic, when demons reigned over the earth.

"Bôte, please," she begged.

"Do not call me by that servant's name. I am Cwen." She drew herself erect, as though taking power from the name itself. "I was sorceress to kings long before even these two were born, and that was long ago. Ask them how old they are."

Alaida looked to Ivo. He shook his head, and stepped toward Bôte. "I ask again, what do you want?"

"A simple thing, Eagle—your daughter in my son's place. And you will give her to me."

"No." Alaida jerked forward again, and Ivo put his arm out to block her.

"Never," he spat at Cwen. "I would die first."

"A hollow vow, since you cannot." The firelight gilded Cwen's gaunt face into terrifying beauty that sent more fear racing through Alaida. "That was the cleverest part of what I wrought, and the most difficult, but I wanted your torment to go on through eternity, like my own. How is it, knowing you will never see the sun again?"

Ivo stepped toward her. "I have grown to love the moon."

"Ah, but you remember how the sun feels . . ." She flicked a finger and golden warmth bathed the cave as though they stood naked beneath a sunlit sky. "The pleasure of a summer afternoon . . ." Another flick, and a cooling breeze riffled past, carrying the scent of new-mown hay. "How the light strikes the waves as you sail home . . ." A flick, and the sound of water rushing past the hull of a ship filled their ears.

Ivo lifted his face to the heat and light that poured down on him, and he sighed.

"It can be yours again," whispered Cwen. "I will free you from the curse. Give me Beatrice, and you can be a man again and live out your life in the sun. In your home. I will love her, care for her, raise her as my own. Say yes, and you can have it all."

Even in her fear, Alaida understood Cwen's offer. *As a man, Ivo could go home.* One word and he would have the sun. All he had to do was give up their child. He would do it. She knew he would do it. *Ah, God, no.*

Ivo opened his eyes and looked deep into Cwen's cold blue gaze. "Take me instead."

"No!" shouted Brand, and Alaida realized she had shouted, too.

Ivo ignored them both. "I will be your son," he told Cwen. "I will give myself over to you, honor you, and learn to love you as a son loves a mother."

"*You!* You think I would want one of the animals that

ripped my boy from me?" Rage shook her so violently that
Beatrice wobbled in her arms.

Ivo dropped his sword and stepped forward, holding his
wrists together as though shackled. "Then take me as slave,
to serve you. To torture as you will."

"Or me," said Brand. "I'm the one who killed Sigeweard,
the one you really want. Spend your venom on me, Witch.
You'll enjoy it more."

"I have other plans for you, Bear," said Cwen in a voice
that made Alaida's skin crawl. "I want the child. She is
young. She will love me as a mother."

"As I did?" asked Alaida, choking out the words past the
tears that filled her eyes and clogged her throat. "Whatever
you call yourself, you are my Bôte, who raised me and cod-
dled me and taught me to sew. My Bôte, who I loved all
these years. Don't you see, you already have the child you
wish."

Cwen's expression softened. "Almost, lamb. But you
loved your mother first, and your grandmother. This one
will love only me."

"And who am I to love?" sobbed Alaida. "How can you
take my child from me when you know how it feels?"

"I'm not going to *take* her from you, lamb. He is going to
give her."

"But he won't. You heard him. Please, give her to me."
Alaida reached out and started forward.

"I could take you both," mused Cwen, "and have both
daughter and granddaughter. What think you, Eagle?"

"No." Ivo dragged Alaida back and set her behind him
once more. "Me, Cwen. That is the offer. Nothing else. Send
Alaida home with Beatrice, vow that your evil will never
touch them again, and I am yours forever."

"How touching. You love her," sneered Cwen. "Little
good it will do you now that your wife has seen you as you
truly are. You have no real choice. Give up your child and
enjoy your life, or refuse and continue in your hell. Alaida
will hate you either way."

"I will take hell," said Ivo. "You get neither of them."

"Of course, I could make her forget," offered Cwen. "All of it. The eagle. What she saw. Even Beatrice."

"I would never forget my own child," vowed Alaida.

"Ah, but you would, lamb, and you would love him then. Give me the child, Eagle, and you can have Alaida along with the sun."

"You offer a great deal, Witch, trying to get me to say yes. Why?"

"Because she must, my lord." Merewyn stepped into the cavern, Tom close on her heel.

Brand's face twisted with concern. "Merewyn. Get out of here."

She shook her head. "I am meant to be here."

"Please, Meri, go. You don't know what she is. Tom, get her out of here."

"Tom, see to your lady," said Merewyn easily. "I do know what she is, *messire*. That is why the Mother sent me."

"Arrogance," sneered Cwen. "Your simple goddess magic cannot match mine."

"I have been listening at the mouth of the cave, great one. I well know what your magic can do." She circled toward Brand, drawing Cwen's attention with her.

Tom reached Alaida's side and took her hand. "I will help you be strong, my lady."

"She wants your soul along with the child, my lord," continued Merewyn. "That's why she offers up your lady's heart to tempt you. Do not let her do it. Refuse her."

"Until my last breath," vowed Ivo.

"My lady, she tampers with your spirit, too. This fear . . . this is her, not you."

"You meddle in things not your business, Healer," warned Cwen.

Merewyn ignored her. "Think, my lady. How did you grow so frightened of your husband?"

"I . . ." Confused, Alaida looked to Ivo, then to Cwen, then back to Merewyn. The healer's calm drew her, and she chose it, let it soothe her tangled thoughts. "I saw him change. Bôte told me he was a demon. She said they would burn me for lying with him. But I kept thinking, he's Ivo, he's my husband. She made me drink . . . to calm me, she said."

"But you grew more afraid, didn't you? She made you more afraid," said Merewyn.

Alaida struggled, trying to think. "I was so afraid."

"Ah, sweet leaf, I would never hurt you," said Ivo. "You must know that. Never fear me."

"Fear him," commanded Cwen, and Alaida whimpered and trembled under the weight of the terror that crashed down on her.

"Leave her be," said Tom. He released Alaida and squared off next to Ivo, between her and Cwen. "She is not afraid of him, Witch. None of us are."

"You should be, boy." Cwen found Alaida over his shoulder. "They will burn you if they know, my lady."

"How would they know?" asked Merewyn. "Would you tell them, my lady?"

Alaida's head felt thick, but not so thick she couldn't answer this. "Never."

"They will know and burn you for it," promised Cwen. Her voice shifted so she sounded like Bôte again. "Or *he* will kill us, lamb, even the babe, to keep his foul secret."

"No," said Alaida. She understood what Cwen was doing now, and she fought to push her out of her mind. "You lie. You have lied to me all along. He loves us."

"His weakness," said Cwen. "And yours."

"Then make it your strength, my lady." Tom turned his back on Cwen and held his fist before his chest, where only Alaida could see, and opened it. "Be strong for the eagle who followed us that day."

Tom was trying to tell her something. *Hand*. He'd left something in her hand. She opened her fist just enough to catch a glimpse of silver, to make out an eagle. She looked to Merewyn, questioning.

"All the strength you need lies within you, my lady," said Merewyn softly. "When you came to me for help, the potion I gave you was only a soothing oil, with no drop of magic in it. All the magic lies here." She made a fist and laid her hand over her heart. "*Here*, as it does in Lord Ivo."

"But I . . ."

"Are you truly afraid?" asked Merewyn. "Do you truly fear your husband?"

"No." Alaida thought she understood . . . But what if she was wrong? What if he . . . *No, that was Cwen.* She drew a shaky breath. "No, I am not."

"But you are," breathed Cwen, her poison wafting once more through Alaida's soul.

"No." She squeezed until the little eagle cut into her hand, using the pain to push Cwen's magic aside. "No. I am not."

Reaching deep, she found the strength to take the few steps to Ivo's side. Sure now, she touched the eagle over his heart and spoke the truth she'd been fighting to remember all day, even as Bôte had driven her deeper into fear. "I am not afraid. I love Ivo. God help me, I do love him, even now."

"And I . . ." Ivo suddenly screamed and stiffened, his back arching like a bow. Foulness streamed out of him in ropes of thick brown mist. Horrified, Alaida watched him strain and choke within the dark cloud. *Dying. He was dying. She'd killed him.* Her scream rose up with his, joined with that of the phantom eagle that formed out of the mist and stretched its wings wide over their heads. It screamed once more and abruptly vanished, leaving only a dull sparkle hanging in the air.

Ivo folded to his knees, gasping for air as Alaida crumpled beside him.

"No!" shrieked Cwen. "No, it cannot be. This is impossible. You don't have it. No one has it. The spell cannot be broken with love alone."

"Your hold on him is ended," said Merewyn. "As is your hold on his lady."

Cwen shifted her grip on Beatrice and dangled her over the flames. "Not yet it is not."

"No!" Ivo launched himself at Cwen, knocking her sideways as he snatched Beatrice from her hands. He twisted midair to land beneath the infant, protecting her as he hit the firestones and bounced away, embers flying around them.

"Enough." The air around Cwen boiled with her wrath. She gathered the seething clouds to her and flung her arm toward Ivo. With a cry, Merewyn dove between them. The thunderbolt intended for Ivo and Beatrice struck her chest and raised her off the ground. She hung there, writhing, lightning crackling over her skin.

"Merewyn!" Brand roared and charged forward. Another flick of Cwen's hand turned him aside and sent his blade spinning away as Merewyn fell to the ground, motionless. Cwen turned toward Alaida and drew her arm back.

"No." Tom's slender body flew across the cave like a spear. He hit Cwen straight on, driving his knife into her chest with a shout as her lightning seared him. They fell back, slamming into the rear wall. Tom rolled away, and Brand surged to his feet, swinging for Cwen's neck.

His blade found only air and smoke. Snarling in frustration, he whirled, seeking the witch. "Where is she?"

Tom came up in a fighting stance, Ivo's discarded sword in his fist, searching, too. "Vanished."

The earth began to tremble around them. Dust and pebbles rained from the ceiling.

"Get out," yelled Ivo. "Alaida. Get out!"

She ran for the entrance with Ivo hard behind her, once more sheltering Beatrice with his body. Behind them, Brand tossed his sword to Tom. "Run, boy." He scooped up Merewyn and dashed out, narrowly escaping as the cavern collapsed around them. The rumbling and shaking continued as the standing stone shifted, dancing, to fill the hole where the entrance had been. The tremors faded away, and the night grew still. It was as if the cave had never existed.

"Meri? Ah, no. No." Brand hugged the healer's shattered body to his chest. "Meri."

Ivo pushed Beatrice into Alaida's arms and ripped off his cloak to spread it on the tufted grass. "Brand, here."

As Alaida clung to her child, repeating her name over and over in sobs of relief, Brand knelt to lay Merewyn on the cloak. Gently, he covered her with his own. "You'll be all right," he whispered, stroking her hair. "I'll take care of you."

Her chest rose in a shudder, and she slowly opened her eyes. A soft smile touched her lips. "You are safe."

"Aye," said Brand.

"Lady Beatrice?"

"Aye. She's safe, too."

Weeping, Alaida knelt to show Merewyn the dusty but sound babe who wailed in her arms. "You saved her, Merewyn. You saved us all."

"Love saved you." She shuddered again, and her breath rattled in her lungs. "My lord?"

"Here, Merewyn." Ivo knelt beside Alaida. "My thanks can never be enough."

"Love her," she said simply, then, "Tom knows. Ask him."

"I will. Peace be with you, Healer." Ivo helped Alaida up and led her to one side. She sobbed against his chest, guilty at the great joy she took in having him and Beatrice alive and well when so much had been lost.

"It is beautiful," whispered Merewyn. The fog had vanished with Cwen, leaving a night so clear the stars seemed to hang in the branches just out of reach. Merewyn's eyes found the streak of milky white overhead. "Woden's Way. I walk it tonight."

"No, Meri. Don't leave me. Hang on. I'll take you home."

"The Mother calls me." She struggled to raise her hand to touch Brand's cheek. "Do not mourn, my love."

"Merewyn, please."

"When it is our time, I will find you." Her hand fell away,

and as the breath sighed from her, she whispered, "Watch for me."

Then she was gone, her eyes still fixed on the heavens. With a moan, Brand gathered her in his arms. Tears glittered on his cheeks, bright as the stars, as he closed her eyes and kissed her good-bye.

CHAPTER 30

THEY MADE THEIR way home through the silent night, Brand carrying Merewyn every step of the way. Ivo put Alaida up on Fax with Beatrice and led them, walking at Brand's side. Tom brought up the rear with the other two horses, and the raven circled high overhead.

A mile before the bridge, Brand stopped. "I'm turning here. She should go home, not to their church, and if I go through the village, there will be questions."

Ivo nodded, knowing what Brand must do to honor Merewyn. "I will come with you."

"No, see to your family." Brand swallowed hard, his jaw ridged with self-control.

"Will you move on?" asked Ivo.

"No. Cwen's not dead. If she comes back, you will need us. I will be there tonight, after I . . ." He stopped, unable to say the words. "Ari can ride Tom's horse and bring Kraken back to me tonight."

He turned and walked away, his back straight and determined as he carried Merewyn home, the raven following silently behind.

Ivo watched till the darkness swallowed them, then turned to look up at Alaida. "How is she?"

"Fine." She peeked under her cloak to check Beatrice. "Sleeping."

"Good. I . . ." He hesitated. "Perhaps I should go with him. I don't know what will happen at sunrise."

"I do." She reached down to touch his hair, a blessing more precious than any priest could give. "The sky will turn rose and gold, and then blue, and the sun will touch this pale hair of yours, and I'll cry, first for joy, and then for Merewyn's passing. It will be all right, my love. You're free of it. Merewyn said so. Even Bô . . . Even Cwen said so."

Merewyn said so. In the sadness that had followed them across the moors, he hadn't troubled to ask Tom, but now he motioned the boy forward. "Merewyn said you'd know. What did she mean?"

"She told me all as we rode after you, my lord, what I must do. And why. She said I must remember, but I didn't know why until . . ." Tom swallowed hard, then looked to Alaida. "Do you still have it, my lady. What I gave you?"

Alaida looked startled, then glanced down at her fist, clenched tight around something. "I didn't even realize I still had it." She opened her hand slowly, and Ivo blinked back tears as he saw what it was she clung to so tightly that her palm bore its mark.

Ivo looked down at the bit of silver Cwen had ripped from his neck so long ago. "You've had this all along?"

"It came from the well, my lord," said Tom. "Aelfwine found it when he cleaned it. Merewyn said Aelfwine didn't know it, but he only gave it to me for safekeeping. I didn't know 'twas yours, my lord, until she told me."

"No. No, there's no way you would." He gave Tom's shoulder a squeeze. "But you guarded it for me, nonetheless." He took his eagle from Alaida and pulled the chain over his head. The weight felt right, there against his chest, as though it had never been gone.

"Why was there such magic in it?" asked Alaida.

"It is my *fylgja*. My . . ." Ivo searched for a word in

French. "My guardian spirit. My father put this on me the day I was born, and Cwen stole it, all those years ago."

"Merewyn—" Tom's voice caught, and he had to clear his throat. "She said Cwen used it to turn him beast, and that the magic could be undone with it, so long as there was also love. Love that knew the truth, she said. She bid me put it in your hand, my lady, saying it would give you the strength to say what was in your heart. And my lord, she said to tell you that all of the others must find their charms."

"There are others, then, besides Brand and Ari?" asked Alaida.

"Nine of us altogether. All the creatures Cwen named." Ivo stared into the night, thinking of the others. "Good men. I will tell you of them, one day soon." One *day*, he thought. He was going to have day after day . . .

"Perhaps we should clean the well again, to see if Brand's *fil*—guardian is there."

"*Fylgja*." It wouldn't be, Ivo sensed, but he nodded. "We'll do that. And we'll search the cavern, if we can dig it out, and the hill fort and any other place I can think of she might have hidden them. And we'll send word to the others to search. With luck, perhaps some will even find them."

"They all must, my lord," said Tom. "Merewyn said that Cwen's magic binds Sir Brand more tightly because he led you that night, that all of you must break the curse before he can be free."

All of them? When it had taken twelve score years to stumble on this single one? *Impossible.*

"Then we will find them *all*," said Alaida firmly, and her determination flowed into Ivo the same way her love had, washing away the doubt.

"We will not stop until we do," he vowed. "But for now, we must get you and Beatrice home. We can ride, now that Brand's gone with . . ." He couldn't say her name. "I'll take Kraken."

Tom handed him Kraken's reins, then mounted Ari's bay, wincing as he pulled himself up.

"Show me that hand," ordered Ivo. Tom held out his

hand, and even by the fading moonlight, Ivo could see his palm was scored nearly to the bone.

"Thomas, you should have said something," said Alaida.

"It only hurts a little, my lady. There were more important things."

"Aye. There were." So far as Ivo was concerned, the boy had already earned his spurs, even if he had to wait to come of age to get them. But there would be time later to tell him that, to thank him again, to reward his courage. A lifetime— but only one. He would have to remember that now, and cherish every moment of it. Every day.

"Come, let's get you and my ladies home."

THE ROOSTERS WERE already crowing as they crossed the bridge and rode up the hill into Alnwick. A shout went up on the wall, and the gates opened wide in welcome. With a sense of relief, Ivo led Alaida into the yard. *Safe.*

In the next instant, that relief faded, strangled by the knot of noblemen clustered around the door to the hall. Ivo quickly scanned the faces, recognizing Flambard, Brainard, de Jeune, and others of the king's council. Ranulf Flambard lifted his hand, and a score of armed knights fanned out across the yard, making a loose circle around the riders. The Alnwick men grumbled, but did nothing—apparently, they'd been warned.

Tom moved up on the other side of Alaida, and his hand drifted toward to Ari's sword, hanging from the saddle.

"Easy, Tom," said Ivo.

A moment later, King William strolled out the door, and Ivo relaxed. He could deal with William. Then he saw the man who walked out beside him.

"Fitz Hubert, you've been warned off my land twice already." Ivo swung off Kraken, giving Neville a steely stare before helping Alaida down with Beatrice. He made sure the babe was well settled in her mother's arms and gave them each a kiss.

"Why is the king here?" whispered Alaida urgently.

' We shall see. Behave yourself." He pressed another kiss to her cheek and led her forward to kneel before the king. "Sire. Welcome to Alnwick."

"Up," said William impatiently. "Is this your lady?"

"Yes, Your Grace. Lady Alaida, who you gave me as bride, and our daughter, Beatrice."

Alaida dipped in courtesy—not as low as she might, but low enough, if William allowed for the child—and voiced a neutral, "Your Grace."

"My lady. Your marshal said you were stolen away by outlaws."

"We were, Your Grace."

"I retrieved them without harm to either," said Ivo.

"And where are your men?"

"Burying bodies, including that of my wife's old nurse, who was part of the vile scheme." He let the Alnwick men absorb that before he looked pointedly at Fitz Hubert. "And speaking of vile, Your Grace . . ."

"Take care, my lord. Sir Neville rides with me this time." William motioned, and Neville stepped forward wearing a smug smile. "He has brought me word of foul deeds at Alnwick. He accuses you of practicing dark magic and consorting with devils. In fact, of being a devil yourself."

"Foulness, indeed . . . if it were true."

"Neville, what lies are you telling *now*?" demanded Alaida indignantly.

Neville's smile only broadened. "None, my lady. Have you never wondered why your husband disappears into the woods every dawn and only returns after dark?"

Alaida shook her head like a disbelieving mother over a child's fancy and turned to William. "If the love of hunting is a sign of devilry, Your Grace, the forests of England are full of noble incubi."

The laughter that rocked the yard twisted Neville's face into a poisonous sneer. "He does not hunt, Lady Alaida. He is a demon, and he turns into an eagle with the rising of the sun and back to a man again at nightfall. I have seen him do it with my own eyes. Truly the Devil's work."

"An eagle?" said Ivo, forcing a smile as his newfound life slipped away. "Surely, Your Grace, you cannot believe such nonsense."

"I do not know whether I believe him or not," said William. "That is why I am here."

Alaida cleared her throat delicately. "I assure you, Your Grace, day or night, my husband is *fully* a man."

Laughter again, most of all from William. Her quick tongue might prove a boon in this, Ivo thought, grateful he'd never tried to tame it. Only the tightness at the corners of her eyes and mouth gave away how it must be costing her to fight the dregs of Cwen's vileness.

William wiped the grin off his face with his hand. "Nonetheless, Lady Alaida, I will know for myself whether fitz Hubert speaks truth. I have enough trouble with devils in the north without leaving a real one sitting in a strong castle. It will be easy enough to settle." William glanced up at the brightening sky, the scattered clouds touched with the rose and gold Alaida had predicted. "The sun rises soon. We shall see what happens. Take him."

Two burly knights stepped forward, jostling Alaida aside as they grabbed Ivo's arms. Ivo fought the urge to struggle, instead giving Alaida an encouraging smile. "Your Grace, my wife has had a difficult day and a more difficult night. Will you let her retire so she is not subject to this?"

William nodded. "Lord Robert, escort Lady Alaida and her daughter to the solar."

Alaida backed away from Robert. "Please, Your Grace, I prefer to stay. It will be most amusing watching Neville's downfall at last."

"Are you certain, my lady? It may be your husband's downfall you witness."

"No, Your Grace, it will not be." Her easy certainty buttressed Ivo's confidence. "I could never love a man who was evil."

"I hope not, my lady. Come, stand by me, and we will discover the truth together."

The rose faded away as the sky lightened and turned

blue. Light painted the tops of distant hills. Ivo steeled himself, as he had each dawn for the last twelve score years, waiting for the pain.

"Be ready," ordered William. "If he does turn eagle, I don't want him escaping before the bishops have a chance at him."

Neville's face was going to split if he grinned more broadly. "I really should let Brand gut you," said Ivo softly, savoring the fear that widened his eyes.

The sun broke the horizon and the first rays of light fell across the yard. The men holding Ivo tensed; their fingers bit into his arms. The great barons crowded forward, avidly searching for the first sign of beak or talon.

The moment passed with no pain, and Ivo's heart began to race with hope. Disappointment filled the barons' faces. Neville shifted uneasily. The sunlight crept toward Ivo, touched him, made him dizzy with the warmth and brightness.

"You see, Your Grace." Alaida pushed through the barons to bring Beatrice to Ivo, and the sun traced her cheek and then the babe's, and it was all he could do to breathe. "There is no eagle except in Neville's foul imagination. This is the third time he has made trouble here, all because I refused his suit and waited for you to give my hand as was your right."

"Is that what this is about, fitz Hubert?"

"No, Sire. No. I saw him change. I swear I did. This is some trick. He's an eagle. An eagle, I tell you."

"An eagle. God's wounds, man, I cannot believe I let you waste my time on this. Get him out of here," snapped William. Oswald and Penda rushed forward to oblige. "In fact, get him out of England. That traitorous brother of mine needs more men to go with him to Jerusalem. With luck the Saracens will rid us of both of them. Sir Neville, you are taking the Cross this very morning. Take him to the chapel so he may make his vow."

A cheer rose from where the Alnwick men were gathered. The two knights released Ivo and took charge of Neville, dragging him off toward the chapel.

"You're a fortunate man, de Vassy," said William, "to have a wife with such faith in you and such a tongue to use on your behalf."

"I have been grateful for both every day since you chose her for me, Your Grace."

"Good. Then you won't mind if I reward her for it. What would you have, Lady Alaida?"

"You know what I want, Your Grace, from the petitions I have sent you. One each month for the last year?"

"Aye. You pester me worse than the pope. I will send word to Windsor, and if your grandfather and uncle will swear homage and convince me they mean it this time, you may have their freedom."

Glowing, she dropped in deep courtesy. "Thank you, my liege."

"Yes. Well." William turned to go inside. "I'll want to look at that tower I paid for, de Vassy, after I break my fast."

"Of course, Your Grace."

Geoffrey summoned the Alnwick men to see to the king and his men, and with a sigh, Ivo wrapped his arms around his wife and daughter. Half sobbing, half laughing, Alaida reached up and ruffled his hair. "See? I told you. I told you."

They stood there a long while, just holding each other, while men and animals moved around them. After a time, Tom cleared his throat. "Look, my lord."

Above the distant woods, gray smoke billowed into the morning sky. Alaida's voice caught. "Merewyn's cottage."

"Her funeral pyre," murmured Ivo. "They will think she died in the flames. Never say otherwise."

"No, my lord," said Tom, then, "Look. Sir Ari."

Ari came whipping across the field and through the gate at full gallop, threw himself off Tom's horse, and ran for Ivo. He skidded to a stop, staring as if he didn't believe what he saw, his eyes brimming with tears.

"You did it," he said. "You did it. We can break it."

"Aye," said Ivo. "We can."

"There's so much . . . The visions. I'm sorry . . ."

"They were Cwen's doing, my friend. Part of her plan." Ivo gripped Ari's shoulders and gave him a hard look, then pulled him close for a quick hug. "The king's here, and all his men. We'll have to talk later."

"By the gods, will we talk!" Ari said in Norse. He switched to French and motioned for Tom to follow, "Come, Squire. I think you know something about my stolen horse."

Ivo squinted down at Alaida, his eyes still unused to the glory of the sun on her face. "What is that smile about?"

"You and Ari. I've never seen you together. 'Twill be strange, having you around all day."

"Aye. Will you like it?"

"God's knees, husband, must you ask?" She threw her head back in laughter that was still half-filled with tears, and her headrail slipped to let the sun touch her hair. It blazed with copper fire, brighter even than in Ivo's imaginings, so bright he had to close his eyes against the incredible beauty of it.

When he dared open them again, her face had gone serious. "Promise me one thing."

"What is that?"

She smiled, that woman's smile that made him glad he was a man, full of heat and promise. "That the nights will not change."

He pulled her close, silently promising the gods that he would honor them forever for this woman they had brought to save him. "On that, my lady wife, you have my vow."

And he kissed her.

Epilogue

TOGETHER IVAR AND *his beloved Alaida moved through the years, raising Beatrice and her five sisters and watching them marry. Together they lived the full measure of their time. And together they died, passing gently within days of each other near the winter solstice in the Christian year 1133.*

Brand stayed nearby, living in the woods as both man and bear to watch over the lord of Alnwick and his lady, until his friends' passing. Then, armed with the knowledge of how to break the curse, he rode forth in search of his men and of the fylgjur *that Cwen had hidden away, taking with him the raven who was his faithful friend, into the cold of winter.*

A hawk screamed overhead, and Ari looked up from his parchment. "Pillocks."

It was growing late. He blew softly across the ink to dry it as he read through the words he'd just traced. He nodded in satisfaction until he read the final word, when his gut clenched.

He hated winter, when the sun stayed in the sky so briefly and the nights dragged out. Winter left him so little time in each of these days of forever.

When the ink dried, he closed the book and fastened the straps. He broke the quill in two and let the breeze take it. The remaining ink, he simply spilled onto the ground. There was no point in saving either. He would simply make more the next time he could spare the time to write. Oak galls came cheaply in the forests of this cursed land, and quills . . . well, there were always quills.

Working quickly now, he checked the horses to make certain they were secure for Brand, then stripped out of his clothes, wrapped them around the book, and tied the bundle behind his saddle. With only moments left, he stepped to the edge of the ravine, where the final rays of the sun were strongest. He stood there, his bare skin absorbing the thin warmth, his heart pounding faster and faster as the pain hit, his arms growing lighter, stronger, longer.

How he loved the sun. It was the last thought that flashed through his mind before he stepped into the air and soared off over the trees, a raven, black as the night into which he flew.

HISTORICAL NOTES

Alnwick Castle (pronounced AH-nik) still stands, serving as the ancestral home of the Dukes of Northumberland. Its large, flat bailey is known from the Harry Potter movies as the place where Hogwarts students learn to fly their brooms. The old well still sits in the courtyard of the keep, and the standing stone still perches on the high ground northwest of the castle—though without visible carvings.

Ivo de Vassy (or de Vesci) was a real man, a Norman lord who was given Alnwick and its lady—possibly named Alda—by King William II after the previous owner was captured in the 1095 uprising. Little is known about Ivo, other than that he built the first castle at Alnwick, had a daughter named Beatrice, and died sometime around 1133. His descendants through Beatrice held Alnwick for some two hundred years, and his great-grandson, Eustace de Vesci, was a Magna Carta surety baron. The de Vesci name still survives in England today.

For all that, no one is quite certain where Ivo came from. Despite much hopeful supposition posted on Internet genealogy sites, historians currently believe that he is *not* the same Ivo de Vesci who rode with the Conqueror.

But then again, historians don't know about Cwen.

For more history and a chance to win a reproduction *fylgja* amulet similar to Ivo's, visit: www.lisahendrix.com.

ACKNOWLEDGEMENTS

My deep gratitude goes to the devoted webmasters of the many Internet sites I consulted in the writing of *Immortal Warrior*. Their dedication, coding skills, and love of the arcane made my midnight searches for that one crucial fact I needed to complete a scene both possible and fruitful. In particular, I would like to thank the Viking Answer Lady, the Jomsborg Vikings Hird website, the reenactors and historians of the Society for Creative Anachronism (US) and Regia Anglorum (UK), and most especially Fordham University's Internet Medieval Sourcebook, where I found the model for the marriage contract, as translated from a 984 A.D. Burgundian document by Dr. Paul Hyams of Cornell University.

And although the Google Books project generates much controversy in publishing circles, its archiving of out-of-print, out-of-copyright books made it possible for me to discover *The History of the Borough, Castle, and Barony of Alnwick* by George Tate (1866, digitized 2007), which I never would have been able to obtain through my local library.

In addition, the usual culprits made this books possible: my husband and children; my good friend and brainstorming pal, Sheila Roberts; my wonderful agent, Helen Breitwieser; and my insightful (and correct!) editor, Kate Seaver. My thanks and love to each of you.

Finally, a special shout-out goes to my critique partner and no-punches-pulled male viewpoint checker, the extraordinary and slightly off-center R. Scott Shanks, Jr. Praise and contracts be heaped upon you.

Lisa Hendrix